HOLLOW STATE

THE STRATAGEM BOOK I

D.L. Peoples

Peoples ✹ Books

Copyright © by D.L. Peoples 2014

All rights reserved
First Edition
No part of this book may be reproduced without written permission except in the case of brief quotations included in critical articles and reviews. For further information please contact the author.

Cover Design by Dane Low
www.ebooklaunch.com

Printing by Suffolk Printing
Bay Shore, New York
www.suffolkprinting.com

Peoples ✹ Books

dlpeoples.books@gmail.com
peoplesbooks.us
https://www.facebook.com/HollowStateDLP
twitter:@dlpeoples

To My Family
For their inspiration, guidance,
unconditional love and support.

Matthew
Evan, Brian, Scott and Jordan
William and Florence
Charlie, Masha and Joe

And to those whose loving encouragement
reaches beyond our years apart.

Joe and Selma
Minnie
Sol and Mary

Acknowledgements

Thank you doesn't begin to express my appreciation for all that my husband, Matthew, has done to make my life and this book complete. Reading, proofing, and sharing his knowledge of all things computer once again exemplified his unwavering support of all my dreams.

I am so grateful to my kids, who are no longer really kids, but are now outstanding young men. First a huge thank you goes to my very wise and talented son Evan Peoples. It may not be easy for a son to critique his mother's work but Evan took on the challenge and my story is exponentially better because I listened to him. Brian who is a wonderful musician in his own right is always willing to offer his support and his exceptional proofing skills. Thanks to my nephew Scott, the computer wizard. His invaluable knowledge of websites and blogs helped this Neanderthal struggle through. And last, but not least, my nephew Jordan, who took care of things around the house so I was free to write for more hours than I should have.

Love and thanks to my parents William and Florence Beitch, who always encouraged me to reach for any star I wanted. Thanks to my brother, Charles Beitch and my sister-in-law Masha Beitch who joined me in my endless discussions on politics, and my nephew Joseph Beitch who has grown up listening to, and putting up with, all those discussions.

A thank you to Michelle Felipe whose encouragement and cupcakes offered me and my family sustenance while I was busy focusing on this book.

I am so grateful and lucky to have Marianne Franzese Chasen in my life. One day when I was feeling particularly defeated she said to me, "You have a bestseller in you." This book is a direct result of that conversation and I will be forever indebted to her.

Where would a writer be without readers? My first readers were Kathy Delaney, Florence Beitch, Matthew Peoples, Masha Beitch, Marianne Franzese Chasen, Roberta Gordon and Evan Peoples. Their enthusiasm and encouragement was a truly valuable gift.

I love and thank the women in my writers group at the Women's Center of Huntington, Amy, Barbara, Beverly, Carol, Cori, Dolores, Eileen, Harriet, Karen, Lois, Louella, Sherri, Stephanie Sue and Susan. Their sage wisdom guided this novel to its fruition. Of this group I have to say a special thanks to Susan Davis for her friendship, support and the many hours she put into both reading, rereading, and discussing the ins and out of this novel. I hope you know how much I appreciate your efforts and how much I always love listening to your words of wisdom.

Special thanks to my many proofreaders who stepped up at different points in the process. My speedy, master proof reader, editor, and cheerleader Amy Conner. Listening to her has been beyond helpful. My first proofreader Maggie Rowe, certainly had her work cut out for her and rose to the challenge and my last proofreader, my mother-in-law, Joan Peoples whose many long hours and attention to detail is truly appreciated.

Thank you to Dane Low at ebooklaunch.com for the truly great cover design. It was such a pleasure working with such a talented and professional artist.

Last but not least, thank you to Suffolk Printing in Bay Shore for the many copies they made of this book for my readers and proofers and for the wonderful job they have done printing this paperback.

This book is a work of fiction. All names, characters, places and events are products of the author's imagination. Any resemblance to real people, businesses, events or places is a coincidence, with the following exceptions:

The Business Plot is an actual historical event. General Smedley Butler was a real and, I might add, a patriotic American hero.

Joe & Selma Gordon are the names of my grandparents. They did not, to my knowledge, do any of the things I have described them as doing. Nor did they say any of the words I have credited them with saying. However, I believe that if faced with this particular set of circumstances they would have stood up to such adversity with the same dogged persistence and concern for American Democracy as exhibited on the pages of this novel, and certainly instilled in me. I have been so happy to have had this opportunity to visit with them again in my imagination, as they have both been gone for far too long.

The Gordon Family

JOSEPH GORDON
Born 1894
Married SELMA GOLDBERG

ABRAHAM GORDON
Born 1913
Married SARA KIRKOWITZ

BENJAMIN GORDON
Born 1934
Married MARY ETHAN

GRIFFIN GORDON
Born 1969
Married MOLLY DANIELS

Griffin's & Molly's Sons
OLIVER GORDON
Born 1994–Married ABIGAIL BAYLOR
ANDREW GORDON
Born 2000–Married KENDALL MARTIN
TYLER GORDON
Born 2000–Partner KRIS MAYER

Chapter 0

Like battered children the people of the United States, collectively, were tired—worn out from a drama that had been set in motion almost a century before. A slippery slope of deception perpetrated on the American people by a litany of presidents who had become actors, and actors who had become presidents.

Decades of promises and lies, wars and thievery, the switch finally pulled, planes slamming into buildings, fingers pointing, tortures human and inhuman. *In Fear We Trust* was the leaders' motto as they shredded the Constitution, and conned the citizenry into taking off their shoes at the airport and checking their rights at every door.

So the people shifted, dunked themselves in tea, steeped in hope of change that never came. Spare change, in fact, was all anyone had left when the ones in control finally finished picking the bones of the American people.

With unquestioned authority, questionable voting machines, and corporations accorded human rights, their plan was complete.

Anyone who dared fight back was silenced.

And the truth? Well, eventually it all came out in the wash—far too late for anyone to do anything about it. They had already taken everything worth taking. Congress no longer even pretended to care about what the American people wanted, and the history books were rewritten to make it seem as if it had always been this way—that *this was* democracy and that this was exactly what our founding fathers had wanted.

A clever ruse. A democracy with all the trappings and none of the substance. Such was the world they created.

Ironically, whether it be with good intentions or bad, the seizure of wealth and power and the subsequent control of a people always comes with a price. Unintended consequences, karma, destiny, providence—call it what you will. In the end, few will win…and many will die.

Part 1

They constructed a reality in which the rest of the world would reside. A hollow state where the citizenry would be considered superfluous and expendable, and the pillars upon which democracy once stood would be an illusion, mere props of a play, staged solely to dupe the public into believing in its existence.

Chapter 1

Sunday, May 12, 2024
Molly & Griffin Gordon
Long Island, New York

The way Molly Gordon and her husband Griffin saw it, the world had become like a rubber band stretched too far. It had to snap, it had to hurt and then, when the pain stopped, everyone would feel better. They were still waiting to feel better.

Griffin and Molly were fifty-five years old in 2024 when the rubber band snapped. Invisible though it was, in debit accounts that stretched to the last penny each month, there were also visible, quite obvious signs that the buffer between the rich and the poor had disappeared.

The plush, green, tree lined streets, and manicured lawns of middle-class Long Island had been replaced by barren trees and unkempt, parched, beige grass. Boarded-up homes surrounded by barbed wire now outnumbered the others, and the public beaches and parks had all been sold to private investors to pay off the debts of bankrupt counties and towns. There was no longer a reason for the main streets and malls of the Island to exist since all the needs of the public could be met by the handful of conglomerates that dominated the market with their mega-superstores, fast-food chains and grocery giants.

But it wasn't only the landscape of Long Island that had changed, so too had the people; and Griffin and Molly were no exception. The once moderately attractive couple now bore the unmistakable signs of the modern middle-aged middle-class. Perpetually slumped shoulders, rapidly greying un-dyed hair, his dark brown, hers light; and their matching brown eyes underlined in shadows, involuntarily displayed a resignation to their unrelenting exhaustion. Thanks to their protracted work hours and a household of rationed food, the ever expanding mid-sections once promised to those of their age were not something Griffin and Molly had to worry about. They were both well-proportioned and looked to be relatively fit, though their pale skin betrayed any thoughts of outdoor athleticism. In public, their well-rehearsed smiles were meant to give the impression that they were happy enough with the circumstances of their life so as not to cause trouble; but their short, homemade haircuts and their clothing, used and reused for more than a decade, were a clear indication that things were not going as well as they pretended.

Though similar looking on inventory, as many couples are with age, Griffin and Molly's presence in the world was decidedly different. Anxious and worried most of the time, Griffin had become a target for every annoyance and conspiracy theory the world could dish out, while Molly's sharply contrasting and pervasive calm was often mistaken for denial. They were the epitome of the emotionally mismatched pair whose only congruence came to be in the intensity of their desire to see to each other's wellbeing. It was not always this way though. In their younger days their emotional lives were more closely aligned.

Back then Molly had loved to dress in fashion, wore make-up every day and routinely colored her hair to a rich blend of blonds and browns. She was an excellent hostess, preparing elaborate meals for her guests and welcoming them into her home with warm and supportive conversations.

Though less concerned about his clothing, Griffin's steadfast nature coupled with his quick-witted personality made him a standout both socially and at work. Everyone wanted Griffin for a teacher and everyone wanted to be his friend.

Against this erstwhile backdrop of financial comfort, Griffin and Molly enjoyed an ease of life that showed on their faces and in the humor they shared. After all, they had done everything right, passing each hurdle, milestones on the prescribed path to success: high school, a decent college, graduation, job, marriage, house, children, and on and on it went…until it didn't.

Both Molly and Griffin recognized that their own

failure to thrive was, in fact, an epidemic of the middle class on which they had perched themselves, albeit precariously at times – an epidemic fueled, quite simply, by greed. Whose greed exactly was up for debate, but each side blamed the other. Perhaps Robin Hood thought it wise to take from the rich and give to the poor, but politicians and corporate heads felt it best to rob from the poor and middle class, and give to the rich. They just pretended they were only taking from the poor.

"The day before the election they told us they were on our side; two days later they raised our taxes and took away our Social Security. When we asked for it back, what did they tell us?" Griffin didn't wait for Molly to answer. "They told us that poor people always want the government to give them free stuff."

Molly rolled her eyes.

"That's what they said just before they lowered their own tax rate and gave themselves tax loopholes you could drive a truck through. Seems to me, it's the politicians and their rich friends who are getting all the free stuff." Griffin's face was red.

As usual Molly listened in silence, waiting for her husband to get it all out of his system.

"Everyone's so busy just surviving there's no time to pay attention, real attention, to what they're doing."

Not that Griffin had much free time either, working shifts that lasted ten, sometimes twelve hours, while only getting paid for eight. He had no choice: there were too many bills. His parents now lived with them, along with his grown children and their spouses; and all in a house that was built for a single family with two children. No explanation necessary: this was the new norm for middle class families who were just poor families in disguise. Invisibly crippled by debt, they lived in neighborhoods where they no longer belonged. The problem was, no one belonged there anymore.

"Evil, self-righteous pricks," Griffin continued but in a whisper, suddenly remembering that even in his own home someone might be listening. "The way they talk you'd think God himself came down and commanded them to take away Medicare and food stamps."

Molly looked at the pain on her husband's face and couldn't help but wish he could stop.

"They pull out their blank checkbook anytime they want to build a new weapons system but God forbid they should take care of their own people. I swear, every time they call us socialists for wanting the Social Security benefits we paid for, I can't for the life of me figure out who voted for these clowns."

Molly listened to Griffin and nodded her head, affirming his words but not bothering to speak. She knew he was right, but she also knew that everything he said ran counter to what the media told her.

"This is just a big game to them, Mol, and we're just the pawns."

Chapter 2

Thursday, May 12, 1938
Joseph & Selma Gordon
New York City

Joseph Gordon and his wife Selma were 35 and 34 years old respectively in 1929, when the bottom dropped out of their world, the whole world according to all accounts on the headlines of the newspapers they could no longer afford to buy.

From the day they met, Selma was the center of Joseph Gordon's world. Short in stature, she made her presence known through her warm personality and her more orange than red hair. Once natural, and exceedingly long, her beautiful tresses had been her calling card, signifying her place in the world. It had also been the reason Joe picked her out of the crowd of onlookers during the Suffrage Parade. There on the sidewalk, overflowing with spectators, Joe had spotted Selma's long braid weaving through the crowd. Though he had yet to see her face, he insisted on the spot that his brother help him chase down the redheaded woman he intended to marry one day.

"He's crazy." Maura, Selma's friend who had accompanied her to the parade and who bore witness to Joe's advances, felt obliged to whisper into Selma's ear. "Don't be a pushover. He's nothing more than a drug store cowboy."

The warnings continued, and at first Selma agreed with her friend that Joe had been far too forward; but there was something about his determination, the novelty of his wit, and his unabashed honesty that fascinated Selma and made her uncharacteristically vulnerable to his charms.

Nevertheless, in an effort to avoid even the slightest hint of impropriety, Selma felt obligated to politely rebuff Joe's request to walk her home.

Joe persisted, though, and not only won Selma's permission to accompany her, but also won her heart that day. Even Selma's father, who vehemently objected to the advances of this un-vetted individual's intrusion into his daughter's life, turned a blind eye to his own concerns after learning of Joe's lofty entrepreneurial goals for the future.

Now twenty-seven years later, Joe's love for Selma, and her hair, had only become stronger. Yes, he squawked when she first cut her flowing tresses into the new bob style without his permission, and yes, thanks to mishaps with cheap henna rinses Selma's hair was bound to look like the color of carrots one day and a dark coppery orange-red the next; but Joe persevered, telling himself that hair grows and dyes wash out. Even if he didn't always like her many transformations, and even if he and his wife didn't always see eye to eye, Joe always believed Selma to be the most beautiful woman in the room, and his devotion to her; just as her devotion to him, never wavered.

Through good times and bad, and now through The Great Depression, the couple weathered their storms together. For Selma that meant that each day, no matter how little money they had or how dark their prospects for the future seemed, there was a smile on her face and a plan to make a stew out of whatever she found that day in the garbage behind the restaurant where Joseph swept the floors.

Joe hadn't always swept floors. Before the Depression he had been a dressmaker, not for the rich people who now ate in the restaurant, but for those who aspired to be rich. People who were just beginning to rise up from the poverty of their immigrant parents, people who believed in their hearts and minds that the suffering was over. Just as Joe had believed.

Though it wasn't the most popular dress shop in the city by any means, his clientele had been growing and he had had big plans to expand beyond the tiny space that held only four sewing stations, a dressing room and two chairs. At the time, Joe had been optimistic.

Each day, as he put his key in the door of the tiny New York City store he had bought with his business partner Sam, Joseph had said a prayer of thanks to the God he was now sure had forsaken him.

All Joe could see now was that he had always done the right thing and it had gotten him nowhere. After all, it was Joe who had quit school at fourteen when his mother died from the illegal abortion of what was to be his twelfth sibling. At the time, his father had been so wracked with guilt at his part in his wife's demise, he could no longer get up in the morning to support the family. So Joe had stepped in. It was also Joe who currently looked after, lived with, and supported his father, a spinster sister, his youngest brother, and his wife's parents in addition to his own family consisting of his wife, son, daughter, a daughter-in-law, son-in-law and four grandchildren. Fifteen in all, including himself, in one home intended for six. Fifteen people who needed shelter, food, clothing and medicine.

"Swatted like flies," Joe would say to Selma. "We were swatted like flies," he'd repeat and shake his head.

It was true. For this burgeoning group of businessmen who were now bankrupt, the only way out of their financial troubles seemed to be either through less than honorable activities or through the window.

Even Joseph Gordon, who had once touted his value system as being above reproach, was not spared the shame of dishonesty in this new world he suddenly found himself occupying.

Almost every day that he worked at the restaurant,

which was only two days a week, three if he was lucky, Joe would hit his broom handle against a slab of meat on the kitchen counter and send it sailing to the floor. No one would notice what the sweeper was picking up, or how he carefully wrapped it in clean paper. They wouldn't notice him taking the half empty garbage can outside or his whistle summoning Selma to come and get the meat so they could all eat for a few more days. That's all they ever asked for, a few more days.

"Gordon!" Joe heard his name called loudly from the kitchen. The maître d', Mr. Marcello, was angry, again.

"Coming, sir."

"Gordon!" Joe was now running, holding the garbage can in one hand and two thoughts in his head: that he had been spotted stealing the meat, and that Selma would run out from behind the garbage cans and get caught. Joe began to retrace his steps in his mind. Where had he slipped up? Who had seen him? Joe could not help but believe that a policeman was standing just inside the door of the kitchen waiting to arrest him. Part of him wanted to run away, but the thought of Selma kept him moving forward. He hadn't whistled yet so she would stay put, he tried to assure himself as fear gushed from his pores and sweat ran down his face.

"Mr. Gordon, Mr. Roberts has not shown for work." So deep in his own thoughts and worry, Joe could barely understand what the maître d' was saying to him. "You will be filling in."

The maître d', who towered over Joe's modest five-foot-seven frame, remained in control of his voice but his eyes showed an urgency Joe had rarely seen. Joe had filled in for a waiter only once before and, though commended for his efforts, he was not asked back until now, three months later. At the time, Joe suspected it was because his father had shown up at work the next day sporting his forgotten lunch and the unmistakable thick accent of a Russian Jew. Until that day Joe's boss, who had never bothered to ask him his last name, believed his jet black, straight hair, dark eyes and olive skin meant 'Joe' was just the Americanized version of Giuseppe. The realization of his true ancestry immediately squashed any possibility that Joe could become a waiter in this type of establishment. However this maître d' was new, barely there two weeks, and obviously knew nothing of Joe's Russian or religious roots.

Rushing back into the restaurant, Joe forgot all about Selma as he moved quickly to wash his hands and find his uniform for the evening. He also didn't bother to look at the faces of the other kitchen workers, first generation immigrants all, whose thick accents would keep them out of the front of the house forever, despite their years of seniority over Joe.

This was Joe's second chance to move up in the

restaurant, to get more hours, tips and a bigger salary to bring home; however in order to do that he knew he would have to prove himself worthy of the position.

Chapter 3

Wednesday, June 12, 2024
Molly & Griffin Gordon
Long Island, New York

One by one Molly and Griffin's neighbors were leaving their homes in the middle of the night in fear. The banks had learned that threats, thugs and barbed wire were much more efficient than the legal process ever could be.

There were never any goodbyes, no "see you laters" or forwarding addresses. Email had become the dead letter office of modern society because there was nothing to write about anymore: their worlds were gone. Everything that really mattered to them was packed into their cars, and the rest was left behind.

Now the talk at every remaining dinner table consisted of two conversations: which friend or neighbor had disappeared during the night, and what things they themselves would be taking with them when they were forced to leave.

Most everyone from Long Island headed south, just far enough to be spared freezing to death in their cars, tents, or makeshift homes during the winter; but not too far south as it had become dangerously hot during the spring and summer months.

No one went west anymore because it had become too hard to live on that side of the country. Ten straight years of droughts, recurrent earthquakes, high temperatures, extreme winter storms, and virulent tornadoes had made living in one's car, even temporarily, a perilous proposition. In many areas where twisters were a daily occurrence, residents adapted by leveling what was left of their houses and living in renovated storm cellars underground. Instead of seeing a row of houses, now all anyone could see were rows of man-made hills protruding from the flat earth like giant ant colonies.

Once considered symbols of wealth and status, sprawling McMansions were now ridiculed and laughingly referred to as "tornado targets." Instead, residents of the Midwest coveted properties with large hills, which implied a more expansive subterranean living space, one that offered better protection from tornadoes and more stability during earthquakes. Almost all new commercial buildings, and in some cases whole towns and mass transit systems, had been constructed below ground.

Since the government cared about a lot of things but not about those who fell on hard times or what little was left of its public land, the two were free to commingle for a fee. Left in the capable hands of private management companies, a 12'x12' patch of dirt could cost anywhere from $20 to $100 a night to rent depending on amenities, which generally only consisted of a public bathroom. Extras like showers and electrical hook-ups were a luxury few families could afford. After all, business was business to the private companies, and if they could get someone's last dime, they did.

Those with no money at all were free to lose themselves in the dangerous woods surrounding the protected campsites. However, small groups attempting to gather together for protection were immediately rounded up and jailed as it was assumed that their displeasure with their circumstances would lead them to traitorous activities.

It was only because Griffin saw it all coming that he and his family enjoyed a distinct advantage over his fleeing neighbors. In fact, he had been prepping his family for years, which was why his basement was now filled with supplies and his safe held a deed to a small patch of land in Pennsylvania. The deed, placed in their son's name and comfortably out of the reach of Griffin and Molly's mortgage company, included three acres and no buildings to speak of, just a very large barn with a patchwork roof.

"Paid in full and suitable for farming!" Griffin had proudly exclaimed to his family. "It's not a big piece of land, but there's enough."

Griffin knew nothing about farming or if indeed his patch of land would be big enough to sustain his family and bring in a little extra income. Nevertheless, he was confident that everything he needed to know was available at the New York Public Library, the last library left in the state and his favorite place to go whenever he had a day off and a few dollars for the train.

"This isn't rocket science, Molly. I can figure it out."

Molly wasn't so sure. What she was sure of, however, was that there wasn't any other choice but to make their efforts work.

As Griffin had planned it, they would initially use trailers for supplies and sleep in tents placed inside the barn to take advantage of the extra protection from the elements the old building could afford them. Eventually they would use the barn for storage and animals, and convert the trailers into homes.

At first Molly considered Griffin's plan to be insane, but now that her friends were disappearing one by one she thought it was pure genius. She believed, or at least wanted to believe, that Griffin had thought of everything and had left nothing to chance. He had even purchased three cows, two goats, three dozen chickens, some sheep, and a rooster, all of which he boarded at a local farm. Griffin had also been saving as much cash as possible, knowing full well that the mortgage company would be raiding his bank accounts after his first late payment.

Molly too had been saving money Griffin didn't know about. A dollar here, a ten there; it wasn't easy, but no one seemed to notice, or just didn't care enough to complain about the extra pasta dishes she had started serving two years ago. By the time they had to leave, Molly hoped they would have enough for something more – maybe more land to grow crops, another cow, or at least a few more chickens. Aspirations Molly viewed as being diametrically opposed to the designer handbags, new cars and family vacations she had once pined for.

Chapter 4

Sunday, June 12, 1938
Joseph & Selma Gordon
New York City

"Joe! Table four. They've been waiting nearly ten minutes," the maître d' yelled in a whisper as he physically shoved Joe out through the swinging kitchen door, sending him sailing into the boy whose job it was to set the tables and pour the water for a few pennies a day. The two barely managed to remain upright.

Joe had been working as a waiter for nearly a month now, thanks to the early demise of Mr. Roberts, the previous waiter. Mr. Roberts had liked the ladies and the drink, and it was rumored that chasing one or the other had been at the root of his untimely death.

"The lady or the tiger." That's how Selma had put it. "Either way, Mr. Roberts was destined to lose."

"Mr. Roberts' loss is our gain, Selma." Hearing his own thoughts out loud, Joe could not help but feel their harsh edge. Yet in these hard times he doubted anyone would begrudge him his sentiments, especially given the reported circumstances of the waiter's death.

As the story went, Mr. Roberts was crossing the street to either make the acquaintance of a young woman he had no business acquainting himself with, or to step into the cocktail lounge that happened to be situated directly beside where the young woman was standing.

What was in his head as he stepped off the curb and into the path of an oncoming car was the topic of discussion at the restaurant for the better part of two weeks following the closed casket wake. The people who knew Mr. Roberts best would have put their money on the woman, if such a wager had been suggested. A fool's bet for sure, given the fact that neither woman nor drink had actually been on Reginald Roberts mind when he felt the need to step off the curb and into the path of a speeding car.

Chapter 5

Friday, July 12, 2024
Molly & Griffin Gordon
Long Island, New York

Some nights, Griffin would go over the plans for the move in his head and praise his own ingenuity. More often, though, he would admonish himself for not planning sooner, saving more, and borrowing less. That trip to Disney, his new car, the kids' tuitions: they all seemed frivolous now. None of it meant anything. None of it would help them survive.

Most nights, Griffin would lie in bed fighting the thoughts that kept him from sleep, beating himself up for being too slow to believe his uncle and the warnings he had sounded from the time Griffin was a little boy. He'd had no idea his uncle wasn't really related to him. All Griffin knew was that until his death Uncle Jack had been in their home every Sunday night for dinner.

"It's just that he sounded so crazy, Molly," he would tell his wife all too often these days. "I didn't believe him. But nobody believed him, especially my father."

"Shut up, old man, you're scaring the boy." Griffin's

father would say the words as gently as possible and smile at the end. Truth be told, Griffin *was* scared. Afraid of the doom in his uncle's tone, and the prophecy that seemed hopeless and inevitable. A horrific story of what was to come that prompted Griffin to lie to his father, say he was fine and not scared, so he could hear his uncle's prophesies again and again, right to the end, over and over, the way kids do until they aren't scared anymore. Try as hard as the young Griffin might to keep his breathing steady and his mind focused, it was his eyes, wide, frightened saucers of blue, edged with white, that compelled his father to silence Uncle Jack yet again.

It was a scene that now plagued Griffin at night, every night; a scene from which he tried to extract every bit of information. A thought, a word he might have forgotten that would lead him to know more and figure it all out. Unfortunately, the extra information never came. He knew no more in the morning than when he went to bed. Griffin would just have to stick with his plan and execute it soon, before anyone outside of his immediate family realized what he was doing.

Chapter 6

Tuesday, July 12, 1938
Joseph & Selma Gordon
New York City

It was the Depression, unprecedented in its breadth and depth, that had brought millions of unemployed, shabbily clothed, poor, sick, and starving families onto the breadlines and into the headlines for the better part of a decade—but not everyone was suffering.

Certainly the people who ate in the restaurant where Joe worked were not suffering in any manner. They drove up in their expensive cars, ordered expensive steaks, and no doubt went home that night to their expensive homes. Joe had wanted that good life more than anyone could have imagined. He had wanted it for himself, but mostly he had wanted it for Selma and for his children.

"People want a lot of things they can't have." Joe thought the words in his head as he waited for the first diners to arrive. Those were Joe's own words to his children, twenty-some years ago, as they squeezed his hands and pulled him through the park in the direction of the cotton candy man.

"Please, Father, pleeease!" Sophie and Abraham would whine in a chorus of pleases purposely slurred for emphasis.

Joe's response of "No" was purposeful too, and meant to build character in his children. A lesson Joe believed one was never too young to learn. Not to say that refusing the whims of his children was easy for Joe. It wasn't, it was just necessary. After all, Joe did not want his children to act like that Peter Pan character. He knew his children did not have the luxury of staying young forever, and strongly believed that the lessons he taught them now, regardless of how harsh they might seem, would serve them well in their adult lives. Now that they were grown, however, he was not so sure he had been correct in his assumptions, since clearly in these hard times the people who were doing the best generally lacked the character he had worked so hard to instill in his children.

So it was with the people who dined at the tables he waited on. Ever since he had started taking their orders two months ago, Joe had been privy to numerous schemes ranging from petty larceny to serious criminal endeavors. Not that Joe could actually be considered a witness or be called to testify against any of these men, as his duties as a waiter allowed for only snippets of conversations for which he would have to fill in the blanks himself. This left Joe's imagination to run wild at times, especially during dinnertime conversations at home. Conversations that left Selma and his children fearing that the head of their household was encountering a malady of the brain generally reserved for the elderly. Though Selma and the children only shared their fears in whispers, Joe could sense their concerns in the glances being exchanged at the end of each of his fill-in-the-blank stories.

Tonight, however, Joe would not have to make anything up because for the first time since becoming a waiter he had been assigned to the private dining room, where he would stay the entire evening. The secluded area, generally reserved for private parties and guests of the owner, was situated behind a set of intricately-carved, oversized mahogany doors and was resplendent in dark woods, red velvets, and gold trims with tiny windows set high above eyes' reach. Joe's work for the evening would be that of a trainee, whose only jobs were to refill water glasses and replace fallen silverware and napkins.

"They are coming!" The head waiter, Gino, was rushing through the dining room straightening napkins, forks, and the bow ties of all the waiters.

Joe felt the nervousness of his boss in the pit of his stomach even though he himself had no reason to feel anxious. His responsibilities that evening were so limited that the chance of his making a mistake was minimal. Nevertheless, the energy in the room was high and Joe could not help but imagine that the dinner guests arriving were of royalty or some other equally high status.

Chapter 7

Friday, July 12, 2024
Molly & Griffin Gordon
Long Island, New York

It was a dichotomy of the most extreme: a hands-off government that had no trouble delving into the privacy of its citizens under the guise of security.

Just like the search engines and social networks of the past, current email providers were sending everyone's personal communications to the highest bidder without consequence. If the word "camera" appeared in an e-mail, the writer would suddenly find himself inundated with ads for the latest, greatest, and cheapest cameras on the internet. Barely a page could appear without the reader first being subjected to the unrelenting product promotion.

Griffin knew this, and also knew that all his communications and searches were being tracked by the government. Nevertheless, he continued using the internet, believing that those who did not were deemed even more suspicious than those who did. So Griffin would email articles and cartoons relating to the mishaps of golfing and parenthood after carefully editing out any words that would have led to him being roused from deep sleep, roughed-up, and dragged into a police station for questioning. Stories of such occurrences abounded but were no longer reported on the internet as, generally, the reporter would suffer the same fate.

Instead, anecdotes in whispers between longtime friends spread the words that could no longer be written without reprisal. Reprisal not only from a government hell-bent on "protecting" its citizens, but also from paranoid corporations whose daily deluge of pink slips rained down on employees like confetti on New Year's Eve.

For Griffin and Molly, both public school teachers who had long since lost their jobs to for-profit schooling institutions, such censorship of their words was abhorrent. Yet their righteous indignation was long gone. Some might say it was beaten out of them, not literally, of course, but rather because of the exhausting efforts needed to maintain their lives and protect their families.

After losing their teaching jobs, Griffin had worked his way up to a management position at a local supermarket and Molly now had two part-time jobs: cashiering at a fast food restaurant, and making calls two nights a week at a telemarketing firm. In spite of their efforts and those of their college-educated, sporadically-employed children, the likelihood of their being able to stay in their home was slim. Not because they couldn't afford their twenty-five-year-old mortgage, but because of everything else.

Skyrocketing gas, clothing and healthcare costs drained their budget. Utility bills had them showering less, adjusting to the sight of a parched lawn, wearing their coats inside all winter and bathing suits in the house all summer. Nevertheless their bills were unbearable.

These days the kinds of food they had grown up on, that even their children had grown up on, rarely graced their dinner table. For lunch instead of cold cuts they ate peanut butter and jelly sandwiches, or sometimes just jelly on bread. Yogurt or maybe a can of soup was a rare but welcome change. Instead of steak, chicken or burgers, dinner consisted of pasta, eggs, or rice and beans. Desserts were no longer served, and the exorbitant price of fruit made it a rare treat reserved for special occasions like birthdays and anniversaries. As time went on Molly learned to prepare a few tasty meals, even though she could not bring herself to take pride in them. After all, their presence on her dinner table was nothing more to her than a visual reminder of what little money they had left.

Griffin and Molly likened their budget to water through a sieve. No matter how much they tried to plug one hole, there were hundreds more where the money flowed through.

"Holy crap, they just charged me to look at my money!" Griffin noticed the four dollar fee labeled 'Balance Inquiry' on his statement. "They charged me four dollars to find out that I have eight dollars left in my account."

Griffin proceeded to punctuate his words with an expletive-filled tirade. This would not be the first nor the last time Griffin would find himself screaming at his bank, which was owned by his employer and operated with an unprecedented, unregulated abandon thanks to a government whose laissez-faire attitude extended to all things corporate. Thus, interest rates had soared to once-unimaginable, loan-sharkian heights, despite an economy the government had deceptively labeled 'Torpid.' New words for old—'torpid' for 'depressed.' Words to take to the airwaves and confuse the public. Words that would ultimately lay the groundwork for blaming the 'lazy' citizenry of the country, who would get what they deserved for failing to work hard and appreciate their birthright as members of a democratic and free society.

Democracy, my ass. Griffin wished he could shout at Congressman Rhine, currently gracing the screen of his twenty-five-year-old, once proudly displayed, and now embarrassingly old, flat screen TV. *Fuck you, Rhine. Go to hell*, Griffin thought to himself, but he dared not say it out loud, even in his own home. He knew better.

Chapter 8

Tuesday, July 12, 1938
Joseph & Selma Gordon
New York City

If Joe had known what was going to happen that night at the restaurant, if he had known what he was going to do, he would have brought his satchel.

The arrival at the restaurant of all twelve men almost simultaneously in separate long, black, shiny cars, looked more like a funeral procession for a head of state than a dinner meeting. As each man stepped out of his respective Rolls Royce in formal dress, Joe could not help but notice how their hats and long coats stood out in defiance of the July heat.

Once in the foyer, each guest was greeted by the restaurant owner, whom Joe had seen only once before. According to the waiters, Mr. Sloukin spent all his time in the basement of the restaurant, "Counting his money." At the time, Joe had viewed their comments as odd, since he had no belief that the restaurant, with its sparse clientele, made enough money to count. It would take a while for

Joe to realize that Sloukin made more money from what he did in the basement than in the dining room.

With their unnecessary outer garments removed and checked, the men moved quickly and with purpose toward the dining room to which they did not need to be led. Though no one diner acknowledged the other with anything beyond the kind of nod afforded to strangers during a stroll in the park, it was obvious they had all been there before.

In rapid succession and without so much as a place card or hand-gestured direction each man took his place at the table.

As a trainee for future such occasions, Joe was stationed in the far right hand back corner of the room. There were four waiters, four busboys and the maître d' to see to the needs of these twelve men, whose faces seemed familiar but unplaceable to Joe. It would not be until later, after listening to the context of their discussions and through the overheard offhand remarks made by the other waiters, that Joe would piece together their identities and the full implications of their words.

"These were no ordinary men," Joe would later tell Selma. "These men make the movies, publish the newspapers, head the banks, run the big corporations and build the bridges."

Under normal circumstances Joe's excitement would have emanated from the fact that he had been in the presence of these powerful men; however, any enthusiasm he might have felt initially was wholly overshadowed by the implications of their words.

"Gentlemen, a house divided against itself cannot stand."

The man at the head of the table was himself standing, commanding the room and speaking with such authority that all the other men nodded as if he were both the author of these words and the purveyor of some sort of new truth. Joe, though, remembered that those exact words had come from a speech by Abraham Lincoln and, even without a high school diploma, he knew that they had been used to encourage an end to slavery and not to whatever this man was alluding.

Joe listened as the speaker skillfully wove amongst his own words a litany of famous quotes positioned in such a way as to imply that their original authors' intents were indeed the new meanings now being assigned to them: hidden messages, he said, reserved for himself and others of elite intellect. Joe saw right through the clever ruse that now obligated each and every guest to accept the speaker's words at face value or be put forth, in front of all, as being of lesser intelligence.

"My friends from Chicago here agree, in fact wholly agree, that our *Stratagem for a New America* makes the most sense for this great country." The speaker looked to his left and gestured toward the three men who were now smiling and nodding in affirmation. "Gentlemen, I ask you, how is it that we continue to allow the general populace, the vast uneducated citizenry of our country, the preposterous privilege of choosing our senators, our members of the house, indeed our president," his voice lifted louder, "when they themselves know nothing of the responsibilities of these esteemed offices for which they are being asked to choose the most qualified candidate? This, gentlemen, is not the seventeen hundreds."

The men in the room all laughed and shook their heads in condescending agreement that things were so much more complicated in 1938 than they had been when the Constitution had granted the less-educated the right to vote.

Remarkably to Joe, none of the waiters or busboys upon whom these insults were heaped showed any emotion. Not so much as a flinch was exposed. Joe assumed it best to follow their lead. Listening intently, he remained stoic and alert, but on the outside Joe appeared to be completely detached.

"Thus, gentlemen," the speaker continued, "I have employed the services of my colleagues from Chicago to help us ensure that our great country is not led astray."

With those words, the man at the head of the table, the one Joe would later identify as being the publisher, took his seat. His movement automatically signaled time for the first course to be served: soup, that would turn cold as the diners' attention turned to the stacks of mimeographed pages being handed out by the youngest of the Chicago contingency.

Stealing surreptitious glances over the shoulders of the diners, Joe could see that the pages consisted of blue-inked words, numbers and maps, the details of which were blurred by the distance Joe was required to stand from the table.

As the Chicago gentleman, who looked to be barely the age of Joe's own son, finished the distribution of his treatise, he began to refer the men in the room to various pages, laying out his plan before them. The discussion, which Joe had trouble keeping up with due to the rapid fire way in which the information was being presented as well as to the fact that Joe had no visual representation to reference, centered on the subjects of elections, business, and banking. As the men flipped through the dull white pages, Joe tried to commit to memory whatever he was able to comprehend from the discussion. A discussion that was filled with unfamiliar words and prospects so disturbing that more than once Joe tried to convince himself he had not actually heard what was being said out loud.

The young speaker, perhaps because of his age, repeatedly quoted his professors, whom he assured his audience were now famous in their respective fields. Nevertheless, what he was suggesting was so outrageous Joe struggled to keep his focus on the speaker's words rather than his own thoughts.

"By seizing control of the vote and placing authority

in the rightful hands of those most qualified to make the thorny decisions of government, we shall be providing an enduring service to this country."

Joe, like most people, was used to the rich taking advantage of the poor, not only during hard times, but at all times. This, however, was taking that advantage to another level entirely.

"Though it would seem a waste of time," the young man continued, "the illusion of a democracy, of a two-party system, must be maintained."

To this, now, some at the table did not nod, though they didn't yet speak up, deferring still to the speaker. Then the young man from Chicago quoted Albert Einstein as if to imply that the Nobel Laureate himself had approved of his plan.

"As Professor Einstein has told us, 'Out of clutter, find simplicity. From discord, find harmony. In the middle of difficulty lies opportunity.' Gentlemen, our current system of government is cluttered, and is no longer working. Why, one need only to look to the streets to see discord. And our wasteful and misguided government has become nothing if not obsolete. Opportunity awaits us. We need only to utilize this plan. In its most pure form it is the simplicity to which this great man refers."

As Joe listened, he found it increasingly difficult to stop the red from rising in his face and the sweat from emanating from his pores.

Had these men not been who they were, Joe would have thought each to be crazier than the next. Their arrogance, and the fact that they felt they could say such things in front of a stranger such as he, someone not on their payroll or beholden to them in any way, led Joe to the conclusion that anyone who might expose their scheme would be stopped dead in his tracks.

Then why, Joe could not figure out, was he even considering the possibility of stealing a copy of their plans?

Chapter 9

Thursday, September 12, 2024
Molly & Griffin Gordon
Long Island, New York

"Why is it," Griffin asked himself over and over, *"that the first born son feels obliged to challenge the father at every turn?"*

Having two of their three grown, college-educated sons unemployed and living at home with their spouses would normally be quite disconcerting for parents who should have been comfortably settling into their empty nest. However, for Molly and Griffin, having their sons and the helping hands they brought with them, made the prospect of their upcoming relocation seem doable. Ironically, it was their eldest son, Oliver, the only one in the family with a good and remarkably stable job, who caused Griffin concern.

Oliver Gordon was the type of child every parent dreams of. With his six-foot four muscular frame, chiseled features, olive skin, and dark eyes he was the epitome of the word handsome. Even his hair had just enough of a wave so as not to be boring. Oliver looked nothing like his siblings who had inherited the average looks, shorter stature, lighter hair and skin tones of their mother. In fact, to look at Oliver, one could see more of his great-great-grandfather Joe in him than any of his living relatives. He was also smart; head of the class, valedictorian smart. That, coupled with his dogged belief that he was always right, was the engine that allowed Oliver to get things done no matter how many obstacles were thrown in his way. It was also why he was such a perfect fit for politics.

Oliver lived and worked in Washington, on the inside of everything Griffin had been taught not to trust.

It was not as if Oliver hadn't heard the stories. Rather it was as if the stories had become fuel for Oliver to prove both his father and his ancestors wrong despite what seemed to be an ever-mounting pile of evidence to the contrary.

"Oliver, your great-grandfather was at the right place at the right time; it was a freak accident of placement that he was there then, to hear the future. We have an advantage, a jump on the others. Why would you go and work for the enemy?"

As soon he had said the word "enemy" Griffin was sorry. It was one of those times that if he could rewind, and put the words back into his mouth, he would have. Now, despite Griffin's attempts to refocus his attention back onto his newspaper, all he could do was play their last phone conversation over in his head.

"What advantage would that be, Father?" Oliver had, as usual, gone in for the kill and not felt satisfied until he had mortally wounded what was left of his father's ego. "The advantage that you are losing your home, going to live in trailers and raise chickens? That advantage?"

Normally, Griffin would have fought back with the truth. He always had. But lately he had grown tired of it never working. Instead he had decided to change the subject.

If Oliver chose not to believe him, to close his eyes to the evidence, and to swear by the propaganda he and his buddies produced like snow during a Nor'easter, then Griffin's hands were tied and he knew it. It was just becoming harder to hang up the phone after one of their conversations, since he knew what was coming, what would happen right after the move.

"Pretty soon he won't be able to talk to us," Griffin had said to Molly.

"I think he'll find a way to speak to us." Molly knew she was lying, to Griffin and to herself.

"We will be classified, Molly. D.E.'s." Griffin had gazed down, unable to look at his wife, as if meeting her eyes would acknowledge some kind of failure on his part to keep his family together.

Molly had no response and found it just as hard to

look at Griffin. She was not used to seeing that level of hurt in any man, least of all her husband. Molly may have been born in the bra-burning sixties, but she still grew up watching *The Brady Bunch, Andy Griffith* and reruns of *Father Knows Best*, where the husbands fixed every family problem in thirty minutes. This, however, was not a problem Griffin could fix. They were destined to be labeled "Domestic Enemies" because they couldn't keep up with their bills. No fixing possible.

"Domestic Enemies. And I've never had so much as a parking ticket."

The fact that not one citizen who had lost a home had actually exacted revenge in any form did not stop the government and the propagandized news media from painting those who defaulted on their loans as "Capable of extreme acts of violence" that were "likely, credible, and imminent." Griffin remembered how those same words had taken hold against the Arab community after 9/11. Now they were being turned on him and much of the middle class. And this week, like all weeks that contained the date 9/11, terrorist rhetoric was at a fever pitch. This despite the fact that not one foreign attack had taken place on U.S. in twenty-three years.

Those who installed cameras, trashed the Constitution, and routinely pointed fingers during congressional hearings claimed ownership of that statistic and declared themselves victorious over the non-existent terrorists. Griffin never understood how the umbrella of terrorism actually grew larger as each year passed without incident. Griffin's confusion also extended to the American people, who were encouraged to cower in the corner and give up more and more of their democratic freedoms while simultaneously supporting the wonders of a democratic society.

Finally able to shake himself from the memories of his talk with Oliver, Griffin moved his eyes back to the paper, which he found equally disturbing.

"50,000 more cameras, Molly," Griffin shouted into the other room where his wife had disappeared to clean up from dinner. Griffin kept her informed of the latest numbers released by Citizens for Surveillance, an organization hell bent on seeing to it that America was "Safe for Democracy."

"What does that even mean? 'Safe for Democracy'?" Griffin was mumbling to himself as he read his newspaper. Paper newspapers had made a significant resurgence in the "I spy" world in which everyone now resided. Online papers tracked your every move—every page you viewed, when you viewed it, how long you viewed it. Their eye scanners even forced you to read specific news stories before you were allowed to read articles of your own choosing. Not unlike the ads one needed to watch before viewing free video clips. Hardcopy newspapers, even though they were filled with the same kind of propaganda as their online counterparts, now afforded people protection to view whatever articles they wished without anyone knowing about it.

"Democracy…" Griffin's thoughts trailed off.

"What did you say?" Molly came back into the room. "I couldn't hear. The dishwasher is on."

"Oh, nothing." Griffin annoyed himself with the fact that their thirty-year-old dishwasher was on its last leg and its noise had, as usual, encroached on his conversation.

"Just 50,000 more cameras and the last nails in the coffin of democracy."

As she walked back into the kitchen with thoughts of where she would store the leftovers, Molly laughed at the juxtaposition between the horror of what Griffin was saying and the matter of fact, sarcastic tone of his voice.

Griffin went back to his paper and began reading an article about the 9/11 ceremonies held in the city the day before. It was the headline beneath, however, that caught his eye.

"New Drone Surveillance Contract Signed." It was an article announcing the commission of a new fleet of drones to patrol the skies over the tri-state area. The article contained interviews with government officials past and present, including some who were in positions of power during the time of the 9/11 attacks.

"They're still trying to rewrite history to make

themselves look like they're the authority on all things terrorism," Griffin said to no one.

The former officials' comments regarding the drone deployment, that begged the public's collective amnesia regarding the fact that the attacks occurred on their watch, raised Griffin's blood pressure beyond reason. Though it was the last line of the article, which stated that the drones would be owned and monitored by a private company and would be carrying missiles "in case the need arose" and "for the protection of our citizens," that was the straw that broke the camel's back for Griffin.

"A corporate-owned drone with missiles, Molly," Griffin said, just loud enough for Molly to hear above the noise of the dishwasher. "A fucking burger corporation is going to be flying over our neighborhood with missiles."

Molly reluctantly walked back into the den, where she couldn't help but notice the red rising in Griffin's face.

"For God's sake, Molly, they own big-box stores, burger joints and sell soda, and now they're going to be flying over our heads with missiles."

Griffin smacked his paper on the arm of his chair and let it drop to the floor so he could flail his arms at will.

"What if we go to the wrong store? Do they blow us up?" Griffin made a tiny explosion sound with his mouth. "Sir, you have chosen the wrong cola." Griffin made the exploding sound again. "Not that burger." Again an exploding sound.

Molly found herself laughing at Griffin. She knew he had given up on staying furious for more than a minute at a time, lest he lose his life to a heart attack or be placed in the psych ward.

"The're watching us, Molly, and there's not a damn thing we can do about it." Griffin bent down to pick up the pages of his paper that he had scattered across the floor.

"Yeah, this surveillance thing was a lot easier to take when it was aimed at the Muslims," Molly said, letting Griffin know he wasn't the only one able to inject sarcasm into all things wrong with their world.

Griffin knew Molly was right. Initially those of Arab decent had taken the brunt of the surveillance and it had seemed as if they always would, but then it was the illegal aliens of whom everyone was told to be afraid. Suddenly ID laws and racial profiling were encouraged as a matter of public discourse by the scared citizens who feared that jobs and votes were being stolen.

The last stage of the plan didn't come, however, until all the prison systems were transferred to a private corporation. For reasons that initially defied logic, the government had agreed to pay the corporation stiff penalties if they did not keep the prison occupancy levels at ninety-nine percent. As a result, all efforts at curbing crime came to a screeching halt, and the war on drugs was intensified to the point that even friends and family members of drug dealers were being thrown in jail without evidence of wrongdoing. That, of course, swelled the United States' prison population, already the largest in the world, to numbers beyond capacity and created a need for even more prisons. More prisons, more money for private prison corporations, which meant more money siphoned into campaign coffers. A closed system fueled by greed and tightly controlled by so few that no one could stop it. Eventually, anyone who might have an ax to grind, like people who complained that their garbage hadn't been picked up, or who voiced opposition to an incumbent candidate or even people whose homes had been foreclosed on, would be considered Domestic Enemies and became fair game for any form of surveillance, with subsequent charges, real or trumped-up.

Thus, Griffin and Molly would soon be marked as Domestic Enemies, a distinction that would be included on their driver's licenses, encrypted in their license plates, noted in the Federal Medical Records Centralized Database, and tagged in the National Financial Monitoring System. All these measures were designed to stop Griffin, Molly and their ilk from escaping scrutiny or allowing them to talk amongst themselves.

These measures not only benefited the prison corporations and elected officials but also allowed the privatized surveillance industry to grow beyond reason. In addition it meant that Oliver, working for the government, would not be able to see or speak to his parents once they became Domestic Enemies. Which is why, whenever Molly overheard one of Griffin's and Oliver's heated conversations, she couldn't help but wonder if both father and son had become increasingly confrontational as a means of severing their relationship before the government did it for them.

Chapter 10

Tuesday, July 12, 1938
Joseph & Selma Gordon
New York City

By the time all the diners had finished their meals, and had retired to the restaurant's bar, Joe had given up all hope of stealing a copy of the Stratagem. Despite the fact that he had no idea what he would do with it, should it have actually come into his possession, he did know that without it, he would never be able to prove the truth about what its architects were planning.

Each night on his way out of the restaurant Joe would pass by Millie, the coat-check girl. She would always be standing there smiling behind the half door, dressed to the nines, full red lips, perfectly quaffed blond hair, and plenty of make-up. Joe would try not to notice her cleavage as he helped himself to one of the little square white mints she left in the dish on the counter next to her tip jar.

Usually, if she wasn't too busy hanging up a coat or flirting with a customer to garner a bigger tip, Millie would lean on the shelf of the bottom door and make Joe stop and talk to her about the unseasonably cold weather or about the goings on in his family. Tonight, however, when Joe passed by the coat room, the door was closed and the mints were gone, despite the fact that the bar was still full of diners enjoying multiple nightcaps.

Confused, Joe leaned his ear toward the door and heard an indistinguishable man's voice and then Millie's muffled words. It seemed to him as if they were arguing, but because he couldn't be sure, Joe felt compelled to move cautiously ahead.

Tentatively grabbing the door handle and pushing it open just a crack, Joe's initial view into the darkened room allowed him to see only shadows moving in the corner, but their words were now clear and their meaning unmistakable. Millie was struggling to free herself from the grip of the man who was holding her captive.

"Let me go." Millie's voice demanded, through her gritted teeth.

"Open your goddam mouth or I'll pull every hair out of your head, I swear."

Without further thought, Joe yanked the door open and the room flooded with light. Now he could clearly see what was happening. Millie was on her knees, pinned between the wall and her attacker and struggling to get away from the man who had firmly wrapped a large lock of her hair around his hand.

"Open, goddam it." Millie's attacker pulled her hair

tighter and drew her mouth closer to his open zipper, using her own hair as a weapon against her.

"What the hell are you doing?" Joe lunged at the attacker, pushing him backwards then landing on top of him. The unmistakable heavily laden smell of alcohol on the man's breath repulsed Joe, and he rushed to get away from it by standing up.

"You piece of shit." Joe's voice was loud and clear as he placed his foot firmly on the man's neck. "Move and I crush you."

The man, suddenly more helpless than his victim, lay still for Joe.

"Are you all right?" Joe turned his attention to Millie and extended his hand to help her up.

"I'll," Millie took a shallow breath, "I'll…" Millie took another breath. "be fine." Millie's words were painfully unconvincing and Joe worried that her injuries were far more serious than visible.

"I'm…fine." Millie insisted as she steadied herself with the help of the wall.

"Good, you go call the police. I'll wait here." Joe pressed his foot slightly lower onto the man's neck. The perpetrators eyes were wide, but he remained still. "He's not going anywhere."

"No police!" Millie gripped Joe's forearm, her fingernails pushed into his skin.

"Why?" Joe looked confused.

Millie pulled herself closer to Joe and whispered in his ear.

"Girls like me don't call the cops, and guys like him, they don't get arrested."

"I saw the whole thing, I'll vouch for your honor," Joe whispered back.

"And who are you? You think because you're a waiter in a fancy restaurant they're going to believe you instead of Diamond Jim over here?" Millie looked down on her attacker and began to fantasize about hurting him by stomping on his face with her heels then repeatedly kicking him in the groin. Her thoughts distracted her.

"Did you hear me?" Joe worked to get Millie's attention back by whispering louder. "I said we could at least try."

In response to Joe's naiveté, Millie offered a weak smile, but even that hurt and she began to rub her head in the sore spot where her hair had nearly been pulled out by the roots. "Don't bother. How many judges da you think this one here has in his pocket?" Before Joe could answer Millie continued." I'll tell ya…ALL of em." Millie emphasized the word, "all" and the heat from her breath filled Joe's ear. "Just get rid of him."

"You're sure?"

"Throw 'em out."

Even though he didn't believe that letting this man off the hook was a good idea, the speed at which he removed his shoe from the perpetrator's neck and pulled him off the floor, left no doubt as to how grateful Joe was to see the whole situation end.

"Get the hell out of here before I call the police, ya scum." Joe's empty threat made the frightened man practically trip over himself as he ran for the door, while pulling up his zipper, and craning his neck behind him to be sure Joe was not following him.

"Good riddance," Millie said under her breath before a momentary awkward, silence left she and Joe to gather their thoughts.

"Well whataya know." Millie had spotted a black leather briefcase left standing next to Joe in the middle of the floor and pointed to it. "Hand me that, will ya?"

Joe obliged Millie and brought the soft, fine leather case over to her.

"For my troubles." Millie wiped her face of the tears that were making her cheeks cold, then undid the leather straps on each side of the case, pushed open the briefcase's latch, and dumped its contents onto the floor. "Spectacles, pens, papers, garbage." Millie took a verbal inventory, while in her mind she critically assessed each item for their worth. Seeing nothing of value she reached back into the briefcase and delved deeper inside, searching its many pockets and pulling at the lining. "Now that's more like it." Millie efficaciously pulled out a fistful of hundred-dollar bills, rolled into a cylindrical shape. "Come to mama." Millie shoved the money into her cleavage and all evidence of her discovery disappeared.

Despite her windfall, Joe could see that the expression on Millie's face did not match her words. A hollow victory, he quickly surmised.

"And, Joe, this is for you. For ya troubles," Millie said before pushing the briefcase back into Joe's hands. "Pawn it, you'll get a good dollar. Or keep it for ya-self."

Joe could see right away that the gift he had been given could not be sold or used, as the attackers initials were clearly embossed into the leather.

"Look through the papers, maybe you'll see some bonds or some stock certificates, ya never know. Go ahead, look."

Millie's disingenuous generosity left Joe feeling somewhat annoyed, but he didn't have it in him to upset Millie. Instead he began looking through the papers as if he cared. Contracts, correspondence, nothing of interest or value, until Joe noticed a thick pile of papers, the cover of which had been tossed face down when Millie had dumped everything onto the floor. Placing the pages right side up, Joe momentarily stared at the cover in disbelief. *Stratagem for a New America*. Without further hesitation, and trying not to let on to his excitement, Joe shoved his prized papers back into the briefcase along with all the others, so as not to arouse suspicion.

"What was that?"

"Nothing," Joe lied, hoping Millie had not read the title on the cover. "Just want to clean up this mess so you can open the door. You know, in case someone wants their coat. Unless you're not all right, then I can stay and help you." Joe couldn't shake the nervous chatter that had come with the excitement of getting the *Stratagem* into his hands so unexpectedly.

"I'm okay now." Millie patted her cleavage then brushed off her dress and cautiously fussed with her hair, so as not to cause herself any pain. Again, Joe could see that the money had brought her no happiness. "I'll see ya tomorrow. Go home to ya wife."

"If you're sure."

Without answering, Millie shoved Joe lightly and pretended to smile, and Joe returned his own distracted smile back at her.

Chapter 11

Friday, October 18, 2024
Benjamin Gordon
Long Island, New York

"If a person who has secrets looks like they have secrets, they won't have their secrets for very long." That's what Benjamin used to tell his grandson Oliver, only Oliver could never figure out why.

Benjamin Gordon was the patriarch of the Gordon family, an unassuming ninety-year-old man whose hazy blue eyes shielded the complexities of his life. He was the kind of man who wore sweaters in the heat of the summer and heavy overcoats as soon as the October chill set in. His grey hair was thick and curly, and a bit longer than most men his age would normally sport, but no one seemed to mind. What they did mind was that every few weeks, and in spite of the sustained protests of his son Griffin and daughter-in-law Molly, Benjamin Gordon would get on the Long Island Railroad and presumably get off at his regular Coney Island stop to make his way to *shul* for Friday night Sabbath services.

Benjamin would tell his family he would be accompanying his best friend Saul home on that Friday night to partake in a lovely *Oneg Shabbat* followed by the eleven o'clock news, then bed. The next day, Benjamin said, he would be playing and, God willing, winning his monthly pinochle game, a game he would play with his four best friends, just as he had for as long as anyone could remember. Benjamin would say he would be eating with Saul and his wife, and sleeping on Saul's couch for the weekend, and that he wouldn't sleep well but he would be fine.

After all these years, his family still worried and Griffin still begged his father to "Stop the foolishness."

Benjamin, however, did not respond to his family's concerns and he never would. Because Benjamin did not go to Coney Island to play cards or to go to *shul*; he was going to attend a meeting. After the meeting, which always ended precisely at 1:30 p.m., Benjamin had plenty of time to hop back on the train to make his way to Amtrak and eventually to Union Station in Washington D.C., where he would meet his grandson, Oliver. Oliver would always be there to carry his bag and grab hold of his elbow, hoping to keep Benjamin steady up the escalators and along the way to one of many cabs waiting at the curb. They would share a late dinner and Benjamin would stay until Sunday morning, when he would do everything in reverse order, attending another meeting in Coney Island and making it home for a late dinner with the Gordons Sunday night.

It was a routine he had established when he had come to live with Griffin and Molly, and one he would not break or share the details of with anyone but his wife Mary.

Chapter 12

Saturday, September 17, 1938
Joseph & Selma Gordon
New York City

It was more than two months before Joe amassed the courage he needed to tell Selma how he had come into possession of the papers entitled Stratagem for a New America. He wouldn't tell her the part about how he had hidden the papers underneath the broken Victrola in the basement, lest she be reminded of his many promises to fix what had once been the showpiece of their living room. The Victrola had been out of commission for three months and stood next to their old Gramophone, which had not worked for at least ten years. Joe had no idea how to fix either, though he was loath to admit it. Now, however, the broken music players had become the least of his problems. For the past month, Joe had been sure that any minute someone would be pounding on his door or, worse, breaking it down, to get to the papers he was hiding. Every day he went over in his mind the possibility that someone had seen him walk out of the restaurant with a briefcase that clearly didn't belong to him, and he worried day and night for his own safety and the safety of his family. It had been a sleepless month.

Today, with everyone else out of the house and off to *shul* and then to the park, Joe and Selma were alone. This was a weekly occurrence of quiet, owing only to the fact that somewhere along the genetic line both Selma and Joe had lost the urge to converse with God at specific times in a specified building. Both had chosen instead to discuss concerns, beg for forgiveness, and rail against injustices in the privacy of their own heads. Despite their parents' protests and their children's pleading for the safety of their souls, Joe and Selma stayed home and took charge of the Saturday housecleaning and dinner. Not that there was much to clean, since Selma kept a spotless home the other six days of the week. Nevertheless, Joe knew that if he wished to talk to his wife he would have to follow her as she moved about the kitchen.

Now, Joe said to himself as he watched Selma scrub the outside of the kitchen cabinets with a vengeance. "Careful, Sel, you'll take the paint off."

Selma just smiled at Joe.

"Selma?"

Selma was opening the cabinet and removing a long stack of mismatched dinner plates, a direct result of combining households for survival. As each relative had moved in with them, each had stored their lives in basement boxes, and their clothing and place settings upstairs. At the time Selma had to explain to Joe the importance of people keeping their own plates, cups and saucers, even if there was barely any food to put on them.

"For three meals a day they can eat from their own plates. Plates are home. We can give them that, the feeling of home, even if they will never be there again."

Perhaps it would have been a small thing to others, but Joe knew that Selma's willingness to put a perfectly-matched dinner table aside for her guests' emotional comfort was a huge sacrifice for a woman who sought perfection in everything she did.

"I need to talk to you, Selma." As the words moved slowly from his mouth, Joe chose to look at the black and white squares of the floor instead of at his wife. "I have..." Before he could get out a third word, the doorbell rang and Selma was on her way out of the kitchen.

Temporarily relieved of his burden, Joe took a deep breath.

"Selma! *Gut Shabbos.*" The loud voice coming from the open door and offering up the Yiddish version of "Good Sabbath" belonged to Selma's cousin Miriam. Miriam was four foot practically nothing with flaming red hair, and a personality and energy to match. She came through the door wearing an orange dress, a purple hat, and carrying two pocketbooks. Miriam always carried two pocketbooks because she always wanted to be prepared. Prepared for what, she never said exactly, but Joe liked to tell everyone she used the second purse to steal their silverware. He claimed her constant chatter was a way to distract them while she robbed them blind. Selma would laugh at the suggestion but, nevertheless, counted the silverware every time she left.

"Yussel, *Gut Shabbos!*" Joe nodded. He didn't like when people spoke Yiddish since Selma always had to translate for him.

"I hear I should say *Mazel Tov*, Yussel?" Joe didn't have time to answer before Miriam continued. "A promotion to waiter? Oy, you should only do better than my cousin Yankel, *Alev Ha-Sholem.*"

"Yes, may he rest in peace," Selma injected, slyly translating for her husband and nodding toward the floor.

"A waiter, like you; but dead." Miriam smiled at Joe.

"How did he die?" Joe loathed the fact that Selma had just asked that question.

"Two veeks ago. Fancy-shmancy car pulls up to the restaurant, knocks the *shlemazel* on his *tuche*s. Oy. Such *mishegoss*. Oy, they needed a spatula to pick him up." Miriam laughed at her own words, but Selma didn't think that needing a kitchen utensil to pick up what was left of her cousin was something to laugh about.

"Come, sit down, Miriam." Selma would change the direction of the conversation by being a good hostess, even if it meant a disruption to her cleaning regimen and a hit to her meager supply of coffee. "Would you like something to drink, some coffee?"

"Water, water, that's all. *Oy gevalt*." Miriam sat down on the always-fluffed pillows of the couch, her feet barely touching the floor while Selma quickly retrieved the water, two cookies, and a coaster, which she placed on the coffee table barely within Miriam's reach. Joe chose the seat as far away from the couch as possible and now wished the old Victrola was upstairs so he could wash out the sound of Miriam's voice with music. Joe toyed with the idea of turning on the radio and pretending to have trouble choosing a station, but knew his actions would be slapped down by Selma, first politely in front of their guest and then with her seldom-seen wrath when they were alone. Joe's last choice was to sit and nod and allow his thoughts to swim in his head, but not the ones about the *Stratagem* or the dead waiter cousin.

"*Oy vey*, Selma." Miriam was speaking without prompting, flipping without warning or reason between English and Yiddish, a litany of ills, complaints and predictions of disaster at every turn. Joe knew that while the Yiddish language lent itself to the joys of the world, the sorrows were patently more than appropriate for these times.

As a means of distraction, Joe started keeping count of how many times Miriam said the word "*oy*." By the time he got bored of that game he was up to twenty-three. Joe's second game was to listen to the Yiddish words Miriam sprinkled through her conversation and count how many he actually knew. *Mechuleh*, which he remembered meant 'bankrupt,' and *tsuris*, which means 'woes,' were words Miriam used multiple times in reference to less-fortunate family members, of which she offered Joe and Selma's parents as examples. Comments that sent Joe reeling and Selma gritting her teeth at him, lest he say something for which she would end up having to apologize.

Joe also heard the word *meshuggeneh* more than once, which was the Yiddish word for 'crazy fool' and the one Yiddish word Joe used as he was finally able to slide the door closed behind Miriam. Luckily for Joe, Selma was already in the kitchen and could not hear him.

"Selma, come down from there!" Joe had entered the kitchen to see his wife balancing on the countertop on her tiptoes as she stretched to reach the tops of the kitchen cabinets. "I'll do that."

"I'm done," Selma told Joe, after assuring him of her safety regarding her precarious climb. Her assurances were based on the fact that she had been accomplishing this feat almost daily for many years. Once Selma was on the floor and Joe was able to contain his fears, he couldn't help but marvel at how the two of them were able to keep secrets from one another despite their close proximity, she her acrobatics routine and he the *Stratagem*.

"Sel, I need to talk to you." Joe was still holding Selma's hand after helping her down from the chair she had used to climb up onto the counter. "I need to tell you something." Joe looked right into his wife's eyes, and his serious tone finally made her want to stop what she was doing and listen.

Joe started the story.

Stratagem for a New America, Joe said as he ran his fingers across the words on the cover. "See, the word 'Stratagem' means it's a trick, Sel. I looked it up in the dictionary. It's like a scheme, a con."

Speaking slowly, to keep Selma from knowing the truth of how worried he really was, Joe told her all the details. But the more he spoke, the more impossible it became for him to remain calm.

"I tried to figure out how to steal a copy." Joe wasn't used to admitting he wanted to steal things. Even when he used to take the meat from the restaurant he would say it was 'borrowed,' insisting that sometime in the future he would pay for all he had taken.

"They put one of these by every place setting." Again Joe looked down at the *Stratagem*, which allowed him to avoid looking into Selma's eyes. "When everyone got up to leave, they all took their copies. There was no way for me to get one."

"But here it is."

"Right, well I'm getting to that." Joe had been so focused on how he would downplay the danger of possessing the *Stratagem*, he forgot that he would first have to explain to his wife what he had witnessed in the coatroom. As he spoke about Millie and her assailant, Joe edited the story for his wife to hear, carefully choosing his words for the sake of decorum, but making it crystal clear he was justified in his use of physical violence.

"And you didn't get hurt?" Even though she knew it had happened over a month ago, Selma looked her husband up and down, as if any damage might still be visible.

"No, I was fine."

"And no one saw you?" Selma couldn't help but feel anxious. "No one else knows about this?"

"Only Anthony. That waiter I told you about, the one with the ten children, he's Millie's cousin."

"She told him?"

"No, I did."

"Why?"

"What if he comes back, Sel? What if he wants his briefcase or his money and I'm not there? I needed someone to watch out for her."

Selma nodded in agreement of her husband's decision to enlist Anthony's help, and then hesitated as she took in the gravity of all that Joe had just told her.

"What did Anthony say?"

"Besides wanting to kill the guy?"

"Besides that."

"He said the men that come to these meetings, they're crazy, every one of them. Said they come here every month from all over the country. Last month it was Washington, before that California, before that it was

Texas. Always different people, always the same plan to take over the world."

"He said 'take over the world'? 'Take over the world.' What does that mean?" Selma hoped having details would somehow calm her fears.

"I don't know. Anthony laughed when he said it, but I can't figure out why. I haven't gotten too far into this," Joe again pointed to the stack of what he estimated was more than five hundred pages, "but it doesn't seem like what they're proposing is impossible. It's complicated though, and I haven't really read enough to know for sure, but what I do know from what I heard them say was that they don't think we should have the right to vote."

"What?" Selma cringed at the thought of this relatively-new privilege being taken away from her. "They can't take that away. Why, who will stand for that?"

"I thought the same thing when they talked about it during dinner, but look at this." Joe opened the book to a picture of a voting booth, and then flipped through page after page of drawings. "See, it's instructions on how to make the machines cast the same vote over and over no matter what lever you press."

Then Joe showed Selma the other page, the page with the letter from the government agency, the one on the most official-looking letterhead he had ever seen in his life. Joe just pointed to it, then let Selma read it.

"What?" Was the first and last thing Selma said,

before making Joe promise to God he would remove the papers from the house and bring them back to the restaurant trash can as soon as tomorrow.

Joe swore to his wife he would do so. He told her the next day he had done so. Though, as it turned out, he never offered her any proof.

Chapter 13

Friday, October 18, 2024
Oliver & Abigail Gordon
Washington, D.C.

"Only fear and arrogance stand in the way of the truth" were the words on the plaque that Oliver had hung in his living room. Every time he saw it there, Benjamin would wonder when his grandson would figure out what it really meant.

When Abigail Baylor first met Oliver Gordon she had been trying to arrange a meeting with his boss, Wilson Rhine, an incumbent senate candidate from the State of Pennsylvania and the perfect person to interview for a story on the environment. Unfortunately, since most of his state was now an environmental disaster, thanks to the legislation pushed and passed by the laissez-faire lawmaker, he was also the hardest person to pin down for an interview on this issue. It was only in their chance meeting at the Penn Club in New York City, where Senator Rhine was holding a discussion and book signing of, *Hands Off My State*, that Abigail was able to talk Oliver into a ten minute interview with Rhine. This was a not a feat accomplished through Abigail's superior powers of persuasion, but rather that Oliver had fallen instantly and insatiably in love with this woman who would, within the year, become his bride.

Strong of will and politically opposed to all that Oliver stood for, Abigail was the exact opposite of everything he should have wanted in a wife. But the tall lanky, stunning brunette with the bluest of eyes and coco brown skin captivated him in a way no other woman ever had. Abigail's unique beauty was the direct result of the juxtaposed features of her white mother and African-American father. It was a curious match and one that could only be explained by those who supported the theory that opposites attract.

"You don't look like a Penn Club member." His comment and her confused response as to what a Penn Club member looked like were etched in Abigail's mind, and she suspected always would be, since it was not just Oliver who had fallen in love that evening.

"An unfortunate pairing," she thought to herself as she dressed in Oliver's hotel room the next morning, leaving her card on his bedside table before he woke. When Oliver called her later that afternoon, he told her the interview was set up, as were their dinner reservations.

Over her salad and his Boeuf Bourguignon, as well as their multiple glasses of wine, each would admit to the other their fears that the previous night's sex had been used merely as a means to an end, instead of for reasons of the heart. Their honesty, which ironically Oliver believed to be the hallmark of their relationship, was a risk for sure, one that each would always be glad they had taken.

From that first night in New York, there never passed another day when the two would not spend hours communicating through low or high tech means and always supposedly in secret, though Abigail doubted that was actually the case.

In Washington D.C., where senators could sleep with interns, lobbyists could marry congressmen, and diplomats could do whatever the hell they wanted with whomever they wanted, real reporters, as opposed to the ones that just regurgitated White House press releases, were persona non grata. Thus for Oliver, who served at the right hand of a senator with presidential aspirations, and Abigail, who tried to fix the world through her investigative journalism, their relationship had to remain a secret for now. A secret they kept from their bosses and from the majority of their colleagues, friends and families. Even the people in their condo complex knew the two only as neighbors who passed pleasantries in the hall, not as a couple who had installed a door that led from his bedroom closet to hers.

The one exception to this information embargo regarding their relationship was Oliver's grandfather,

Benjamin. 'Gamps,' as Oliver had called him since he could speak, had been coming to Washington once a month for years to continue the supportive relationship that had become the antithesis of Oliver's relationship with his father, as well as the means by which he learned to tolerate his father.

How many times had his grandfather insisted to Oliver that his father was indeed proud of him, that his father loved him, that opposites could love one another, offering his own relationship as well as Oliver's as proof? Examples, with which Oliver could not argue. After all, his grandparents, though painfully in love, could debate the color of grass; and he and Abigail, despite their feet being firmly planted on opposite sides of the Washington divide, were certainly in love with each other. Nevertheless, every time his grandfather came to visit Oliver would reenact word for word the latest argument and bone of contention between himself and his father, which Gamps would inevitably smooth over with a call for compassion and an occasional reality check.

"Particularly painful assault on your father this week, so I hear." This time Oliver's grandfather brought up the subject as he stepped off the train. "Your father's got too much stress. I'm worried." Benjamin held on to the subject, but did not have to go much further with his concerns because by the time the pair had made it to the cab

Oliver was apologizing to his grandfather and promising to call his father that evening to apologize to him as well.

"Now it will be a good weekend," Benjamin Gordon exclaimed to himself in the cab.

"A good weekend." Benjamin said again, as soon as he detected the comforting aroma of Abigail's chicken soup wafting through the hallway of Oliver's apartment.

Abigail was not Jewish, but she could cook any dish so well that any ethnic group would be proud to take her in as one of their own. Benjamin was extremely pleased, not only because his grandson had chosen to marry a woman with superior culinary skills, but because he had also chosen one who possessed a good heart, intelligence and a quick, oftentimes hilarious wit, which he assured the couple would see them through good times and bad.

"Honey, we're home." Oliver whispered into the room as if there were a baby asleep nearby.

"Gamps!" Abigail had taken to calling Benjamin in the familiar vernacular of the family, and welcomed her adopted grandfather with a hug, followed by instructions to sit for a big hot bowl of chicken soup.

"Matzo balls, they should be like lead weights. No, fluffy, like feathers. They should drop to the bottom of the pot like stones. They should rise to the top and bob." Abigail imitated the ritual matzo ball argument that took place between grandchild and grandfather and always preceded the sounds of 'ummm' as each slipped into the silence of eating.

"Look, I've customized your balls." Abigail was speaking and laughing at her own joke, all the while wondering if she should be making a dirty joke in front of Gamps. "Soft for you." Abigail put the plate in front of Benjamin. "And hard for you." Abigail put a second plate down in front of her husband, but not before winking.

"Whoa, Abby," Oliver shifted his eyes towards his grandfather. "It's *Shabbos*, for God's sake!" Oliver pretended to scold his wife, but his involuntary smile and escaping laugh betrayed him.

Benjamin laughed too, but seemed more interested in heading right for the soup and the homemade challah bread.

Throughout the dinner there was, as usual, more laughter and discussions about food, family, and travel, as well as stories from Oliver's and Abigail's wedding, which had taken place outside the country and off the radar. By dessert, the subject of work would come up, which for these two Washington insiders meant politics.

Usually, and Benjamin readily admitted this, he would first ask Abigail about her work, the story she was working on at the time. He would start with, "So what corrupt politicians are you trying to hang now?" He would say it lightheartedly with a smile, and Abigail would answer back seriously and at length.

Poor Oliver, Benjamin thought at these times, because his grandson would have to listen and have no choice but to love his bride anyway.

Most of the time Abigail would not notice her husband's discomfort as she accused this politician or that of one bad behavior after another, ignoring the fact that her husband might have just had lunch or shared a drink with the man she was now calling a traitor, fool, idiot or downright evildoer. As far as Abigail was concerned, you could depend on politicians to do two things: give themselves praises and give themselves raises. Everything else they were sure to screw up.

When Abigail was finished with the latest news of impending doom, it was Oliver's turn to update his grandfather on the status of the legislation he was working on for Senator Rhine. Benjamin would listen to his grandson intently, but also never failed to notice that, no matter how often his new granddaughter would roll her eyes at the mere mention of the senator's name or how many times she had to excuse herself to calm down, when all was said and done and the dessert dishes were in the dishwasher, Abigail was in love with Oliver again. Maybe more so.

"I think I'll turn in." That was always Benjamin's signal to his grandchildren that political discussions for the evening were over and that the eleven o'clock news was coming on. However, tonight after he had given his requisite hugs and kisses, Benjamin stopped his walk toward the bedroom and turned around.

"Do you ever wonder why all those stories you write don't change anyone's mind? Did anyone in Washington ever come up to you and say, "Hey, Abigail, thanks for that information, I had no idea that what I was going to vote on would destroy the environment. I think I'll change my vote." Abigail listened to Benjamin's words, but before she could respond, the conversation switched to Oliver.

"Oliver, did you ever wonder how your boss got reelected? He voted to do away with Medicare and Social Security. He voted to raise taxes on the poor and middle class, and left the rich to count their money. How does someone like that get reelected?"

"If you raise taxes on the rich, they don't create jobs, Grandpa."

Suddenly demoted from 'Gamps' to 'Grandpa,' Benjamin knew he had hit a nerve. "What jobs, Oliver? How many years has it been since they raised taxes?"

"If we had raised taxes, it would be worse, trust me."

Trust me. In his mind Benjamin laughed at his grandson as he remembered what his own grandfather used to say. *Only a fool trusts a politician – ask any politician's wife.*

"Your brothers are out of work, I and your other grandfather were forced out, your parents lost their teaching jobs. Where's the 'trickle down'?" Benjamin bent his fingers around the last two words.

"My brothers are lazy, and the only reason my parents aren't teaching is because they refused to switch schools."

Benjamin remained calm, stuck to the facts, and hoped that Oliver could handle the truth.

"Your brothers are not you, I will grant you that; but they are both college graduates and have been willing to take any job if there was one. As for your parents, they refused to switch to the private school because working there would have made all their agreements with the union null and void."

"So what? Without a public school what's the point of the union?"

"Null and void their retirement, Oliver." Benjamin couldn't help but emphasize his grandson's name because of his inability to see the bigger picture. "What little there was left of their retirement accounts after the public school system was declared bankrupt would have been lost. As it is, they ended up using most of the money to put your brothers through college, and to keep up with the mortgage payments."

Oliver didn't know this about his parents and didn't know why he didn't.

"Oliver, tell me," Benjamin questioned, even though he already knew his grandson's thoughts, "you believe that the millions of people who are out of work are all as lazy as you seem to think your brothers are?"

Oliver didn't even have to think. He knew the answer was yes and said so.

"So if their motivation for staying unemployed is laziness, then do you also believe that it is easier to live hand to mouth than to work?"

"Absolutely. You don't even have to get dressed in the morning. Hell, you never have to get dressed."

"And all those homeless people, the ones living in cars and in the woods, those people are lazy too?"

"More so."

"So you believe it's easier to live without a roof over your head or food on the table?"

"Generally. But what's your point?"

"I'm just surprised. I've never really thought that it was easier to be homeless than it is to go to work. I'm just a little surprised you do."

"It's easy enough; that's why we got rid of the shelters. They can either make it work or they can go to work: we're not going to coddle them anymore."

"And if you lost your job you wouldn't mind living the lazy life?" Benjamin tried not to sound sarcastic.

"Me? Well no, I would hate that; but I'm not lazy, so it would never happen to me."

"And how do you know that?"

"Because, I told you, I'm not lazy."

"That's what I thought." Benjamin was frowning.

"What? You're not happy to hear that I'll never be a burden to society? That I'm a hard worker and that I'm smart enough not to fall into the traps my parents fell into?"

"And you believe that too, Abigail?"

Abigail wanted to say no, but the truth was that she, like many Washington liberal thinkers, had removed herself far enough from the poor to be able to regard those who spent their evenings dumpster-diving as being too lazy to work. Unlike the environment and the wildlife she believed needed protecting, she viewed people as being in charge of their own fate.

"Yes. Well, maybe not all the unemployed are lazy, but I'd say the majority are."

"There are jobs out there, Grandpa, for those who want them." Oliver slid his response across the room with conviction, despite the fact that he had no facts to back it up.

"You are aware that if it wasn't for your parents, I'd be living on the street?"

Benjamin's grandchildren remained silent.

"Do you consider me lazy?"

Abigail and Oliver answered simultaneously and emphatically that Benjamin was not lazy.

"Well, I guess I'm a victim of circumstances?"

Oliver nodded his head yes, but was unable to make the connection his grandfather wanted him to.

"No, I'm not a victim of circumstances. I was screwed. I did my part. I paid into my Social Security fund, and I was promised I would get a certain amount back. I had a contract with the Federal Government, and your Senator Rhine broke that contract."

Now Oliver had a good answer for his grandfather. He had written at least fifty speeches for his boss on this very subject.

"Well, technically, they didn't take it from you because it was a socialist program that never should have existed in a free democratic and capitalistic society in the first place. Arguably, the whole program was unconstitutional right from the get-go, and it was headed for bankruptcy from the very beginning, just like all Ponzi schemes."

"So it was a Ponzi scheme?"

"Essentially."

"That's how you see this?" Benjamin wanted to get angry, but held himself back as a means to an end.

"It's not like you weren't warned, Grandpa. Everyone was warned, for God's sake. Your father was warned, but no one listened. In the end it came down to math. You can't take money out of a bankrupt system. Even you can appreciate that."

Even you? His grandson's condescension swam around in Benjamin's head. *Even you?* Benjamin was used to such scorn directed at Griffin, but now that the loaded gun was pointing at him it was much harder for him to remain calm. "You saw the numbers, the facts and figures from the Social Security reports? And the total was zero?"

"Well, no, but there would have been only enough money to last another ten, maybe fifteen years at best, so they cut it off before the damage had become too great."

"I'm not sure what you mean by the damage being greater than what happened. Oliver, I lost everything. Do you know what that did to me and your grandmother, to lose our home, everything we worked for?" Perhaps Benjamin had gone too far. It wasn't in his plan for Oliver to see his eyes fill with tears. "We got statements every year that said how much money we had invested in our retirement. It was our money that we worked hard for, not some socialist handout."

Benjamin couldn't look up, but if he had he would have seen the struggle in his grandson's eyes, his working to understand why his grandfather was saying these things. This was the first time Benjamin had ever alluded to not being on board with all that Oliver did, and Benjamin knew he was shaking his grandson's world. But he also knew that once the family had moved and was put on the D.E. list Oliver would no longer be allowed to have any contact with his parents, and Benjamin wanted his grandson to know exactly what he would be giving up his family for.

"You make it sound so black-and-white. It's not, Grandpa. You don't understand."

"I understand perfectly, though I disagree. It all

comes down to black and white, but in Washington what's black is white and what's white is black. We can continue this discussion tomorrow." Benjamin decided he needed to stop, and moved toward the bedroom without turning to look back at his grandchildren.

* * *

There was no chance that Oliver and Abigail would enjoy a good night's sleep. For hours the two spoke in hushed tones, first dismissing Benjamin and then acquiescing to some of his truths.

"What did he mean by 'How did Rhine get reelected'? He got reelected because he's good at what he does." Oliver worked his brain to affirm his belief in the relevance of his work.

Abigail didn't answer Oliver; she was too busy concentrating on Benjamin's assertion that her writing about the environment didn't make any difference.

Neither one focused on the homeless or on the poor or on the Social Security money that Benjamin had lost; instead both stayed focused on the value of their highly-self-regarded positions. When they finally fell asleep they did so out of the exhaustion they felt from spending hours internally defending the legitimacy of their jobs.

* * *

"Lovely day, children!" Benjamin knew by the looks on their faces, even before he had finished his words, that he had caused the disruption in his grandchildren's thoughts and sleep that he had intended, though, he might have been somewhat disappointed if he had known how focused the two had been on their own careers over the more substantive issues he had raised.

"I made the coffee and got some bagels and lox from the corner." Between sips of black coffee and savored bites from his bagel, Benjamin continued his cheerful one-sided conversation.

"Poll has Rhine up by 20 points." Benjamin read the headline from the newspaper. "Huh. Another park in Maine and one in Pennsylvania given to Cyborge Gas. Huh – just gave it away. Two more prisons are going up in Virginia – two? Huh. Oh, six more drone fleets ordered – excellent." Benjamin's sarcasm was obvious and intentional.

"She doesn't let me have lox anymore, you know." Benjamin was referring to his wife, and the fact that one bagel, piled high with lox as this one was, contained more salt than the doctor said he should have in a week.

For their part, Oliver and Abigail took turns smiling at the conversation their grandfather was having with himself, all the while picking at their own breakfasts between wide yawns and thoughts of getting back into bed. When Benjamin had finally finished the better part of his breakfast and the newspaper, he decided it best to dive back into the conversation he had begun the night before. His intent to introduce his grandson to the truth about elections was not something he was looking forward to, although his biggest concern right now was what Oliver might do with the information.

Chapter 14

Saturday, November 12, 1938
Joseph & Selma Gordon
New York City

Though enough time had passed to assuage any fears Selma might have had regarding the Stratagem, Joe believed that if his wife knew the papers were still in the basement she would not hesitate to dispose of them herself this time.

Even if Selma wasn't home, there was usually someone else in the house who might have informed her of Joe's time spent in the basement. Then Joe would have to come up with a good excuse for what he was doing. He knew Selma had all but given up on the items she had placed downstairs for him to fix. Instead, she now chose to believe that one day, after the Depression was truly over, they would be able to afford a handyman to come in and repair all that had been broken.

Joe, on the other hand, was not as convinced that the Depression would ever end. Yes, he knew he was exceedingly lucky to have a job at all and lucky to have been promoted to waiter, but the fact remained that his wages were meager, the hours sparse, and the tips were surprisingly low considering the clientele. At the end of the month, after food and rent were paid, there was not much more than a few dollars left over for the other necessities of life.

"Just let me get a job. A few hours a week," Selma would beg Joe each time they got to the end of the month with nothing more than spare change in their pockets but Joe would not hear of it.

It was not as if Joe thought his wife incapable of work. He just believed a married woman's job was her home and family, and that was enough. In fact the only time Joe ever wished his wife would go out and work was on those occasions when he wanted to read more of the *Stratagem*. In the months since he had obtained the document, he had barely scratched the surface of the plan because, truth be told, his limited education didn't allow for much more than a reading of the words and not necessarily their understanding. Joe had slightly better success deciphering the diagrams, though because of the limits of his mechanical know-how he would not actually be capable of performing any of the tasks as instructed in the illustrations.

Eventually, Joe came to the conclusion that he needed another way to approach the situation, one that would bypass Selma's watchful eye and get him the knowledge he sought. Immediately, and with a feeling of annoyance at not having considered this before, Joe thought of Sam.

Chapter 15

Tuesday, November 12, 2024
Molly & Griffin Gordon
Andrew & Kendall Gordan
Long Island, New York

They called it the "Office of Encumbrance" because they didn't want to just come out and say how much they loathed old people.

Sunday night family dinners were different now. Window shades were closed and television volumes were raised as calendars were pulled out for review, leaving dates discussed, the farmer's almanac consulted. Money was counted, usually by the grandparents and only in silence. Checklists and building plans were brought out, covering the spots on the table where Molly used to place the food. Meals were now served from one pot in the kitchen, usually pasta or eggs, and there would be no side dishes.

"The tomato sauce is all the vegetables you need."
"There is broccoli and cheese in the eggs, you don't need

more," Molly would say to her children before they asked, because she felt she knew what they were thinking.

Molly never had to worry about what Griffin's parents Benjamin and Mary were thinking, as she knew exactly how they felt. Almost daily for the past two years, they had inundated her with their gratitude at just being able to live there. Even Molly's own parents, when they were still alive, routinely gushed with appreciation for taking them in.

"Now that was a shell game if ever there was one." Molly remembered her father telling her that April day in '22 when he was forced into retirement. "I paid into Social Security my whole life and the politicians..." Molly noticed her father wince when he said the word 'politicians.' "and the politicians used my money, your mother's money, your money and everyone's money to build jails; beautiful, new, private, corporate-run jails. But don't worry, they tell me, because see, in with this pink slip..." Molly's father had pulled out a small pink slip and what looked to be a white business card.

"For Your Retirement"

Her father read the bold print on the first line then adjusted the white card back and forth so he could see the small print.

If you can no longer afford your apartment or home or need money for food, you must apply to the Office of Encumbrance for assignment within the next 48 hours.*

"'Assignment.' You know what that means, Molly? It means go live in one of those old *fakakta* jail cells."

Molly had seen the news reports of happy seniors in brightly-colored cells with real furniture and pastel-colored bars on the windows adorned with lacy curtains. The reporter had touted the use of real doors on each "apartlet", healthcare on site, awesome security, and assurances that the bars and barbed wire had remained to keep unwanteds out rather than to keep seniors in.

"And here, look at the fine print, the note at the bottom, Molly. This. Read this."

Molly remembered taking the small piece of paper from her father's shaking hand, seeing his eyes, his cloudy, barely-blue eyes and reading the tiny printed words out loud.

*If you have any living children you are <u>AUTOMATICALLY</u> <u>DISQUALIFIED</u> from receiving Encumbrance Benefits.

Molly knew this was part of the "Family First" initiative that touted the use of family resources before government resources. A concept that sounded good until you considered the realities of families.

Of course Molly would take her father and mother in, and she said so immediately as her father took out his handkerchief to wipe his eyes. It was not until that night, when the reality of the conversation she had had with her dad had set in, that Molly allowed herself the image of her father and mother living in a jail cell and dining at picnic tables in a room with hundreds of other old people, eating off of tin trays and drinking out of metal cups like criminals. An image that made her feel physically sick.

"The real criminals are the politicians who stole our retirement money. Griffin's been right all along." At the time, Molly had said that out loud to no one, and knew she owed Griffin an apology. Of course she had pretended to support him and his ideas with her silence. However, up until this point, until it became as real as her father's tears, Griffin's words had just been warnings of things to come.

When Molly shared her thoughts with Griffin that night two years ago, and talked of how difficult her conversation had been with her father, her husband's response was so immediate she knew this wasn't the first time he'd had the thought.

"We need to make a plan, Molly. We need to survive without the help of the government."

"Or in spite of it," Molly had added through her clenched teeth.

That's when it started for Molly: her saving pennies, serving one-pot meals, reading books on raising chickens and milking cows. That's when she started spending her evenings in the basement reviewing the food inventory with her daughter-in-law Kendall, a job the two of them now shared.

Kendall had married one of Molly's twins, Andrew, right out of college. At the time Andrew was working and had avoided the plague of unemployment that had engulfed the vast majority of his classmates.

However, thanks to the Supreme Court ruling that determined that life begins two weeks before conception, outlawed contraception, and forced women to prove their innocence in the loss of a child through miscarriage, Kendall could not find a job. Corporate risk managers fearing that women would shift the blame for any miscarriages on to their employer, decided long ago that the only way to avoid criminal liability was to not employ females of childbearing age in the first place.

Two years later, and still five years short of being able to collect unemployment benefits, Andrew lost his job too. The old requirement of having to work eighteen consecutive months to collect unemployment had gone out the window with the forty-hour work week and the child labor laws. They were all considered too restrictive in the 'emergency' that was this economy. The new, more lax requirements allowed companies to get significantly more work out of their employees while avoiding messy regulations. As a result, profits rose to unimaginable heights while salaries dipped to never-before-seen lows.

The American Dream, such as it was, had died and it had become painfully clear to everyone that no matter how hard they worked there was no way to get ahead.

The days of small business entrepreneurship ended on the day corporations opened their own deregulated banks and choked off credit to anyone who might compete on even the smallest of scales.

With no other jobs in sight and little hope for the future, the newlyweds moved in with the Gordons. Kendall's family was not an option. As the youngest of seven children, Kendall was not welcome to bring yet another mouth to feed into a home that already housed more residents than beds. This mandate was actually fine by Kendall, who saw her in-laws' plans to become self-sustaining organic farmers as the first ray of hope she had seen since graduation.

"I never envisioned Andrew and I as a cross between the homesteaders on *Little House on the Prairie* and the out-of-place New Yorkers on *Green Acres,* but here we are."

"Yes, here we are," Molly responded to her daughter-in-law between checks on the inventory sheet.

"When we leave, you'll have to do this yourself." Kendall let her words hang in the air. She knew that the revised plan was for her, Andrew, Tyler, and Kris to leave as soon as spring broke, while Molly and Griffin were to stay behind and continue to work until the bills overwhelmed them.

"It won't be a problem. You'll be taking most of the food and supplies with you. There won't be that much left to inventory." Molly tried to reassure the young girl by acting nonchalant about the circumstances that had kept her stomach tied in knots most days.

"You'll be okay, then?"

"Why would you think I wouldn't be?"

"Oh, no reason," Kendall lied.

"We'll be fine, trust me." Molly moved toward Kendall to hug her, allowing the hard wooden clipboard to come between them. "We will be fine." Molly looked into her very young daughter-in-law's eyes, and Kendall hoped she wasn't lying.

Chapter 16

Friday, December 6, 2024
Oliver & Abigail Gordon
Washington, D.C.

When the person you have depended on your whole life suddenly disappears, the world as you knew it is gone forever.

When Benjamin first told him about the *Stratagem*, Oliver began to worry that his grandfather had teetered over the line into senility. However, when his grandfather explained why he had never told anyone else about it and promised to bring a copy as proof, the possibility that the aforementioned treatise actually existed seemed almost plausible. Now, one month later, after giving much thought to his grandfather's words and doing some preliminary research of his own, Oliver had once again become apprehensive.

"Where is he?" Oliver called loudly to Abigail as she struggled to raise her eyes above the heads of the masses that had just departed from the inbound Amtrak train from New York.

"I can't see him," Abigail shouted back against the

sound of the train pulling from the station, and then she grabbed her husband's hand as a defense against a crowd which seemed determined to shove them apart. It was a sign of connection she rarely exhibited in public, but one she made an exception for lest she lose sight of her husband, too.

"This is the right train, isn't it?" Abigail asked, even though she knew the answer.

"2:05, that's what he said," Oliver shouted back as a train on another track left the station.

Within minutes the crowd that had filled the platform was almost non-existent. Oliver tried using his cell to call his grandfather; but Benjamin's voicemail immediately picked up, signaling to Oliver that his grandfather had once again forgotten to charge his phone.

"No answer," Oliver told Abigail as he pushed the phone back into his pocket. Without discussion the couple instinctively began to scan the area around them and further down the platform. There were no grandfathers anywhere. A few businessmen looking at their phones, a group of teens hugging, and the destitute who cleaned in the station all day in exchange for being able to sleep in abandoned railroad cars at night, but no grandfather.

Oliver walked over to one of the cleaners and inquired about Benjamin, describing him to a tee. The worker, a man who looked to be in his thirties, and surprisingly clean-shaven, pointed to the stairs that led up to the concourse. At Abigail's insistence, Oliver offered the man a ten dollar bill. An unnecessary gratuity in Oliver's mind, given the fact that anyone could have pointed up the stairs and in most cases have been correct. Especially since the platform was now practically empty.

With no other choices possible, the couple moved up the stairs to the massive concourse where thousands rushed about, all as if they were going to miss their trains. Again, Oliver tried Benjamin's cell phone, which got him the same results.

Normally, Oliver would want to be methodical and walk the parallel lines of the concourse using the floor tiles as his guide until he found his grandfather. Conversely, Abigail's preference would have been to run through the expanse of the concourse willy-nilly, screaming Benjamin's name until he answered. Instead they stood, frozen to the ground in fear, silently calling his name in their heads while scanning the unfamiliar faces of the crowd, as if somehow their grandfather would just appear.

Chapter 17

Thursday, December 8, 1938
Joseph & Selma Gordon
New York City

Mario Impolitanio was a wealthy man who had come to America in 1894 after the collapse of the Italian Bank and the ensuing political unrest. His belief that assimilation and education were the keys to success led him to legally change his family's last name to Smith and to arm all ten of his children, including the girls, with college degrees. Additionally, his experience with having barely escaped his hometown of Sicily with his wealth intact prompted Mario, and subsequently his children, to hide their gold and cash under their mattresses, in their wallets, and in cement encasements buried in their backyard. Even if something happened in one of their many hiding places, the Smiths could sleep soundly knowing there was always a lot more money hidden someplace else.

Sam Smith was Mario Impolitanio's eldest son, a short, stocky man who credited his wife's meatballs for his need to lengthen his suspenders after every meal. Sam was the father of twelve children, sported two college degrees, one in economics and the other in accounting, and just happened to be Joe's best friend and former business partner.

Luckily, with the help of his father's wealth and home

banking system, Sam was able to weather the Depression while he waited for America's, and more importantly his own, comeback.

Sam's real concern, however, was for Joe, who had rebuffed all his offers of financial help. In fact, Sam had pleaded with his friend to take some money instead of taking "that job" in the restaurant.

Joe's family had brought some things from the Old Country too, but in their case the Old Country was Russia, and instead of money they had brought an intractable pride, a pride that would have Joe live on the street before admitting that he needed money.

So beyond the need to see to his family's financial wellbeing, Sam's motivation also extended to making sure Joe got out of the restaurant and back into the dressmaking business where he belonged.

The ground beneath Joe's feet was slippery. The sudden drop in temperature overnight had turned yesterday's rain water into a thin sheet of ice on the sidewalk. It was an unusually cold December morning with a frosty air that penetrated to the bone. As he walked through the streets of New York, Joe's left hand held his scarf up against his mouth while his right forearm pressed the large envelope beneath his coat, a reflex reaction for protection against both the chill and thieves. Considering Joe's intended destination was ten blocks away, such weather would normally send him from the street onto the trolley, but it was the end of the month and his remaining pocket change had to go toward necessities, not the convenience of traveling to Sam's house in the warmth of the street car.

By the time he knocked on Sam's door, Joe could hardly feel his fingers, which was why the Smiths could barely hear his knock. Their concern that something must have gone horribly wrong in the Gordon home for Joe to venture out in such weather was immediately assuaged by his assurances that everything was fine.

"Thank God," Joe added. Then he inquired as to the well-being of the Smiths.

"We are doing well, considering."

Sam did not have to continue his sentence. "Considering" always came right before the words "the Depression" whether it was said out loud or not.

"I'm so glad you're here."

Joe noticed Sam seemed particularly happy to see him, but attributed the warm welcome to the length of time the two had been apart.

"Come, come to my study." Ignoring their usual routine of coffee and conversation around the kitchen table before the start of work, Sam quickly ushered his friend to a room of sculpted woods and books and living memories of their previous meetings. Joe immediately noticed that nothing in the room had changed, and moved to sit down at the mahogany table next to the warmth of the fireplace in the same high-backed, black leather chair as always.

"We're going back into business, Joe," Sam blurted out to his friend before Joe was even settled in his chair. In the excitement of the moment, Sam's plan to ask Joe to join him in his new business venture had inadvertently come out like a foregone conclusion.

"A couture clothing line for the *zaftig* women of New York. They have more money than they know what to do with, and they're always trying to fit into dresses made for women half their size. You can make beautiful dresses for them."

Sam went on to assure Joe he could raise the necessary capital. Considering they were still in the throes of the Depression, Joe wondered if that entailed digging up some of the gold in Sam's backyard. Either way, he trusted that his partner could come through with the cash.

"In fact, I was going to call you today about a store on Fifth Avenue." Sam told Joe the particulars of the small shop, the owner of which had fallen on hard times and was willing to make a deal that they could not pass up.

For Joe, the juxtaposition of the frightening matters that lay within the papers he had just placed on the table and the joyous news that perhaps his dream would be coming true left him silent.

"How is it possible my partner has no words?"

Instead of answering, Joe got up from his chair and threw the biggest hug he could muster around his friend and once-again business partner.

"I will take that as a 'yes'."

"You can take that to the bank, sir," Joe quipped with a wink, knowing full well Sam's abhorrence of banks.

As the two men began to talk of meetings and plans and ways to accomplish what, just minutes ago, he would not have believed possible, Joe wanted nothing more than to revel in the excitement of their new venture. Thoughts of rushing home to Selma and letting her know that soon they would not have to worry about putting food on the table and clothing on their backs filled his imagination. For the first time in a very long time, Joe started to believe that everything would be alright again. Even the *Stratagem*, which periodically begged for his attention like the flames of the fireplace leaping at his side, seemed less important.

"Lunch, gentlemen?" Sam's wife placed a silver tray with a variety of sandwiches and fresh cups of coffee on the table, and before either could look up from their work she was gone.

"Thank you, Lydia!" Sam called after his wife, having no idea if she had heard him.

"Where has this day gone?" Joe had expected to be home hours before and felt lucky he had chosen to visit his friend on a day he was not also scheduled to work.

"I think we've done all we can for now, at least until we can take a look at the shop." As Sam began collecting and organizing all the papers strewn about the table, he noticed the large envelope sitting in front of his friend.

"What is this, Joe?"

Joe answered by removing the document from the envelope and sliding it toward Sam. After reading the title, *Stratagem for a New America,* out loud, Sam's curiosity led him to turn the page and read in silence.

With Sam engrossed in the contents of the *Stratagem,* Joe kept himself busy by once again reading through the business plan they had just developed. By doing so he hoped to make the dream of a new business more real in his mind, as well as stave off the anxiety of waiting for Sam's response.

"Where did you get this?" Sam spoke while he continued reading.

Although Joe didn't want to answer without Sam's full attention, he could no longer hold his thoughts in, and told the story of how he had come into possession of the papers. He listed the participants of the meeting, which he knew would verify the credibility of the document.

"Genius," Sam said under his breath and he continued reading for at least thirty more minutes until he abruptly stopped. "Get rid of this. That's my suggestion."

"But you have to tell me why you think…" Before Joe could finish his sentence, he was interrupted.

"The die's been cast. There's nothing you can do. Best to stay out of it."

"So you want them to get away with it?"

"You have no choice in the matter. According to this, it's just a matter of time before everyone will be going to the polls and pulling those little levers for nothing."

"And you're okay with that?" Joe was not happy with his friend's nonchalant attitude. Sam just shrugged.

"It's really rather brilliant, when you think about it." Sam flipped to the map of the United States where stars marked the locations of the *Stratagem's* targets. "See, here are the districts up for grabs in the battleground states. They all have voting machines, and all the voting machines are warehoused between elections. How much money do you think it would take for a watchman to turn the other way while they tamper with the machines?"

Joe wasn't at all sure, but told Sam he suspected it wouldn't take much.

"Right. Watchmen don't make much of a living, and these guys..." Sam tapped on the stack of papers with his index finger, "these guys roll their cigars in hundred dollar bills. Paying off night watchmen, even thousands of them, would be nothing compared to what they are planning to make."

Sam then went on to explain to Joe how, thanks to the way the Electoral College worked, all they had to do was target specific portions of battleground states and they could make the presidential election go any way they wanted.

"They have it all figured out. They can even choose their senators, congressmen, governors; anyone they want to get elected, will get elected."

Sam could see Joe still didn't understand so he flipped through the pages of the *Stratagem* to the map of New York.

"See, each polling area is labeled 'Republican,' 'Democrat,' or 'battleground.' The Xs are the warehouses in the battleground areas. Bribe the watchmen, adjust the machines to vote for the candidate of your choice, and you have your winner. And they don't even have to fix every machine to win, just enough to ensure a majority for their candidate."

"This seems like a lot of trouble to go through."

"It will make them rich."

"They're already rich."

Sam didn't blame his friend for not catching on, as Joe's roots in poverty had left him without a clear understanding of the minds of the wealthy.

"In order to continue to make money and foster prosperity you have to be able to maintain control over your own wealth. You can't just delegate that responsibility to some employee of the government, especially a government that likes to coddle its citizens and put restrictions on business."

Joe figured out right away that Sam was referring to Roosevelt's administration. He had seen more than one editorial condemning Roosevelt's policies, calling him a socialist, and demanding an end to the New Deal.

"Come to think of it, these might be some of the same men who were involved in the Business Plot."

In his mind Joe perused the headlines of the newsstands and recalled reading the stories about a plot to overthrow the government. General Smedley D. Butler had testified that he had been recruited by some of the richest men in America to mobilize half a million retired servicemen to get rid of Roosevelt. The thought that the *Stratagem* might be an offshoot of what they called the Business Plot sent a chill down Joe's spine, and brought the reality of who he was dealing with to the forefront.

"Joe, they all got away with it. They could have been hung for treason, but not one of them spent so much as a night in jail. Doesn't that tell you something?" Sam paused for a minute, then continued. "They're going to make this happen, and I am telling you they are willing to kill anyone who tries to stand in their way, even if it means killing the president."

"They said that?" Joe was annoyed with himself at having missed that part.

"Indirectly." Sam flipped through the pages again and read an excerpt from the page now in front of him "'… fates of death as suffered by previous presidents were no more severe nor random than the fate that shall be suffered by one who strays from this plan.' I think it's implied."

"Evil." Joe felt justified in putting the group of them in this one category.

"You could say that; and from your perspective, I suppose they are."

"My perspective? You don't agree?"

Sam thought about how he might respond to his friend without causing a rift in their friendship. "I certainly don't want to pay more taxes. Do you, Joe?"

"No."

"And we don't want the government to tell us how to run our business, do we?"

"No."

"Well, that's all they're asking. They want to be able to run their businesses and do what they want with their money without the government stepping in to tell them what to. They believe, and arguably they are right, that what they are doing is for the good of the country."

"So you think that fixing elections is good for America?"

"Consolidating the real power of the United States and giving it to the best and the brightest might very well be in our best interest, especially since the general populace will not even know they're doing it."

"How can you say that?"

"I said might be – I didn't say it was, or that I supported it."

Sam's backpedaling for the sake of their friendship was obvious to Joe.

"But here, see this. They look to the Founding Fathers—Washington, Franklin and Adams—for support of their viewpoint."

Joe remembered hearing quotes from the famous men during the meetings that, at the time, he had believed had been taken out of context.

"The Founding Fathers were rich men, so it's not so far-fetched to believe they wrote the Constitution to favor themselves to some degree." Sam didn't know how to make his words sound better to Joe but kept trying. "All I'm saying is, that you may not agree with the methods they are planning to use, but you may not be as opposed to the results as you think you might be."

"Sorry, I can't agree with you." Joe was in fact now more than annoyed with his friend. Yes, he had conceded many times that there were numerous differences between their lives. Their homes, their education, their clothes, even the food that made it to their respective tables, spoke to their different circumstances. However, this was not the same: this felt insurmountable. Sam's reluctance to condemn the men involved with the *Stratagem* felt like a ringing endorsement, a feeling that cast a bright light on the philosophical divide that he knew came down to how each of them had been raised and how they viewed the world.

With every passing second of thoughtful silence, the chasm which had always existed between the two men deepened, and both Joe and Sam began to question how they had ever become such good friends. Yet friends they were, a fact that prompted Sam to push aside their differences and warn his friend once again.

"It really doesn't matter what you or I believe; right now, the only thing that matters is that you wash your hands of this whole thing and get rid of this. I don't want you to get hurt."

Briefly, Joe entertained the thought that his friend was telling him to ignore the *Stratagem* for selfish reasons, so there would be no one to stand in the way of executing the plan, but as he listened further Joe realized that Sam could be right.

"If they find out you have this, who knows what they would do? If they don't kill you they could have you carted off to jail on some trumped-up phony charges, and if you're lucky one of their judges will throw away the key." Sam pretended to kiss a make-believe key, then throw it across the room. "If you're not lucky the headline will read, *Joe Gordon Sent to the Gas Chamber for Treason – Gordon's Wife and Kids Say He's Innocent.* I'm telling you, Joe, burn it." Sam put the manuscript back in Joe's hands. "Burn it and let's get back to business."

Joe just nodded his head as if to affirm his friend's words and hoped, as he placed the papers back into the envelope, that Sam would not suggest they immediately toss the manuscript into the fire. While Joe had always trusted his friend like a brother, unlike Sam, Joe believed these men needed to be stopped and that he could do something to stop them. Joe wanted more time to think, even if it meant, and he knew it did, that he was taking a risk.

Chapter 18

Friday, December 6, 2024
Molly & Griffin Gordon
Long Island, New York

The call came to Oliver's cell phone just minutes after he and Abigail had ridden the escalator back up to the concourse level of the train station. Without hesitation, they walked to the nearest ticket counter and boarded the next train for New York.

"He's sleeping now." Oliver was peering through the crack of his grandfather's bedroom door when his father came up behind him. "How did you get here so fast?"

Oliver responded to his father's whispered question by whispering back that he and Abigail happened to be near the train station and happened to time everything just right with the train schedule.

"He'll be happy you're here when he wakes up. Come, let's get some coffee."

Both men moved to the kitchen table where Abigail

was surrounded on all sides by coffee cups, cakes, cookies, and Oliver's inquisitive family.

"Where are you from?" Molly started.

"Originally Newark, then Rockville." Abigail assumed everyone would know she meant Delaware, then Maryland.

"What do you do?" Kendall inquired of this new female in the home.

"I'm a reporter for the Green Ledger." Abigail assumed everyone would know she meant the progressive online newspaper that focused on environmental issues.

"How did you meet Oliver?"

"Do you live near one another?"

"Where did you get those shoes?"

"How long have you been dating?"

The questions kept coming until Oliver suddenly made an announcement he had not planned on making. "Abigail and I are married."

Abigail's eyes widened at her husband's unexpected declaration.

"We're married." Abigail reiterated her husband's words, albeit more timidly as she pulled her wedding and engagement rings out from their hiding place on the gold chain underneath her sweater.

While the women of the family moved closer to appraise the rings for value and taste, the men, with the exception of Griffin, gathered around Oliver to deliver handshakes and congratulations.

Noticing her husband's reticence and the rising anger in his face, Molly moved as inconspicuously as possible to Griffin's side.

Despite her own confusing mixture of feelings at her eldest son's announcement – shock, disappointment, and anger among them – Molly recognized the need to push her personal feelings aside for now.

"Not now. No fights. Your father..." Molly told Griffin in a ventriloquist's whisper, which she punctuated by shifting her eyes toward the room where Griffin's father was recovering.

"But..." was all Griffin got out in response before Molly grabbed his arm and pushed her nails through the threads of his sweater, giving her husband no other goal than to stop the pain before he bled.

"Fine," Griffin said as he pulled his arm from his wife's grip.

"What's all the commotion?" Oliver's Grandma Mary entered the room with a glass for water and a washcloth she was intent on freshening for her husband. Even though he had wanted neither when he had been awake, and would use neither now that he was asleep, her actions would keep her occupied, and for now that was all that mattered.

"Grandma, this is Abigail." Oliver seemed unusually nervous as he walked his wife over toward his grandmother.

"So this is your wife."

Oliver seemed surprised.

"Do you think your grandfather and I don't talk?"

Molly and Griffin continued their silence as feelings of betrayal swelled inside them. Both felt as if they were about to burst, he into anger and she into tears.

"Congratulations, children." Grandma Mary placed a swarm of light kisses on Oliver's, then Abigail's, cheeks, before squeezing the last drop of moisture from the washcloth and exiting the kitchen.

"Ask your father to tell you about the schmucks at the hospital," Grandma yelled back from the hallway. Oliver's grandmother was not one to mince words. She told everyone whatever she thought, whenever she thought it.

Griffin, never one to disobey his mother, began describing the scene that had taken place at the hospital that morning.

"After we told them your grandfather didn't have insurance they ran his credit history and quickly figured out he wouldn't be able to pay, so they wouldn't admit him." Griffin had mixed feelings about mentioning the insurance issue since he knew it was Oliver who had pushed the bill that demolished Medicare and transferred the responsibility for coverage into the privately managed Senior Network Insurance Plan Exchange. Unfortunately, unlike Medicare, the cost of a SNIPE was so prohibitive only the very wealthy could afford such coverage, so most people, like Benjamin, just had to learn how to do without doctors.

"SNIPE bullshit," Andrew said under his breath, hoping his brother would hear him and feel at least a twinge of guilt.

Oliver, however, felt no such pangs of responsibility, believing his family to be the anomaly, their insurance wounds self-inflicted. They had simply not signed up correctly, he presumed, since their experience was exactly the opposite of the testimony of proven efficacy submitted directly to Oliver's office by SNIPE's own actuaries. Additionally, and there was no denying this, the savings posted to the federal balance sheet under the new plan were significant. Oliver didn't bother to explain any of this to his brother, as, clearly, Andrew did not understand public policy.

"But they said that aspirin was enough to take care of a stroke," Kendall chimed in, not believing what the doctors said to be true, but wishing it could be. "They said it was as good as anything they could give him."

Seeing the worry on his wife's face, Andrew held his tongue and allowed his father the opportunity to continue.

"They gave us the papers to sign, the ones absolving the doctor and the hospital of any liability should something go wrong. Not that we could afford a lawyer if it did." Griffin couldn't help but roll his eyes. "Then they handed your grandmother the bill. Three thousand dollars for the ambulance ride and a one hour stay, which included no tests and a diagnosis they refused to treat. That's when Grandma lost it."

Griffin told the story of his mother's anger, born of her fear for her husband's life.

"I told her I would handle it. I thought she was going to have a stroke herself. I begged her to calm down. But you know Grandma."

Oliver shook his head, knowing that telling his grandmother to calm down was like telling her to stop making chicken soup. She would do neither.

"Then all of a sudden she started swinging that big black shiny purse of hers and yelling at the doctor. 'Schmuck' was the nicest thing she called him." Griffin got out of his chair and continued telling the story while imitating and exaggerating his mother's voice and movements.

"The doctor kept pretending he wasn't scared, probably because she was half his size. But he kept backing up and holding his arms out for protection. Then she got just a little too close and –WHAM– right in the groin with her purse, and over he went!"

Everyone around the table started laughing at Griffin's perfect impression of their grandmother.

"After writhing on the floor for a few minutes, the doctor got to his feet and ran for the nurses' station. I really thought he was going to call the police, especially when she followed him out of the room and started screaming for him to come back so she could put her cane up his *tuchas*!"

The image of their very old, very feisty grandmother chasing a young doctor with her cane made everyone laugh even harder, and Griffin was grateful he was able to give his family a brief respite from the tension that had been building all day.

Griffin, himself, was not as lucky, however. The weight of the ambulance and hospital bill, which he had no way of paying, as well as his son's marriage revelation, had stifled his ability to reap any personal benefit from the humor he had evoked for his family.

Chapter 19

Monday, December 16, 2024
Oliver & Abigail Gordon
Washington, D.C.

It was a temporary truce, at least as far as Oliver was concerned. He and his father were getting along for the first time in many years, thanks to the frequent visits, phone calls, texts and emails updating him on his grandfather's condition.

"Thank God your brother's husband is a physical therapist. He's working wonders with your grandfather." Oliver thanked God, too, but remained silently concerned that the herbal remedies Kris had added to his grandfather's rehab plan amounted to little more than hocus-pocus medicine. As the only member of the Gordon family to have traditional health insurance through his employer, the U.S. Government, Oliver still believed strongly in traditional medicine.

"We'll be there on the twentieth and stay through New Year's." Oliver's intention to spend his holidays with his family for the first time since leaving for college was a direct result of his grandfather's illness, and not some expectation he felt necessary to fulfill now that he was a married man.

"We're doing the annual grab-bag. Homemade gifts only. Grandma Mary will call you on Friday with your grab-bag names."

"I'm not sure Abigail is very artsy, Dad."

"You know the drill. There's always something someone can do. No cop-outs."

Oliver didn't bother answering. He knew there was no stopping a Gordon family ritual. Once the family participated in an activity more than one time it was deemed a 'tradition' and there was no way around it. Mini-golf on every vacation, Monopoly during every blackout, and homemade gifts for Chanukah. End of story.

"Call me if there are any changes; I have a speech to get to." Oliver quickly hung up the phone without apology, and had to literally sprint through the halls of the Capitol to get to his boss's 9 a.m. speech on the Senate floor. After that, the day would continue like most, with Oliver running back to his office by 9:30 to respond to a pile of emails before handling a steady stream of constituent meetings. In lieu of lunch, Oliver would hit the private Capitol gym where he would move from treadmill to treadmill brokering deals with reps and lobbyists.

The gym, however, was just the warm-up for Oliver's day. There were speeches to write, office staff to meet with, upcoming votes to review, a reception for his boss, a fundraising dinner for the party, and a nightcap with Monty.

'Monty' was Oliver's nickname for Mark Montgomery, a junior senator from Maine with whom he had become fast friends. A bond tightened by the fact that they had been fraternity brothers at Syracuse, as well as last-string members of the football team, missing each other's presence on the field and in the frat house by only two years. Though Mark was the older of the two, he knew less about Washington than most, and his politics were painfully liberal. At least that was how Oliver chose to describe him. Nevertheless, the two friends took great pleasure in fighting over policy issues, playing touch football on weekends, and cheering on their alma mater. It was a bond that became so close so quickly that Monty was the first person Oliver had told about Abigail.

"What's wrong with you, old man? Fuck Rhine," Monty would say. He told Oliver to fuck his boss a lot, mostly when he was being asked to vote for one of his "crazy conservative bills." At least that's how Monty described them.

Oliver would always reply in kind with the same four letter word aimed at one or another of Monty's fellow liberal caucus members, and then not give it another thought. Since conservatives had held a lock on all branches of government as far back as he could remember, Oliver considered his ability to routinely sway minority

Democrats as job security. Not to mention the fact that '28 was right around the corner, and Rhine was going to throw his hat into what was shaping up to be a very large presidential ring. By that time, Oliver wanted the senator to view him as indispensable.

It was a well-thought-out strategy that Oliver had had for a very long time. Trouble was, thanks to his grandfather, Oliver was no longer sure his plan to win the presidency for his boss was one he could actually deliver on. If it were true, if the things his grandfather had shared during his last visit to Washington were actually happening, then no matter how many brilliant speeches he could write, how much support he could garner, or how many states he could lock up for a win, the decision regarding who would be the next person to occupy the White House might already have been made.

Chapter 20

Friday, December 20, 2024
Molly & Griffin Gordon
Long Island, New York

In the process of making things happen for their eldest son Oliver, sending him to a private college, then Harvard Law, making sure he always had a nice car and an apartment off campus, Molly and Griffin had drained their savings accounts. At the time, Oliver had agreed to pay it all back, with interest, as soon as he secured employment at one of the big law firms he seemed destined to work for. Then Molly and Griffin had planned on using that money to pay for the twins' college educations. Certainly, with a Harvard law degree, Oliver's promise seemed as good as gold. However, sometime during his last semester of law school Oliver had decided to work in D.C. as a public servant. Though the salaries of those who worked for Congress were respectable, they were minimal compared to the compensation afforded by private law firms and would not be enough, according to Oliver, to live off of and repay his debt to his parents. When Griffin and Molly disagreed with their son's choice of profession, Oliver temporarily cut off all communication with them and invited only his grandparents to his graduation.

Griffin and Molly never actually lost hope that the son they had raised so well would one day come to his senses and pay them back, but that day had never come. Instead, with nothing left in the family's savings account, as well the untimely end to financial aid and single digit interest rate loans for students, Griffin and Molly had no choice but to dip into their retirement accounts if they wanted their younger sons to be educated. In order to retire they would have to remain employed until they were 70, or win the lottery.

Unfortunately, just three months after the twins' college graduations, both Molly and Griffin lost their teaching jobs to a private online home school called the "New Online School for Education." As part of the Public School System's bankruptcy settlement, the union gave away half of the Gordon's retirement fund, the part they hadn't spent on college tuition.

Though both Molly and Griffin were offered teaching jobs with the online school, hidden in the fine print of the emails that contained their offers was the loss of the rest of the money in their previous retirement plan, a fifty percent salary cut, and no future retirement benefits. Additionally, and this was the part that actually became the tipping point for the lifelong educators, they would not be doing any actual teaching. With all the lessons being taught by actors whose costumes, props, and special effects made the online experience seemed to be aimed at preschoolers even at the high school level, and with all testing and grading automated, the only thing teachers were doing anymore was answering student questions. It was a requirement of the job that would have obligated them to be on-call twenty-four hours a day, seven days a week.

Griffin and Molly rejected the job offer and found equally unsatisfying, but slightly more lucrative, jobs. Nevertheless, without their teaching salaries every month had become a struggle.

Oliver, on the other hand, did not struggle when it came to money, nor was he surprised at his father's dismal financial situation. In fact, ever since his graduation from college, Oliver had made it his mission to protect himself from a similar fate.

Oliver's condo in Washington was not of the same caliber most in his position owned. Instead he purchased three smaller condos, lived in one and collected rent from the others. He never bought expensive suits or drove expensive cars, like others of his ilk. Oliver's bank and retirement accounts had experienced a steady and substantial climb, not just from his frugal ways, but from his dipping in and out of the stock market. Oliver was good at seeing 'trends' as he called them, though most with a law degree would consider what he did 'insider trading.'

No one in the family knew of Oliver's investments, or that he had the means to help his family and chose instead to condemn them as followers of his father's misguided decisions. Looking in from the outside, people might be tempted to label Oliver's behavior as selfish, arrogant and narcissistic, at the very least; but that would be because they wouldn't understand. Not that Oliver understood it himself, as he stood behind the walls of his opinions. Only his grandfather Benjamin actually understood that all of Oliver's talk, the bravado that enacted edicts of condemnation against his father, was no more than the fear of ending up like him—not so much poor, as afraid.

Oliver's need to keep his world orderly and in control,

and his need to stand with the powerful and keep himself financially secure, were the only ways he knew of to keep himself in sharp contrast to the 'Henny Penny' way he believed his father had chosen to live his life.

It was an ironic twist of fate that saw both father and son afraid of the same thing: a government out of control.

When Oliver and Abigail arrived at the Gordons' home, something immediately seemed amiss to them. Although it was the first night of Chanukah and just five days before Christmas, the only signs of the season were a lone menorah and a lit, but undecorated, Christmas tree standing in the window. Missing were the ornaments, the stockings over the fireplace, Santa's cup and cookie plate, the garland, the Christmas cards hung on yarn above each doorway, his mother's dreidel collection, and his grandmother's old school menorah with the candles that never got lit because his mother was afraid they would burn the house down. All of it, along with the smell of his grandmother's pot-roast wafting through the air, was missing.

Instead, the job of Chanukah and Christmas had clearly been replaced by the business of packing.

"Mom, what's going on?" Oliver wanted an explanation.

"Your father lost his job this morning. They're withholding his last paycheck. They say he won't get it for five months, so we won't be able to make the next mortgage payment."

"Five months?"

"They have to do an ex post facto tax assessment. I'm sure you know about it." Molly's fake smile bent back to a frown as she tried unsuccessfully to hide her disgust.

"Of course I know about it, I wrote the bill. I just don't get why it's going to take five months."

What Oliver didn't know was that the private accounting firm the government had contracted the audit work to, was failing to meet the terms of their no-bid contract.

"This is *your* fault?" Oliver's brother Andrew, who had been silently bringing boxes back and forth from the living room to the garage, stopped what he was doing when he heard his brother admit to the part he had played in the troubles they now faced. "I should have known this was your dirty work."

"Hey, it's not my fault the unemployed skip town and don't pay their taxes at the end of the year. We just made it impossible to cheat the government."

Admittedly, when Oliver had written the bill at the urging of his boss, he could not find any compelling statistical data to back up the need for such legislation. Stemming the tide of faceless tax cheats was always a favorite topic for constituents who never saw their own missteps regarding the tax code as anything but justifiable.

Oliver had no idea that Rhine had suggested the bill because of his close financial ties with the CEO of the accounting firm now doing the contract work.

"They don't skip town, they get evicted. If they don't pay their taxes, it's because they have no money to pay them with!"

As always, Andrew had become infuriated by his older brother.

"And, just so you're clear, yes, this is your fault." Andrew pointed to the boxes filling every corner of the room. "You and your friends in Washington did this."

Oliver was used to being blamed for the failings of others, so his brother's accusation slid quickly and cleanly off his back.

"You can make this a big deal, but a law requiring companies to accurately assess their employee's taxes and withhold them accordingly is not wrong."

"It's a big deal because Mom and Dad need the money." Andrew's voice had become very loud.

"So does the government. Or should we go back to the days of unpaved roads?"

"Ha, unpaved roads. That's what you use as an example of what our illustrious government does with our money? Do you really want to discuss how many bridges fell down last year, or how many people died because of it?"

"That was domestic terrorism."

"Domestic terrorism. You guys are still clinging to

that bullshit story?" Andrew's rage grew. "The reason those bridges fell is the same reason all the roads are filled with potholes. The reason why the snow never gets removed from the streets, and the reason why half the traffic lights are out. You and the other buzzards in Washington left our infrastructure in the hands of private companies who promised they could deliver the work faster and cheaper than the government, and what happened?"

Andrew didn't bother to give his brother time to answer before he continued.

"They didn't deliver. None of them did. The contractors couldn't do the jobs at the prices they promised, and your underpaid 'oversight' guys took kickbacks to lie and say the work was done when it wasn't. Now everyone's pointing fingers and not a goddamn one of them will admit it was all a bunch of bullshit right from the start. Now our dad's check is going to take five months because no one, including you, gives a shit." Andrew's voice had become hoarse from the stress of yelling.

Oliver, on the other hand, held the steady cool of a seasoned politician, a tactic he had learned from watching Senator Rhine in action. And just as his boss would do, Oliver was about to calmly suggest to his brother that if he didn't like what his elected representatives were doing he could always vote them out of office. Luckily for everyone, Abigail cut off her husband's thoughts by interjecting a question to change the direction of the conversation, a characteristic of a good reporter, if not necessarily of a new daughter-in-law.

"What happened? Why was Mr. Gordon let go?"

Although her question was clearly directed at Molly, Andrew's wife Kendall, who was busy filling boxes in the far corner of the room, chose to answer for her.

"They found out Mom was shopping at Stuffs Food."

"Mom's not allowed to shop in Stuffs Food?" Abigail was confused.

"Dad works for BUYnEAT. Well, he used to work there."

"So?"

"You can't shop in a competitor's store. It's a rule."

"How can that be a rule?"

"Well, not a written rule, but, trust me, it's a rule."

"How would they know?"

"It's easy to track employees through the direct deposit systems set up by the BUYnEAT Bank. The bank charges nothing for debit card transactions and exorbitant fees for withdrawing cash, so no one uses cash."

"So then the company knows everywhere you shop, everywhere you go, and everything you do that involves money?" Abigail had caught on fast to a system she had been shielded from by working for a small, most would say radical, environmental online newspaper.

"So it's true, you were there?" Oliver's tone with his

mother was accusatory and sparked a second sudden and virulent response from Andrew.

"This is still fucking America, isn't it?" Again Andrew didn't give Oliver an opportunity to answer his question before continuing. "Oh, I forgot, you and your Washington assholes just like to pretend we live in a free society."

"You're beginning to sound more and more like Dad each day." Oliver skillfully moved the conversation away from the political and right to the personal.

"If you think that's an insult, and I'm sure you do, it's not."

"Look around, I think even you can admit he's made a few mistakes." Oliver's tone was calm and biting.

"What exactly did he do that was so wrong? What? He raised us, clothed us, took us on vacations, bought us our first cars, and sent us to college." Andrew was getting louder again. "And what did you and your political hacks do to him? You closed his school, let them syphon off his retirement money, taxed everything in sight, ditched Social Security and Medicare, and now you are going to steal his goddamn house. But you still blame him, you fucking asshole!"

In his fury, Andrew pulled a vase out of a carton and threw it across the room, missing his brother's head by inches and crashing it into pieces against the wall.

"Enough." From the hallway a voice unsuccessfully

straining to whisper called. "Take it outside if you must, but not in here. You're upsetting your grandfather."

Normally they would have stopped fighting and apologized to their grandmother, but Oliver believed neither was necessary and Andrew did not have the presence of mind to do so. Instead they continued battling in quieter tones with their teeth clenched and their voices barely above a whisper.

"Washington didn't steal anything from anyone," Oliver muttered. "If anything, there's less government now. And you're damn right, I am proud. Proud that we have finally stopped the socialist handout machine. You and dad are just used to getting all the government freebies, and now that they're gone, you two obviously can't manage on your own. It's a shame really. I warned you both."

Molly, no longer able to listen to her sons fight without taking sides and jeopardizing what was left of her relationship with Oliver, chose to leave the room.

"You warned us? You screwed us. The government isn't any smaller, it's just been outsourced. Everything Dad said all along has been true, and thank God he didn't listen to you and your political crap machine. If he had, we'd have nothing now. At least we have someplace to go and some land to build on."

Andrew had been down this road before with his brother, and never got anywhere. All Oliver saw was the fact that his father had spent more money than he made. All Andrew saw was that the government had taken more than his father had to spare.

"Yes. Dad's a fucking financial wizard. Good luck with that farm."

Oliver used his most sarcastic tone, and accented the word 'farm' by using quotes he made with his fingers.

Though he had every intention of continuing his verbal attacks on his brother and father, Oliver noticed his mother return to the room with tears in her eyes, and for the first time saw the devastated faces of Kendall and Abigail.

"Please, boys." Molly sounded defeated, and suddenly Oliver realized where his punches had been landing. "I don't want any more fighting." Molly's words were interrupted by her sobs as she returned to her packing. "We have too much to do to be fighting like this."

Wiping her tears with her hands, Molly worked to pull herself together so she could talk to Oliver before Griffin returned home. Though she had always had a better rapport with her eldest son than her husband had had with him, Molly did not believe for a minute that she could make him do anything he did not want to do.

"We can't take your grandparents with us now." Molly spoke in an apprehensive tone, deliberately allowing her son to feel he had the upper hand. "So we were hoping they could stay with you and Abigail until it gets warmer and we've built some decent shelter for them."

Molly considered her use of the word 'shelter' as a description of where they would soon live. In all her life, she had never used any words besides 'apartment,' 'house' or 'home.' Now everything had come down to 'shelter.' One more thought that summoned the need to hold back her tears.

"Of course they can come live with us." Abigail didn't wait for her husband to respond. She assumed her offer would stop her mother-in-law from any further crying and make Oliver look good, in even Andrews's eyes. In fact, Abigail was ready to promise Molly the world if it would get everyone to calm down.

"You could take the train up from D.C., and then your father said he would rent a car for all of you to ride back in."

"Not necessary: we'll take care of everything." Again Abigail was controlling the situation, believing she was saving her usually-strong husband from having to show his vulnerability to his mother's tears.

In the space between Abigail's offer and Molly's thanks, thoughts of the other grandparents, Molly's parents, silently made their way through the room. They would need no arrangements and no accommodations because both had died earlier that year. The police had called it an accident and were satisfied with their version of how her parents' car had slipped off the side of the road and flipped multiple times.

"He was old," the cop had said to her before hanging up the phone, as if that would be all the explanation she would need as to how something like that could happen. But it wasn't. Instead, Molly would be left to wonder forever if her parents, or maybe just her father, believed they had become too much of a burden on their only daughter. In the new Social-Security-less society, retirement was a time of abject poverty for all but the very rich. So for Molly's dad, who had always been a proud, hardworking, and independent man, dying in a fiery car crash would be significantly more tolerable than the promise of a pauper's future.

"Molly, you should see what we got." Griffin broke the quiet upset of the room as he came bounding through the front door with Andrews's twin brother Tyler and Tyler's no-longer-legal husband Kris. All were red-cheeked, wrapped in scarves, and pulling off their gloves as Tyler began describing what had just transpired.

"The Masons are leaving tomorrow. They're headed south to their daughter's place, so they told us we can have whatever we want from their house." Tyler spoke in a controlled tone, lest anyone believe he was excited about the misfortunes of their longtime neighbors, a couple even older than his grandparents. He was excited inside, though, every time he thought of all they had been given.

"We got two wood-burning stoves, Molly. Remember, they had one in the den and one in their basement?" Griffin was bursting with excitement and couldn't help but begin listing the inventory of unexpected but very welcome items. "A couple of rolls of insulation from their attic, some wood from their deck, well, what used to be their deck." Griffin was grinning ear to ear. "Fans, a barbeque grill, two toilets, fixtures, light bulbs, nails, tools, wallboard, a bathtub, tile, and windows. Windows, Molly, they gave us their windows. And bricks. We have bricks!" Griffin laughed at the fact that one of his trailers was now filled with all the fixings for a house.

Not trusting their sudden brush with good fortune, Molly shared her worries. "Are you sure we can get it all past the checkpoints?"

Molly knew the checkpoints between states and around major cities had originally been set up to keep terrorists out. However, private security firms contracted to man the borders realized early on that they would need more than suspected terrorists to fill their privately-owned jails. Luckily, new legislation granted them the power to randomly review the contents of any car or truck if the driver was suspected of transporting materials from a foreclosed home.

"Yes." Griffin interrupted Molly's train of thought, which was currently filled with worry. "We're leaving before the mortgage is even due, and they still own their house free and clear. They just don't want to spend their last dime on taxes, so they're letting it go." Griffin didn't want to seem as happy as he was, but this influx of much-needed tools and supplies was quite a relief for him.

"Yeah, they want to be able to continue eating." Kris lent some sarcasm to the mix.

"It will be fine, Molly." For once Griffin was too happy to fret over what the government might do to him. "We'll have our paid-up mortgage bill, so they can't touch us. There's no rule that says we can't take our own stuff if the mortgage is actually paid." Griffin paused to smile. "At least, not yet."

In his head, Oliver quickly reviewed the bills on his desk and clearly saw SA5777 in his mind. The legislation, touted as an economic stimulus bill, and embraced by retailers and politicians alike, would soon prevent all citizens from crossing state lines with used building materials and furniture. No one cared to notice that the bill significantly increased the parameters of the search and seizure rules, or that the border patrol was the driving force behind the lobbying efforts for the bill.

"You know, if I hadn't gotten fired today I never would have seen the Masons packing up their car." Griffin's dazzling optimism was an unfamiliar treat for everyone.

"Karma." Abigail thought it best to reinforce the positive vibe that had finally entered the room.

"Karma." Oliver reiterated under his breath,

gratefully acknowledging, if only to himself, that the law on his desk was not yet a fait accompli, and therefore was not yet another excuse for his brother to fight with him.

Though Oliver could now see firsthand the hardship such a measure might have caused his family, he thoroughly believed that the law of unintended consequences applied to every piece of legislation, even the most benign.

Look, if we all started to worry about the impact of EVERY law on EVERY Tom, Dick and Harry, face it, nothing would get done in Washington. Oliver remembered using that argument whenever he felt the need to defend his viewpoint on any bill. Today, however, he thought it best not to share those thoughts with his family.

"Oliver, Abigail! When did you two get here?" Griffin moved to the other side of the room to offer unusually large hugs to his son and daughter-in-law. "I guess you heard." Instinctively Griffin's eyes turned away from his son's.

"Yes, he did." Andrew interjected with a tone angry enough to arouse Griffin's suspicion and to turn his happy mood into one of concern.

"What's going on?"

"Nothing, Griffin, everything's fine. Oliver and Abigail are going to take your father and mother until we get things set up on the farm."

Griffin didn't believe his wife's assurances that everything was fine, but his mind was so full of plans for the move he decided it best to ignore what was going on in the hopes that it might resolve itself and that he would not have to get involved.

Chapter 21

Sunday, January 1, 1939
Selma & Joe Gordon
New York City

Unconsciously attempting to walk off the tension that continued to build in his mind and in his body, Joe paced rhythmically back and forth across the black and white linoleum tiles of the kitchen floor. His face was redder than Selma had ever seen it before; his voice louder than usual.

"Let me get this straight, Selma." Joe could not help but keep his hands fisted. "How did Myron find out about the *Stratagem*?"

Selma had had no idea that telling her mother would have started a chain reaction of gossip and innuendo that would run through the family like the flu. She had sworn her mother to secrecy and her mother had taken the oath. Now Selma didn't know what to tell her husband and opted for the truth.

"And from your mother where did it go?"

"My sister Tess." If Selma had believed her husband a violent man, she certainly would have ducked at that point as everyone knew Selma's sister Tess to be a world class *yenta*.

"And from there?"

"I don't know, Myron maybe. Maybe Harry, I don't know."

"So they all know now, Selma? They all know? All your brothers and sisters, and everyone at the party last night knows?"

"I didn't think it was a problem to tell her. You said you threw out all the papers. That's what I told her, that the papers were gone. That's what she told them, I'm sure!"

"My God, Selma, my God. Do you know what you have done? I'm sure by now Tessie, the human telegraph, has gotten the word out to the whole neighborhood. The butcher, the shoemaker, who knows, maybe the President of the United States knows by now." Joe pretended to pick up a phone receiver. "Hello, Poland, this is Tess. Have you heard what Joe Gordon has?"

Normally, Joe and Selma would laugh at a Tess imitation, but this time Joe's decision to use his own angry low voice and not the raspy higher-pitched voice he usually used was nothing to laugh at.

"What am I going to do?" Joe said to no one. He wasn't through lamenting and he wasn't through pacing, landing each footstep harder than the one before.

"What is there to do? The papers are gone, you can deny it all and…"

Selma's quick fix solutions that assumed Joe had disposed of the *Stratagem* were worthless to him. Joe's lies by omission had caught up to him and all he could think of to do was to blame his wife. By the time Joe left the room, Selma was crying.

Chapter 22

Friday, January 10, 2025
Oliver & Abigail Gordon
Washington, D.C.

The newlyweds had spent their entire Christmas vacation helping Oliver's family sort through a lifetime of memories, most of which had to be discarded due to space limitations. For the first time, Oliver's parents were forced to shift their view of their possessions from one of sentimentality to one of survival.

The only consolation for Oliver and Abigail was in the knowledge that this would be the worst holiday they would ever spend together, and that all others to come had to be better.

Between the physical labor and the pervasive feeling of loss everyone was exhausted. Yet resting, taking a break, a real break, was not an option. No one slept normally anymore. Sleep came when they were too tired to stay awake a minute longer. Once asleep, though, Griffin insisted that the fallen not be disturbed for a full seven hours.

"'We can't afford to get sick.' That's what he said, Abby. He said, 'We can't afford to get sick.' Then he looked right at me."

"What are you thinking? You think that he's blaming you for not having health insurance?"

"Everything. He blames me for everything."

"I think you're getting paranoid, Oliver."

"No. He follows all of Rhine's votes in the Senate. He knows exactly what I'm responsible for."

"Now you're giving yourself too much credit."

Oliver couldn't help but wonder if Abigail was right. Maybe he did give himself too much credit, a thought he immediately dismissed because, like most people in Washington, much of Oliver's power, his success in the political arena, derived from his ability to keep his ego intact. Any cracks in that dam were a dangerous thing.

Which is why Oliver had chosen not to bring up the subject of the Stratagem. By his grandfather's own admission, the plan as outlined would render his strategy for getting his boss elected president a moot point if the powers that be had deemed otherwise. So, despite the fact that his grandfather had been scheduled to bring proof the Stratagem to Washington the day of his stroke, Oliver kept quiet, hoping that all memory of the document was lost in the stroke-damaged portion of his grandfather's brain.

"Oh, no!" Abigail began to run through their adjoining bedroom closets and into her old bedroom. "Ahhh!" she pretended to scream, but not too loud as Oliver caught her around the waist and easily managed to wrestle her to the bed, mainly because she didn't really have any desire to struggle.

They would each blame the other for missing the last train to New York that night, and each insisted that the other call with their apologies and assurances that they would be on the six a.m. train the following morning. A stalemate that was broken only after the best of three highly competitive games of Rock, Paper, Scissors had determined that Oliver would make the call.

"You cheated," Oliver said after he put out his scissor hands to Abigail's slower-arriving rock.

"You lose." Abigail gloated as she handed Oliver the phone and then listened to him make his excuses regarding late work obligations that he blamed on his wife.

"What?" Abigail whispered a yell at her husband as she punched his arm lightly then leaned back against the three white pillows propped against her fake mahogany headboard.

As Abigail sat naked, listening to her husband get the latest news from New York, she thought about her own concerns earlier that evening, about how their life was about to change. Suddenly it came to Abigail that providing for and taking care of their grandparents was going to be the easy part. It was this, what had just transpired, their spontaneous, private, intimately personal time that Abigail wasn't sure she would be able to manage without.

"Oh, well." Abigail said out loud to herself, just as Oliver hung up the phone.

"What?"

"Nothing. I was just thinking about your grandparents coming to live here."

"I know, food, water, heat, electricity, it's all going to cost us more. Especially the heat. God, those two are always cold. I'm going to have to put a lock on the thermostat."

"No, I meant, this, us, this place." Abigail motioned her now extended arm, like a game show hostess might display the room as if it had been won as a prize.

"Yup, in a few days this is going to be their room, and you're sitting naked on their bed." Oliver smiled.

"I'll change the sheets." Abigail rolled her eyes at her husband who had, himself, chased her into the room and onto the bed.

"No, I'm serious Ol, it's going to be like having kids." The gravity of what she and Oliver had agreed to was coming more and more into focus. "Well, not little kids, more like teenagers who can be left alone, but not for too long. And they can certainly make their own food, but they won't be going shopping for it." As she spoke, Abigail's worry increased.

"Don't forget stubborn, opinionated, and argumentative like teenagers." In an effort to ease Abigail's mind, Oliver smiled at his additions to her list.

"Are you talking about you or your grandparents?" Abigail quietly laughed back at Oliver.

"Are you talking about you or your grandparents?" Oliver mimicked his wife's voice, then rolled over and closed his eyes. The image of his grandparents inhabiting his apartment resisted his demands to visualize something else, a resistance that persisted until the sum of his thoughts slipped into the succor of the void before sleep.

Chapter 23

Saturday, January 11, 2025
Molly & Griffin Gordon
Long Island, New York

When Oliver and Abigail didn't show up on Friday night, the mood in the Gordon household was decidedly depressed. Everyone began believing that Oliver was about to once again renege on a promise made to his family. When Oliver and Abigail didn't show up on Saturday morning as they had subsequently promised, depression turned to anger and the accrued resentments began to spill out.

"He's so fucking selfish." Andrew whispered his thoughts to his brother, who did not have to hear the actual words to know what his twin was thinking.

"Did anyone really expect he was suddenly going to change because he got married?" Tyler was a bit less angry and more logical.

"I think Mom thought so." Andrew could have cried at the thought of his mother's disappointment, but continued lifting the heavy boxes into the trailer that had been pulled into the backyard away from the street cameras.

"You know, I feel sorry for his wife. She has no idea who she married."

"What are you two whispering about?" Kendall was bringing out a box from the kitchen, which made Andrew momentarily anxious.

"Those are too heavy." Only he and Kendall knew of his wife's pregnancy, and Andrew didn't want her jeopardizing it by lifting boxes he could just as easily handle.

"We were just saying we feel sorry for Oliver's wife. She has no idea," Tyler answered his sister-in-law.

Kendall hadn't even known the Gordon family when Oliver had reneged on his promise to become a lawyer and pay his parents back for his college education. However, over the years she had heard all the stories, and had been privy to the anger and resentment that flowed so deeply through the younger Gordons.

She's so nice too, Kendall thought to herself but chose not to comment out loud. Instead Kendall decided to refocus the discussion and her husband's frustration.

"Mom and Kris are almost done packing the kitchen, let's go help them finish it up."

Without waiting for a response, Kendall led the way back into the house just in time to hear that Oliver and Abigail had arrived.

"They're here Molly. Oliver's here. They're here." Griffin was so relieved to see his son and daughter-in-law pull up in the rented minivan, six hours late, that he overstated his happiness, a fact that just made his younger sons seethe.

Finally, Molly thought to herself as she came out to the front steps to offer a warm, though fake, greeting for her son as he got out of the van. Not that she wasn't happy to see him: she was always happy to see her sons. She just didn't trust that this visit would start off any smoother than the last, especially given Oliver's decision to ignore all the promises he had made to the family with regard to his arrival time. Molly also knew that Oliver's lack of apology, due to his absence of guilt or remorse regarding his tardiness, would only add fuel to his brothers' already-angry fires.

This was not what Molly wanted for her sons; in fact she did everything she could to keep them as close as possible. It just never worked. Griffin had blamed it on the wide gap in their ages, inadvertently caused by Molly's inability to conceive for so long. Others told Molly it was bound to happen because twins were always different from the rest of the family. Understandably set apart for their specialness, they said. However Molly believed her own truth, which was that Oliver was a child who was bright and handsome, reasonably athletic, and seemed to have everything handed to him on a silver platter. In Molly's experience nothing upsets younger brothers more than an older brother who places the bar too high and keeps raising it. Not that Andrew and Tyler were slouches: they had made their own marks on the field and in the classroom, but they never recognized their own accomplishments as anything more than catching up with Oliver.

"Oliver!" Benjamin joined Molly on the front step, leaning on a cane but looking significantly healthier than he had looked only a week before.

"Gamps." Oliver left Abigail in the van and ran to his grandfather lest he try to manage the steps unaided.

"Drive the car around back, then come in, sit down and relax. There's plenty of time to pack the car. We're not leaving until Monday."

At first, Oliver believed his grandfather was confusing his days, and didn't think much of the comment until his grandmother confirmed their leaving date and time as Monday at 10:00 a.m. Though they showed no outward emotion, both Oliver and Abigail realized immediately that they had not even gotten into the car yet and they had already had their first dose of what life with their grandparents was going to be like: unpredictable, unbending, and, worst of all, disruptive to their work.

Part 2

Dear Senator Rhine,

As you know, our Domestic Enemies Apprehension Device, or DEAD for short, uses algorithms to screen and profile individuals, then takes physical measurements such as heart rate and breathing to determine criminality. It relies on parameters congruent with normal measures of human emotions, anxiety, frustration, and excitement, and subjects them to interpretation as being related to crime and terrorism. As a contractor for the U.S. Government we are proud of our DEAD program and its success in capturing tens of thousands of individuals who have posed an immediate terrorist threat to our country.

Additionally, our state-of-the-art domestic and foreign prison facilities, operated by our U.S.A. Global Prison Systems subsidiary, have effectively handled the ever-increasing number of captures; and our outstanding work release labor programs, located in allied countries throughout the globe, have become models of productivity and profitability for America.

We are writing to you today to remind you of the two upcoming Senate votes regarding the implementation of our new security program. The first vote scheduled for January

25, 2025 will extend the powers of our service providers at checkpoints and enable them to detain the children of terrorism suspects (COTS) for transfer to our new COTS facilities to be located in Denver and Pittsburgh. As you will see in the enclosed brochure, each of these planned institutions will securely and efficiently house five thousand COTS, thus relieving the overburdened, dysfunctional, and costly foster care system.

The accompanying appropriations bill, which includes the land grants and tax abatements, as discussed at our last meeting, will also likely come out of committee and up for a vote within the next two weeks.

We look forward to your continued support of our mission, and if you or your colleagues have any further questions please join us for dinner on Saturday, January 23, 2025 at 7:00 p.m. in the Boca Raton Hightower Hills Ballroom. For flight arrangements, lodging, and tee off times please contact my secretary Giselle.

God Bless America

P.J. McKing, CEO, The McKing Corporation

Chapter 24

Friday, January 17, 2025
Molly & Griffin Gordon
Checkpoint

Andrew, Kendall, Tyler and Kris had left on the thirteenth of January, and had arrived safely at the farm. All Molly and Griffin had to do was leave by Tuesday the fourteenth and arrive with the truck before the sixteenth. Otherwise, their missed mortgage payment would place them on the domestic terrorist watch list. Even when the truck broke down in New Jersey and stalled them for an entire day, they thanked God they still had plenty of time to get to their destination.

It wasn't until the border stop, their last before Pennsylvania, that the couple allowed themselves to shed the weight of their sadness over all they had just lost and to feel the excitement of their future. The fulfillment of all their planning and the possibilities that lay ahead were right over the border and now within reach. In conversation and thought the couple began to recognize the gravity of it all.

"One more checkpoint, another hour or so, and we're there." Griffin leaned over to Molly and planted a quick kiss on her cheek.

"Andrew said they're making a lot of progress on the construction."

"Who would have thought our college boys would be swinging hammers?"

"Or that we would be living on a farm." Molly laughed to herself. Not a city girl, but certainly not a country girl, she had yet to see a non-domesticated animal outside the confines of a zoo.

"I think we're going to love it." Griffin's heart felt lighter as he said it.

"I think it's going to be hard work."

"We've been working hard, Mol, and where has it gotten us?"

"True." Molly couldn't help but catch on to Griffin's happiness. "You're right. It's going to be good."

"Here we are, Molly. Smile and breathe," Griffin warned his wife as he turned up the air conditioning and inched the car slowly to the front of the checkpoint line. At this point in the trip Griffin didn't have to tell Molly how to act or remind her that passing checkpoints required a bribe, a cool head, steady breathing, a little bit of a smile, and turned-up air conditioning, since the machines measured sweat even in the dead of winter. Nor had they forgotten to take the anti-anxiety pharmaceuticals advertised on late night TV and available for self-prescription since the dissolution of the FDA in 2019. Heavily-medicated, Molly and Griffin believed their checkpoint etiquette was foolproof.

"Sir, hand me your papers." Like all the other guards at all the other checkpoints, this guard was dressed in army fatigues and wore a helmet. Behind him stood two more men in army gear carrying machine guns; but instead of casually carrying their weapons in the crooks of their arms pointed toward the ground, as all the others had, these guards had them pointed toward Griffin's head.

Overzealous, Griffin thought, but he didn't attach any more significance to their behavior than the possibility that border guards in the suburbs were more nervous than city guards.

As Griffin handed the paperwork through the open window with the toll on top and the expected bribe money on the bottom, just as he had done at all the borders and bridges before, he expected to be home, at his new home, within the hour.

When the guard informed the couple they would need to step out and away from their vehicle, Griffin believed he had not offered a large-enough bribe, and reached into his pocket to add more cash to the pile, an action which prompted the guards to feel a sense of justification for what they were about to do anyway.

"Get out!" The guard screamed as he flung open the door and shoved the unresisting Griffin to the ground.

Molly's mind struggled to make sense of what she was witnessing as a half-dozen guards surrounded her husband and began their attack. All attempts by Griffin to shield himself from their onslaught were useless. Their bare fists, steel-toed boots and nightsticks thrashed through his skin, bloodying his clothes and the ground.

Molly's revulsion instantaneously made her sick to her stomach, a feeling immediately overridden by her need to help her husband. But as she exited the van she herself was thrown to the ground, punched, and then forced to watch in horror as the agents continued to pummel her now barely-conscious husband until he didn't move.

"Another domestic terrorist caught," a voice proclaimed through the PA system, a spectacle for all to see, a warning for bystanders.

Molly heard the crowd cheering on command, as she watched one of the agents, his right hand fisted and held high, his left foot firmly planted on her husband's lifeless back.

The onlookers jeered as they proceeded to drag Griffin along the ground by one leg, leaving a trail of blood across the pavement.

"And another one!" The voice announced even louder as the agents pulled Molly to her feet and walked her away, her screams of her husband's innocence held inside the dirty rag the gloved agent held to her mouth.

Chapter 25

Wednesday, January 18, 1939
Joe & Selma Gordon
New York City

It had been eighteen days since Joe had found out that the entire Gordon clan was privy to his possession of the Stratagem, and Joe could only pray that his ability to tell a good, convincing story, or in this case a lie, had enabled him to stop them from leaking the information outside the family.

Now that Joe no longer trusted Selma's ability to keep a secret, he felt no need to tell her the details he had learned from Sam about the *Stratagem*, or mention that he had placed it back in the basement. He also decided that he was still too angry to speak to her, so beyond directives such as "Pass the sugar, please" Joe levied a language embargo against his wife.

Selma, never having dealt with such a silence in her marriage, continued speaking to Joe as if nothing had happened between them, much like when she conversed with a dog, believing in the validity of the conversation but not actually expecting a response.

On those occasions when Selma might have needed her questions answered and Joe returned not so much as a nod for a response, Selma had taken it upon herself to answer for him. In fact Selma had taken to having whole conversations without Joe ever saying a word.

"How would you like your eggs, Joe? Why, Selma, my dear, I would love my eggs sunnyside-up, if you wouldn't mind. Oh, and by the way, you look lovely today. Well, thank you, Joseph, that's very sweet of you to notice."

This stalemate, which had been going on for weeks, had become as uncomfortable for the other members of the Gordon household as it was for Joe and Selma. Consequently, more than one relative had stormed out of the room after witnessing the lopsided conversation between the couple.

In addition to his silence, Joe had taken to heading directly over to Sam's after his shift at the restaurant to continue working on their business plan and to start sketching his designs. Usually Joe would fall asleep on Sam's couch, and come home the next day with just enough time to wash up and change for work.

On his days off Joe would travel to the garment district before sunrise, perusing the many fabric vendors' wares for samples and returning to his basement to sketch the beautiful designs he was inspired to create. What surprised him about this process, though, was the fact that despite his anger and all his efforts to avoid contact with his wife, Joe could not stop envisioning her in each of his many designs. More than once he imagined Selma walking into his dress salon with a trail of women behind her, all begging Joe to make them the same beautiful dress that his wife was wearing. Selma, slim and petite, would of course be an inaccurate depiction of the women he was designing for, the ones with the less-than-svelte bodies. Nevertheless, Joe knew that the patrons of his shop would buy the dresses anyway, believing they looked just as good as Selma even if their mirrors begged to differ.

Sam believed that, too, all the time telling Joe, "As long as the rich have no doubt that their wealth makes them superior to the rest of us, they will never comprehend a reason to entertain our opinions. We will give them what they want and, no matter how they look, we will keep still about it."

Luckily for Joe, and thanks to Selma, he had been having considerable practice keeping still about everything.

Chapter 26

Friday, January 17, 2025
Molly & Griffin Gordon
Unknown Location

As they pushed Molly into the van that would transport her to jail, she heard them say that the DEAD Program had worked once again. Immediately Molly began berating herself for not being able to outsmart the dependably inaccurate system.

Griffin woke up again. He had been moving in and out of sleep, perhaps unconsciousness, for hours. How many hours, he had no way to judge and no one to ask. In fact, he didn't know how he had gotten here, tied, maybe handcuffed, he wasn't sure anymore. His wrists were numb and attached to the back of the hard metal chair he sat on. He didn't know he was bleeding from his face, from inside his ear and his head because the intensity of the pain from his leg bore through all of it. It was an excruciating physical pain that still paled in comparison to the devastating emotional torture he felt whenever the sounds of Molly's sobs came through the thin walls of the interrogation room.

Molly had tried to stop herself from crying, from remembering, but even through the haze of her pain the trauma of witnessing her husband's battering and the memories of the torture she endured, kept pushing forward. They had stripped her of her clothing, slowly, painfully, until she stood naked. Then they abused and humiliated her, forced her to watch their brutality, until she no longer felt that she existed beneath her own skin.

Finally, after hours of their cruelty they left her alone, in an empty room, handcuffed to a chair, naked and beaten, spattered with blood and bruises, cold and starving. All that was left of Molly's world were the reflexive moans of her husband through the thin walls, and the memories of his warnings.

"Well, fuck the Constitution." Molly could still hear his words the day he found out that those charged under the DEAD program could be held indefinitely. "All they have to do is say the word 'terrorist' and then it's screw habeas corpus."

It was clear to Griffin that the constitutional rights of Americans had been lost forever under the government's alphabet soup of repressive initiatives. NDAA, EA, FISA, AUMF and their many modifications, in the form of amendments, had given the government carte blanche to spy on and indefinitely 'detain' its citizens without reading them any rights or letting them set foot in a courtroom. Seemingly innocuous actions, like buying food in bulk or sweating too much when driving past a DEAD checkpoint, could now land even a loyal American in a federal prison cell.

ACLU lawyers, who should have called into question the imprecise nature of the DEAD program, found their hands equally tied. Since DEAD terrorists essentially had no rights, and many had even been stripped of their citizenship, lower court judges routinely thwarted all attempts made by prisoners to obtain legal representation by making it clear that the attorneys themselves risked prosecution under the ambiguous umbrella of offering "material support" to the enemy.

"What's the point? Let's just move. Let's get the hell out of this country and try to find someplace where there's an actual democracy." Molly now remembered Griffin's frustration and couldn't help but wish they had actually taken his thoughts seriously.

"Maybe one of those places we went to war with so they could be free and democratic. How's South Korea sound?"

"I think it's rainy season."

"Iraq?"

"Definitely not rainy season."

At the time, Molly and Griffin had ended up resorting to sarcasm as a means of dealing with their feelings about the duplicitous nature of the U.S. Government's policies. Today, however, Molly could not find that place inside her willing to poke fun at her fears. Thanks to the ACLU's inability to break through the terrorist façade, white middle-class men and women had joined the ranks of the minorities and the poor in not being able to defend themselves against being wrongly accused of a crime. For Molly and Griffin, just like the hundreds of thousands of Americans who were being left to languish under a privatized version of civil rights, there would be no lawyers, there would be no trial, and there would be no freedom.

Chapter 27

Tuesday, January 24, 1939
Joe & Selma Gordon
New York City

Maybe it was the fact that the lease for the store on Fifth Avenue was going to be signed that day, or maybe it was just getting too difficult to live in a state of silence. Whatever it was, Joe began speaking to Selma that morning as if nothing had happened.

"Today we sign the lease." Joe proclaimed loudly as he rose from the table and inadvertently pushed the back of his chair into the nearby Hoosier cabinet.

"Joe, careful." Selma cringed at the thought of her beloved white cabinet being chipped. "Joe, sit, eat." Selma hated the thought of wasting their precious food.

"Can't, Sel, got to go," Joe said before he flew out of the kitchen and, seconds later, out the door.

Though Selma had been generally left out of the plans for Joe's return to the dress business, she believed she knew enough to be worried.

What if he quits his job? What if the business fails? What if the bank closes and they lose their loan money? What if? What if?

The normally positive thinking Selma could not eke out a single encouraging thought, no matter how hard she tried to distract herself with her chores. A bad omen, she believed, since experience told her that whenever this feeling of doom overwhelmed her, something horrible was inevitably around the corner. It had happened right before she had miscarried her second child, before each of her grandparents had died, and the night before Black Tuesday. Although Selma had acknowledged long ago that she possessed the gift of clairvoyance, it was in fact only half a gift, one that let her know that tragedy was on the horizon, but did not inform her of the particulars of said tragedy. Which was why Selma's assuming that the disastrous news heading her way had anything to do with Joe's business was nothing more than a futile stab in the dark, aimed at controlling the uncontrollable, a failure of prediction she would only be able to make sense of after it was far too late to do anything about it.

Chapter 28

Wednesday, January 22, 2025
Andrew & Kendall Gordon
Tyler & Kris Mayer-Gordon
Gordon Family Farm, Pinewood, Pennsylvania

No one had heard from Molly or Griffin since the fifteenth of January. Whenever Andrew tried to call his parents both their cell phones would go right to voice mail, and calls to the neighbors yielded no information other than the fact that they had left days ago.

"Yeah, looks like they trashed the house. Left everything on the front lawn. The windows are all boarded up, and they put a barbed wire fence around the yard like they always do." Their old neighbor, Harry Minkon, spoke to Andrew in the same tone that one usually reserves for wakes and funerals. "There's a foreclosure notice posted."

The images of his childhood home desecrated, as Harry described it, pained Andrew.

"My home's gonna be the next one. It's only a matter of time." Harry went on to explain that he had been laid off, and that he and his family would likely be heading down south to Louisiana sometime next week.

"They say the fishing's good down there. I think we'll do okay."

Andrew remembered his father telling him about all the wildlife that died every time a big oil rig spilled its contents into the Gulf. From listening to his father speak about it, though, Andrew was never quite able to figure out if the dissolution of the government agencies overseeing the drilling was a good or a bad thing.

First, Griffin would assault the oil companies with a generous spattering of expletives.

"Even when the government was watching, their behavior sucked. It's not going to get any better now that there's no one out there even pretending they give a shit. It's like believing that a kid who steals candy when someone's watching won't steal any if no one's watching. It's fucking asinine!"

Then, just when Andrew thought he knew who the enemy was and began to hate all things oil, Griffin would rail just as hard against the EPA.

"At least there's no government asshole standing up there ten minutes after an oil spill saying 'pass the shrimp'," Griffin would cringe at his own words. "Go ahead, let your kids go swim in the sludge, 'look, it washes off with dish soap.'"

Eventually Andrew came to the conclusion that the

problem wasn't a matter of government versus business, but rather a lack of ethical behavior and common sense.

Either way, Andrew didn't think going down to the oil contaminated Gulf was a great idea. Though, when he thought about it, choosing the best place to live based on how polluted the environment was would eventually eliminate all fifty states for one reason or another. Even Pennsylvania, whose water supply had been destroyed by hydro-fracking, would have been a bad choice if Andrew's father and grandfather had not come up with a viable rainwater purification system.

"Back in '05 our illustrious Congress, in their infinite wisdom, literally stopped the EPA from enforcing the clean water laws and gave the fucking big oil and gas companies a free pass to shit in our drinking water," Griffin had said the night they chose Pennsylvania. He then went on to explain to his family, in less colorful terms, the system he and Benjamin had devised to work around what had been destroyed.

"I hope you find your parents, Andrew. They're good people." Before he hung up, Harry said he was going to stop paying his cell phone bill to save money, so this would likely be their last phone call. He nevertheless encouraged Andrew to look him up if he ever made it down south. Andrew in turn wished Harry good luck and knew it was likely they would never speak again.

Next, Andrew made the call he dreaded.

"Hi, Oliver, it's Andy." Andrew hated that he had to tell his brother his name, hated that Oliver would not know who it was just by the sound of his voice.

Oliver hated that Andrew was calling for the first time since he had moved out of the house and had to resist the urge to pretend he didn't know anyone by the name of Andy. The possibility that something might be wrong never crossed Oliver's mind as the people he cared most about, his wife and grandparents, were all conveniently within view.

"I'm calling because..." Andrew couldn't help but hesitate, a hesitation that caused Oliver to get even more annoyed than he already was.

"It's Mom and Dad," Andrew continued. "They're missing."

Oliver didn't know what to make of those few words and wasn't sure he wanted to. When it came to his family, the 'ignorance is bliss' approach had always worked in the past, and Oliver had no reason to believe that this policy would not continue to serve him well.

"No one has heard from them or seen them for three days," Andrew continued, moving his story forward slowly and choosing his words cautiously. "We spoke to them once when they were leaving Delaware. They had a flat tire, stayed the night, and told us they were on their way. But that was..." Andrew stopped for a second to regain his composure, which was rapidly slipping. "That was it. Their phones are going to voice mail."

Oliver's mind didn't yet register concern, only annoyance.

"Did you check the GPS tracking in their phones?"

"Turned off."

"That's impossible." Oliver's tone was condescending. "GPS works even when the phone is turned off." He knew this because he had urged Rhine to vote for the law that kept the tracking device activated at all times. Of course, Oliver was well aware that the bill superseded citizen's privacy rights, but he had believed that the end—the ability to find lost phones, hikers, and kidnapped children expeditiously and economically—justified the means. What Oliver didn't know was that the senators who had proposed the bill had ulterior motives. Needless to say, the GPS surveillance industry that grew up around the tracking software was never mentioned in the bill or on the Senate floor before or after the passage of the legislation. In fact, the only time it was ever mentioned again was at election time.

"You know what that means, don't you?" Andrew's words brought Oliver's thoughts away from Washington and back into the conversation. "It means they have most likely been arrested at one of the checkpoints."

Shit, Oliver thought to himself. He hated when his brother was right. GPS systems could only be disabled by checkpoint guards, meaning that his parents, worse than that, his mother, were likely in the hands of Homeland

Security contractors. Although Oliver had heard all the stories of torture, sexual abuse, and starvation he had never had a problem with it. After all, anything it took to get information that might stop the kind of attack that had happened in New York twenty-four years before was fine with Oliver. The only problem he had now was that he did not want the same rules to apply to his mother, and could think of no way to make her an exception. Legislation had wrapped up all the loose ends years ago by immediately revoking the U.S. citizenship of all captured terrorists, thus stripping away any rights that might see them go free on a technicality. It had been a good idea at the time, and he still believed it to be, except for the fact that now they had his mother, and his mother wasn't a terrorist. She was just a mother, whose biggest fault, as far as Oliver was concerned, was that she had married the wrong man.

"So he's really made a mess of things this time."

"Your anger is irrelevant," Andrew said. *Yet expected*, he thought to himself. "We need to find them before they get shipped off to one of those fucked-up overseas prisons."

"Those prisons work very well. And you're welcome."

"I'm welcome?" Andrew restrained himself.

"Shipping terrorists overseas stops them from being able to track each other's whereabouts, and we get more bang for the buck: cheaper land, cheaper building costs, cheaper food and lower pay scales."

Oliver's argument left out the part about bribes, corruption, and the work release programs that had detainees working more than fifteen hours each day, seven days a week and earning the U.S. a per-prisoner profit of two-thousand dollars a year.

Though Andrew really wanted to call his brother a fucking jerk, what he wanted even more was to get his parents out of jail.

"You know everything about everything in Washington, and you know everyone." Andrew deceitfully stroked his brother's ego. "Can you find them?"

To Oliver, Andrew's words felt too much like pleading, and they just added to the feelings of repulsion he had toward his brother.

"How the fuck am I supposed to know?"

That was the only response Oliver could think of, as the truth of his life was that, although he wrote speeches, he never actually set foot on a podium; and, although he wrote laws, he never spent a day in a courtroom; and, though he was in part responsible for the legislation that created the checkpoints that had ensnared his parents, thanks to the Senate parking sticker that attested to his upstanding citizenship, he, himself, was not subject to their scrutiny. As a bystander to the world he had helped to create, Oliver had just admitted to himself and his brother that he had no idea how things actually worked.

"You don't know? You work for the goddamn

government. You wrote the laws that sent our parents to prison! What the fuck do you mean, you don't know?" Andrew couldn't believe what he had just said, and was now furious at himself for yelling at the one person who might be able to get his parents released.

"I don't know. It's not my fucking department!"

Oliver raised his voice back at his brother and stirred the attention of his grandparents and his wife, who he now saw were listening intently to his conversation. As if his day had not already been interrupted enough, Oliver would now have to explain to his grandparents that their son and daughter-in-law were missing, likely arrested, and may have been shipped off to a foreign prison. The stress of this imposition made Oliver's anger rise, and it was all due to the stupidity of his father.

To get off the phone, and because his grandfather was listening, Oliver shifted his tone and promised his brother he would do some research and make some calls.

"Gamps, Grandma..." Oliver started, then told his grandparents the truth, mistakenly employing the 'quick and painless' approach as if he were pulling off a bandage instead of delivering devastating news.

Chapter 29

Wednesday, January 25, 1939
Selma & Joe Gordon
New York City

The white shirt and black tie that had once offered Joe a small sense of accomplishment over the dirty clothes of a porter, now made him feel as if he were being strangled. He no longer wanted to serve the rich their pastas and meatballs, their veal scaloppinis and their everything parmesaned. All Joe wanted to do now was make dresses.

It had been a very good day. A long day that included a trip to the fabric shop, hours of sketching, and a shift at the restaurant. With, just two more city blocks to walk, Joe was happy to be almost home. The house would be quiet, Selma would be asleep, and he could get some much needed rest.

"Joe."

A male voice, from behind, caused Joe to take a startled breath and to reflexively look back over his shoulder.

In the shadows cast from the oil fueled street lamps, Joe did not recognize the man, nor did he feel it wise to approach his caller on the empty street. Instead, Joe quickened his steps towards home and moved at a pace he hoped would be hard to catch up with. But he was wrong, and the stranger's second request for attention came with a hand held firmly around Joe's arm.

"I know about the *Stratagem* and the meeting in the restaurant."

Joe pretended to ignore the man's words, but the anxiety they caused spread through his body, weakening his legs and making him sweat into the freezing January air. Nevertheless, Joe willed himself to move forward, faster. Mere steps away was the corner, where he hoped to find someone, anyone, who might bear witness to what was happening. But the cross street was as empty as the one Joe now stood on and, with the stranger's grip tightening, all he could think of was to free himself in any way possible. Joe lurched forward with a miscalculated overcompensating force that landed him head first over the curb and into the street.

Shocked by his ill-fated attempt at freedom and recognizing the danger, Joe tried to catch his breath, tried to get to his feet. But it was too hard. His head was pounding and his legs felt like lead. Within seconds Joe realized he had a choice. He could either grab the hand of the stranger now offering to pull him to safety or be run over by the car that had come out of nowhere and was careening towards him.

Stretching, Joe reached for the stranger's hand and painfully pulled himself to a standing position just as the speeding car reached him and knocked him back to the ground.

Chapter 30

Monday, January 27, 2025
Oliver & Abigail Gordon
Washington, D.C.

Even though Oliver wanted no part of his parents' arrest debacle, as he could only see it as casting a stain on his otherwise spotless record of patriotism, he believed himself to be a person who lived by his word. If he promised to deliver a vote, he would make good on it. If he promised to love his wife forever, he would never even entertain the prospect of divorce. And if he promised his brother he would look for his parents, then that is what he would do, albeit begrudgingly.

By the time Oliver hung up the phone for the seventh time he could muster no rational reason why he had run into a proverbial dead end. Though, admittedly, he had started out low on the information totem pole as a means of avoiding those whom he might know personally, this was certainly not the kind of outcome Oliver was used to.

Not only did Oliver's contacts admit to their personal lack of knowledge regarding a system that they had ostensibly helped put into place, but they also offered him no suggestions as to who might possess such insight.

Oliver made six more calls before becoming resolute in his decision to call General G, the commanding officer in charge of Homeland Security's Domestic Terrorist Division, a decision born of Oliver's genetically-instilled desire to succeed at everything and one that demanded he allay all apprehensions set in motion by those with which he had previously been in contact.

General G was one of thirteen generals who comprised the Government Safety and Preservation Commission, a group charged with overseeing the wellbeing of the United States Government. Any threat, foreign or domestic, came under the watchful eyes and unprecedented powers of this superior-ranking group of men. Due to the high threat nature of their positions, the actual identity of each of these male generals was kept in the strictest of confidence.

The military, with the blessing of the Supreme Court, had become nothing but a paranoid male bastion of testosterone, determined to save everyone from a world they perceived as hell-bent on destroying the American way of life. Those who dared to speak out in dissension likened the group to The Wizard of Oz, portraying the generals as nameless, faceless puppeteers controlling the unsuspecting masses. Some even questioned the actual existence of the group, choosing to believe instead that one general, or

"The Wizard," as they referred to him, controlled everything under the guise of the Commission. Such suspicions were dismissed as easily as the questions of Martians and Yetis, yet likewise lingered in the public consciousness within the realm of "what if."

Oliver, however, never questioned General G's existence nor his ability to meet him personally.

Chapter 31

Friday, January 27, 1939
Joe & Selma Gordon
New York City

By the time the family made it to the hospital Joe was being released. Refusing the doctor's recommendation to stay overnight, Joe's decision to leave was based purely on the fact that he had no money to pay for further care, rather than any kind of medical prudence.

"The doctor said bed rest for a week; it's been barely two days." Selma's level of frustration with her husband was mounting as she pulled his dress shirt from his hands and gently, though persuasively, pushed his torso back against the pillows.

"Owww," Joe whispered, hoping his wife would not recognize the intensity of his discomfort. He was still suffering from headaches and his body, especially his back, hurt intensely whenever he moved, though the most severe pain came from his regret over maintaining possession of the *Stratagem*.

"Well, how's the patient?"

Both Selma and Joe gasped with fright. Under normal circumstances Sam's unannounced entrance into the room would have merely been a surprise, but the traumatic events of the last few days had left the couple teetering on their last nerve.

"Sorry, didn't mean to startle you both. Abe let me in." Before Sam could make any further apologies for frightening his friends, Selma hastily walked past him, exiting the room without the courtesy of a smile or comment.

"What's wrong with ...?" Sam whispered as his eyes turned toward the door.

"She thinks you, I mean the business, had something to do with my accident," Joe whispered back to his friend.

"What?" Sam answered, "Me? The business? What are you talking about?"

Joe was immediately angry at himself for bringing the business into the discussion, and stumbled about inside his thoughts looking for another answer that might seem plausible to Sam. He didn't want to admit that Selma believed their business loan had come from an unscrupulous source, any more than he felt it wise to confess that his accident had been a direct result of his possession of the *Stratagem*. Such truths, Joe feared, might cause Selma to dispose of their marriage and Sam of their partnership.

"I'm sorry about Selma. It's nothing, really." Joe's solution to apologize to his business partner, instead of answering the question directly, only frustrated Sam further and made him more demanding.

"Joe, what is going on?" Sam said as forcefully as he could in a whisper.

Feeling cornered and believing he had no choice, Joe began his story.

Chapter 32

Friday, January 31, 2025
Molly & Griffin Gordon
Location Unknown

They had both been in custody for two weeks and were feeling physically and mentally worse than either had ever felt before. Partly because they were in pain, partly because they were being deprived of everything they knew and counted on in their daily lives, but mostly because they were being deprived of each other.

They were never asked about leaving their home, about where they were headed, or about the mortgage that was now overdue. There was no mention of the building materials or if the cash they had hidden in the truck had been found. In fact, for the first five days they were asked nothing and, worse, were told nothing. Sometimes left naked, sometimes clothed. Starved, then fed. Left outside in the January night in a brick 3'x3' enclosure in t-shirt and shorts without shoes. Made to stay awake for days on end with music that blared non-stop. Cursed at, hit with sticks, beaten up, and violated. The Gordons had been treated to a variety of techniques designed to make them feel out of control and helpless, and it was working.

Both were ready to tell the state secrets, the combination to the safe, the location of the jewels, the maps, and their list of spy contacts. They would have given up any of those things, if they had had them.

However, as far as Griffin could tell, he had nothing the government might want, and he could not think of anything he had done that was actually illegal. Nevertheless, whenever he had the presence of mind to do so, Griffin would retrace his steps to see where he had gone wrong, what, if anything, he might have done to arouse suspicion or, worse, break the law. As he played each scenario out in his mind and came up empty time after time, Griffin couldn't help but wonder if another member of the family might have tripped him up. More than once Griffin was unable to push away the possibility that Oliver, in sharing one of his usual negative comments about his family and specifically about Griffin, had inadvertently said the wrong thing to the wrong person. Someone who might have misinterpreted Oliver's feelings of being left out of the family's plans as some sort of secret plot against the government.

That was the story Griffin told himself to explain how it might have happened that they had ended up in this prison. What he could not explain was how those who were his captors could justify their actions. What might have been told to them, or what could they be telling themselves, that would make them believe it was acceptable to torture another American citizen, or for that matter another human being?

Ultimately, when he was no longer able to process these thoughts, Griffin would give up and concede his worst fear. That evil had indeed triumphed.

Chapter 33

Friday, January 31, 2025
Andrew & Kendall Gordon
Tyler & Kris Mayer-Gordon
Gordon Family Farm, Pinewood, Pennsylvania

There had been very little snow in Pennsylvania that year, just like last year and the year before that. Flurries mostly, no accumulations. Only the highest elevations caught real snow here and there, but generally it would melt almost as fast as it fell. Resorts that had once drawn skiers with their fine-powdered slopes and the perfection of man-made snow, had struggled for years against the elements to keep their mountains blanketed in white. When all else failed they tried promoting a new sport called slush-boarding, and desperately tried to legitimize mud-wrestling by demanding it be considered a viable Olympic sport, but to no avail. Thanks to the weather and the virtual disappearance of the middle class, patrons who had always occupied their rooms and filled their coffers were gone. The only snow-covered ski resorts left were the small, exclusive, havens of extravagance in northern Canada that catered to those still able to afford a vacation.

Perhaps it was the stress of knowing their parents were missing and that the one person who might offer some help in finding them was reluctant to do so. Perhaps it was the unrelenting chill that leaked through every crack and crevice and into their bones. Perhaps it was the rationed electricity in the form of four outlets. Or the rudimentary bathroom. Or maybe it was the realization that their lack of building and farming experience could not be overcome through the use of books and common sense as they had been previously assured by their father.

Most likely, though, it was all those things together that dulled the younger Gordons' initial sense of adventure and hindered their ability to fashion a livable home out of what was left of the dilapidated farm they now owned. Consequently, progress was slow and tensions were high. Construction deadlines were lengthened and expectations were reluctantly, though continually, lowered. Even Andrew and Tyler, whose cemented bond as twins had grown stronger over the years, found themselves at odds over everything from the proper way to fix a hole in the roof to what vegetable should be served with dinner.

It was, in fact, only through the rational thoughts and protestations of their respective spouses that the two brothers were able to find amicable solutions to the innumerable problems that arose each day.

"He's on the roof again." Tyler couldn't help the annoyance that came through in his tone.

Kendall chose to answer with a grin and a silent prayer for her husband's safety before cutting diagonally across the four peanut butter and jelly sandwiches she had been preparing for lunch in their makeshift kitchen. The kitchen, which also served as the living room and bedroom area, was a freshly-built wood-framed freestanding box, inside the huge old barn. Covered in heavy plastic sheeting on all sides and heated by a wood-burning stove, the three hundred square foot room would not normally have been considered adequate living space for two couples. However, given the fact that the four of them had spent their first week in a tent they had pitched on the floor of the barn, all they felt was gratitude for this small but comparatively more spacious room with the plastic flap door. It was the barn roof that the Gordons were far less enamored of. Each time it rained another hole made a way for water to drip through. Last night, during the latest of the multiple rainstorms they had endured since their arrival, Kendall had counted six new places where the water had puddled on the plastic roof of their room.

"What's with him?" Tyler continued, trying to engage his sister-in-law in a conversation she didn't want to have. "He dragged Kris up with him this time. What does Kris know about fixing roofs?"

"About as much as any of us." Kendall hoped that was enough for Tyler, but she could see by his still-frustrated expression that it wasn't. "Just be grateful it hasn't snowed yet."

Tyler knew his sister-in-law was right and that she was likely as worried as he that the alarmingly-unreliable roof would rupture and spill those they loved onto the floor below. So he vowed to himself not to cause Kendall any more grief.

Out of desperation for a better way to deal with his worries, Tyler, the self-proclaimed atheist of the family, suddenly found himself offering up a silent prayer for his brother and his husband's safe return to the ground. He also added a second prayer for his parents, knowing that if they ever caught wind of his sudden flood of prayer requests, his mother's response would be *I told you so,* while his father's more practical response would have been more like *any port in a storm.*

The ability of his parents to occupy his head and offer up commentary when they were apparently lost somewhere in the outside world gave Tyler pause and caused his sadness to resurface. Instinctively, he looked at his phone. There were no missed calls, no yellow envelope in the corner indicating a text message, and no red mouth signaling a voice mail message. Tyler sent up a third prayer in as many minutes, that they would be able to afford to keep up the monthly payments on their phone, at least until his parents were found.

"No word from Oliver?" Kendall knew exactly why Tyler was looking at his phone.

Tyler shook his head and wondered if it was worth calling again. It had been more than a week since their initial conversation and only twenty-four hours since their last. Tyler knew Oliver was getting increasingly irritated with each phone call and had worried out loud to Andrew that their brother might halt the search for their parents altogether if pushed too far.

As a matter of habit, Tyler checked his text messages and voicemail one more time before shoving the phone back into his pocket.

Chapter 34

Thursday, February 2, 1939
Joe & Selma Gordon
New York City

Joe wasted no time taking off his fedora and overcoat and placing both on the dusty floor of the empty space he now co-owned. A signal of his readiness, in spite of his reticence, to get to work.

There would be no pleasantries exchanged between the two partners that day, no mention of the weather, enquiries as to the health and well-being of each other's families, or discussions regarding the playoff prospects of the Rangers. Sam was still too angry at Joe, and Joe still too angry at Sam, to discuss anything besides business. Instead Sam prodded Joe directly into a discussion about how they might set up their space. Sam said he wanted their business to exude the same glamor, elegance and sophistication as all the other Fifth Avenue couture clothing salons, but had no idea how to accomplish such a feat on the shoestring budget allotted by their bank loan.

If not for the current rift in his marriage, Joe would

have immediately responded to Sam's dilemma by offering the services of Selma as the solution. Generally Joe boasted of his wife's God-given ability to make a silk purse out of a sow's ear. After all, it was she who had enabled their home, with its furnishings, bric-a-brac, and paintings, to look as if the Gordons had previously lived a grander life than their current address would suggest. Selma's trick of trash collecting in the most upscale neighborhoods, before the trash collectors got there, allowed her to take others' perfectly good cast-offs into her own home where, with just the right positioning or a little shoe polish, she was able to hide all the nicks and scratches that might have given away her secret. It was not just Selma's ability to turn a discarded table or chair into an item to be treasured, but also her skill at choosing the perfect piece for the precise spot.

Unfortunately, given the current state of his marriage, there was not a chance that Selma would agree to help decorate the shop. The stress brought on by this thought as well as the realization that perhaps he had done irreparable damage to both his marriage and his business, caused the muscles in Joe's back to tighten around his bruises and made him wince.

"What about Selma?" Sam threw Joe's own thoughts into the air.

"I will not have my wife work." Joe deflected with an argument separate from the one that was going on in his mind.

"It's not work, it's decorating. Just how many times have you told me of her genius in this area? It would be a shame to waste such talents." Sam's ability to convince people to do what they had no intention of doing was how he had succeeded in securing their business loan during a time when banks had barely enough cash on hand to deal with their regular day to day transactions, let alone lend money.

"They agreed to hand over thousands of dollars to a man whose previous business failed? Does that make sense to you?" The situation had, once again, aroused Selma's lingering suspicions regarding Sam, and prompted her to question their business dealings.

Ultimately, however, no matter how many times Joe tried to convince his wife of the legalities of their current business venture, even going so far as to show her the bank paperwork he himself had co-signed, nothing could convince her. In fact, Selma's perusal of the documents and her knowledge that her husband's signature on the dotted line was not backed by any tangible assets, just furthered her belief that the business was based on a backroom deal and forged paperwork. From Selma's perspective it was only a matter of time before gangsters came to collect on a deal gone awry. Being summoned to the hospital, seeing her husband in pain, had just confirmed the inevitable scenario Selma had previously laid out in her mind.

"Well, we can talk about this all later." Sam alerted

Joe that their conversation was not over. "I have to pick up that fabric you ordered and then I'll be back. In the meantime you can take over for me."

Sam handed Joe his broom and dustpan.

"Thanks." The last thing Joe wanted to do was clean. What he had planned to do when he came in this morning was set up his tiny studio office and then work on his sketches. Nevertheless, he took the tools handed to him and began sweeping up the mess that had been left by the previous tenants. By the time his partner walked out the door, Joe was so deep in thought about his admission to Selma and Sam about his accident , he no longer cared about how much he didn't want to be sweeping the floor.

"I don't really know what happened next, whether he let go or if somehow I freed myself from his grasp. Either way, I found myself lurching forward and that's when I fell into the street."

Joe played those words in his mind over and over again. He had stopped his story there, and decided not to finish the true account as he knew it to be. Selma and Sam already knew Joe's fall into the street had precipitated his getting hit by a car. The truth that the car came from nowhere and that the driver actually sped up as he approached Joe, were not things he wished to share. Nor did he share his confusion as to why the stranger ran away. Initially, Joe suspected some collusion between the driver and the man on the street, until he realized that their purposes were indeed at odds, with one man seeming to want Joe to know more and one wanting Joe to know nothing more, ever. Joe's realization that he was somehow caught between these two evils had left his nights sleepless and his days filled with anxiety, a fact that helped him view his decision to leave Selma and Sam in the dark as an exercise in altruism rather than what it was: a dangerous, misguided lapse in judgment that would keep them from fearing what they both needed to fear.

Chapter 35

Wednesday, February 5, 2025
Oliver & Abigail Gordon
Washington, D.C.

Abigail didn't want Oliver to go to the meeting with the General since she knew there was always the possibility that he too would not return.

"I'm here to see the General." Oliver had ignored his wife's warnings and was now speaking into an old-fashioned intercom system.

"Sit down, Mr. Gordon."

The voice that came back at Oliver through the little beige box with one black button labeled "talk" was male, stern, and demanding. Oliver was not used to being treated in what he perceived to be an arrogant manner, and had to restrain his instinct to demand more from the voice. Normally Oliver would want to know how long he would have to wait for the General, and why he was not being offered a beverage and some small talk. However, he had been warned repeatedly by everyone, not just his wife, that in this particular situation it would be necessary to check his ego at the door. All exchanges, he was told, needed to be respectful, and everyone he came in contact with needed to be addressed as one would address a member of the military. Thus Oliver's instructed response of "Yes, sir" was so uncomfortably out of character for him he had to force himself to sit down instead of instinctively heading directly for the door.

Causing further discomfort for Oliver was the immediately noticeable lack of stuffing in the seat of the worn leather chair he sat on. Oliver could tell the formerly well-made and expensive chair was, in fact, a victim of age rather than poor workmanship, not unlike the rest of the furnishings in the room. As Oliver repeatedly shifted his weight in search of a more suitable position, he couldn't help but think about the sharp contrast between this dimly-lit, windowless, paneled office and the bright, ultra-modern, glass and chrome building he had initially entered.

Also obvious was the one very old-looking camera conspicuously perched near the ceiling and directly facing Oliver. Certainly the antithesis of modern covert surveillance systems, the capabilities of this motionless device were a far cry from the security measures in place in the rest of the building. Replete with metal detectors, eye and fingerprint scanners, hidden cameras, two-way mirrors, and random pat downs the facility was an exemplar of modern security.

Even more curious to Oliver, though, was the wooden door that ostensibly stood between himself and the highest echelons of the military. This seemingly flimsy ingress, conspicuously lacking in reinforcements and locks, was, on face value, less secure than a typical bathroom door.

It was as if they ran out of money or the desire to protect him. Oliver made a mental note to tell his brother this thought next time they spoke. Tyler would want to know these kinds of details as proof that Oliver was telling him the truth regarding his meeting with the General. Unlike most people Oliver came in contact with, Tyler always needed proof that the words coming from his brother's mouth were indeed factual. Ultimately, however, Oliver believed the best proof of his actions would be his parents' release, something he was sure he could make happen despite the warnings of his colleagues, who were not convinced Oliver's plans to broker a deal with the General was the way to go.

"These guys don't make deals. They give orders," Monty had warned him only yesterday. Monty may not have been a Senator for very long, but as a member of the Armed Services Committee he had, in his short tenure, learned that the Generals called the shots. All the shots.

Oliver's steadfast arrogance, as well as his belief that everyone, including the General, had a price, was a tough nut to crack. So tough, in fact, that the Senator's well-intentioned warning had fallen on deaf ears.

"I've got this, Monty," had been Oliver's shorthand response to his friend.

Now that Oliver was here, though, and waiting far longer than he had ever waited for any Washington official or insider, he began to question whether the meeting with the General would actually take place, especially after thirty, forty-five, and then sixty minutes had passed. Despite his frustration, Oliver forced himself to remain seated. Leaving, he knew, would be perceived as a failure by his friends and family, a thought even less tolerable than the feeling of being ignored that was rapidly rising within him. A feeling Oliver dealt with by checking his email for the fifth time and wrapping himself in thoughts of his own importance by envisioning his office door in the Capitol with his specially-made impenetrable locks, obvious proof of his superiority over the general.

Suddenly, a voice from the speaker interrupted Oliver's thoughts and told him to come in.

After hesitating just enough to push his frustrations aside, Oliver made his way through the paneled door to a room no bigger, brighter, or any more modern than the ten by ten room he had just been in.

In the middle of the office a man sporting a thick, untrimmed mustache, an unruly half head of hair, and civilian clothes sat behind a beige metal desk conspicuously dented on all sides. The cheap plastic name plate facing Oliver informed him that this stranger, who didn't bother to look up at him, speak, or shake hands when he walked into the room, was Mr. Melvin Bash, Assistant to the Assistant General. Instead of pleasantries, the annoyed-looking Assistant to the Assistant chose to continue his work of flipping through the stack of papers and photos lying atop the open manila file in front of him.

"Be seated," Mr. Bash finally instructed.

Oliver reluctantly obliged, and promised himself never to acquiesce to such rude behavior in the future.

"Mr. Gordon, I see congratulations are in order. Abigail made quite the beautiful bride."

Mr. Bash's comment, which sounded more sarcastic than congratulatory, stopped Oliver's anger in its tracks and pulled his breath from him.

From across the desk, Oliver now recognized a photograph of Abigail in her white, flowing wedding gown. There were other wedding photos too, of himself, their hotel room, the plane, their luggage and the Justice of the Peace.

As Oliver watched in silence, the stranger in front of him continued flipping through page after page, photo after photo, offering an upside-down view of Oliver's life in reverse chronological order.

There were pictures of Oliver in his office, at the supermarket, inside cabs, cars, bars, meetings. He saw himself playing football and golf, and at home with Abigail; pictures apparently taken through the living room window.

There were photos of Oliver in Union Station with his grandfather, and photos of his visits with his parents. There were even pictures dating back to college and high school. Oliver couldn't move.

"The General will not see you, but consider yourself lucky that you will be allowed to return home to your wife." Mr. Bash looked up for the first time since Oliver had entered the room. Staring directly into Oliver's eyes he continued, "Your decision to come here was a poor one, Mr. Gordon. I expect you will be making better decisions going forward."

Oliver could honestly swear he had never seen such an intimidating look on any man's face. Any inclination he might have had to question Bash's authority collapsed.

"My parents…" was all Oliver managed to say before being cut off.

"I know why you are here, Mr. Gordon, and, though I am loathe to waste my breath on further explanation, suffice it to say, the Government will do what it is supposed to do and what it needs to do with regard to your parents. Just as it does with all citizens of the United States. They will be granted no exceptions because of who you work for."

Without the insight needed to recognize that his actions were being controlled by his fear of failure, and at the risk of overextending the limits of his welcome, Oliver made one last attempt to gain some traction.

"What does that mean…Sir?"

"It means you will leave now and tell no one of our meeting." Bash slammed his fist on the desk as he rose from his chair. The sound of hollow metal drawers reverberating pushed through the floor and into Oliver's body. "Unless you would prefer to move to an interrogation room and discuss this?"

As the anger rose in the face of the man across from him, a stack of printed, stapled pages sailed across the desk landing perfectly in front of Oliver, allowing him to read the title, "Natural Gas Drilling, Funding Bill S4993, Conversation with Senator Mark Montgomery, 13 of February, 2024."

Quickly, Oliver scanned the document and recognized the conversation between himself and his friend the Senator. Their discussion, which had started in a nearby park just before one of their regular Sunday morning touch football games and continued later on that day over lunch at a nearby pub, was accurately depicted on each of the pages. Even the comments he and Monty had made regarding the Syracuse basketball game playing on the big screen television, the suitability of the waitress as a date for Monty, and the impromptu interactions they had had with other patrons were all part of the transcript. Every conversation he had that day was there.

Everything.

Perfectly transcribed, and causing fear to flow

through his body. The more Oliver read the closer he came to his own incrimination. Not that offering huge sums of money to bolster one's campaign in exchange for a vote wasn't the norm in Washington: clearly it was, and had been for decades. However, in this case, the money Oliver had offered under the table on behalf of Senator Rhine and the corporate entity that would benefit most from Mark's yea vote on the controversial drilling project in Maine was bugged, recorded, photographed, and now printed on the paper in front of him. A fact that could only mean one thing for Oliver. Jail.

Suddenly, Oliver could not shake the imagined image of himself sharing a cell with his parents. If there was a way out of this Oliver knew it had already been offered in the form of an expedited exit and indefinite silence. So without further ado, or so much as a goodbye, Oliver took Mr. Bash up on his offer and hastily left the office.

Chapter 36

Wednesday, February 5, 2025
Andrew & Kendall Gordon
Tyler & Kris Mayer-Gordon
Gordon Family Farm, Pinewood, Pennsylvania

They sat around the kitchen table, made from the wood of an old door, eating a warm but not-so-hearty dinner of canned soup and crackers. They expected the topic of conversation to be the same as always, a critique of the day's accomplishments followed by a to-do list for the following day.

"With the roof done we can start to focus on the interior structures." Tyler and Kendall let out a sigh of relief at Andrew's comment. They could finally stop their relentless litany of prayers petitioning for the safety of their elevated loved ones.

"Though the bedrooms would be the easiest and the quickest rooms to construct, I think we should hold off." Andrew was in his usual take-control mode. "I know we need privacy, but let's face it we're all too exhausted at night to do anything but sleep." Everyone silently nodded their head in agreement with him. "So, at this point, heating three separate rooms would be a waste of energy."

"He's right." Kendall found herself chiming in and taking some control from her husband. "I've been thinking about the design of the house, and I think for now it should be one big room with sleeping lofts so we can use one heating source for the whole space. Like *Little House on the Prairie.*"

Kendall was suddenly proud of the time she had spent watching the old reruns.

"The hot air will rise, making it even warmer up there than down here." Kendall continued to sell her idea. "Eventually, when we can afford it, if we can afford it, we can add bedrooms; but for now I think our time would be better spent focusing on the bathroom. I am so sick of washcloth showers and heating up the bathwater on the stove."

"What, you don't want an outhouse like they had on the prairie?" Andrew decided to tease his wife, despite the fact he intended to alter his plans based on the merits of her suggestions. "Fine. Kris and I will go over the plans for the bathroom tonight and start working on it tomorrow." Andrew had found his foothold of control again. "Tyler, you and Kendall start working on revisions to the floor plan; see if we can make lofts instead of bedrooms and…"

Before Andrew could finish his sentence a call came through on Tyler's phone. Without needing to be asked to do so, Tyler brought Oliver's voice through the phone speaker and into the now-silent room.

"What's the word, Oliver? Did you see the General?" Again Andrew took it upon himself to take the lead.

"No I didn't, I…" Oliver stopped to remember the lines he had rehearsed in the car driving home from the General's office. "I decided not to see the General." Oliver wished that could be enough for his family, but he knew it wasn't and continued. "The government will do what it is supposed to do, and what it needs to do, with regard to Mom and Dad, just as it does with all citizens of the United States." Oliver's words were taken straight from Bash's mouth and he started to feel sick repeating them.

"What are you talking about? You were supposed to see him. You had an appointment." Andrew was not about to let Oliver get away with what sounded to him like his usual Washington bullshit.

"Uh, I have to go, but I'll call you." Oliver's staccato words immediately followed by his hanging up left no time for further discourse.

"What? Oliver, wait!" Andrew screamed into the unresponsive phone. "Oliver. God damn it!"

Without being prompted, Andrew redialed the phone, but that call and all the others after it went to voicemail. Even the fifteen expletive-filled text messages left by a frenetic Andrew went unanswered.

"I shouldn't have left those messages." Andrew was

already regretting the texts. Some were pleading, most were angry, all seemed justified at the time despite the fact that everyone had tried to stop him.

"No, you shouldn't have, but he deserved it." Kris lent his support to the visibly-shaken Andrew.

"None of this makes sense." A somewhat calmer Tyler finally shared his thoughts. "He had an appointment. He told us more than once."

"You make it sound like it's so unusual for our black sheep brother to lie." Andrew still had plenty of rage left to throw at his brother, despite the fact that he had become remorseful for his own actions.

"No, I know he has no problem screwing us over; but negotiating deals is his thing. He's really good at it. Think about it. It's who he is, it's all he does all day, every day." Tyler was thinking out loud. "Oliver never admits defeat. Of course he said he changed his mind, but I don't think he did. Why would he? Talking to the General was the only solution; he knew that, we all knew that. No, he didn't change his mind; something went wrong."

"What kind of something?" Andrew was quick to ask his brother but wasn't sure he wanted to know the answer.

"I don't know. The only thing I know for sure right now is that if Oliver couldn't get to Mom and Dad, no one else is going to be able to."

There it was. The truth no one wanted to hear. Tyler had put it out there into the room. An inevitable result no one saw coming. They had bet on their brother to change the course of fate, and instead, Oliver had delivered back to them their worst fears.

Chapter 37

Sunday, February 5, 1939
Joe & Selma Gordon
New York City

The newly-installed business phone let out its first loud, unfamiliar ring and startled Joe out of his own thoughts.

"Joe!" Hearing Selma's voice on the other end of the phone, Joe's hope that he was about to conduct his first piece of business, perhaps schedule his first appointment, was immediately dashed. Instead, he was charged with the imposition of trying to figure out why his wife was wasting the cost of a phone call when she could easily have taken the trolley down to the salon to speak to him directly.

"Joe, the man from the street, he called here to speak to you." Selma's breathless words ran together. "He wants to speak to you, Joe. He's coming to the salon now. He's coming to see you now!"

"What, Selma? Slow down, slow down. What did he say?"

"He asked if you were home, and he said he needed to speak to you about business."

"How did you know it was him?"

"I didn't know who he was at first, but it was him!"

"Slow down, tell me everything."

"Okay, okay. I told him you weren't home. Then he said he met you on the street last week, and that he would go talk to you at the salon. He's the one, the one from the street. Call the police Joe. Make them come before he gets there, or lock the doors, or leave, Joe leave please. Before he gets there!" Selma's thoughts moved in as many directions as her instructions.

Instinctively, Joe could not think to do anything but calm his wife and assure her of his future safety. He would, he promised, speak to the cop on the beat and ask for his assistance.

"I'm coming down." Selma didn't believe Joe would speak to the policeman any more than he would stop and ask for directions.

"No, Selma! Stay home. I've got this handled."

Joe's words were firm, his decision final. He did not want his wife in harm's way, even though, without wanting to recognize it, he had been putting her in harm's way all along.

"I will call you when he leaves," he said. "Now, don't worry Sel. I will be fine."

In the face of this sudden threat to Joe's very existence, Selma's belief in her obligation to obey her husband, as outlined in their marriage vows, suddenly disappeared.

Without plan or significant thought she threw on her hat and coat, pulled on her gloves and galoshes, grabbed the last coins from her emergency money, and stuffed them into her change purse as she ran out the door. It wasn't until she was on the trolley and halfway to Fifth Avenue, that Selma realized that the umbrella she had left at home would have made a decent weapon should it have become necessary to defend her husband. So for the rest of the ride and during her run to the salon, Selma thought of nothing else but what she might use in its stead.

Chapter 38

Wednesday, February 5, 2025
Oliver & Abigail Gordon
Washington, D.C.

"What's wrong?" Abigail looked at her husband's face and immediately wanted to know why it was void of color.

As Oliver made his way around the room closing all the curtains, he answered his wife's questions. No, he was not sick, not really, and no, he had not had an accident, and no, no one was dead. At least he hoped that was the case. What the truth was, however, he was not willing to share just yet.

"I'm fine, everything's fine," Oliver said in a make-believe happy tone he usually reserved for children.

"I'm good," he reiterated as he grabbed a pen and wrote:

No matter what you read here you are not to respond out loud, just read and respond back in writing.

Abigail read the words on the page and nodded her head affirmatively, a signal to Oliver that he could continue.

Didn't see the General, just an assistant, a civilian named Melvin Bash. He had pictures of us, a whole file full, and transcripts of our conversations.

Abigail grabbed the pen out of Oliver's hand and responded to her husband on the same piece of paper.

What kind of pictures? What conversations?

Fearing too much silence might pass between them, and in an effort to satisfy anyone who might currently be listening to them, Oliver started an irrelevant discussion about a shopping list while he communicated with his wife on paper, a back and forth real and make-believe conversation with more questions than answers, more frightening thoughts than comforting ones.

Finally, and without saying as much, both Abigail and Oliver had had enough and ended their silent communication by ripping the transcription of their words into minute pieces of paper, placing them in a frying pan, and setting them on fire.

Conversation flambé, Oliver thought to himself as he mingled what was left of the charred pages with the fireplace ashes and soot, remains from what he feared might be their last romantic evening.

The realization that she and Oliver were justified in what seemed to be overzealous paranoia sent a chill up Abigail's spine she could not shake.

"Coffee?" she asked as she poured herself a shaky cup to ward off the cold that was rapidly spreading to her bones. A futile effort she suspected, since she was pretty sure that her body sensations had nothing to do with the actual temperature of the room.

"No. Okay, yes." Oliver changed his mind, suddenly feeling the cold himself.

"I'll take it in the living room. I'm going to do some work," Oliver announced to the microphones he assumed had been planted among his belongings.

As Oliver settled himself down on his overstuffed leather chair and put his feet up on the hassock, he couldn't help but take notice of Abigail slowly pacing back and forth across the kitchen floor. Her long, slow steps, her slumping posture, and the deep frown that had spread across her face worried him. Oliver's customarily comfortable seat suddenly felt as if all the springs had been sprung out of place. This feeling was followed by the realization that it was not his chair but his home and his surroundings that were causing his discomfort. Much like the sensations that follow a robbery, the invisible presence of strangers in his space surrounded him, overwhelming his senses and dominating his thoughts. Instead of taking this time to consider what other incriminating information might have been garnered by the General, Oliver scoured the room from his chair, futilely trying to guess where all the bugs had been hidden.

Chapter 39

Sunday, February 5, 1939
Joe & Selma Gordon
New York City

Selma spent a significant portion of the trolley ride praying she would not find her husband dead on the floor of the salon.

"Please, God, please keep my Yussel safe. Please keep him safe." Selma repeated the words as her mantra, over and over, under her breath but out of earshot of any of the passengers of the sparsely-filled trolley.

"Selma?" Joe was both annoyed and reflexively happy to see his wife walk into the salon. "I told you not to come."

"He's not here?"

"No, no one is here. It's just me."

Nevertheless, Selma looked tentatively around the salon. Perhaps she had seen too many gangster movies, but there was nothing inside her that said it was out of the realm of possibility for someone to be hiding around the corner with a gun trained on her husband.

"No one's here," Joe reiterated as his annoyance deepened.

"Where's the cop?" Selma shared her own frustration with her husband's dishonesty.

Immediately, Joe changed the subject to that of the decor, lest they get into yet another argument that promised to get them nowhere.

"Do you like this beige wallpaper or would you prefer the green striped paper with the flowers?" Joe held the two papers against the curtains knowing full well that such questions would engross Selma in the decorative decision-making process and away from any imagined danger that might be lurking near. It was a short-lived distraction that held her attention until the bell at the front door suddenly announced the arrival of customers.

"Can I help you?" Joe asked the stylishly-dressed couple moving toward him. The presence of the woman disarmed the fears Joe and Selma had been carrying, and allowed both to smile for the first time that day.

Despite the fact that the space they now stood in was clearly a work in progress and not a couture clothing salon open for business, Joe was convinced that these were the salon's first customers, and he was ready to design the perfect dress for the woman who stood before him. Right away Joe began eyeing her voluptuous physique, measuring her curves in his head and placing, in his mind's eye, a swatch of turquoise fabric against her pale skin and wavy dark hair.

"I suspect you can help us," the man said as he removed his hat and became suddenly recognizable. Joe's unconscious instinct to back up and pull at his wife's arm confused Selma. Suddenly she was frightened without knowing why.

It was, however, the stranger's reach into his pocket that pushed Joe to shove his wife behind him and slowly reach in his own pocket for the letter opener he had placed there just in case, a precaution that now seemed ridiculous in light of the perceived threat they were facing.

"My card." Oblivious to the fear emanating from the Gordons, the stranger pulled his card out of his pocket and offered it to Joe. Almost relieved, Joe perused the raised black letters on the small white rectangle of paper and read the words "Martin Muchanskie." Beneath the name Joe read "Manhattan World News, Editor in Chief."

Pulling his thoughts together, and quickly surmising that killers do not hand out business cards, Joe took a deep breath and passed the card along to his frightened wife.

"So what is it I can help you with, Mr. Muchanskie and…" Joe hesitated, not having been introduced to the woman who stood before him.

"Forgive me, Mr. Gordon. This is my wife, Fanny."

"A pleasure." Joe tipped his head forward. "And this is my wife, Selma."

Selma moved out from behind her husband, slightly embarrassed but exceedingly relieved at this sudden turn of events.

"I have an urgent matter to discuss with you. However, I think it best we speak in private. Is there a place we might go?"

Joe saw to it that Fanny Muchanskie would be looked after by Selma, and then showed Martin Muchanskie the way back to his office.

"Watch your step," Joe warned his guest.

Walking through an obstacle course of ladders, paint cans, and brushes, Martin Muchanskie felt compelled to apologize for his obvious interruption.

"Will you have a seat?" Joe, embarrassed, offered Muchanskie a seat on a paint-splattered bridge chair, but both ultimately chose to stand for different reasons; Muchanskie so that he would not dirty his fine clothes, and Joe so that he would not be at any disadvantage to his guest.

"Let me get right down to business."

Joe liked the idea of Muchanskie putting his cards on the table and then leaving as quickly as possible. The emotional rise and fall caused by this man's presence in his life had left Joe physically drained.

"First off, I am sorry for frightening you on the street the other night. I hope we can put that incident behind us. I'm certainly relieved to see you are back in good shape."

Joe chose not to answer. Being prompted to remember the events of that evening caused his body to tense and his ribs to ache again.

"When we first met, admittedly, I handled things

poorly. I hope that what I have to say will fully make up for my initial misstep."

With Muchanskie addressing his business at a much slower pace than promised, Joe kept his growing impatience to himself.

"I have it on good authority that you have come into possession of a document known as the *Stratagem for a New America* and I would like to offer you some insight regarding the text, and ask for your assistance."

Joe neither confirmed nor denied Muchanskie's claim, and worked to keep his expression from telling the truth.

"As you probably know by now, the information you possess was not meant for the eyes of the general public, and in fact your ownership of said document has put you in a considerable amount of danger."

"And how is it that you have come to this hypothesis?" Joe was still interested in playing his cards close to his vest.

"Oh, I am quite sure of all I have said," Muchanskie said with conviction.

"Suppose you are. What does it matter to you what I might have in my possession or what danger I might face because of it? After all, with the exception of our brief encounters, we are strangers."

"Admittedly. However, my interest is not in the knowledge of what you possess, nor in the backlash it might cause you." Muchanskie recognized the callous nature of his words but continued on. "I am actually interested in gaining an understanding of your position on the *Stratagem* and if you might be interested in joining the cause."

"The cause?"

Muchanskie, irritated by his own choice of words, backtracked slightly. "Never mind the cause. I first need to know your position."

"I believe it would be in my best interest to know yours."

"Touché." Muchanskie laughed at the correctness of Joe's response. "I'm sorry; trust does not come easily to me these days. In fact I am sure that given the contents of the manuscript, which by the way you still haven't admitted to be in possession of, you can appreciate my caution, and, indeed, I can appreciate yours."

Joe gave Muchanskie a nod and nothing more.

"Given the probability that our respective fears will lead us to nothing more than a stalemate, let us just suppose for one moment that you are in possession of the aforementioned papers, and that you recognize the inherent dangers and sheer travesty of allowing the plans as written to move forward."

"We could do that." Joe hoped he would not regret letting his guard down slightly.

"Then let us also suppose, that I am representing

a group of men in possession of the other parts of the *Stratagem*."

"Other parts?"

"You were unaware that there is more to their plan than is in your possession? My understanding is that you possess the election section. There is also a full volume concerning legal matters, you know, police, FBI, judge appointments, tipping the Supreme Court, things like that. The third volume has to do with banks and the stock market as well as manufacturing and retail. That one details how they intend to use their newspapers, movies, and radio to influence the general public and cover up what they are doing.

"I don't know why I assumed this was just about the elections."

"Likely because it seemed like enough of a threat, I suppose."

"I suppose…" Joe didn't realize at first that he had dropped his evasive stance, and now became worried about the fact that one more person in the world knew for sure he had a copy of the *Stratagem*.

Can't put this genie back in the bottle. Joe pressed himself to let go of his inner apprehensions and forced his attention back into the room just as Muchanskie had begun telling him how to get to Graham and Metropolitan Avenues in Brooklyn.

"We're meeting on Monday, 6 p.m." Muchanskie told Joe the exact address and the apartment number.

"Remember it; don't write it down." Muchanskie's words were said as a warning.

Joe nodded.

"And don't tell anyone. Not even Selma or Sam."

Caught up in the excitement he felt at finding likeminded men willing to take on the authors of the *Stratagems*, Joe chose to ignore the fact that Muchanskie knew things he seemingly had no way of knowing and quickly dismissed a fleeting thought he had about the possibility he might be being lied to or set up. Instead, all Joe could think about right now was how he was going to get to the meeting the following Monday without having to tell Selma the truth.

Chapter 40

Thursday, February 6, 2025
Andrew & Kendall Gordon
Tyler & Kris Mayer-Gordon
Gordon Family Farm, Pinewood, Pennsylvania

Due to their universal lack of sleep, their day would be a sluggish one: minimally productive, and starting with lunch at noon.

"No luck?" Kendall hoped Andrew would look at the phone one more time.

Andrew, feeling no such need, offered only a negative shake of his head.

"Has anyone thought of anything we might do?"

Unconsciously determined to restore the strength that had been lost to last night's emotions, all three men allowed Kendall's question to go unanswered and her frustration to build.

"Andrew, we need to figure this out!"

"Kendall, right now I have nothing." Andrew wanted to have an answer for his wife, but even more so for himself. He wanted to know where his parents were, and he especially wanted to know that they were safe. "Is there any more hash?"

"No, not unless you want to ruin the inventory." Kendall's fist on the food always gripped tighter whenever any of the Gordon men frustrated her.

"Come on, Ken. We didn't even get breakfast today." Kendall hated when her husband whined, so ignoring his request for more food had just become that much easier.

"There must be something we can do."

"Fine. If my brother doesn't call back by tomorrow, I'll try and get in touch with Grandpa and see what he has to say. He always knows what's going on with Oliver." As Andrew expected, his response was enough to convince his wife to open up another can of corned beef hash.

"I think I'll get to work on the bathroom after lunch and…" Andrew's thoughts regarding the day's chores were interrupted.

"Is someone knocking?" Kris may have been the first to hear the sound coming from the barn door but he was not the first to his feet. Instead it was Andrew and Tyler who moved in sync, the rapid sound of their wooden chairs scraping against the unfinished wood floor revealing their urgency.

Given the recent turn of events, going to the door was now a fear to be faced, which was why everyone was particularly relieved to find out that the visitor was a woman who looked to be in her sixties. Despite her innocuous-looking clipboard, her grey hair and her introduction as a modern day schoolmarm named Shirley, the visitor was not asked to make herself comfortable or brought into the warmth of their living space. Instead, all four Gordons stood with their uninvited guest just inside the entrance and began answering the many questions posed by this quasi-official of the state.

"It's just the four of you living here, right?" The official responded with an air of suspicion to Andrew's assertion that there were no other residents occupying the farm.

"No children?" The woman inquired as she perused the space with a sharp eye, as if the Gordons might be hiding a child behind a post or somewhere up in the rafters.

"No, none," Andrew answered, silencing his inner dialog of resentment toward this woman's questions and her presence in his space. State officials, even older ones with grey hair, were not to be messed with, a fact ingrained in all four of them from childhood.

"Is there something wrong with you?" The woman looked directly at the young woman's midsection, which Kendall tried to hold in without being too conspicuous. As much as she had been anxious to see her belly swell, now both Kendall and Andrew were grateful she was not yet visibly pregnant.

"It's for the form. If you don't have children they need to know why."

Kendall was well aware of what the woman was getting at. Ever since it had been determined by the courts that life began two weeks before conception and that using contraception ran the risk of killing babies that might have been conceived during intercourse, the only way to obtain illegal condoms or birth control pills was through the black market or if you could afford to bring them back from Europe on a private jet where your luggage wouldn't be searched.

For young couples like Kendall and Andrew the only method of birth control now acceptable to the government was the *Abstinence Protocol* as described in the booklet that had come with their marriage license. Considering how often the prescribed method had failed because young couples in love were unable to exhibit the necessary sexual self-restraint needed to prevent procreation, Shirley's skepticism was not unfounded.

"You see," Shirley continued without being asked, "some people hide their children so they don't have to pay for their education. If you're married and you don't have children I need to tell the government why. That way they won't suspect anything is amiss."

Andrew figured the word 'amiss' was code for the illegal use of contraception or for an illegal abortion, which could land both himself and his wife in jail for murder.

"It's really for your protection." Shirley smiled.

Protection, Kendall repeated in her head, knowing

there was nothing protective about the laws when it came to a woman's uterus. Out of fear, past experience, and on cue, Kendall smiled at Shirley and thanked her for her concern.

Try as he might Andrew couldn't help but return an angry glance at this stranger who was perusing his wife's body for defects.

We have a silo full of condoms and we fuck like bunnies all day and all night and she never gets pregnant! Now you and your clipboard get the hell out of my home and don't let the barn door hit you in the ass! That's what Andrew imagined himself saying.

"There's probably something wrong." Kendall now took over for her husband, whom she sensed was struggling to maintain his composure. "We don't have health insurance, Shirley, so we can't..." As Kendall continued pretending to have an undiagnosed problem with her fertility, her teary eyes, slumping body and folded arms at her waist, as if in physical pain, became the perfect body language accompaniment to the quiet, melancholy tale she was telling. Everyone but Shirley knew she was overacting.

"I'm sorry, dear. Maybe someday you will be blessed." Shirley's upset was visible as she patted Kendall on the shoulder and then turned to leave, but not before firmly depositing one of her brochures in Andrew's hand.

"What an ass!" Andrew waited until Shirley was in

her car, safely out of earshot, before beginning his tirade. "Who the fuck does she think she is?"

As Andrew dealt with his resentments by throwing the brochure to the floor, Kendall, who had been composed in front of Shirley, now felt all her fears rise to the surface.

"Stop, Andrew, please stop."

Though there were times Kendall could deal with her husband's anger, Andrew could now see by his wife's expression, this was not one of them.

"What's wrong?"

"I'm just thinking about Janie."

"Who's Janie?" Kris had not heard the name mentioned before.

Hoping to save his wife from further upset, Andrew chose to tell his brother-in-law the story. "She's a friend of Kendall's who had a miscarriage. They charged her with fetal homicide because she didn't use prenatal care, which she couldn't afford. Since she also couldn't afford the public defender fees, she had no choice but to plead guilty. We haven't heard from her since she was sentenced. No one has, not even her husband or her parents."

Kris had heard of numerous instances of how the Supreme Court decision as to when life begins was being used to justify the suppression of women, and to fill the coffers of the for-profit prison system. Without realizing Kendall's fear of miscarriage and the inevitable incarceration which would follow, Kris added his own horror story of legislation aimed at protecting fetuses.

"Yeah, my cousin Amy had an ectopic pregnancy and the doctor didn't bother to tell her because he couldn't do anything about it. Saved himself from going to jail, but my cousin died. It's crazy, a fetus growing in a woman's tube isn't viable anyway."

"Neither are fetuses that haven't been conceived yet." Andrew added that bit of irony to the mix.

Kendall felt a chill rush up her spine and questioned the doctor's allegiance to the Hippocratic Oath. "Whatever happened to 'do no harm'?"

"I think it only applies to their wallets, not their patients," Kris said, referring to the fact that doctors were no longer willing, nor obliged, to save their patients' lives if it meant that the procedure in question would pose a risk to their practice.

On their way back to the kitchen, and in an effort to distract herself from her own worries about not being able to afford medical care, Kendall picked up the school brochure Andrew had thrown to the floor and began to read.

"Look at this."

Right on the cover alongside a smiling child presumably involved in an online lesson was the warning they all knew of, but had never actually seen in writing. Kendall pointed to the thick, bold, black letters which were nearly an inch high and highlighted in yellow. "Parents of children not enrolled in school will be subject to fines of up to $100,000 and mandatory imprisonment."

Seeing it in writing shocked both Kendall and Andrew out of their long-held belief that they could skirt the system and homeschool their children.

"I guess our kids will go to NOOSE."

Andrew knew the correct acronym for the National Online School of Education was 'NOSE' but added a second "O" so that everyone would know how he felt about being mandated to utilize the inferior, privately-run, publicly-mandated educational system.

"The cost for one year is $2,000 per child." Kendall saw her plans for a large family slipping from her grasp. "Plus books, tutoring, field trips…"

"Field trips? Virtual trips or real ones?" Tyler didn't know whether to laugh or be annoyed for his brother and sister-in-law.

"That's what it says, but it doesn't give details."

"How much is OS?" Andrew's curiosity regarding the difference between the online school costs and the traditional form of schooling known as Old School temporarily overrode his anger.

"OS is $24,000 a year?" Kendall could not believe what she was reading.

"Well at least the online schools save money." *At least they're allowed to have a child to educate,* Kris couldn't help think to himself, knowing that if he wanted children he would have to pretend he had prayed his gay away and then marry a woman to make it official.

"There's no real savings." Kendall countered. "The government subsidies for the NOSE schools brought taxes right back up to where they were before. Only now, instead of all that tax money going back into the community through salaries and equipment, it's going directly to the CEOs."

"CEOs have to eat too," Andrew said, smiling at his wife while knowing full well she had been quoting his father verbatim.

Kendall gave her husband a fake punch in the arm then felt the need to continue.

"It's not just about the money. It's the ridiculous education, the crazy versions of history and the 'science' that isn't science at all. They don't teach anything of value. They'll get our kids ready to flip burgers, not much else."

"Don't worry Ken, after our kids finish learning that the world is flat, that the cavemen rode dinosaurs, and that the sun and the planets revolve around the earth, we will tell them the truth."

Andrew may have been smiling, but Kendall knew he wasn't kidding. They had both heard the stories from her father-in-law about NOSE's obfuscation of scientific facts aimed at dumbing down the population. She also knew that if she and Andrew did not intercede, their children would be destined to believe that electricity was a miraculous and unexplainable phenomenon, and that the increasingly-destructive weather patterns and rising sea levels had everything to do with a lack of religious fervor and nothing to do with global warming.

"And history," Kendall continued, recalling her father-in-law's angst over all that was missing from the online school's social studies lessons. "There's no dissent. No demonstrations." Kendall went through her list of examples starting with Women's Suffrage and included the Civil Rights Movement, Voting Rights Act, Vietnam War protests and Occupy. "It's like they never happened, they're all gone. The only things left are Bible stories and events that incited war."

"It's always been that way. History is what the writer says it is." Tyler's comments admitted him back into a conversation he wasn't sure he was entitled to weigh in on. *After all*, he reasoned in the back of his mind, *I'll never have kids, so I'll never have to worry about this.*

"Maybe, but it's never been this bad." Based on her father-in-law's belief system, Kendall assumed she was right.

"How would you know? How do you know what you don't know?" Tyler waited for his sister-in-law to answer, and then continued when she didn't. "Government depends on the ignorance of its citizens. Protests are the first thing they erase from history so people won't recognize how well they can work. The Flint Sit-Down Strikes of 1936 were never mentioned when we were going to school. And the Battle of Blair Mountain, you never hear about that."

"Blair Mountain?" Kendall had no idea what Tyler was talking about.

"Huge union victory, and a whole slew of elected officials got voted out of office."

"How do you know all this if no one else does?"

"Grandpa used to tell me the stories. And it was all online for a while too, until the internet laws."

Tyler didn't need to explain further. The series of internet laws that had taken hold over the past ten years effectively blocked the free flow of information by enabling the government to arbitrarily take down any website simply by claiming copyright infringement. Owners of the sites not only had no recourse, but were generally fined or jailed depending on the nature of the material and how badly the government wanted the information silenced.

"We should write it all down," Kendall said out loud before appreciating the implications of her suggestion.

"Yeah, Kendall, that way we can all go to jail." Tyler's response came with his teasing smile but inadvertently directed their thoughts back to their parents. All at once an overwhelming feeling of worry seemed to be caving in on them again.

"All right, all right. I think it's time we all got back to work." Andrew tried to save his loved ones from their emotions. "Let's go, we've lost too much of the day as it is."

Let's go, we've lost too much of the day as it is. Andrew's planned emotional rescue came to a sudden halt as he heard the words repeat in his head, this time in his father's voice. *Let's go, we've lost too much of the day as it is.* Andrew could see his father rousing them all as they packed for their move. He remembered Griffin's unwavering determination and his blind optimism about a better future. Andrew couldn't help but worry that his father might never see his masterful plan come to fruition.

In an effort to stop his own thoughts, Andrew instinctively grabbed his tool box and headed to his latest construction project with a newfound energy and determination. It wouldn't be until much later that evening, when he took stock of all they had completed that day, that Andrew would realize he was not the only one who had been driven by his father's words.

CHAPTER 41

Thursday, February 6, 2025
Molly & Griffin Gordon
Unknown Location

Without a clock or the ability to see a sunrise from their windowless cells they had no way of knowing that they had been imprisoned for twenty-two days. During that period they had been moved countless times. Transferred from one facility to another, one state to another, unknown distances on buses and trains. Always under black hoods, the smells and sounds around them offering no solid clues as to time, direction or place. Today, however, on this twenty-second day of their captivity, things were going to change—and change dramatically.

For the first time Molly and Griffin were given clothes, real clothes, and socks and sneakers. For the first time they were comfortably warm from head to toe. Trays with food were also brought to their respective cells, though each hesitated to eat at first, fearing that poisoning was to be the pièce de résistance of their torture.

After breakfast Molly and Griffin were ushered up eight flights of stairs and into separate elevators, where each of their captors pressed the button for the forty-second floor. Following the lightning-fast elevator ride that left their newly-filled stomachs at their feet, Molly and Griffin were led through a waiting room and into a small, unattractive old office. Un-hooded, the couple glimpsed for the first time what living in hell had done to each of them, a vision that would have brought both to tears if they had been allowed to look for more than a second. However, they immediately brought their eyes straight ahead as instructed. Too terrified to disobey and look toward one another, even out of the corner of their eyes, each settled instead into the chair to which they were led and faced a man behind a desk. The man, whose name plate informed them that he was Mr. Melvin Bash, Assistant to the Assistant General, did not bother to look up at them, choosing instead to rifle through the files in front of him.

Chapter 42

Monday, February 6, 1939
Joe & Selma Gordon
New York City

Generally Joe would have told Sam about the meeting in Brooklyn, but Muchanskie had warned him not to, and until now Joe hadn't even thought to ask why.

"I'm the creative partner in this team. I have no interest in this. They're just numbers on a page." Joe put the balance sheet back on the desk in front of Sam. "Just tell me how much money I can spend on the fabric for the samples and—oh, look at the time." Joe pretended to be surprised, when really he had been watching the clock on the wall all day. "Selma is expecting me." Sam summarily ignored Joe's concern as he placed the balance sheet back in his partner's hand.

His excuses didn't work, and it took another hour before Sam concluded their business. By that time it was after six o'clock and Joe was sure the meeting had started without him. Nevertheless, he headed for the subway, and endured an anxious, though uneventful, ride under the streets of the city to the Brooklyn address.

It wasn't until Joe had climbed the Metropolitan Avenue Subway Station stairs to street level that the smell of burning wood and the sounds of sirens caught his attention. As he moved closer to his destination the air thickened with falling ash that mimicked flakes of snow. In no time Joe found himself directly across the street from the building he had intended to enter, only instead of going inside he was watching it burn to the ground.

A multitude of thoughts and emotions swirled inside Joe's head as he became mesmerized by the firemen's fruitless efforts to fight the out-of-control blaze. He watched as they struggled with ice-clogged hoses and carried stretcher after stretcher of blanket-covered bodies out of the flames. Joe doubted anyone trapped inside could have survived the intensity of the inferno, and he felt compelled to say a prayer for the safety of the men he did not know but was supposed to meet with that evening. He also kept looking desperately around the crowd for signs of Muchanskie, and eventually he tuned in to the crowd's commotion for any information he might garner.

Though the rumors were many, they centered only on the causes of the fire, rather than on those who might have been caught in it. From explanations such as a roast in the oven left unattended for too long, to a drunken brawl knocking over an oil lamp, Joe tried to find the truth. The last supposed cause of the fire, the one that mentioned foul play, set off a chain reaction of thoughts in Joe's mind, ones he desperately tried to push aside.

Suddenly Joe saw the words as if they were written in his mind's eye:

And don't tell anyone, not even Selma or Sam.

All the questions Joe had—how Muchanskie had known he had the *Stratagem* in the first place, where he had gotten his phone number, how he had found the salon that wasn't even open for business—flooded Joe's thoughts.

Why did Muchanskie ask me to meet with these men?
Who is Muchanskie, really?
Why did I trust him?
Was there actually a meeting?

Then Joe's thoughts moved to the most unsettling questions of all.

Was I supposed to be in that building? In that fire?

None of Joe's questions could be answered now, and the chances of his learning more this evening had literally gone up in flames. Muchanskie was nowhere to be found.

As the fire raged on and the body count climbed, Joe's fingers and toes became numb from the cold, prompting him to walk back toward the subway entrance where his fears for the safety of his loved ones grew.

Though the subway car had plenty of empty seats, Joe's anxiety forced him to stand. As he shook with the motion of the floor and gripped the strap hanging from the ceiling tighter than he needed to, Joe berated himself for his decisions. How, he wondered, could he have been so gullible as to listen to a total stranger over the advice of his wife and his partner? He also questioned whether he should be afraid of the other subway riders, and began perusing each individual as they stepped into the car. Joe hated this feeling, hated his thoughts, and wished for the first time that the subway had a bar car like the Long Island Railroad did.

"Sir? Sir?"

Joe missed a breath then spun around, completely unaware of how the man now standing next to him had gotten there without his noticing.

Just then the subway came to a stop.

"You dropped this." The stranger handed Joe a glove.

Before Joe could respond, the man slipped through the closing subway doors and onto the platform, seemingly disappearing into thin air.

Confused and not wanting to place a stranger's possession into his own pocket, Joe inspected the leather article for any signs of ownership. An exercise in futility, Joe would realize, only after he had reached inside the glove and discovered the note that had been left there for his benefit. In defiance of his own judgment and reason, Joe unfolded the white rectangle of paper and read the message.

Chapter 43

Friday, February 7, 2025
Oliver & Abigail Gordon
Washington, D.C.

Once you know the government is watching you, how do you get them to stop?

Oliver entered through the door with the engraved name plate that said "Senator Mark Montgomery" and, after exchanging pleasantries with the senator's staff, was given quick entry to his friend's office.

"Ollie!" The Senator was genuinely happy to see his friend.

"Monty, how are you?"

"I'm good."

The two friends completed their greeting with their secret fraternity handshake before being seated across from each other, the Senator behind his oversized mahogany desk and Oliver in front of it.

"How about those Skins?"

Even though he had not seen his friend for over a

week, Mark nevertheless assumed Oliver had seen the first of the playoff games the night before.

"I told you the extended season was a good thing." Oliver never missed an opportunity to prove to his friend that doing away with the player unions meant more games to watch and ultimately more money pumped into the economy. Advantages, Oliver maintained, far outweighing the protestations of critics, like the Senator, who believed that player fatigue was to blame for the recent tenfold increase in player injuries.

"I'm not going to pretend that I don't enjoy the longer season, but..." The Senator stopped himself from engaging in yet another frustrating argument for and against unions. If Mark had learned anything in his short tenure as a Senator it was that on Capitol Hill most issues were thought of as black and white in nature, and finding the greys of compromise across the aisle was as elusive a goal as finding the Holy Grail.

"So what else is new? How's Abby?"

"She's good."

Before they ran out of small talk Oliver decided it was time to address the real reason for his visit to the Senator's office. Positioning his left index finger over his mouth, Oliver used his right hand to place a note on the desk. It was a note just like the one he had placed in front of Abigail last week, requesting that the forthcoming information be read silently in its entirety and that all responses be put in writing.

Confused, apprehensive, but extremely intrigued, Mark was willing to take the note despite the fact that he had watched a disproportionate number of his fellow lawmakers be taken down through litigations built on entrapment. If he couldn't trust his best friend, Mark quickly reasoned, then there would be no one else he could trust. After replying with an affirmative nod to Oliver's request, the Senator was handed another note in a blank white envelope.

As Mark read the letter, the two friends continued to engage in trivial conversation. Despite having to simultaneously maintain two thought processes, both managed to keep their dialog and voices at a normal steady volume and pace while Oliver impatiently monitored Mark's facial expressions for any signs of disbelief.

Monty,

I am sure you are curious about my secrecy and the use of this antiquated form of communication. However, I find myself needing to discuss this matter by a means that cannot be spied on, hacked into, or otherwise stolen by the government et al, and can, when all is said and done, be shredded and burned...

Oliver's letter continued, recounting the details of his meeting with Bash and including the fact that all his actions had been recorded and documented. The letter also stated that the transcripts and pictures contained previous interactions he had had with the Senator and raised the distinct possibility that people might be also be following Mark as closely as they were following Oliver and his wife.

I am at a loss to discover why the military should be watching me so closely. Over the past week I've gone over my actions at work and at home in an effort to decipher what might be of interest to them, and I have come up with nothing. Rhine is an ardent supporter of everything military. All my speeches favor strengthening our forces through funding, and you know I have never wavered from that.

At this point Mark started to seem nervous and stopped just long enough to jot down some notes on the page before continuing on.

Uncharacteristically, Oliver shared with Monty his fears regarding his parents' safety and what life had been like for himself and Abigail since finding out that he was being spied on.

When you believe every word you speak and every movement you make is being recorded, life gets very complicated. Everything I say has to be thought out in detail. Often I find my conversations grinding to a halt, fearing that my words might be twisted maliciously and give rise to consequences for myself or my family at a later date. Even a simple trip to the supermarket feels different under scrutiny. At times it has gotten so difficult that I have begun to question whether staying in D.C. is the best choice for Abigail and me.

What Oliver left out of the letter was that since

finding out about the pictures from their honeymoon, his wife had refused to have sex with him. Abigail had no doubt his assurances, regarding their bedroom being free of cameras and bugs, were based on his horniness and not on verifiable facts. Instead, Oliver put a positive spin on his currently-strained relationship by saying in the letter that sharing their thoughts on notepads, which they had adopted as their primary means of communication, was not as bad as one might have predicted, and that he and Abigail had gotten quite good at holding two conversations at once.

Reading between the lines, however, Mark couldn't help but believe this situation was having a negative impact on his newlywed friends. Particularly troubling to Mark was the end of the letter where Oliver's denial grew thick in defense of his ego.

When Senator Rhine becomes President Rhine, I will be in the position to call Bash onto the carpet and have the power to punish him accordingly.

Oliver, perhaps naively, also stated he believed that getting rid of Bash would ultimately stop any future attempts to spy on him. Mark, who knew so much more about the workings of the military than Oliver, was quite clear that taking down one man, in this case Bash, meant nothing. There were always hundreds, presumably thousands more Bashes waiting in the wings ready to follow orders and do whatever they were told to do. Any misconception on Oliver's part that Bash was the end of the line was a dangerous one, and would leave him open and vulnerable. Eventually Mark would need to straighten Oliver out about this, but for now there were bigger issues to consider. The Senator still had no idea why Oliver was being watched and to what extent he himself was being followed, or for that matter who could help him figure it out without his questions getting back to the military. More disturbing to him was the fact that his instincts were telling him there was more to the story than Oliver had put into the letter; an intentionally missing piece of the puzzle, perhaps, but more likely something in Oliver's subconscious that he was not yet ready to give up. Either way Mark suspected that finding out the truth was going to be critical to his own safety as well as to his career.

Part 3

It started innocently enough. An American deemed 'traitor' and 'terrorist' on foreign turf killed by a drone, excused as necessary and justifiable. Everyone agreed the world had just become a little safer.

Then the drones came back from their overseas missions and "forgot" to turn off their cameras, taping citizens of the United States as they went about their business. Illegal as wiretaps without subpoenas, the images were reviewed and those citizens deemed to be doing wrong were jailed. Americans were told to feel safer.

Soon the drones were extolled as heroes, scouting forest fires, surveying hurricanes, and warning of tornadoes. Though quite the novelty at first, they had become as commonplace over city skies as seagulls at the beach and were perceived as innocuous. No one mentioned that as the military was watching people in the path of natural disasters they were also recording their movements, and keeping files on each of them.

Even in the suburbs, where the drones routinely dotted the skies and made special appearances at public gatherings, flying in thrillingly complex formations with their mesmerizing neon-like signs promoting colas, gas, and water, everyone believed they were just something to notice and nothing to fear. Few suspected that the individuals looking up were also being looked down upon, or that the signs were designed to camouflage the on-board hidden cameras and sensors as well as their substantial weapons capability.

Griffin was one of the few who knew right from the start what was going to happen and warned his family accordingly.

"If the government ignores their own laws, their own Constitution, no matter what their motive or how patriotically-justifiable they believe their actions to be, it's a genie that can't be put back in a bottle. Eventually one instance will turn into more, and then more, until there no longer needs to be any justification. It just is."

As usual, no one had taken Griffin's warnings and predictions seriously. No one believed these wonders of the sky would ever be used for malevolent purposes against America's own citizenry. Unfortunately, by the time they figured out that Griffin was right, it was too late.

Chapter 44

Friday, February 7, 2025
Andrew & Kendall Gordon
Tyler & Kris Mayer-Gordon
Gordon Family Farm, Pinewood, Pennsylvania

It was too easy to let their guard down on the farm. Without street cameras recording their every move, they started to forget about watching the depth of every breath they took.

"Don't look up." Andrew said to Kendall as emphatically as one can in a whisper between clenched teeth and a fake smile.

"Why, what's…?" Reflexively Kendall started to do exactly what Andrew told her not to do and moved her eyes toward the sky.

"Here look at this."

Andrew grabbed Kendall by the arm, pulling her down towards the ground so forcefully she lost her balance. Luckily for Andrew she also lost her desire to look up.

"What? What's so important you had to knock me over to see it?"

"See, look here, down here."

Andrew pretended that what he wanted to show his wife was only visible if she would lie down on the overgrown, winter-dead, grass poking out of the hard ground. Reluctantly, but feeling like she had no other choice, Kendall complied with her husband's request.

"So, are we looking for a needle in a haystack or did you get me down here for a roll in the hay?"

Andrew laughed tentatively at Kendall's joke, then moved on top of her as if he was in fact looking for the intimacy his wife had teased about. From a distance, from above, at least no one would be able to see his expressions or read his lips.

Initially Andrew had written off his father's warnings regarding drones as pure paranoia. Now Andrew not only believed his father's predictions, but took them so seriously he was now face down in a frozen field trying to communicate the danger to his wife without causing her to panic.

"Don't say anything, don't move, don't do anything but smile," Andrew whispered.

Kendall smiled warily, which was the best she could do under the circumstances because now her husband was making her nervous.

"There's a drone above. It was here a little while ago,

but it circled back. We're going to walk back inside like nothing is wrong, and whatever you do don't look up."

Andrew gave Kendall a few seconds to absorb what he was saying before he continued. "It's probably nothing, but, just in case, act like you do at the tolls: calm, nonchalant. You know the drill."

Kendall did know how to act at the tolls so the sensors would not pick up any nervous behavior, but she knew almost nothing about drones or why Andrew was scaring her so. Nevertheless she agreed to Andrew's request, and rose to her feet in sync with her husband.

Gripping her hand tightly and with a smile on his face, Andrew led his wife back into the barn and to what they believed to be the safety of their living space, where Tyler was reviewing the plans for the sleeping loft.

"What'd you two see out there, a ghost?" Tyler quipped, not wanting to believe that something was actually wrong.

"A drone." Kendall answered first, still not fully aware of why she should have been so afraid.

Chapter 45

Tuesday, February 7, 1939
Joe & Selma Gordon
New York City

The note that the stranger had furtively tucked inside the glove given to Joe on the subway informed him of an upcoming meeting in an alternate location and was unsigned. Joe would have to decide if it was more dangerous to attend the meeting than it was to stay home. Either way, it was a decision he would have to make on his own.

Leaving his precious coffee to grow cold, Joe repeatedly scanned the newspaper's scant list of names of those who had perished in the fire. Though he was positive that he had witnessed in excess of twenty stretchers of blanketed bodies being loaded onto the van labeled "Office of the Coroner for the City of New York – MORGUE," the newspaper list claimed that the number of deceased totaled only five.

"Joe, stop reading. Your breakfast is already cold."

"Then it doesn't matter if I stop reading, now does it?"

Selma had no idea that Joe's unpleasant response had to do with the article he was reading. Instead she assumed his attitude, as well as his preoccupation with the newspaper, had only to do with the worry that always accompanied his forays into entrepreneurship. She therefore decided her best course of action would be to change the subject.

"Rose called. Said she was walking by the Ethel Barrymore Theatre yesterday afternoon and who do you think she saw?"

Joe didn't respond or even look up from his paper. Undaunted, Selma continued.

"Walter Huston. Can you imagine that? In the flesh: Walter Huston."

Even Selma's mention of the Broadway star elicited no response.

"You know he's in 'Knickerbocker Holiday.'" Selma couldn't help but start humming the tune *September Song*, a popular ballad from the show.

Nothing.

"It's about Roosevelt, you know. They say he's a fascist. They think he's another Mussolini. "

"What?"

Joe looked up from his newspaper, annoyed. Having incorrectly concluded that Selma was insinuating, much as Sam had done, that Roosevelt and his policies were fascist, his response to her was biting.

"You don't know what you're talking about, Sel. He's a Democrat." Joe retreated behind his paper once again and finished his thought under his breath. "Trying to pull this country out of the garbage can the Republicans put us in. Calling him a fascist. Huh."

"You're not listening, Joe." Selma didn't allow the fact that her feelings had been hurt to stand in the way of defending herself. "I said that's what 'Knickerbocker Holiday' is about. You know, at the Ethel Barrymore. Rose said she saw Walter Huston. Did you hear any of what I said?"

Joe didn't hear his wife. All his attention was once again focused on the details of the article, and the stark differences between what he had seen last night and what was being reported in today's paper. His inability to make sense of the disparity was drawing him oddly closer to the idea of attending the next secret meeting rather than being rational and maintaining a safe distance from it.

Chapter 46

Friday, February 14, 2025
Molly & Griffin Gordon
Location Unknown

Even if Griffin had known it was Valentine's Day, there was no way to communicate to his wife how much he loved her and how sorry he was for getting her involved in the situation they now found themselves in.

Last week's meeting with the Assistant to the Assistant General Melvin Bash had not gone well. Though Griffin was able to justify that the beating he received afterward was a small price to pay for seeing Molly and knowing that she was alive, he still had no way of giving them any information about Oliver or Rhine.

The subsequent interrogation of Molly, though less violent, was equally unproductive for Bash, who later confided to his underlings that he found the whole thing too messy and considerably more frustrating than it was worth.

Bash hated working within arm's reach, preferring to remain anonymous by making things happen from a distance. Ordering surveillance, taking out suspected terrorists with a drone strike, or sending the command to blow up a building was all in a day's work and quite preferable to him. After being in the business for thirty years and seeing most of his colleagues "disappear" following one inadvertent misstep or another, Bash had become justifiably paranoid. So much so that the only time he felt safe these days was when he was alone in his office.

Bringing the Gordons in was neither his idea nor a good one as far as he was concerned. Bash could not care less what a lackey like Oliver Gordon was or was not doing for Senator Rhine. Rhine was the dirtiest lawmaker in the Senate, and they had all the evidence they needed to get anything they wanted from him. As far as Bash was concerned his boss was being unnecessarily overzealous.

Nevertheless, Bash knew his boss would not be happy to hear he had come up empty-handed, and decided it would be best to lie. He would throw a bone to the Assistant General by making up a plausible account of their meeting.

I'll just take a piece of intel we already have and add to it, Bash thought to himself, praising his own ingenuity. *Genius, I'm a genius.*

He continued his self-praise by making the words into a song he sang out loud.

"Genius, genius, I'm a genius,

Genius, genius, fucking genius,

My great big brain will make me famous,
The boss' brain is up his anus..."

Bash continued his song as he rifled through pages and pulled out a document accusing Rhine of all manner of indiscretions. All he needed to do was choose one that had happened so far in the past it was unlikely anyone would care at this point.

"This should do it," Bash said to no one in his empty office, and he set out to write a phony transcript of the made-up conversation, a chore that took him less than ten minutes.

After that, Bash sent a communication to the prison ordering them to withhold Griffin's food and sleep for three days due to his lack of cooperation during the interrogation. This was despite the fact that Bash had believed Griffin when he'd said he did not have any information to share.

Chapter 47

Saturday, February 15, 2025
Oliver & Abigail Gordon
Washington, D.C.

Their decision to go out to dinner to celebrate their first Valentine's Day together in spite of all that was going on in their lives was one they regretted almost immediately. Fearing everything they said was being recorded, and recognizing that passing notes would look ridiculous in public, their conversation centered on the décor of the restaurant.

For Abigail this was the worst Valentine's Day she had ever celebrated, even worse than the time her college boyfriend had broken up with her between the main course and dessert. At least that time she had been able to yell at her partner, make a scene in the restaurant and throw the wine in his face. At least that time she had had an outlet for her rage.

With nothing to say and no longer hungry, the couple left after one drink, drove home, undressed, and went to bed without speaking – an uncomfortable silence born of resignation. It was not until the next morning that one would notice the other was missing.

Hollow State

Oliver awoke before his alarm clock and without even opening his eyes he knew Abigail was gone. Nevertheless, he instinctively reached for his wife and then quietly called out to her. Getting no response he was loathe to open his eyes, as it would simply confirm what he already knew.

As he read the clock that said 6:00, a feeling of panic swept over his body. It was a feeling he had not experienced since he was a child, when he had thought he'd lost his mother in a sea of shoppers. As much as Oliver wanted to be able to believe that whatever was going on was not a result of any foul play, that his wife was safe, just like his mother had been, his still half-asleep thoughts would not hear of it, going instead to entertain the most primal of fears. *My mommy is gone, my wife is gone.* This time, as during the last, he became furious with himself for letting go for too long.

It was not until he had finally managed to get to his feet and come to his adult senses that he realized his wife had placed a note right beside him on her pillow. Oliver's heart began to slow for the first time since awakening.

* * *

I LOVE YOU OLI but this is too hard – you know it

is. I have to do what I can to fix this – make things better for us. See you tonight.

* * *

Abigail had dotted all the i's in her note with hearts, hoping that Oliver would notice them but not judge them childish.

Unlike the laser focus he utilized at work to detect the most minuscule of details unscrupulous senators tried to slip into the thousands of pages of legislation he reviewed, when it came to his personal life Oliver hardly ever noticed or questioned anything.

So when Abigail had told him she had a wonderful close-knit family that lived in California, Oliver never even questioned her about the fact that she chose not to tell them about their marriage, or enquired as to why she never visited or spoke with them.

There were times her husbands inattentiveness to the details of her life would bother Abigail, but mostly she was grateful for it. For instance, the fact that Oliver had never asked her about how she was able to maintain the role of 'upstart environmental reporter' without being imprisoned never seemed to cross his mind. Even when his friend Monty had mentioned it, Oliver chose to jokingly write off the peculiarity as attributable to her good looks.

It was for that reason Abigail believed the note she had left her husband, though severely lacking in detail and explanation, would be enough for him, and gave it not another thought as she wound her car through the streets and circles of Washington toward the government building that housed the office where her husband had been to see Bash the week before, and her in-laws had been just the day before.

CHAPTER 48

Wednesday, February 15, 1939
Joe & Selma Gordon
New York City

Joe had always believed that his steadfast adherence to telling the truth and to following the letter of law, even when it made his life more difficult, was part of being a good person and a good citizen.

However, given the fact that he had stolen the Stratagem, routinely lied to those he loved, and was willing to put everyone he cared about, including himself, in harm's way, Joe couldn't help but worry that his moral compass was broken. This was a worry he carried until he finally came to the conclusion that good and bad, and right and wrong, were not isolated choices, and that what defined a good citizen and a good person clearly depended on who was in charge of the definition.

Joe's imagination had led him to believe that behind the wooden door he had just knocked on was a smoke-filled room of angry men arguing about how to save America.

"Come in," the little girl in the blue sailor dress said to Joe as she opened the door. She was no more than three, maybe four years old and her blonde hair had the tightest curls Joe had ever seen.

"Dining room," was all she said as she pointed, then skipped in a straight line down the hall, leaving Joe to close the door behind him and walk through the first opening to his left.

The room Joe entered was large, much larger than his own dining room, and the walls were covered in the kind of French wallpaper Selma coveted. The men and women, about twenty or so, were sitting and standing around the large table laughing. Joe immediately assumed he was in the wrong apartment, and prepared to make an apology for his intrusion, when Martin Muchanskie walked up to him in the way old friends do, extending a hand for a handshake followed by a big slap on the back.

"Joe, old man!" He turned. "Hey everyone, this is Joseph Gordon!"

The group stopped their conversation to look up and smile at the newcomer. Joe smiled, though he was not happy with the fact that Muchanskie had exposed his name to all these strangers so quickly.

"Pull up a chair. We were just discussing the weather."

Joe couldn't help but wonder if 'weather' was some kind of code word for something else, as he couldn't imagine what might be funny about the freezing temperatures that returned every evening as the sun went down. The same cold that had practically caused him to lose his fingers to frostbite the night he had stood on the street watching the fire. However, as the conversation moved on, Joe noticed that weather was indeed only one, of all manner of things they talked about, without any mention of the *Stratagem*.

"Patience, we will get there," was all Muchanskie said in answer to Joe's many questions about the previous meeting and the fire.

"Patience," Muchanskie reiterated before his and everyone's attention turned to a knock at the door that brought the same little girl running to open it.

Ushered in was the girl's grandfather, Joe quickly learned, a stocky man who used a polished black walking stick for no particular purpose that Joe could see. He also wore a homburg and spoke with a thick, indistinguishable, multinational accent that seemed to be Eastern European at its core.

"Father, this is Joseph Gordon." Muchanskie introduced Joe right away.

"Mr. Gordon! Call me Uncle Bernie, everyone does. Come have a drink. Everyone, join us!"

"Joseph, hand me your glass!" Muchanskie was pouring servings so generous, Joe worried he might become too inebriated to make his way home.

"That's fine," Joe cried out, putting up his hand when the glass was half-full, a signal Muchanskie ignored.

Over the course of the next few hours, the food and

alcohol continued to flow as others arrived with piled-high dishes of mouthwatering, ethnically diverse offerings and multiple bottles of liquor. Joe mingled and ate, pretending he was drinking as much as the others when in fact each trip he made to the bathroom was an opportunity to further dilute his drink and maintain the impression that his glass was always full.

Between bites of food and sips of what now was essentially a glass of water, Joe quickly realized how much he had in common with the other members of the group, and that they shared similar viewpoints on a variety of subjects, especially politics. He also learned there were twelve new members there that evening, and half the people in the room were either relatives or neighbors on this very block. No one he spoke with mentioned the fire from the other night, even when Joe nonchalantly hinted at his desire to discuss it. That was the only thing that seemed odd to Joe. The rest of the evening seemed perfectly normal to him.

Three hours into what seemed to be nothing more than a party, the music, which had grown in volume, was turned off, the children were scurried upstairs and put to bed, and the curtains were drawn. As the women removed the food from the table, Muchanskie passed out literature and everyone but Uncle Bernie sat down.

"I'm very gratified to see the new members here

tonight, and for their edification we will review the minutes of the last meeting before moving on to new business."

Despite his thick accent, Uncle Bernie's ability to command the attention of the room was obvious. To his audience, comprised mostly of first generation Eastern European Americans like Joe, the sound of Bernie's voice was an intelligible and cohesive blending of old and new.

"Before we begin I would just like to say that it warms my heart to see so many of you willing to fight for our American democracy."

Everyone, including Joe, nodded in agreement at Uncle Bernie's words.

"Those who believe it is within their purview to take over the functions of our government as if it were only their own, to the exclusion of everyone else, must be stopped."

A chorus of applause ensued as Uncle Bernie pulled out his handkerchief and wiped his moistened eyes. Joe couldn't help but notice that most of the women in the room had begun to cry.

"They've only had the right to vote for nineteen years. It means a lot to them," the man behind Joe leaned forward and whispered into Joe's ear. Joe answered silently back by nodding, and began to feel choked up himself as the memory of Selma's own fear of losing the vote came to mind. *I wish she was here to hear this*, Joe thought, suddenly feeling unhappy with his decision to leave his wife at home.

As the meeting progressed and the subject of the *Stratagem* finally came up under 'new business,' Joe was grateful he had limited his alcohol intake and kept his wits about him.

"Thanks to Joseph Gordon we now have access to all the pieces of the puzzle. All three documents have been found."

Another round of applause ensued, and Joe was both pleased and surprised to learn that he had the only copy of the third *Stratagem*.

"By dividing their plans into three independent sections and conducting separate meetings in different parts of the country, they believed they could keep the details of their entire plan, as well as their ultimate goal, elusive. It seems, ladies and gentlemen, that we have outwitted them."

Again the room filled with applause, and Joe found himself taking particular delight in the word "outwitted." With much relief, Joe now believed the title *Stratagem* had been the perfect choice. Although it now looked as if it would be the authors of the *Stratagem* who were going to be deceived.

Chapter 49

Saturday, February 15, 2025
Oliver & Abigail Gordon
Washington, D.C.

As Abigail allowed the escalator to raise her the three stories to the General's office, she stared out through the giant wall of glass that made up the front of the building. This wasn't the first time she would wonder why they had built what seemed to be such a fragile and transparent structure to house the workings of the strongest and most secretive military machine the world had ever known.

"Daddy!" Abigail's resolve to be angry at her father floated away the minute she saw his green eyes and pepper gray hair, which, as always, formed the perfect complement to the dark blue of his uniform.

"Abby, my girl." The General could never be formal with his daughter, and could also never be angry at her. At most, his frustrations with her lasted maybe ten minutes before falling apart into apologies for his own gruffness, a soft side those under his command would never have believed existed.

"Still working Saturdays I see."

"There are no weekends in the military." The General gave his daughter the same response he had given her all her life. The one he had used every time he had to miss a soccer game or a play.

"How are Mom and the twins?"

"Good. They miss you, you know."

"I know."

"And when will you be coming by the house?"

"That depends."

"Abigail Marie." The General accented his daughter's middle name and rolled his eyes, predicting she was about to trade her presence at dinner for something he had already told her he couldn't deliver. "If this is about –"

"Dad, wait." Only Abigail had the power to stop her father in his tracks. Even her teenage twin sisters, as charming and manipulating as they could be, could not hold a candle to their older sister when it came to their father. "I know you said you couldn't help Oliver's parents. I told you I understood." Abigail didn't understand and her father knew it.

"I just wanted to thank you for helping Oliver get that appointment. You did know the General wouldn't see him?"

"No, but I had a feeling." That he had even asked a favor of another General was further than he felt he should have gone in the first place, so the fact that it didn't work out was not an entirely unexpected outcome.

"Did you know they showed him his dossier? I thought only you were having him followed. They're following him too?"

"Apparently."

"Why?"

"Rhine."

Abigail shook her head, annoyed once again that her husband was working for the man who had the distinction of being the most crooked senator of them all. "No scruples. Not a one," Abigail said under her breath before continuing. "What I don't understand is why Bash told Oliver they were following him. Now that he knows, he'll be of no use to them."

"They've pretty much figured out by now that Rhine's not interested in letting your husband in on his business dealings, or his profits. Bash just wanted to scare Oliver off, make sure he never came back again. I take it his plan worked?"

"Oh yeah, he's going crazy trying to figure out why he's being followed. He's convinced this has something to do with his parents."

"That's what Oliver thinks? That this is about his parents?"

Abigail nodded in response.

Though he didn't want to share his thoughts with

his daughter, the General couldn't help but laugh to himself at his son-in-law's entrenched belief that the people he had chosen to surround himself with were somehow above reproach.

"He won't even let me speak in our own home. He has me writing everything down." Abigail smiled because she had no choice but to recognize how ridiculous her life had gotten because of the secrets she needed to keep. "You've got to help me, Dad. I have writer's cramp." Abigail held up her hand and bent it like a claw, causing her father to laugh at her.

"Just a little while longer, Abby. We have to leave things as they are. No arousing suspicions. And we need to make sure your husband keeps his nose clean. Here." The General passed Abigail a card that read simply:

Irvine Pincus

555-111-2278

"Who's this? One of your spy friends?"

"Pinochle."

"And you want me to call him?"

"No. Just tell your husband you had him do a sweep and he got rid of everything. Can you do that?"

"But won't Bash hear us talking about calling in Pincus and wonder what's going on?"

"We'll have our guys get rid of those parts of the transcript. You just have to convince your husband that it's done."

"My husband won't question my word." Abigail loved the sound of the words *my husband* and smiled at her father so he might know that.

Satisfied that she had found the solution to her problem, Abigail said goodbye to her father and then planted a big kiss on his cheek before heading for the door.

"Remember what I told you to say, Abigail."

"Got it, Daddy." Abigail smiled and then winked at her father before pulling the office door shut behind her.

Hearing his daughter's footsteps clear the area, the general picked up his personal cell phone and called his friend Irvine.

"Irv. Yeah. Uh-huh. Uh-huh. Excellent. Right. Okay, see you then."

As he hung up the phone, the general sat back in his chair and thought about how grateful he was that this was all almost over.

Chapter 50

Saturday, February 15, 2025
Andrew & Kendall Gordon
Tyler & Kris Mayer-Gordon
Gordon Family Farm, Pinewood, Pennsylvania

It was rare that all four of the Gordons made it into the town of Pinewood proper. Without fences, locks, or other security measures it was just too risky for all of them to leave the farm for extended periods of time. In fact, now that their presence was known and gossiped about by the few hundred inhabitants of the tiny town, and the drones had made a habit of flying over their property, there wasn't much a Gordon could do without the world knowing about it. At least that's how it felt to the four of them.

"Did you stop at the post offices?" Tyler enquired of Andrew.

"Yea."

"Both offices?"

"Both. It's all on the table."

"Travel to two post offices for one family's mail. I'm sure we can thank our asshole brother for this one, too,"

Tyler mumbled under his breath, loud enough for everyone at the table to hear.

Andrew didn't know if Oliver had anything to do with the dissolution of the U.S. Postal Service and, though he agreed that ending home delivery and dividing the service into official and non-official mail services so citizens had to drive from one mail office box to another was idiotic, he decided to refrain from getting sucked into Tyler's annoyance.

Without further instigation Tyler began opening the indistinguishable official blue envelopes.

"Why do they seal these things if they're going to read them first anyway?" Tyler tore at the envelopes harder. "Anthrax, my ass," he said under his breath, but again everyone heard him.

"Don't you feel safer now that all the mail is placed in officially-sanitized envelopes?" Andrew's tone was appropriately sarcastic.

"Yeah, safer." Tyler was barely listening as he started reading through the letter they had received from the Town of Pinewood Department of Public Works.

"Oh, great."

"What?" Andrew didn't really want to know.

"Listen to this."

Andrew could tell from Tyler's body language and the way he was now gripping the letter that it was going to be bad news.

"'Welcome to the Town of Pinewood.'"

"Better late than never." Andrew pretended to smile.

"'As residents of the town you are entitled to the following services'...blah, blah, blah...blah, blah, blah...oh here it is. 'As you know, the water in this area has been deemed safe for drinking.'"

"Safe? Have they smelled that shit?" Kendall picked up her plate and brought it to the sink.

"I know. Listen to this, 'Many residents prefer to receive their water by delivery. For a small monthly rental and hook-up fee, the town will deliver a 150 gallon sanitized drinking water tank. Enclosed you will find a list of the official water distributors for the Town of Pinewood. Please feel free to contact them directly after your tank has been set up.' Idiots."

"It took them a month to offer us clean drinking water?" Andrew was finding it harder and harder to hold back his anger.

"There's nothing wrong with the water, remember?" Kendall shook her head, infuriated that the authorities would pretend the water was safe to drink when everyone knew it was so toxic you could light it on fire. "Thank God we have our own water system."

"You can thank Dad and Grandpa for that one."

Though Andrew was now singing their praises, he had done his share of cursing as he installed the system that would store copious amounts of rain water and then purify it all. "It should be finished tomorrow. That reminds me. I bought that pipe we needed. It's in the car."

"I'll bring it in later." Kris was anxious to get the job done. He hated drinking bottled water because it was nothing more than the same foul-smelling, rusty brown liquid he could get from the tap, the only difference being that bottled water was laced with chemicals to make it look clean. Kris also knew that water companies were free to make their plastic bottles out of any carcinogenic material they wanted, so he had recycled all the glass bottles he could find, filled them with filtered water and brought them to the farm.

"I'll just be glad when the system is up and running," Kendall added, knowing but not saying that there was not much of the filtered water left in the glass containers, and they would soon have to resort to the water in the plastic bottles they had brought as backup.

"Oh shit, look at this." Tyler had opened another letter and began reading it aloud.

Dear Resident of the Pinewood Fire District,

It has come to our attention that you have failed to pay the fire prevention fee assessed for your residence and property. As of February 12, 2025, your grace period as new residents will end, at which point you will no longer be covered. Should you experience a fire situation you are still required to contact the station number listed below and the department will respond to the call immediately. Please be aware however, that our presence on site is strictly a precautionary measure to assist our department in protecting any and all adjoining public or contracted lands.

As you know, due to the unseasonably warm weather and the possibility of summer droughts we encourage you to reconsider your decision to forgo coverage and look forward to serving you.

Blakely Barns
Fire Chief
AMCOR Fire Fighting Services

"That was days ago. What if their 'safe' water started the house on fire?" The irony hadn't escaped Kris.

"So according to this Blakely guy, if our house is on fire they are going to just watch it burn to the ground?" Andrew tried to wrap his head around the facts.

"Yea, apparently when old Blakely and his good buddies show up in their yellow slickers, with their spanking new fire engine red truck, all they are going to do is roast marshmallows."

"Excellent." Andrew sounded defeated. "I'll go back to town tomorrow and bring them the money. How much is it?"

After rummaging through the envelope for the invoice stating the Gordons would have to pay two hundred dollars a month for fire protection, Tyler reluctantly shared the news with his brother.

"Two hundred dollars? A month?"

Tyler hated when Andrew had been pushed too far, and really hated being the bearer of this bad news. Usually, it was Oliver who pushed him over the edge. The only recourse Tyler knew of was to change the subject, but Kris beat him to it.

"I think we need to make a garage in the far corner of the barn." Kris looked right at Andrew who was showing his anger by crumpling up the letter he had taken from Tyler. "That way we can transport whatever, or whoever, in or out without anyone seeing."

The daily whir of the drones overhead was something none of them could get used to, and though they didn't believe they had anything to hide from the government, the mere presence of the drones had incited a level of paranoia that pushed them to be more secretive than necessary.

"We can start on it now. It will be done before dinner." Kris was optimistic.

"Done before dinner?" Andrew wasn't so sure.

"Absolutely. There's a door there already. We just need to tweak it a bit and figure out how to lock it, and then frame a room inside with plastic sheets to seal the fumes off."

Tyler had, in the past, jokingly referred to Kris as the "half-assed fix-it man" due to his spouse's difficulty staying focused long enough to complete the bigger construction jobs. However, that same impatience also made

Kris perfectly suited for figuring out how to get makeshift jobs, like this one, done in a hurry.

"Let's get to it!" Andrew led the charge for the three men, believing that the only way they had a chance of finishing in time for dinner was to get started immediately.

"Hey. What about the dishes?"

"I'll do dinner," Andrew called back to his wife, adding, "I promise."

"Or you will be sleeping on the floor." Kendall shouted after them, even though she was she was pretty sure her husband was already out of earshot.

Kendall really didn't mind doing housework because she had figured out early on that she didn't like swinging a hammer. The whole process bored her quite quickly, so washing a few dishes, which took only minutes, was far preferable to her than a day of construction and the accompanying blisters and backaches. Today Kendall would use the extra time to tackle the disorganization, dirt and clutter of the living space that she was becoming increasingly less tolerant of. She also believed, optimistically, that her in-laws would be released one day soon, and wanted everything in its place for their arrival.

As the sound of drills, hammering, and the occasional indeterminate noise continued to play in the distance, Kendall turned the radio to its highest volume and tuned it to an oldies station that played mostly nineties music. Then, in an attempt to raise the cleanliness to a level she had never bothered about before, Kendall got on her hands and knees to scrub the cheap linoleum floor covering their main living area.

Why clean today if it's just going to get dirty again tomorrow? Kendall remembered what Tyler had said to her, and silently admonished herself for having listened to him as she worked to remove the layers of dirt that had accumulated over the previous weeks.

"Kendall? Kendall!" Kendall had been so deep in thought it took a while for her to notice her husband standing there with a peace offering in the form of a bouquet he had made out of weeds and winter grass tied with an errant piece of wire. The bunch, of what amounted to nothing more than dead stalks, looked beautiful to Kendall.

"They're wonderful!" Kendall was overwhelmed by his gesture.

"Sorry about the dishes. I'll do better."

"This is so sweet."

"I promise to take care of my dishes from now on."

Andrew helped his wife off her knees and handed her the dried offering. As a gesture of normalcy Kendall brought the bouquet to her nose, breathed in deeply and pretended to be pleased with the smell.

"Mmmm – smells like the dead of winter."

"That's not normal, Kendall." Andrew laughed at his wife.

"Normal? What's normal?"

"You're right. We've lost our home, had to move off Long Island, my parents are in jail, drones fly over our heads day and night. Heck, we're living in a freaking plastic room inside a barn with a cow in the next room!"

The unexpected sound of the cow mooing, shockingly on cue, stopped Andrew in his tracks, and both he and Kendall laughed until they could barely catch their breaths.

Chapter 51

Wednesday, March 1, 1939
Joe Gordon
New York City

As instructed, Joe arrived at Bernie's law office after hours, Stratagem in hand.

The gold letters on the plate glass door spelled out the names of the firm's ten partners. Bernie Wasenfeld, Esq. was first on the list. The office itself was spacious, more spacious than most in the city. It was also well-appointed, with leather chairs, finely carved wood desks and signed oil paintings hanging on all the walls. To Joe it was immediately obvious that someone had spared no expense in decorating Bernie's office, and he couldn't help but wish he had that kind of money to spend on the décor of his own dress salon.

"Mr. Gordon? I'm Mona, Mr. Wasenfeld's secretary." The young woman, neatly dressed in what Joe quickly assessed to be expensive business attire, shook his hand. "This way please."

Joe was surprised to see a secretary still working at

this late hour, and was even more surprised to be greeted by Bernie at the door of his office.

"This one's for you." Bernie began to pour his top shelf scotch whisky into a finely cut art deco glass.

For Joe, who had rarely had any liquor since finishing off the last of his pre-Depression stash, utilizing what precious little money he and Selma had to restock his bar had not been an option. This was despite the fact that many a night he had longed to employ the distinctive properties of alcohol as a means of dulling the sharp edges of his problems.

Now for the second time in a week he was being handed a free glass of scotch, and all he could think about was the importance of keeping his wits about him.

"Have a seat and a drink while my secretary makes copies of this. It's going to take a while." Bernie exchanged the drink for the *Stratagem*, which Joe hesitantly put in the lawyer's hand.

"It's fine. My secretary is one of us."

Us, Joe thought to himself, still not sure he knew enough about who "us" was to feel comfortable handing over the papers.

"You know, Joe, I have to admit I am anxious to get a look at your section of the *Stratagem*. It's the last piece of the puzzle and I'm counting on it to explain everything."

Joe guessed that Bernie was right. After all, his copy contained the specifics of how the conspirators intended to rig the elections by tampering with the voting machines.

"There's quite a bit in there," Joe replied without going into the details. "How did you get ahold of the other two parts?" He felt that offering up his information entitled him to get his own questions answered.

"It's an interesting story. It has to do with my philosophy about loyalty." Bernie took a gulp of his scotch.

Joe had no idea where Bernie was headed with this.

"You see, Joe, here's the thing. Most rich men think their money can get them anything they want."

"Can't it?"

"Almost." Bernie lit a fat cigar and offered one to Joe who refused. "But they can't buy loyalty." Bernie puffed twice. "And I find it rather humorous that they consistently believe they can."

Joe wasn't quite sure why Bernie was laughing and wondered if it had more to do with his alcohol consumption than his wisdom.

"I shouldn't laugh. They can't help it; it's the way their minds work. A man who will do anything for money assumes everyone else will."

"Well, if a man gets desperate enough, he will do pretty much anything for money." Joe immediately thought of how he used to steal food from the restaurant so that his family wouldn't starve. Unconsciously, he took a gulp of his scotch to wash down the usual pang of guilt that accompanied these thoughts.

"Oh, I agree. People will do things for money; but

you can't buy loyalty, and, as it turns out, in business as in life, loyalty is everything."

Joe had not expected a philosophical discussion. He just wanted to know where the other parts of the *Stratagem* had come from. Nevertheless, he had no intention of trying to stop Bernie.

"Here's how it goes, Joe." With his elbows on his desk and his hands animated Bernie told the story of a rich friend named Percy who had bribed a judge years ago in order to get a 'not guilty' verdict.

"Forward twenty years and old Percival finds himself in front of the same judge. Only this time Percy is broke, lost all his money in the stock market. Do you think the fact that he bribed the judge twenty years ago will get him off?"

"Probably not."

"Definitely not." Bernie's voice grew suddenly loud and his arms flew into the air, startling Joe.

"Now let's say instead of money my friend Percy had worked for that same judge. Helped him get elected to the bench, not by writing fat checks, mind you, but by working on his campaign, really working. Handing out leaflets, going door to door, sharing his contacts, organizing fund raisers, the whole megillah. Do you think the judge would have put Percy in jail ten, twenty even thirty years later?"

Joe took a minute to think about what Bernie was telling him.

"No," Bernie yelled. "Of course he wouldn't put him in jail. Because the judge's loyalty came from Percy's loyalty to the judge. Loyalty begets loyalty."

Bernie winked, then leaned back in his oversized leather chair, which creaked to emphasize his movement.

"So what does all this have to do with the *Stratagem*, you're asking yourself?" Bernie was right, Joe was waiting for the connection. "Well, I'm getting to that." Bernie winked at Joe again. "Now, I'm not a betting man, Joe, but I would bet my last dollar on the fact that if the plans outlined in the *Stratagem* were to come to fruition, there would be no way for anyone but a rich man to get ahead in this country."

"I'm not so sure it's not like that now." Joe had become even more cynical since his discussion of the *Stratagem* with Sam.

"Oh, undoubtedly even now it is easier to get ahead, or should I say stay ahead, if your last name is Rockefeller or DuPont, or if you're a Hughes or a Getty. Yes, you can pretty much write your own ticket. But getting back to my story. Let's say for argument's sake, and this is just a 'for instance,' I'm not saying this is true. But let's just say I helped the secretary of one of the men who went to a couple of the *Stratagem* meetings. Maybe a man who, oh I don't know, runs a whole bunch of newspapers."

All the supposition was not fooling Joe, he knew exactly who Bernie was talking about.

"He pays his secretary, I'll call her Marla, he pays Marla quite well; thinks it buys her loyalty. But me, I help Marla with a few legal issues gratis. I meet the family, invite her to dinner, we get friendly. So who does Marla choose to be loyal to? Her employer?"

"No. You."

"Correct, Mr. Gordon. Give that man a cigar." Bernie spoke in a voice like a carnival barker and Joe couldn't help but laugh.

"Now here, Joe, here's where it gets interesting. About two years ago Marla tells me that her boss is going crazy over Roosevelt. Hates him with a passion. Says he's been going back and forth to Germany, and she's getting worried. She thinks he's part of a plot to kill FDR."

Bernie took a big gulp of his drink, finishing what was left in his glass, then poured himself another. "More?" he asked Joe.

"No, thanks." Joe was still nursing his more-than-half-a-glass.

"Where was I?"

"Kill FDR."

"Right, right. Damn memory. No fun getting old, but I guess it beats the alternative, right, Joe?"

Joe smiled at Bernie, impatient to hear more of the story.

"I tell Marla to eavesdrop, listen to those calls from Germany; and she does. Lo and behold, she finds out that they weren't going to kill Roosevelt after all, but they were working on a Plan B to replace the Business Plot."

Joe couldn't believe that Sam had guessed right, and he couldn't help but wonder what else Sam had been right about.

"Her boss went to the first two meetings and asked her to make copies of the *Stratagem*; naturally she made an extra one for me."

Bernie pulled copies of the first and second *Stratagems* out of his desk drawer and tossed the heavy stacks in front of Joe.

"See, Joe, that's loyalty."

Joe nodded, affirming Bernie's belief.

"But how did you find out I had the third copy?"

"You have a relative who works in the newspaper business?"

Suddenly the pieces were falling into place and everything was finally starting to make sense to Joe.

"You know Leo?" he asked.

"No, but my secretary's friend does. Your cousin Leo; apparently he's quite the *yenta*."

"All my wife's relatives are." If it hadn't been such a serious matter Joe might have joked about that fact, but instead he felt it was best to distance himself from Selma's quirky family by changing the subject. "And the fire. Did these people have anything to do with that?" Joe pointed to the *Stratagems*.

"The Brooklyn fire?"

"There were others?"

Seeing the worried look on Joe's face and sensing his fear, Bernie focused on the Brooklyn fire.

"Yes, Brooklyn was aimed at us. Someone wants us to stop meeting, there's no question about that."

"People were killed because of these?"

"None of our people."

"Innocent people. Their names were listed in the paper."

"Whoa, slow down cowboy. I think we can clearly agree on a few things here." Bernie kept himself calm in the face of Joe's rising angst. "First, you can't trust what you read in the paper. Did you not notice that there were quite a few stretchers brought to the morgue truck, but only a few names listed in the paper?"

"Yes."

"Sometimes you can't trust even what you see with your own eyes."

"What does that mean. Of course I can trust what I see with my own eyes." Joe was annoyed at the insinuation that he had not seen what he had seen, but Bernie just smiled between puffs of his cigar.

"The stretchers you saw were not carrying people. No one died in that fire. The names, well, they were real people, they just didn't die in the fire."

"Stretchers with no people? Names of real people who aren't dead? And no one noticed?"

"You didn't, and you were standing right there." Bernie chuckled. "Don't worry, the dead won't be showing up around here any time soon."

Bernie told Joe how he was in the habit of helping clients disappear. Not all his clients, just the ones facing fixed trials and long sentences under the gavel of a crooked judge.

"Crooked judges, they're like cockroaches, Joe: you step on one, there's fifteen more right behind him."

Bernie went on to tell Joe that seeing to it that no one went to jail because someone had bribed a judge had become a personal goal of his.

"They call me the Robin Hood of the legal system."

Bernie looked across the room at a statue of the famed character he had placed on a table under a shining light.

Joe was too preoccupied recalling the events that had transpired the night of the fire to notice Bernie's glance at the statue.

"If people were not on the stretchers then what was?"

"Copies of the *Stratagem*. We had loads of them in the building when they set it on fire. Oh, we have copies elsewhere but we didn't want to risk the possibility of someone finding an errant copy not destroyed in the fire. This just seemed to make the most sense at the time."

Bernie's voice was matter of fact, as if everyone had the resources to pull off a ruse that required a significant network of police and coroner employees to be on board.

"The point is, Joe, that as powerful as they think they are, we are becoming just as powerful."

"How?"

"We're right next to them and they don't even know it. They think we're just their lowly employees: their secretaries, stenographers, maids, cooks, chauffeurs, doormen, janitors. They have no idea we are watching them."

All of a sudden Joe noticed that Bernie's face had changed from the warm and welcoming look it usually carried to one more akin to that of a gangster.

"We knew, for instance, about that car that tried to run you over. We stepped in, you know, to protect you."

A chill spurred by the memory of the dark street and the speeding car pushed Joe to grab for his drink and take a quick gulp.

"How did you protect me? I got hit by that car."

"You didn't die, did you?" The smile that followed Bernie's words seemed misplaced. "One of our guys was behind the wheel. He had to make it look good to keep his cover, but, like I said, you didn't die. You can thank your cousin Leo and his big mouth for putting you in front of that speeding car."

Joe took multiple gulps of his drink the way Bernie usually did, something Joe was not used to doing. The drink hit his stomach and his head simultaneously and removed the filter that stood between his mouth and his emotions.

"So they're still out to kill me? Why didn't you tell me they were still out to kill me? Why didn't Muchanskie? You've known all the time and you let me walk around like everything was okay?" Joe could not deny he had sensed the danger. More than once he suspected he was being followed, but had never placed the thought so securely in his mind as to not be able to pretend it away, something he would no longer be able to do.

"What would you have done if I told you? Would you have actually come here, walked the streets of New York with your copy of the *Stratagem*, or would you have destroyed it? Maybe you would have disappeared, skipped town, or, worse, confronted your newspaper cousin, the one with the big mouth. No, I couldn't take that chance."

"That was not your decision to make. It should have been my choice." Joe could feel the alcohol moving out to his extremities making them feel weak, his body warm. All at once he regretted drinking so much that his anger did not sober him up.

"You sound like you've been nursing some sort of delusion that you are master of your own destiny. Surely you know by now that no man has been given that luxury. Not even these guys." Bernie glanced down at the *Stratagems*. "Though they are certainly going to great pains to try to get it. Can you imagine anything worse than the fears these men possess? Look what they are willing to do to assuage them."

Even though Joe had never considered an insatiable lust for money and control as something that stemmed from fear, he suspected Bernie was right since at this very moment his own fears were making him want to grab for anything that would calm him down.

"If we are going to find a way to stop this thing, and I will be honest, I'm not sure we can, then we will need all the information we can get our hands on. And then –" As Bernie continued to speak, Joe barely listened. Try as he might, he could not control his anxiety.

It wasn't until Bernie once again mentioned his watchful eye, and assured Joe of his safety and the safety of his family, that Joe's full attention moved back to the conversation.

"You are just going to have to trust me."

"I'm not convinced that's such a good idea." Joe could still feel the fear vibrating through his body.

"It was you who leaked information to your cousin about the *Stratagem*. We picked up the pieces on that one."

Suddenly Joe's forgotten anger at Selma regarding her gossiping about the *Stratagem* came rising to the surface.

"Let's just say we will continue to protect you and your family, and we have more than the law on our side. Just go about your business and make believe everything's fine."

"You expect me to pretend nothing's going on, that my life is normal?" Joe watched as Bernie nodded in affirmation. "Do I have a choice?"

"No."

Joe smacked his empty glass onto the wooden desk. "Hit me." Joe said with resignation, prompting Bernie to grab his now half-full bottle of scotch and pour.

As the amber liquid rose slowly toward the rim of the tumbler, Joe came to the realization that he was involved in a giant game of cat and mouse. Much to his chagrin he was apparently playing the part of the cheese.

Chapter 52

Saturday, March 1, 2025
Oliver & Abigail Gordon
Washington, D.C.

Abigail made up quite a story for her husband, telling him how she had found Mr. Irvine Pincus and employed him to make their home free from surveillance. Convincing Oliver was far easier than it should have been and Abigail realized, not for the first time, that her husband was susceptible to the belief that there could be an easy solution to a difficult problem. It was a disappointing aspect of his personality, but one Abigail was more than willing to overlook it if it meant they could finally get back to having conversations out loud and living what they considered to be a normal life.

"Maybe we should go visit them?"

"Who? My grandparents? They're coming home soon enough."

Oliver was thrown off by Abigail's return to their previous conversation.

"No, your brothers. Maybe we should go see them."

"What for?"

"Because they are your family and it would be nice

for you to tell them in person that you've done all you can to get your parents out of prison."

Oliver had no desire to see his brothers and was not about to explain to them the details of what had transpired in Bash's office.

"I have too much work, Abby. I'll just keep deleting their texts."

Abigail hid her displeasure before deciding to put what was left of her lunch in the garbage and return to her goal of straightening the apartment before Oliver's grandparents returned.

Chapter 53

Sunday, March 2, 2025
Andrew & Kendall Gordon
Tyler & Kris Mayer-Gordon
Gordon Family Farm, Pinewood, Pennsylvania

As far as Kendall was concerned, there was nothing better than the early morning hours before anyone else was awake. Sitting by the window, sipping her tea and reading a book was a routine she had followed since she had been a teenager at home. If she let herself, she could remember the sound of her mother's footsteps, still heavy from sleep, padding down the hall past her room to the bathroom, then back again toward the stairs. Her mother's descent to the kitchen always pushed Kendall to read faster, fight to get through just one more chapter before the crescendo of sizzling bacon, brewing coffee, her father's deep voice, and her arguing siblings drew her to the table. They were simple memories, of the sort that Kendall prayed would one day be a part of her unborn child's life.

"It's all hooked up. Finished around midnight." Andrew was filling a glass of water from the newly installed tap in the kitchen.

"Good; we can put all the bottled water back into storage." Kendall was relieved that Griffin and Benjamin had designed a special filtration system that took into account that the water in Pennsylvania, whether it fell from the sky or was pulled up from the ground, was no longer fit to drink, even when filtered through traditional methods.

"I wonder if Oliver would be willing to drink tap water?" Andrew queried Tyler, who was just taking his first sip of his morning coffee.

"He only drinks that spring water shit in the glass bottles that costs more than gas. I think it's like $10 a bottle," Tyler answered, not knowing that he had in fact underestimated the cost of the water his brother was used to drinking.

"Speaking of our brother, have you texted him lately?" Andrew knew Tyler was still texting Oliver multiple times a day.

"Twice so far this morning. He never answers."

Chapter 54

Tuesday, March 4, 2025
Oliver & Abigail Gordon
Washington, D.C.

The same mix of impatience and naiveté that had Oliver believing his home was free of listening devices had also given him the idea that the Capitol Police should scan his car and office for bugs.

"You did what?" Mark Montgomery was livid.

"I had the new Capitol Police search my office for bugs. You should do the same." Oliver was speaking out loud and freely.

Mark grabbed a blank piece of paper from Oliver's computer printer and started frantically writing.

What is wrong with you? You suddenly think those stupid rent-a-cops can be trusted?

Everyone in Washington knew that the well trained, highly skilled public servants charged with protecting and serving the Members of Congress for more than two centuries had been replaced by a completely incompetent private security firm. The fact that legislators and their staffs had taken to carrying their own guns, despite laws that prohibited them from doing so, was a true testament as to how bad these replacements really were. Ultimately, a number of Senators and Congressmen had resorted to hiring their own security forces, culled from retired servicemen. Unfortunately for Oliver, his own boss had proudly boasted about being the first to sign the Privatization Pledge, and was therefore not willing to endure the embarrassment of admitting that replacing the Capitol Police with a private firm had been a bad idea.

"I think they are capable of turning on a machine and walking around an office waiting for it to beep." Oliver's tone was sarcastic and he refused to follow Mark's lead, speaking out loud and recalling for his friend how he had watched as the officer moved through the space with a wand that was supposed to light up every time it came anywhere near an electronic listening device.

DID THEY ACTUALLY FIND ANYTHING?

Mark wrote in angry, oversized capital letters to emphasize the fact that he already knew the answer.

"No, but..." Oliver stopped himself, finally willing to consider the fact that perhaps he had made a mistake and wondering how the attention to detail he normally paid to his work life had so seamlessly slipped by him.

Okay. I'll call the guy Abigail used to get the bugs out of the house. Oliver joined his friend in writing his responses.

Did he find any bugs in your house?
One.
Who is he?
I don't know.

Mark rolled his eyes and shook his head before writing down an admonishment of his friend's willingness to trust strangers, followed by some questions he doubted Oliver would be able to answer.

Who does he work for? What are his credentials?

Oliver shrugged his shoulders.

Don't bother calling him. We'll borrow one of Sherman's guys.

Oliver laughed at his friend's suggestion.

We have no choice!

The discussion between the two friends continued until reluctantly, and after much prodding, Oliver agreed to let Mark ask Senator Sherman for a favor.

Long known for his support of the outdated principles of the Democratic Party, principles the party itself no longer stood by, Sherman at 85 years old had become a lightning rod for everyone's anger and the perfect catalyst for the propaganda machine. Without Sherman those fanning the flames for the cause of conservatism would have nothing for comparison. No one to demonize and throw into the fire.

During any given debate it was not unusual to hear one or more Senators, on both sides of the aisle, calling his ideas the work of the devil and insisting he hurry up and meet his maker down below. Some preferred a more direct approach, suggesting they should just shoot him and get it over with.

Such threatening gestures, which would in the past have kicked off an inquiry by law enforcement or mandated a stay at a mental institution, went virtually overlooked by those with any authority. Ultimately, Sherman was forced to assemble his own army of bodyguards made up of a crack team of former Capitol Police Officers, Navy Seals, and CIA agents.

Although Oliver's use of a Sherman employee would not go over well if Rhine got wind of it, Oliver felt backed into a corner. Though he was loathe to admit it, even to himself, this time Mark was right.

Chapter 55

Thursday, March 16, 1939
Joe & Selma Gordon
New York City

On Joe's way out of the office, Bernie's secretary, a woman named Mona, handed back his copy of the Stratagem and pushed a piece of paper with the information about the next meeting deep into his pants pocket before winking at him. Mona's actions left Joe a captive audience to her long, lean, stockinged legs and the seductive sway of her hips as she crossed the room toward her desk. Joe wished she hadn't done that.

As Joe perused the spacious living room for familiar faces he couldn't help but notice the décor. The stark white of the carpet and furniture was intensified by the mirrors that covered the tabletops and walls. All around the room delicate figurines sat atop glass shelves and large white statues stood precariously on marble pedestals. Joe quickly determined that Mona was not a woman who was looking to be a housewife or a mother.

"Drink?" Mona asked, as Joe followed her to the bar in the living room.

"Yes." He answered her without thinking. Of late Joe had become accustomed to drinking alcohol.

"Joe, this is Harry." Mona gestured with the drink she held in her hand and inadvertently spilled alcohol from her glass onto the plush white carpet at her feet.

Ignoring Mona's upset over the carpet, which was now splashed with yellow, Harry loudly introduced himself again, pushing his large hand into Joe's and pumping harder and longer than necessary.

"Harry K. Bacon, Assistant District Attorney. Nice to meet you."

Harry reached into his pocket and pulled out a white business card, which he placed firmly in Joe's hand.

Immediately Joe could see that Harry was a far younger man than his hyperbolic introduction and imposing size might suggest. Even his business card with the Seal of New York, and his impressive Assistant District Attorney status suggested he should be older than his appearance.

"Any relation to Joe Gordon, the Yankee?"

Joe had been asked the question too many times since the fledgling ballplayer's debut on the Bronx field last year. Now, however Joe saw that particular question as a welcome distraction from talk of the escalating war overseas and the dangers in his own backyard presented by his possession of the *Stratagem*.

"No, but I wish I was. I'd love to spend some time in a box." Joe didn't share that even the fifty-five cents for a seat in the stands was out of his reach these days.

"Season opener is April twentieth. You'll come as my guest."

Although such an offer seemed a premature gesture from this virtual stranger, Joe found himself unable to refuse box seat tickets to see his beloved New York Yankees. Joe's immediate acceptance of Harry's offer then led to a thorough discussion of the team's roster and their prospects for a World Series berth. It was a full twenty-five minutes before the subject of the *Stratagem* came up. Harry asked Joe how he had found his copy of the document and, in turn, Joe felt comfortable asking Harry how he came to be involved in the committee. Once again the words 'Business Plot' entered the conversation.

"Any way you look at it, those men committed treason." Harry seemed increasingly animated as he spoke about how the lawmakers in Washington had betrayed the Constitution and their constituents by sweeping the matter under the rug.

Joe found Harry's desire to be on the right side of the law refreshing. From their discussion Joe got the distinct impression that Harry would not approve of some of the things Bernie did, even if Bernie was able to frame his actions as a means to right a wrong.

As the evening progressed, and other members of the committee joined the conversation, Joe found himself increasingly comfortable sharing details of the *Stratagem* meeting and his personal opinions about their plan. By the time Bernie arrived an hour later, Joe had accepted a lunch and two dinner invitations, one of which would involve Selma. Joe would have a week to explain the truth to Selma, but for now he could distract himself with the goings-on at the meeting.

Right away Bernie mentioned the absence of Stan and Marty from their midst. The two men had not been heard from since leaving the last meeting, and currently the police had no leads as to their whereabouts. Bernie's own admission that his investigators had so far come up with nothing brought a quiet hush into the room.

"Well, what do you think happened to them?" A short, stocky man who had positioned himself next to Joe prodded Bernie.

"Gentlemen, let us not fool ourselves. We have gotten involved with some very powerful, and ultimately very dangerous, men. Did anyone not realize this when we started meeting?"

"We may have all known what we were getting into, to some extent." Another gentleman sitting in the white club chair across from Joe rose to make his point. "But,

Bernie, you assured me, and I assume you assured all of us, that our safety concerns were being taken seriously and that you were handling the details."

The room erupted with the sound of men and women agreeing amongst themselves. Bernie took a substantial swig of his drink before answering.

"Ladies and gentlemen, please let us not forget that no group can expect their security patrol to be everywhere at once." Bernie hated such admissions of fallibility. "However, it is important to remember that we have foiled many plots against our members, and indeed saved many of your lives."

The word "many" stuck in Joe's head and brought his feeling of vulnerability to the surface. Without the copious amounts of alcohol he had consumed at the two previous meetings Bernie's words sounded less reassuring. Silently, Joe admonished himself for his own gullibility at having felt as safe as he was told to believe he was.

By the time the meeting was over a deep sense of worry had spread throughout the room. Joe couldn't help but wonder if the disappearance of two of their members might cause a glitch in their efforts to fight the tyranny proposed by the *Stratagem*. For Joe, however, these new developments would mean a renewal of his previous habit of looking over his shoulder every few steps and suspecting every stranger who came anywhere near him. He also knew this resurgence of insecurity would make it more difficult for him to convince Selma he was doing the right thing.

Chapter 56

Friday, March 28, 2025
Oliver Gordon
Washington, D.C.

As soon as Senator Rhine, got it into his head that he was going to throw his hat into the presidential ring, he immediately stopped participating in what he called the "messy business of Washington" and began fundraising. Thus, in addition to all his other responsibilities, Oliver now had to do the work of a senator.

This was why, when Senator Adam Sherman called Oliver to his office, Oliver assumed it was to hear about yet another inane bill being proposed by the ultraliberal lawmaker from Vermont.

As he entered the small, windowless office of the senior senator located in the basement of the Capitol Building, Oliver was feeling winded. It had been a long walk from Rhine's office.

"Have a seat." Senator Sherman pointed Oliver to a chair made from a tight grouping of branches that seemed, at face value, to be extremely unstable. Hoping that the strings holding the chair together were strong enough to keep him from landing on the floor, Oliver directed his full attention to his surroundings. He had been in the outer office before to drop off one or another piece of legislation that he had no doubt was destined for the senator's circular file, but Oliver had never been invited into Sherman's private office. Though he expected to see pictures of the senator's home state of Vermont, he was surprised to see all the pictures of Sherman with U.S. Presidents, dating all the way back to Dwight D. Eisenhower, a personal favorite of Oliver's for his role in putting the kibosh on twelve straight years of socialist Democrats. His was an admiration shared by many young conservatives, whose history books omitted the fact that Eisenhower had continued and expanded many of the New Deal programs like Social Security.

That Sherman was smiling on a golf course while Eisenhower putted seemed especially astonishing to Oliver, who had no idea that liberals had not always been held in such contempt and at arm's length as they now were.

"So, Mr. Gordon, I take it you're here in your boss's stead. Too busy raking in money for the big campaign?"

Oliver didn't doubt Sherman knew what his boss had not yet officially announced.

"I have a few piece of legislation here that you and your boss will likely dismiss."

As Sherman leaned over his desk to hand over the

pile of papers, Oliver couldn't help but notice how different his own mahogany desk was from this one. Sherman's desk was considerably smaller and made of natural, unvarnished oak. Though the rough edges and imperfections of the wood spoke to the senator's love of all things natural, all Oliver saw was Sherman's lack of concern for making a decent impression.

"What's the bill?" Oliver supposed he might be able to forgo reading all six hundred or so pages if the description offered by the senator proved the bill to be as repulsive as all his other bills were these days.

"Replaces KPOFCA."

Oliver couldn't help but laugh before responding. "We're not going to do that."

"And why not, Mr. Gordon? Why do you think government contractors should be excused from disclosing whose campaign they're funding, or what lobbyists they're employing?"

"Politics should be kept out of the decision-making process of awarding contracts."

"I'll agree with you one hundred percent on that – KPOFCA doesn't keep politics out."

"It ensures integrity."

"How?"

"Well, for instance, say one of your weed-eater groups wants a food service contract. We wouldn't have to know if they had given you money or lobbied for some public land they're so fond of. Integrity."

Sherman loved the ability of conservatives to disparage organic farmers by calling them "weed eaters" in public, then privately insist that organic vegetables grace their own tables.

"OK, well, it doesn't really work that way. You know that, don't you?"

Of course Oliver knew that although a company wasn't subject to financial disclosure, most offered up that information if it was to the company's benefit.

"The bill's not perfect." Though Oliver enjoyed the concept of perfection, he was enough of a pragmatist to accept that this wasn't the first bill, nor would it be the last, that didn't live up to its intention.

"Well then, read this one," the senator pointed to the bill in Oliver's hand, "and maybe you'll see it will do a better job of watching where the money is going."

"Is this it?" Oliver no longer saw the point in prolonging his visit with the senator. He was sure his boss would not vote for Sherman's bill.

"This is it. Just do me a favor and read it."

Oliver nodded and got up to leave, then remembered what he had wanted to tell Sherman.

"I want to thank you," Oliver said in almost a whisper, and he winked at Senator Sherman.

"For what?" It had been decades since anyone in the Senate or any of their staff had thanked him for anything.

"For your guys. The sweep." Even though the senator's door was closed and they were alone, Oliver continued to speak cryptically.

"What the fuck are you talking about?" The senator assumed Oliver was being sarcastic and made his frustration clear.

"You know, sending your security guys to check my office for bugs."

"Why would I do that?"

"Because Montgomery asked you too."

"Why would you think that?"

"Because he said you did." Oliver's confusion grew with each word he spoke.

"Hold on."

When the senator got up and left the room, Oliver assumed he had gone to check with his security people to confirm they had done exactly as Monty had said they had: rid Rhine's office of listening devices.

While he waited impatiently, Oliver read through all his emails and then began quickly flipping through the pages of Sherman's bill, scanning for any words that might automatically negate the legislation right from the get-go. Seeing none right away, he promised himself to read through the whole thing thoroughly that evening at home as a personal favor, in return for the use of Sherman's security people.

Then Oliver was bored.

Part 4

Over the course of the previous ten years it had been estimated that the prison system in the United States had tripled in size, to an occupancy rate somewhere in the range of 35 million people. Without any oversight agencies or Census Bureau statistics, though, there was really no way to tell for sure if only ten percent of America's citizens were behind bars. Further complicating any attempts to count prison populations were the contracted overseas penitentiaries, which accepted boatloads of incarcerated individuals at a time.

The boats, old cruise ships that were barely seaworthy and were fitted with prison-style cells, were dens of physical violence and abuse. What food there was to be had on board was sparse and teeming with mold or bugs: usually both. Since ships were not gender-specific, gang rapes by guards, as well as prisoners who had earned the privilege, were routine occurrences. Eventually barbed wire had to be strung around the edges of the boats to stop the resulting lemming-like suicides.

Not that the landlocked prisons of America were any better. Beatings were as uncontrolled as the lice, cockroach, mosquito and rodent populations ;and torture techniques, utilized to encourage obedience, left most prisoners looking for a way to die.

Illness, both physical and mental, was a given. Outbreaks

of tuberculosis, HIV/AIDS, polio, typhoid, whooping cough, West Nile virus, malaria, severe acute respiratory syndrome (SARS) and mad cow disease forced most prison guards to wear gloves, masks and condoms.

Those prisoners who were brought in with preexisting conditions were unmedicated and out of luck. Considered a costly liability, prisoners with illnesses like asthma and diabetes quickly ended up as fertilizer for the farms that surrounded the prison land or as eternal passengers on the decommissioned prison ships docked on the ocean floor.

Chapter 57

Friday, March 28, 2025
Molly Gordon
U.S.A. Global Prison Systems, Confinement Center #1F,
Washington, D.C.

Everyone knew someone who had gone to prison. Most people knew of three, sometimes four, people behind bars. Molly had previously known five: two teachers who had disappeared after a union protest ten years before, a neighbor down the block who had apparently left home without his wallet and mandatory ID card, the florist who had been jailed for growing marijuana plants that were never actually found, and then there was Molly's next door neighbor, Maria.

Maria had been brutally raped on the way home from the mall the previous July. The neighborhood video and drone surveillance for the county monitored by the Suffolk County Sovereign Crime Squad (SCSCS) – the private force that had replaced the Suffolk County Police Department – should have recorded the two squad cars that cut off Maria's car and sent it sailing into a ditch. It should have recorded the four squad members pulling Maria out of the car by her neck and taking turns raping and beating her. It also should have shown the officers throwing her onto the ground in front of the hospital emergency room, leaving her there to be scooped onto a gurney while they went unquestioned by a hospital staff who knew better than to ask. The cameras should have seen it all, but who would ask them to look? Not Maria.

Instead, Maria left the country for three weeks to visit her parents in Italy and promised them she would to return to Europe permanently after tying up her affairs in the U.S. Unfortunately, while back in the States, Maria visited her gynecologist for her yearly checkup and told him of the rape and, in passing, her trip to Italy.

Maria was promptly arrested at her doctor's office and charged with the murder of her unborn child. Though there was no actual proof that Maria had ever been pregnant, her doctor's suspicions that she had sought an abortion in Italy and his fear of retribution for not reporting his suspicions were all that was needed to put Maria away.

"I was raped by the squad," Maria had whispered in Molly's ear the day before she left for Italy. "Don't tell anyone I told you." Molly remembered the look of panic on Maria's face as she spoke.

Now the woman sitting next to Molly, reminded of her former neighbor.

"Maria?" Molly's whisper was barely audible.

"Molly?" Maria whispered back, moving her eyes to the side but keeping her head pointing down at her tray. "Is it really you? What are you..."

Maria stopped speaking abruptly as the guard moved toward them. Not wanting to arouse suspicion, she took a sip from the metal cup and held the dirty-tasting water in her mouth while Molly slid a bite of the composite meat off her fork with her teeth and began to chew. Both were afraid to swallow, believing the lumps now occupying their throats would make them choke.

"Ladies." The guard slid the word sarcastically past them as he pressed the barrel of his shotgun slowly across each of their backs. A chill rose up Maria's spine. She had immediately recognized his cologne and the sound of his voice and remembered where he had placed the barrel of that gun before he had forced his way into her and gotten her pregnant. *This will teach you to kill a baby.* Maria heard his words as if he were saying them to her now.

No one at the prison had bothered to ask Maria how she had gotten pregnant inside the jail. She assumed they watched the videotape of the rape just like she had been forced to watch tapes of other prisoners being violated.

When the guard finally moved on to the other side of the cafeteria, Molly swallowed what was left of the pulverized meat in her mouth. The taste, if there had ever been any, was gone. Molly had learned to eat the food, all of it, no matter how rancid or bug-infested it was. It was better to be sick to her stomach all night than to be beaten for wasting food.

"Why are you here?" Maria whispered.

"I'm not sure," Molly lied to her friend, preferring

not to implicate her son as the reason for her capture. It didn't matter anyway; what was done, was done.

"Where's Griffin?"

"I don't know, I saw him a week ago, or maybe it was two, or three... I don't know." Molly let a tear slide onto her tray.

"What group are you in?"

"I was just transferred to 48K."

"Good, we're together. I'll see you at free hour tomorrow."

Before she could answer, Molly heard the sound of a man clearing his throat and felt his hand wrap tightly around her forearm which he then twisted. An excruciating pain moved up through her arm and into her shoulder. Within seconds she was on the floor, her face smashed against the concrete by a boot that had slammed into the back of her head.

When she woke up the next morning, Molly ached, her head throbbed, her arm pulsated with a tortuous pain and there was blood everywhere; on her, on her clothes, and on her sheets. She knew from experience that there would be no doctor or help of any kind; all she could do was lay there and pray that God would see fit to kill her.

Molly never saw Maria again. She never knew what happened to her friend. How they woke Maria up in the middle of the night, dragged her to the interrogation room and made her watch the video of all they had done to Molly that night while she was unconscious. After that Maria never uttered another word; even when she gave birth, she did so silently.

Chapter 58

Friday, March 28, 2025
Oliver Gordon
Washington, D.C.

*In most arenas the sight of black block capitalized letters on the cover of a red folder marked **'CONFIDENTIAL'** would stop a person, but in Washington such a warning of secrecy was like an open invitation to pry. So it wasn't until after he had picked up the folder atop Senator Sherman's desk, flipped through the photos and finished reading the report, that Oliver questioned his decision to do so.*

"What the fuck are you involved in?" Oliver's face was red both from anger and from running up the stairs and down a maze of hallways.

Startled by Oliver's unannounced and raucous bull-in-a-china-shop intrusion on his space, the senator from Maine became immediately defensive. "What's wrong with you?"

Oliver slammed the office door and moved aggressively toward his supposed friend. "What's wrong with me? Me?" Oliver took a breath and tried to gather his thoughts into a cohesive order. "You said you had Sherman's men sweep our offices?"

"Yeah, I did."

"OK, well, no, you didn't, but let's move on." Oliver pulled a picture he had taken from the file out of his pocket and unfolded it before handing it to Mark.

"There's a report that goes with this, Monty. It's all about you and my boss skimming off the top of the arms deliveries and shipping it all to the highest bidder. What the fuck?" Oliver backed away from the senator's desk and then began pacing back and forth across the center of the office.

"Where did you get this?"

"What's the difference? It's the truth, there's no denying it. They have the proof and the pictures."

"Who's they?"

"I'm not at liberty to say."

The senator himself had used that line on numerous reporters; now it was being used on him and he didn't like it.

"Are you angry with me for not including you in the deals, or are you suggesting you've suddenly developed a moral compass?"

"Fuck you." The person Oliver was speaking to bore no resemblance to his good friend, the friend he'd thought he knew so well.

"You know how it is, Gordon. You either play or you can't stay."

"What does that mean?"

"Money doesn't grow on trees, my man: cash wins elections, it's the only way to win. Your boss was kind enough to…"

"Cash for what?"

"For ads, bumper stickers, you know." Mark winked at Oliver. "You know."

"No, I don't know; but what I do know is that you sold arms to our enemies. To fucking terrorists, for God's sake!"

"Enemy today, friend tomorrow. Wait ten minutes and the international political landscape changes. Everyone knows that. That's why no one trusts us anymore."

"That's no excuse. Today you sold weapons to our enemies!"

"That's pretty funny, coming from Rhine's bitch."

"What's that supposed to mean?"

"Oh, please, you've been in bed with the King of K Street for how many years?"

"I've never sold arms."

"No, you sold votes. You got Rhine's buddies everything they ever wanted, and it didn't matter who or what died in their wake. Go to war for oil, destroy the water with fracking, pollute the air with coal, kill marine life with oil spills, cut down the forests, mine the shit out of everything. You didn't give any of it a second thought."

"I worked within the system. You're stealing."

"So taking people's land away from them isn't stealing?"

"It was leased and purchased."

"The people were given no choice. And when they were paid, they were paid shit."

"I didn't kill anyone; you can't say the same."

"Is that how you sleep at night? You didn't personally hold a gun to their heads? That's the yardstick you're using?" The senator followed his words with a condescending laugh, then added, "You're such a prick."

"And you're a traitor." Oliver looked at his old friend. He could feel the heat rising in his face. "Iran-Contra, does that ring a bell?"

"Yeah, they all got probation, pardons, blah, blah, blah; and Reagan skated by, acting dumb. For God's sake, he was a fucking actor. That's why they picked him in the first place." The senator laughed again. "You do know that was around forty years ago? It's not even in the history books anymore."

"There's still enough people around who remember it."

"Those idiots were like the fucking Keystone Cops. They were amateurs."

When the senator laughed again, Oliver couldn't help but notice the anger behind it.

"We're not going to get caught."

"You just did." Oliver plucked the picture out of Mark's hand and headed for the door.

"Wait!" The senator wasn't asking.

"What?" Oliver had his hand on the doorknob.

"You won't tell anyone." Mark was smiling.

"What makes you so sure?"

"Who do you think you are dealing with here?"

Oliver stopped to think about the question he had just been asked. Who was he dealing with? Certainly not his friend, the one he had believed to be so liberal. The person who had touted the evils of corruption and said in every speech he made that he was on the side of 'the working man,' 'the little guy.' Rhine was not the person Oliver thought he was either. The man who swore by fiscal conservancy and capitalism was stealing from the government and selling arms to dictators.

"Who? Who am I dealing with?"

"Let's just say you don't want to find out."

"What does that mean? Are you threatening me?"

"Let's just say you don't want to find out," Monty repeated.

Oliver opened the office door with a force that made it slam into the wall and its glass crash to the floor. Although Oliver could ignore the damage, as well as the shocked looks on the faces of Senator Montgomery's staff, he couldn't ignore the words being shouted by his former friend.

"Don't do it! Remember Jim!"

Chapter 59

Friday, March 28, 2025
Griffin Gordon
U.S.A. Global Prison System, Confinement Center #1M,
Washington, D.C.

Compared to his previous cell, this one was luxurious. At twenty feet square it was twice the size of the previous room, and this one had running water and a real toilet instead of a bucket. Yes, this was luxury.

Griffin spent nearly twenty four hours a day in his cell. Sometimes he was given a book to read; most times before he got to the end it was taken away. Griffin finally figured out that he should read the last two chapters of the books first, so he could stop being curious as to how they ended. What he couldn't figure out was how and when his captivity would end, though he suspected, judging from the things he had overheard from other prisoners, that it wouldn't.

"Gordon!" The guard was banging his stick against the outside of the metal door.

"Gordon!"

Griffin was in the middle of another nightmare.

"Get up. You have a phone call."

Griffin tried to pull himself out of his dream and toward the voice calling to him from the background, the one telling him he needed to wake up to answer the phone.

All at once his lids lifted, but the bright fluorescent light above him forced them to close again. Once more he tried to open his eyes, this time willing them to withstand the light.

"Phone call." The metal door reverberated louder.

The day he had arrived at the prison, Griffin was told that phone calls were never allowed.

"Oh, except if a family member dies, then you'll be allowed to receive a two minute phone call," the guard had told him with a smile.

Now all Griffin could think of was who might be dead.

It did not immediately cross his mind that the guard was doing this as a ruse to wake him out of a dead sleep into a frightened state, even though they had done the same thing for the past five nights.

The previous night they had opened the slit in his door and released a four foot snake into the room. When the creature started sliding across Griffin's uncovered legs it woke him out of a sound sleep; he leaped from his bed screaming amidst roars of laughter from the guards watching on the cameras outside his door. Much to the dismay of the guards, after his initial shock, Griffin showed no fear of the reptile, which he realized was a relatively harmless nonvenomous snake. It was not until they threw a rat into the mix, ostensibly offering it up as a feast for the snake, that Griffin felt fear again, leaping to stand on his bunk, toes curled under, until his new cellmate had caught and devoured dinner.

Chapter 60

Friday, March 28, 2025
Oliver & Abigail Gordon ~ Benjamin & Mary Gordon
Washington, D.C.

No one on his staff could explain why Oliver left work early that day or why he wasn't answering his texts and his emails. All they knew was that their boss had stormed red-faced into the office cursing under his breath, that he had filled his laptop case to the brim with files, and that he had carried the rest out in a box. Anyone who tried to speak to him was ignored.

By the time Oliver got to his apartment, Benjamin had filled the younger man's old backpack, the one he had used in college, with a weekend's worth of clothes, saving enough room for his laptop. The impromptu trip Benjamin suggested seemed to Oliver to be a perfect opportunity to get out of town for a few days and clear his head. A 'lucky coincidence' was how Oliver viewed his grandfather's suggestion. It wasn't.

Although advanced in age, Benjamin had no trouble noticing when things were out of place, which was why he noticed as soon as they stepped onto the train headed for Philadelphia that he and Oliver were being followed.

The lean figure of the gentleman who had settled into a seat just a few rows back was wearing jeans, a white shirt, dark sunglasses, and a black sport coat with a bulging breast pocket.

By taking an aisle seat and utilizing the mirrored pill case he carried for just such an occasion, Benjamin was able to watch the gentleman watching him.

After a few minutes Benjamin quietly informed his grandson of the situation, and Oliver became as frightened as his grandfather had expected him to be.

"We're being followed? Oh, shit," Oliver whispered beneath the sounds of the idling train and the baby crying next to them. "Who is it? Who's following us?" Oliver put his fingers to his mouth and began to chew on his nails, an old habit that only surfaced in front of his grandfather.

"I suspect one of your Washington buddies sent him."

"Oh, shit, oh, shit." Oliver's words were garbled between his fingers. *Let's just say you don't want to find out.* Monty's words moved through Oliver's head. *Don't do it! Remember Jim!*

Of course Oliver remembered Jim. Jim Dugan, Rhine's former aid, Oliver's predecessor. As far as the newspapers were concerned, Dugan had fallen off a mountain cliff while hiking in Guatemala. Though anyone who knew Dugan, including his wife of twenty years, believed the possibility of the forty-four year old dragging his three hundred pound body up a mountainside was a preposterous idea. At the time Oliver hadn't cared how ridiculous it all sounded. Marcia Dugan's loss was his gain. But now he couldn't stop thinking about it.

"Shit, oh, shit, oh, shit." Oliver couldn't stop himself from repeating those words, and wanted desperately to stand up and scour the seats for the person who looked most like a hit-man,\; but his grandfather had made it very clear that they both needed to act as if nothing was wrong. This was not the first time Benjamin had been followed, so he was very clear about what needed to be done.

"We're getting off the train," Benjamin said as he pulled his grandson's chewed fingernails away from his mouth to stop him from exposing his nervousness further.

"Why? He'll just follow us. You can't outrun him."

Resisting the desire to roll his eyes, Benjamin instead went on to explain the details of their impending escape, which he choreographed spontaneously as he spoke.

"Does he have a gun? Do you think he has a gun?"

"No, we'll be fine," Benjamin lied. "It's all about timing and execution, brains over brawn," he continued. "But you have to stay calm."

Try as he might to listen to his grandfather's request to remain composed, Oliver found he had no control over the feeling of unreality that was overwhelming him and making the tips of his fingers and toes tingle as if they were about to go numb.

"Oliver, *now*." Benjamin issued the signal for Oliver to get up and start implementing their plan, but his grandson didn't move.

"Oliver, *now*," Benjamin repeated, this time accompanied by a furtive shove that successfully aroused Oliver from his fearful thoughts and pushed him into action.

"I'm going to get a soda," Oliver said out loud, as instructed by his grandfather.

"No, you'll miss the train." Benjamin pretended to be concerned that his grandson would not be back by the scheduled departure time, which now was only seven minutes away.

"I'll be fine. I'll be right back. Do you want anything to drink? A magazine?"

"No, I'm good. Hurry."

Oliver threw the straps of his backpack over his shoulders, happy he had listened to his grandfather's advice about traveling light. As he rushed off the train and onto the platform, he resisted the urge to look back to see if he was being followed. Instead he continued doing exactly as his grandfather had instructed and headed toward the concession stand.

With five minutes to go, Benjamin got up to use the men's room and immediately detected, by way of his peripheral vision, that his movements were not going unnoticed. Though he was relieved the man following them had apparently bought into their ruse and remained seated, Benjamin had not yet ruled out the possibility of an accomplice standing on the platform, and sent a quick message to God to watch over his grandson.

In the small, dimly-lit, urine-reeking cubical Benjamin relieved himself quickly then washed his hands with sanitizer. Upon exiting the bathroom, instead of going to his seat, he pretended to be reading the old poster entitled "Safe Train Travel" hanging next to the open train door. Ironically the notice included a warning by the Department of Homeland Security about the importance of reporting any suspicious people or packages.

With less than a minute to go before the scheduled departure time, the engineer's recorded voice began signaling **"*All aboard!*"** and Oliver, hearing his cue, began to race back toward the train while Benjamin called through the open door for his grandson to run faster.

"*Twenty seconds to door closure,*" the mechanical-sounding voice announced.

"Hurry!" Benjamin called out to Oliver and everyone turned to look at Benjamin, who believed those who were noticed were safest.

"*Ten seconds to door closure – step away from the doors. Eight seconds to door closure – step away from the doors.*"

Reflected in the window glass Benjamin could see

the man seated behind him. No longer pretending to hide behind his paper, he was watching for Oliver's safe delivery back onto the train.

"Five seconds to door closure – step away from the doors." The voice was louder now. ***"Three seconds to door closure – step away from the doors."***

Oliver had made it to the train and held his arm out to Benjamin. Then, instead of grabbing onto Benjamin's hand and entering the train as everyone watching had anticipated, Oliver gripped his grandfather's palm securely and pulled him out through the doorway just as the final warning sounded and the merciless doors slammed shut. Without showing his pleasure, Benjamin watched the slow-moving train leave the station and silently enjoyed the distraught look on the face of the man he had just outwitted.

"Oliver, I'm in need of a ride." Benjamin smiled at his grandson. "Okay if you drive?"

Still out of breath from his staged run and the accompanying upset, Oliver nodded instead of speaking.

"I'll arrange for a car while you catch your breath," Benjamin added.

As his grandfather whispered cryptically into his phone, Oliver breathed deeply and tried to make sense of what had just happened. This was not what his life was supposed to be like right now. He should have been in his office reviewing legislation, writing speeches and answering the flood of messages he was currently ignoring. He should be thinking about how to get Rhine elected president and making plans to hang out with Monty this weekend. Instead he was running from a man they had sent to follow him, maybe kill him.

Seeing his grandfather hang up the phone, Oliver quietly announced, "Philadelphia, here we come."

Benjamin leaned toward his grandson's ear and said, "Coney Island."

Chapter 61

Sunday, March 26, 1939
Joe & Selma Gordon
New York City

Joe couldn't believe how well it had gone. Contrary to his expectations, Selma seemed to have no trouble with the fact that Joe was meeting with people about the Stratagem, and didn't seem concerned that he still possessed his copy of the document as well as the two other parts. She even agreed to go out to dinner with one of his new friends, and to accompany Joe to the next meeting.

Joe had no idea what was responsible for his wife's sudden turnaround, but decided to chalk it up to his newfound power of persuasion. It never occurred to him that the names he had dropped, those of an Assistant District Attorney and some prominent New York lawyers and businessmen, had lent considerable weight to his argument to get involved with the committee.

Selma's first *Stratagem* meeting was on a Sunday afternoon in March. Unseasonably warm, the kind of day that whetted a New Yorker's appetite for the coming of spring. The time of year when apartment dwellers released themselves from hibernation to enjoy sunny, warm walks in the park, where the scent of blossoming flowers alternated with the street smells of cars and horse manure. It was that kind of day.

Since Joe had been working days at his dress shop and maintaining night hours at the restaurant, Selma actually welcomed the opportunity the meeting gave her to go out of the apartment for something other than groceries.

Dressed appropriately in a powder blue suit with a long skirt and matching hat, all of which Joe had designed and tailored himself, Selma moved effortlessly through the meeting, introducing herself and making all manner of small talk.

"Everyone has been so nice and so welcoming..." she pulled Joe aside to let him know of her approval, "except for..."

Selma stopped her words in midstream and looked in the direction of Mona. Surrounded by three men, she was leaning seductively against her white baby grand piano with a drink in one hand and a cigarette sticking out of a long black holder in another. Every so often her exaggerated laughter would disrupt the room and everyone would automatically turn to see Mona batting her lashes at one or another of the men in her ever-increasing circle of admirers.

"Does she only talk to men?" Selma followed the

comment by a laugh to mimic Mona, but quieter so that only Joe and not the whole room would notice.

"Shhhh… Selma. She's not so bad. She's nice, in fact, when you get to know her." As soon as the words left his mouth, Joe knew he had said the wrong thing. The look of outrage on Selma's face just confirmed his belief.

"How well do you know her?"

Selma's words may have come out as a question but there was no mistaking the fact that they were meant as a condemnation.

"I do not know her. I just met her," Joe said in as convincing a tone as he could muster whilst whispering.

Selma looked away from Joe and took a sip of her drink.

"Look, Sel, you have nothing to worry about." Joe put his hand on his wife's shoulder and turned her around. "Look at her. She's, she's an actress, she's not real," Joe whispered the words Selma needed to hear. "But go easy on the alcohol. You haven't had anything to drink in a long time."

The glass in Selma's hand was now empty and Joe worried his wife would be as seduced as he had been by the ethereal feeling of intoxication that would ultimately lure her to crave more than she could handle.

"I'm fine, Joe. This is only my second glass."

Joe marveled at the ease with which alcohol had taken hold of his wife, as it had for him.

"Last call before the meeting starts!"

Selma immediately headed to the bar for a refill before seating herself next to Joe on the couch.

"Sel," was all Joe said between his gritted teeth.

Selma said nothing, but instead took one more sip before placing her glass on the coffee table coaster, just as Uncle Bernie began to speak.

"I am so pleased to see we have new members joining us tonight."

Bernie went on to introduce each of the three fledgling members, including Selma, to the larger group. Selma tried not to blush when her name was called.

"I've promised to update you on the whereabouts of our missing committeemen."

Selma turned sideways to face Joe and kept her eyes focused on him. She knew immediately he had purposely neglected to tell her the story about the missing men.

For his part, Joe had hoped the issue would not be brought up during the meeting and pretended not to notice his wife's piercing stare boring into his cheek.

"Stan and Marty are safe, their families are safe, all is well and that's all I am permitted to say about the matter." Bernie paused for the inevitable applause that would prove his lie believable. No one questioned Bernie further about the issue, and even if they had he wouldn't have been able to tell them the truth: that by the time they had been thrown into the East River with bricks tied to them,

Stan and Marty had already buckled under the pressure of the torture inflicted upon them and told their captors everything they knew about Bernie and his organization.

As Selma listened to Bernie talk further about security issues, she realized that having prominent members of the community in the group meant nothing in terms of protection for her family. Any safety they might have derived from being associated with a single powerful public official, local influential businessmen, or even some police officers who were part of the group, was insignificant when compared to the power brokers of the *Stratagem*.

What none of them could have predicted, however, was that the men responsible for the *Stratagem* were about to make a move intended to stop Bernie and his organization from ever standing in their way.

Chapter 62

Friday, March 28, 2025
Oliver Gordon
Benjamin Gordon
Washington, D.C. to Coney Island, New York

"What better place to figure out what to do than in the birthplace of democracy, Philadelphia," Benjamin had told his grandson. What Benjamin had not told him was that Philadelphia was just a ruse. Heading to their real destination, Coney Island, had been Benjamin's plan all along.

"Stop here." Benjamin stuck his arm out the car window and placed his hand on the old steel pole planted into the sidewalk cement. Within seconds the old graffiti-filled garage door in front of them lifted open.

"Turn here." Benjamin pointed. "Over there, there's my space. Over there."

It was the last of the five-hour-long list of instructions given by Benjamin to Oliver. Instructions that had taken them from the train station, through the Harbor Tunnel, to I-95, over the Delaware Memorial Bridge, up the Jersey Turnpike, over the Goethals and Verrazano-Narrows bridges, and along the Belt Parkway to the final labyrinth of Coney Island roads with names like Shore, Mermaid, Neptune, and Surf, lest anyone forget the small seaside town's proximity to the ocean.

Throughout the trip Benjamin had refused to answer any of Oliver's questions, something he knew he could get away with only because of the mutual respect and trust the two had built over multiple decades. Now that they had arrived at their destination Oliver tried once again to find out what his grandfather was up to.

"What are we doing here? Who are we meeting with? Why are there so many expensive cars in this parking lot?" Oliver's litany of questions spilled out as he parked their subcompact car in the ample parking space.

"Patience, we're getting there," was Benjamin's only response as he grabbed the door handle and lifted himself slowly out of the uncomfortably small car opening.

Chapter 63

Sunday, March 26, 1939
Joe & Selma Gordon
New York City

Because the meeting ended relatively early and the weather had turned to spring, Selma and Joe decided to exit the subway early to walk the few extra blocks toward home. The mood they shared was light, though Joe suspected Selma's was fueled somewhat by the remnants of alcohol still floating through her system.

"It was so good to get out of the apartment." Selma's desire to be away from home was as strong as Joe's was to get back there. "We should eat out."

"There are a lot of things we should do, Selma, but eating out is not one of them." Joe was always thinking ahead, planning and budgeting. Although he never wanted to deal with the financial details of business, at home he had mastered the art of knowing where every penny went.

"What's going on there?" Selma was looking ahead at the next block, where a crowd had formed and cars seemed to be blocking the street.

"I don't know, Sel, I can't see that far." Joe seemed annoyed, a signal to Selma that he was getting hungry.

"It looks like it's in front of our house." Selma barely got out the word 'house' before she and Joe began running toward home, where smoke was billowing from the roof.

By the time they had run the first half block, two fire engines had passed them with sirens screaming. Joe could not help but remember the fire he had watched in Brooklyn, the stretchers put into ambulances and the morgue vans. As Joe ran he cursed himself for picking up the *Stratagem* and he cursed Bernie for downplaying the danger; but mostly he prayed, promising God he would go to temple in exchange for the safety and wellbeing of his family. Selma was making similarly useless promises. Useless because even before they pushed through the crowd and reached the front stoop, their fates had been decided.

Chapter 64

Friday, March 28, 2025
Oliver Gordon ~ Benjamin Gordon
Coney Island, New York

As he walked up the stairs from the parking garage to the lobby, then down a long corridor to the elevator, Oliver couldn't help but be reminded of the old apartment building his grandparents had lived in, the one in Queens where the beige corridors had been frighteningly dark because all the hallway windows faced up against the brick façade of another building. Oliver had always walked quickly down those well-worn linoleum-floored hallways, his fearful imagination running amok from the sounds of foreign tongues and unfamiliar aromas. It was not until he had reached their door, the high gloss red door with its peephole, that Oliver had relaxed, knowing that a delicious home-cooked meal waited just beyond the sound of the triple locks.

The ultra-modern elevator with its chrome interior, voice-activated controls, and smooth comfortable ride was a far cry from the old, paint-peeling, musty-smelling lobby. As they stepped off the elevator on the second floor, Oliver immediately noticed someone had put a lot of money into the smooth grey walls and white marble floor. Oliver followed his grandfather's uncharacteristically quick steps down the brightly-lit corridor. Their destination, a red door labeled 2 BE, was the only residence in a building that had once contained 16 apartments. Before Benjamin could place his hand on the sterling silver doorknob the door swung open and a large, imposing man greeted them.

"Welcome, Mr. Gordon. May I take your overcoat?"

"Reginald, this is my grandson, Oliver."

Though Oliver's training had taught him to quickly size up a room, get to know his surroundings, scope out the invited guests, and disregard the hired help, Reginald's presence was difficult to ignore.

"Welcome, Mr. Gordon."

Concerned that his own hand might easily be crushed, Oliver apprehensively shook the hand the six-foot-eight man extended to him.

"Your coat, Mr. Gordon?"

Oliver obeyed Reginald's request then followed his grandfather into the living room, the grandness of which surprised him. The stark white backdrop of freshly-painted walls and the mile-high ceiling created a perfect blank canvas for the modern curves of the apple green furniture, the museum quality artwork and the black baby grand piano that stood in the corner. If there were any windows there was no way to see them behind the opaque white curtains. The two hundred or so invited guests barely filled the expansive room as they mingled, wine glasses in one hand and hors d'oeuvres in the other. From the way they were dressed Oliver gathered they were the owners of the expensive cars in the garage. All in all it seemed to him that these people, like the apartment in which they had gathered, were as impressive as they were out of place in this decaying Coney Island neighborhood.

"Benjamin!" A small man about the age of Oliver's grandfather approached the two with a raised glass as if he were about to toast them.

"Terry, this is Oliver."

"Oliver!" Terry seemed to want to raise his glass to everyone.

"Look who's here, Lila!" Terry pulled a woman who was clearly involved in another conversation toward them. "This is Bennie's grandson, Oliver."

"Nice to meet you." A small, stocky woman, whom Oliver assumed was Terry's wife, nodded at the two of them.

"Benjamin is here!" Terry shouted as loud as his old vocal cords would allow and the response, as far as Oliver was concerned, was exaggerated and overwhelming.

Chapter 65

Sunday, March 26, 1939
Joe & Selma Gordon
New York City, NY

The crowd gasping, water gushing through large hoses and hitting the building, police whistles that never stopped, booted feet running...

In the silent horror that engulfed Joe and Selma, all they could hear were the screams of their family and the friends they loved.

The scene in front of their apartment building was unlike any the witnesses had ever seen before. They would later tell Joe that the fire had spread quickly, too quickly to have been an accident, an errant match or a fallen candle, too quickly for the older residents of the building to have escaped or even the young and healthy ones to outrun the flames.

As each stretcher passed in front of Joe and Selma their old lives slid further and further out of reach.

More than once Joe caught a glimpse of Selma's face awash in tears as she bore witness to the horror of the barely-recognizable faces of those she loved covered in soot and destroyed by flames, charred bodies missing clothing, skin, limbs. More than once Joe had to turn away to breathe, feeling he might die himself on the spot.

As the sun dropped from the sky and the street lights were lit, they waited helplessly; waited for the flames to be extinguished, the bodies to be accounted for. The push and pull of grief twisted through their thoughts, forcing them to count. This one survived, the rest did not. They refused to speak the names of the deceased aloud, as if hearing them would make it final and negate the possibility that at some moment in time they would both wake to catch their breath and find that it had all been the most terrible dream.

Chapter 66

Friday, March 28, 2025
Oliver Gordon ~ Benjamin Gordon
Coney Island, New York

As the crowd parted and Benjamin made his way up to the makeshift podium, Oliver couldn't help but notice that his grandfather had handed off his cane to Terry and that the spring had returned to his step.

"Friends." Benjamin spoke into the small karaoke-like microphone, then bowed his head and waited for the silence that came quickly. "We are here today as friends, partners in our grief for those we have lost."

Oliver noticed those around him had their heads bowed, their eyes closed.

"Relatives and friends, whose only crime was to insist their stolen democracy, their birthright, be returned to them." Benjamin pulled out a handkerchief and wiped his eyes. "What this country was, what it was supposed to be, will be again."

Oliver expected the compassionate speech to be followed by cheers and clapping, maybe a rousing chorus of

God Bless America. Instead the mood in the room was a somber one as another man offered his grandfather thanks before taking the microphone.

"We have come to a critical point. Our tipping point." Oliver did not recognize the commanding voice at the microphone, though the mannerisms and something about the man's face seemed familiar.

"We've waited too long!" a voice yelled out from the crowd.

"Perhaps. However we have voted fairly every step of the way and agreed to abide by the majority's wishes." The speaker then went on to remind the heckler, apparently named Jarrod, that their collective patience would soon be rewarded.

Oliver was shocked at the way the heckler had been acknowledged, not as a nuisance, but rather as someone who had forgotten the rules. Oliver had become quite used to watching those who spoke out wrestled to the ground.

"All along we have made our choices, and none have been made lightly." The man continued with his speech as the crowd listened intently, especially Oliver, who tried to make sense of what was being said.

"We have tried every other method, considered every possible scenario; anything to avoid taking even one life; and yet it has come to this." Oliver noticed tears streaming down the face of the man next to him and then others.

"What we will do is what needs to be done, before it's too late and all that was is lost forever."

Oliver had no idea what this man was talking about and wanted nothing more right now than to spend time with his grandfather to find out.

"Since this is likely the last time we will see each other for quite a while, I wish you all safe journey." The man lifted up his glass to his audience.

"Safe journey," the audience repeated, raising their glasses.

As everyone drank to their safety, the man exited the stage and Benjamin returned to Oliver's side to continue introductions to at least a hundred strangers who seemed to know his grandfather and his family intimately. After a few hours of mingling without purpose, something a Washington insider never did, Benjamin finally agreed to talk to Oliver.

Ushering him out of the living room, into an upstairs bedroom and away from any possibility of being listened to, Benjamin told Oliver what he believed his grandson was finally ready to hear.

Chapter 67

Sunday, March 26, 1939
Joe & Selma Gordon
New York City, NY

If you asked Joe and Selma to recall how they got to the hospital or how the envelope filled with money and labeled 'For the Hospital Bill' got into Joe's pocket, neither would be able to recall. The only thing that mattered to Joe and Selma was seeing to it that their grandson Benjamin, the only one in their apartment building to survive the fire, would still be alive in the morning.

"Mr. Gordon." The nurse on duty lightly shook Joe out of his sound sleep and he jumped with fear, believing that his momentary lack of attention to his grandson had led to his death. "He's awake."

As Joe gazed with relief at his grandson's open eyes his first instinct was to share the good news with Selma, who had also fallen asleep during their vigil.

"Sel, Sel, Selma." Joe tried to shake his wife out of sleep. "Sel, Sel, wake up. Bennie is awake!" Selma moved only as far as Joe moved her. Her eyes remained closed.

"Selma!" Joe screamed as a new panic hit him. He gripped her hands and fell to his knees, his heart beating enough beats for both of them. Sweat poured from his forehead.

"Grandma?" Benjamin called, stirring in his bed.

"Selma! Selma! No…Selma…No, don't leave me… My God, Selma…No! " Joe's screams echoed through the halls of the hospital, bringing doctors and nurses running to his side; to help him up; to take her away.

Part 5

The massive building jutting out of the flat surface of the Utah desert in plain sight was oddly juxtaposed with the concealed, highly secretive nature of its inner workings. Though the three billion dollar surveillance operation was ostensibly going to be used to trap and record data of foreign threats, it was quickly clear that such a big building to follow a few thousand would-be evildoers around the world was overkill. Within ten years the building and its land had been sold for pennies on the dollar to a private contractor, U.S. Spy Corp, the go-to company for tracking those who might wish to cause harm to America. Between generous tax incentives and the free supercomputer that came with the building, the deal would eventually swing a few billion dollars in the contractor's favor. On the bright side for the Government, the facility would finally be utilized and its full potential realized in the surreptitious tracking of the comings and goings of millions of American citizens.

The fact that reading private emails, tracking posts on social media, hacking into personal computers, and tapping the phone calls of citizens violated even the most basic tenets of American democracy was inconsequential to these self-aggrandizing 'guardians of public safety,' who consistently lied to the public about their activities. Even during a Congressional hearing called by posturing politicians feigning concern for the rights of their constituents, Spy Corp senior management swore under oath that their snooping was limited to foreign-born terrorists. Luckily for these disingenuous executives, when the truth finally came out in the form of hacked files and stolen documents, the body of men sworn to protect the Constitution, the now-less-than Supreme Members of the Court, decided to protect the Spy Corp spies and put the whistleblowers in jail. A wise decision on the part of the Supreme Court considering that, as U.S. Spy Corp's logo clearly stated, "Everyone has a secret to hide" and Congressmen and Supreme Court judges generally had more to hide than most.

Ultimately the collective realization that the spying would continue and that the internet had literally become a net used to gather and manipulate data to support phony criminal prosecutions, led people to leave the social networking sites in droves. The corporate heads of these sites, angry at the mass defection and lack of loyalty displayed by their customers, managed to eke out their last bit of profit by selling all their customers' files. Not their most current files, but rather the information the internet corporations had assured the public they had not been collecting and saving all along. Files spanning the decades prior to inception of the U.S. Spy Corp facility. All the social network companies had to do before selling the private conversations of their customers was change their privacy agreements again, and there was nothing anyone could do about it.

In the end the public realized that their betrayal had been paid for by their own tax dollars and had no choice but to view the Spy Corp building with its massive surveillance tower flanked by five-story buildings on each side as a big middle finger to the American people.

Chapter 68

Friday, March 28, 2025
Oliver Gordon ~ Benjamin Gordon
Coney Island, New York

Benjamin began the story he had been promising to tell his grandson.

"In 1933, in the middle of the Great Depression, there were some very rich and powerful businessmen. You know the kind." Benjamin smiled and Oliver nodded at his grandfather's words. "Well, they hated Roosevelt and his policies. So much so they tried to overthrow the government."

"Ha," was all Oliver said with a smile, but Benjamin knew his grandson's response came from a view of the world that told him such a feat would be impossible.

"Remember, this was 1933, before there were cameras on every corner, wiretapping, drones, even before television."

Hearing the word 'wiretapping' Oliver became uneasy and shifted his weight, a move of discomfort not lost on his grandfather.

"They intended to stage a coup using disgruntled World War I veterans who were out of work and angry," Benjamin continued. "You've heard of the Bonus Army?"

Oliver had not but nevertheless felt the need to insist that his grandfather must be mistaken about the World War I veterans, who were nothing if not proud Americans.

"You can be a proud American and still be unhappy with the direction of the government."

"I'm not sure that's true, Gamps."

"I shouldn't be surprised at your attitude, considering your whitewashed education."

"Should I be insulted, Gamps?" Oliver smiled at his grandfather.

"No, it's certainly not your fault. It's no coincidence your Ivy League, doctoral level education is so lacking. I can assure you it was a purposeful omission from your history classes. But I'm getting off the subject here." Benjamin went on to explain to his grandson the history of the Bonus Army and how the men behind the coup fully intended to exploit the veterans for financial gain. It was a story that both appealed to the history buff in Oliver and shocked him, as his lack of knowledge of such a story was certainly not due to a lack of interest.

"The whole thing might have worked," Benjamin continued, "but for a Major General Smedley Butler."

"Smedley?"

"Yes; you don't hear that name much anymore."

"I like it. Maybe Abigail and I should name our first child Smedley." Oliver laughed at the thought, but Benjamin continued focusing on what he needed to tell his grandson.

"Major General Butler was critical of Roosevelt and his policies, so they tapped him to lead the Bonus Army in the coup. What they didn't know was that Butler would never serve as a traitor to his country, no matter how much he disagreed with the President. Ultimately he turned them all in. Named names, testified before Congress."

"Did they believe him?"

"They actually did, but because the men behind the failed coup were some of the richest and most powerful men in the country, I mean they owned everything worth owning, including the newspapers, they were never prosecuted. In fact, the newspapers did a nice smear campaign against Butler."

"How do you know all this?"

"He knew my grandfather."

"Grandpa Joe?"

"Yes."

"So no one went to jail?"

"No. My grandfather said they forged a deal to make it all go away. All they had to do was pledge their support to Roosevelt and his policies."

"It's amazing what the threat of hanging for treason will do to change a person's mind," Oliver responded.

"I guess in those days even wealthy people had to worry about things like that. Not anymore."

Happy to see his grandson was finally beginning to grasp what had been going on right under his nose, Benjamin felt free to move forward with his story.

"Well, Roosevelt's problems may have been over, but things didn't end there. All the banking regulations, the social programs, the WPA, the health and safety measures for workers, even taking control of all the gold in the country, it just fueled the resolve of the Strategists to reverse the course the government had taken. In public they may have been supporting Roosevelt, but in private they were making plans to get back what they believed had been stolen from them, and this was their resulting plan."

Benjamin pulled out the micro disc that contained all three parts of the *Stratagem* and handed it to Oliver.

"The papers my great-great-grandfather found?"

"That's right. And when the *Stratagem* authors found out my grandfather and the others had gotten ahold of their plan, they figured it was time to kill or be killed. They knew Roosevelt wasn't going to give them a second chance at messing with democracy. So they went after my family and, well, all the families involved." Benjamin abruptly stopped his story to listen the footsteps coming down the hallway. Oliver, on the other hand, having heard no noise outside the door, found his grandfather's pause annoying and the subsequent knock on the door startling.

Chapter 69

Friday, March 28, 2025
Oliver Gordon
Benjamin Gordon
Coney Island, New York

The young man at the door handed Benjamin his written agenda for the next twenty-four hours and then left without a word. After reading the list and committing it to his remarkably- sharp ninety-one-year-old memory, Benjamin rolled the paper up into a wad and tossed it into the flames of the room's sleek gas fireplace.

"Where was I?" Benjamin asked, and then remembered before his grandson could answer. "Oh yes, well it was the worst night of my life, Oliver." He shook his head slowly. "Except for my Grandpa, my whole family was gone, stolen from me. I was only six years old and I remember it like it was yesterday." Benjamin looked away from his grandson and up to the ceiling as if the scene was being projected like an old movie onto the flat white surface.

"I was playing with my sister Irene; she was two years

older than me. A good sister she was." Benjamin closed his eyes to look at the sister he loved so much. "Oye, a *shana medala* she was."

Oliver did not know much Yiddish, but since coming to live with him his grandmother had taken up the habit of greeting Abigail each morning by holding her cheeks between her hands and declaring her a '*shana medala*' followed by the words 'beautiful girl.'

"As far as I was concerned, the sun rose and set with Irene. I loved her, my Irene."

As Benjamin continued talking about the times he had shared with his sister, Oliver silently rationalized to himself that his own resentments and sustained anger toward his brothers was a natural occurrence between male siblings.

"'Edgar Bergan and Charlie McCarthy,' that was her favorite radio show, but mine was 'Captain Midnight.' Whenever I would start to get scared, Irene would squeeze my hand and she could make me feel safe. But not that day. That day she had no power to save me and I could not save her." Benjamin's breathing became labored.

"We were in the hallway rolling the Spalding back and forth. Then we smelled something. Both of us just thought it was our mother burning dinner. It made us laugh until we saw the flames and started screaming. My mother, may she rest in peace, started yelling our names, but the air was thick with smoke, we couldn't get to her. When Irene fell to the floor I dragged her to the front door, but it was on fire so I tried to pull her back. Then I fell. Next thing I knew I was in the hospital, and my Grandpa Joe was screaming at my grandma to wake up. But she was dead, too."

Oliver wanted to say something, but no words would come out.

"They said my grandmother died of a broken heart. Doctors didn't know much those days, but in her case I believe they were right."

"Gamps, if you want to stop ..." Oliver couldn't help but picture the scene in his mind, putting himself in his grandfather's place and feeling the kind of pain he should have felt years ago when he chose to disconnect himself from his family. "We can stop, Gamps, if this is too hard."

"Hard? This is not hard. What's hard is losing your mother and father, your sisters and brothers, your cousins and aunts and uncles and three of your grandparents all in one day. Hearing them scream for help and not being able to do anything to help them." The tears ran down onto Benjamin's lap and he made a conscious decision not to wipe them. "Hard is finding out that the bastards who killed your family..." Benjamin paused. "That the bastards raised their own children to be even bigger bastards."

Oliver had never heard his grandfather curse. He had never heard most of the things he was hearing tonight.

"There were fifteen fires that week, Oliver.

Seventy-eight people died. And there was not one police report. No investigation, no mention of it in any paper."

Oliver began to grasp the gravity of what his family had been involved in and what his grandfather had gone through.

"By then the Strategists owned the police, just like they owned the papers. As soon as I was well enough to travel, we left."

"Is that why you moved to Canada?"

"Yes. Grandpa and the others who were left wanted to go back to Europe, they all did, but there was Hitler. Besides, the same men who were chasing us were doing a brisk business over in Europe with the Nazis."

"How do you know that?"

"My grandfather had been a waiter for ten years during the Depression." Benjamin believed that was enough of an explanation until he saw the puzzled look on Oliver's face. "Only rich people were eating out in those days, so Grandpa knew lots of things that never made it into the newspapers."

"Traitors." Oliver was half-talking to himself. The images of Rhine and Montgomery floated through his mind.

"Once the U.S. declared war on Hitler and those men only pretended to pull out of their business dealings, yes, they became traitors. But remember, they didn't see themselves that way; they believed they were just good businessmen caught in the middle of a political ruckus caused by Roosevelt and his Socialist agenda. They thought he was the traitor."

"Nevertheless, there's a line." Oliver heard himself saying the words that had been said to him more times than he was comfortable with. *There's a line*, Senator Sherman had said to Oliver when he tried to stop the defunding of the Centers for Disease Control, and again when he had begged Oliver to stop Rhine from giving the gas and oil companies carte blanche over land belonging to private citizens.

There's a line, Gordon. We don't let companies seize the land of private citizens just because some corporation wants it.

It's a matter of national security, man. I'm sorry, but we need to keep this ship running.

Fuck that, this ship's running aground! People have a right to keep their own damn land. Read the Bill of Rights, you asshole."

Sherman had stormed out of Oliver's office that day, slamming the door behind him. Just like Monty, Sherman had tried to condemn Oliver for doing his job, but Oliver wouldn't hear of it.

You can't compare giving private corporations the power of eminent domain to Hitler's land grabs. It's completely different: U.S. citizens are paid for their land.

Having legitimized his past actions in his head, Oliver turned his attention back to his grandfather.

"Look, these men thought Hitler was going to take

over. The war in Europe was going gangbusters and the Third Reich's propaganda machine was so strong even the American papers were endorsing Hitler. More importantly, though, the war was making these guys a lot of money, so their belief in Hitler involved some wishful thinking on their part."

Benjamin wiped his forehead with his handkerchief before continuing. If Oliver had not been so engrossed in his grandfather's story he might have noticed that Benjamin was starting to get more upset. "But if Nazis didn't take over, which obviously they didn't," said Benjamin, "then the *Stratagem* was to be their alternate plan. They would tamper with American voting machines in targeted districts in the swing states so they could select the president of their choosing. That's why my grandfather came back from Canada, to try to stop them."

"That's crazy. It wasn't enough that practically his entire family, our entire family, was murdered because he was involved in this whole thing, but he was willing to gamble with your life too?" Oliver's outrage spilled out into the room.

"You don't understand."

"Oh, I understand. He was an asshole."

"You might want to reserve your outrage for the men who killed our relatives." Though he felt the need to correct his grandson, Benjamin understood that the risks his Grandpa Joe had taken had hit too close to home for Oliver.

"Sorry, Gamps, you're right." Oliver wasn't sure he was, but he was sorry he had upset his grandfather.

Benjamin slowly stood up from the edge of the bed he had perched himself on. "I'll leave you to read through the Strategem."

Suddenly it dawned on Oliver that perhaps there was a reason he couldn't get past Bash even with all his connections. "Is this why they arrested Mom and Dad? Were they looking for this?" Oliver held out the tiny piece of plastic that held the contents of the *Stratagem* in his open palm.

"Your father took me to the train station the last time I was supposed to come see you, remember?"

"The day you had the stroke."

"I didn't have a stroke."

"Yes, you did. I saw you."

"You saw me pretending to have a stroke."

"What? Why would you do something like that?"

"Your father and I were being followed."

"By whom?"

"Doesn't matter. The point is, I swallowed this, then pretended to have a stroke. I knew it would get the two of us safely out of the station and I also knew that since I have no health insurance they would never do enough tests to know I really didn't have a stroke."

Oliver didn't know whether to be angry at his

grandfather for causing him so much worry or to applaud his genius. "Does my father know?"

"No."

"He doesn't know any of this?"

"He knows some. Doesn't know about this, though." Benjamin pointed to the tab. "He has no idea there are still copies of the *Stratagem* in existence, and, no, he's never been here. He believes my trips to Coney Island were to play pinochle. Only your grandmother knows."

"Why didn't you tell him?"

"To protect him. I never wanted him to have to choose between saving himself and me. Now that he's in custody, I'm glad I made that decision."

"And me? Why are you telling me?"

"Because very soon it won't matter."

"What are you saying?"

Benjamin smiled. "Well, my grandson, it is getting late, and I have a meeting. You read this through and we can talk more in the morning." Benjamin had made his excuse to exit.

Chapter 70

Saturday, March 29, 2025
Oliver Gordon
Benjamin Gordon
Coney Island, New York

Oliver had wanted the restful night's sleep that his exhaustion had promised. Instead all he got were naps between nightmares. Most of his bad dreams took place on the train, replays of what had happened that day but with different outcomes, all of them awful. Sometimes Rhine and Monty were after him, chasing him through the Capitol, guns drawn. The last nightmare of the evening was the one where they shot his grandfather. That one was so bad it pushed Oliver to sit up in bed and deal with his real fears in as unrealistic a way as possible.

In his mind, Oliver conjured up a scenario that would allow him to continue working for Rhine and not endanger himself or his family. He would see Monty on Monday and say he saw nothing wrong with syphoning off the top of gun shipments. He would acknowledge that elections were an expensive proposition and that sometimes rules needed to be broken for the greater good, for the cause. Then he would insist he was happy that Rhine would have enough money to run for the presidency.

Staring into the blackness of the room, Oliver imagined himself saying all those things to his friend and then relished the image of Monty shaking his hand and cutting him in on the deal.

Oliver didn't remember falling asleep after that, but nothing else could explain the fact that he opened his eyes to find the sun shining through the window and his grandfather standing over him.

"Oliver, so what do you think of the *Stratagem*?
"It was interesting."

"Interesting? You sound like it's no big deal."

Oliver was still barely awake and was annoyed at having to have this discussion without his first cup of coffee. "It's an old plan; we don't even use those voting machines anymore."

"Right, now we use the touch screens and before that we used the paper ballots. There's no difference: it's all been corrupted."

Oliver was barely listening to his grandfather as he grabbed his phone. Still nothing. His email contained only spam-like messages, most of which were articles related to the environment forwarded from Abigail. Oliver erased them all before reading them. All he could think about was the fact that no one was speaking to him and that the plan to save his job, the one he had thought of in the middle of the night, would never work because it was already too late.

"Oliver, listen to me."

Oliver's attention came back to his grandfather "Okay, so they had a plan."

"It wasn't just any plan. It was a plan to corrupt our entire system of democracy."

"Well, it's obvious they didn't succeed."

"Oh really? And how would you know that?"

"Because somewhere along the line someone would have noticed."

Benjamin held in his desire to laugh at his grandson and instead maintained as serious a tone as he could muster. "People noticed."

"No, they didn't."

"They were dealt with. Losing candidates who should have won were written off as sore losers and exit polls were deemed inaccurate. Those who figured out what was going on were labeled conspiracy theorists. The whistleblowers were written off as disgruntled employees with an axe to grind. Most were branded as traitors and were never heard from again."

"Not that I don't trust you, but I'm having trouble believing all this."

"You should have trouble believing it, it's so outrageous it wouldn't be normal for you to accept it on my say so. But I do have proof."

"You have proof that the elections are rigged?" Oliver began to squirm.

"Here." Benjamin handed Oliver a stack of papers.

"You don't expect me to read all this now do you?"

"No, when I go to my meeting later you can go through it all. For now I can tell you briefly that the information in your hand includes testimony from individuals who worked for voting machine manufacturers and software developers. The evidence is pretty damning."

Benjamin read his grandson's face and knew immediately he was not being believed. "Their testimony and statements parallel the exit polls."

"We don't do exit polls, they're illegal." Oliver jumped on his grandfather's proof, knowing it must be wrong.

"They're only illegal since 2018 when people started noticing just how many races were falling outside the margin of error. Talk of fraud was growing so they had to stop the exit polling."

"No, they made it illegal because the news reporters were leaking the results of the exits before the polls closed and it was influencing the elections."

"That was the reason they gave, but that wasn't the real reason. The polls were the best method, well the only method we had, of uncovering voter fraud. They're how our own government decides whether or not another country's election is legit."

Benjamin could tell he had not changed his grandson's mind, but he had no more time to argue his point. He would just have to hold out hope that the documents would convince Oliver. "Get dressed. We have a breakfast meeting in twenty minutes."

"What kind of meeting? I thought we were going to talk more."

"We will. Now, get dressed." Benjamin said it in a tone that expected obedience.

Since escaping whatever danger was lurking on the train yesterday, Oliver no longer viewed the man who stood before him as a typical, somewhat feeble, old grandfather. Now he believed Benjamin to be strong of mind and will, with quite a bit of stamina and a limitless number of secrets.

Despite Oliver's attempt to shower and dress quickly, Benjamin showed his impatience at his grandson's fastidious grooming habits by tapping his foot and periodically pulling his Grandpa Joe's pocket watch out to check the time.

"We'll be having breakfast with some friends of mine."

"Friends? These are friends of yours?" For some reason, despite their obvious adoration of his grandfather, Oliver was under the distinct impression that what was going on, whatever it was, had to do with business, not friendship.

"You're either my friend or my enemy."

Oliver had never heard his grandfather use such black and white terms, and was intrigued.

"Just one more question." Oliver begged his grandfather's indulgence.

Benjamin stood still, waiting for his grandson to ask.

"How did you know the man on train was following us?"

"I told you this wasn't the first time I've been followed; you learn the signs." Benjamin stopped for a second to consider how much more he wanted to say. "We had intelligence. We knew you were being followed. That's why I bought tickets to Pennsylvania and not Coney Island in the first place. They're still combing the city of Philadelphia looking for you."

"What the fuck?" Oliver said to himself.

"Oh, and he did have a gun, but I didn't want to scare you. I needed you to focus on the plan, not on his gun."

Oliver's eyes widened.

"Yes, that's the response I was trying to avoid." Benjamin smiled.

"I think I owe you an apology," Oliver finally said.

"What for?"

"Last night I convinced myself you were wrong; that the man on the train wasn't after us. I was trying to figure out how to get my job back come Monday morning."

"I didn't just meet you yesterday, Oliver. I know how much your job means to you."

"I know, but I should have believed you and I shouldn't want to go back there."

"Well, despite your beliefs to the contrary, you're only human and us humans are not perfect. Remember Angie, who lived on the corner?"

"Yeah."

"How many times did she leave her husband? The cops would come on Friday night to arrest Mike for beating her, and you'd see Angie and Mike on the front lawn together by Saturday morning smiling and laughing, her with a black eye and him with the red marks from the handcuffs still visible on his wrists."

Oliver shook his head and remembered how he had judged her injuries as something Angie deserved for being so stupid.

"And your Aunt Betty, do you think she stopped eating hotdogs or fries after her heart attack?"

"No?"

"No, she didn't. Because people aren't logical; they don't follow the rules of common sense."

"Yeah, but seeing the picture of Monty stealing the guns should have done it for me. And I should have believed you about the man on the train. But last night, I swear I was all set to go back to my office Monday morning. "

"People don't have epiphanies like they do in the

movies. You're not some character in a novel. Our brains don't really work that way. We're a species that's uncomfortable with change and when we feel like it's being forced upon us we work like the dickens to maintain the status quo, even if we have to lie to ourselves and even if it's not in our best interest. Angie kept lying to herself about her husband so she wouldn't have to get a divorce or move or be alone. And your Aunt Betty told herself she could eat anything she wanted to as long as she took a baby aspirin every day. Maintaining the status quo."

"Well, not me."

"You say that now."

Oliver was annoyed at his grandfather for not believing him. "No, I mean it. I'm not kidding, Grandpa. Fuck them."

"I don't blame you for being angry and frustrated, but the fact of the matter is you liked your job and the people you worked with. And you were good at it, really good. So don't be surprised if you still feel a temptation to go back. I'm not saying you'll go back, I'm just saying you might be tempted."

"Maybe after Rhine and his buddies are in jail."

"I wouldn't hold my breath."

"Why, you think Sherman's not going to expose them?"

"It's more complicated than that."

"Well, if he doesn't and if they don't go to jail, then I'll never be safe. Am I even safe here?"

"I can promise you that there is no place safer for you to be right now. Come, let's go, we're late."

Chapter 71

Saturday, March 29, 2025
Oliver Gordon
Benjamin Gordon
Coney Island, New York

As he finished dressing, Oliver couldn't help but worry that he was getting too used to following his grandfather's lead. In his mind he began to count how many cryptic comments he had let go without even trying to get more information.

"Oliver, this is Michael, Anne, Irvine, and Craig." Benjamin pointed to each member of the group one by one. "Michael is Vice Chairman of our 'pinochle' group, and Anne's his wife and Director of Security. Irvine is Communications Director, and Craig is Irvine's son and our technical guru."

Oliver shook each of their hands, while taking note that everyone at the table was younger than his grandfather by at least a generation. They all seemed to be contemporaries of his parents, with the exception of Irvine's son who looked to be about Oliver's own age. He also noticed they were all well-dressed in clothing made by a variety of high-end designers, which immediately made him feel more comfortable.

"Oh, and this is General Baylor." Oliver turned around, surprised to hear his wife's maiden name and shocked that an out-of-uniform general was in their midst.

"Retired," the general corrected Benjamin as he shook Oliver's hand.

"Have we met before, General?" The fact that Oliver had never met any of the generals did not dissuade him from believing there was something familiar about the man standing before him.

"No, but you know my daughter." The general winked at Oliver, whose confirmation of familiarity made him forget to stop shaking the general's hand.

"Oh, sorry." Oliver realized his mistake and pulled his hand back.

"That's quite alright, son. And how is my daughter these days?"

Oliver was speechless. He wanted to answer this man, who was presumably his father-in-law, but the information would not process fast enough to allow him to.

"I see you're surprised?"

Oliver nodded his head affirmatively, but without speaking. As far as he knew his in-laws owned a vineyard in California, a story that had coincided nicely with Abigail's love of the environment. Though Oliver wanted to address the deception apparently perpetrated by his wife, there were far too many irons in the fire already to start focusing on a glitch in his personal life.

"Have a seat, everyone." Benjamin directed his comment to Oliver and the general since the others were already seated. "Oliver, we will be in meetings all day today and tomorrow, but I've brought this group here right now for your benefit, to bring you up to speed."

Oliver wished he had asked more questions the night before so he would know what he was being brought up to speed about.

"I want to start by apologizing for all the secrecy. As you will come to understand, our methods were neither random nor meant to be devious. In fact they were actually meant to protect you."

If Benjamin was trying to make Oliver feel better, being more mysterious was not the way to do it. The out-of-control feeling Oliver had been experiencing for the past twenty-four hours intensified and landed in his leg, which shook rapidly under the table until his grandfather gripped his knee. Counterintuitively, Oliver grabbed the pot of coffee and started pouring the dark, rich, anxiety-promoting brew into his cup.

"As I told you, when my Grandpa Joe got to Chicago he started going to the *Stratagem* meetings again." Benjamin started the conversation. "Even as a child I accompanied him. The group was small and stayed small for a long time until second and third generations of pinochle players joined us."

"Pinochle?"

"The thing is," Irvine fielded the question, "at first, pinochle was just a code word our grandfathers used because the game involves hands called 'tricks,' and the definition of 'stratagem' is 'trick.' But then they realized it was also a good cover since no one ever questioned them about attending a weekly pinochle game. They would hold their business meetings first and then they would play."

"We all played. From one generation to the next. And we're all pretty good at it too." Anne added to her husband's comments as she pointed to the overflowing trophy cases that lined the walls of the dining room. "Most of us play in tournaments, and we usually win."

"But lately we've been far too busy to indulge in games." Benjamin reminded everyone about returning to the topic at hand.

"So you've been meeting for years to play pinochle with the hope of one day taking down the richest, most powerful men in this country?" Oliver didn't mean to sound condescending, but the whole thing seemed ridiculous to him. He was, however, relieved to see that no one appeared to be offended by his words since everyone at the table, including his grandfather, started laughing.

"You want to field this one, General?" Since strategy was the general's strong suit it felt to Benjamin like a good call.

"Certainly, Ben."

Oliver still couldn't get over the fact his father-in-law was one of the generals, and that his grandfather was the general's friend.

"As the men responsible for the *Stratagem* went around rigging elections, building alliances, and stacking the deck in their favor, we were right next to them filling the number two spots in the same organizations and gaining their trust so we would always be privy to their plans. It wasn't until the seventies, when they really made inroads into the White House, the CIA, FBI, and DOD that their shit started hitting the fan."

"By 'shit' you mean Reagan?" Oliver sounded profoundly upset over the insinuation that one of the greatest presidents who ever lived was supposedly part of some kind of plot. *Obviously*, Oliver thought to himself, *I'm the only Republican here.*

"He was an actor. Not a president," Craig passionately interrupted the general. "And, come on, if that fact in and of itself doesn't send up a flare, what about his Alzheimer's? You mean to tell me that not one fucking Cabinet member ever noticed that the man with his finger on the *button* had any symptoms? No one thought to sound that alarm?"

"Maybe when he said, 'I don't recall' during the Iran Contra hearings he was telling the truth." Anne laughed at her own joke, which she had skillfully positioned to stop

Craig from saying too much of what they all knew about the administration that had irreparably damaged the country.

"It wasn't just that," the general continued in a calmer tone. "That's when they made their move, tested the waters to see what they could get away with."

"By 'get away with' you mean…?" Oliver asked, not expecting to be convinced.

"Ask yourself, what's the difference between Daniel Ellsberg and Bradley Manning? Ask yourself, what's the difference between Watergate and the Iran Contra or even Iraq?" The general didn't have to wait more than a second for Oliver's expected response.

"Uh, night and day."

"Maybe in the details. The who, what, when and where. But here's the thing. Before Reagan, if a president was even close to the fire, he got burned a la Watergate. Now a president can personally throw the logs on a fire and the only people who get burned are the people who saw him do it. They couldn't make Ellsberg's information about the Vietnam War stick: that should have been a warning. Instead they just closed all the holes, better insulated themselves. They had their business-friendly man in the White House, had the CIA and FBI pretty well covered by then, and Defense was wrapped up thanks to decades of the Cold War. They also had plenty of their followers voted into Congress and onto the local courts, so when Iran Contra came up, Reagan skated."

"I don't recall…" Craig reiterated his disgust, but the general continued, apparently ignoring the young man's interruption.

"Fast forward to 2001 and 9/11, and 'terrorism' became the magic bullet. Anyone who didn't fly the flag to the right was immediately branded a terrorist. Even a decade later, when the lies about the war with Iraq were exposed, and thousands of American servicemen and more than a hundred thousand Iraqis lay dead, it didn't even show up as a blip on the radar of Congress, let alone garner the attention of the American mainstream media or more importantly the justice system. And since then, anyone who has tried to do anything about government corruption has been branded…"

"A member of the Tin Hat Society, "Craig added before the General could finish his thought.

"They were branded terrorists, or traitors. Sometimes socialists," The General corrected Craig but not before giving the young man his most disapproving glance. "Unfortunately, governing through intimidation and fear, trashing the Constitution, wiretapping, video surveillance—these formed only the tip of the iceberg."

"It was the Supreme Court that was the tough nut to crack." Benjamin so seamlessly took the lead from the General it looked to Oliver to have been choreographed and rehearsed many times before. "Whether you agreed with the Supreme Court or not, they were usually pretty good at grounding their opinions in what seemed to be a sound legal interpretation of the Constitution. But even that changed. A bad ruling here, another there, and eventually they were all bad. At that point everything, and I mean everything, was up for grabs because they knew they could litigate anything they wanted right up to the highest court and get their way. Local towns and school districts, utilities, parks, state universities, power at every level was made to do their bidding regardless of public opinion and regardless of party affiliation. Republican, Democrat, it didn't matter anymore. You either played by the rules of business or you didn't play."

"Surely you must have noticed that with few exceptions there's not been much difference between Democrats and Republicans for a while now?" Anne couldn't imagine this was the first time Oliver had considered the possibility.

"No. I see a definite difference," Oliver said, automatically remembering the many votes his friend Monty had refused to cast in Rhine's favor, and ignoring the fact that Rhine and Monty had ended up working together on the arms scam.

"What you're seeing is a show," Michael chimed in. "They're putting on an act. No matter who is in the majority, in the end business gets everything it wants and just about everyone gets reelected."

"Not everyone gets reelected." Oliver was insulted at the

insinuation, not the first he'd heard recently, that what he did for a living had no impact on his boss's reelection bids.

"Those who play the game get reelected and those who, for whatever reason, don't want to play anymore are either encouraged to quit or are defeated." Though Michael spoke with authority, Oliver did not want to be convinced.

"Or eliminated." Benjamin took responsibility for saying out loud what the other members of the committee knew to be true.

"Look. I get the story about my great-great-grandfather. There were a few big businessman back then and they pulled the strings. I don't doubt that." Oliver was agitated beyond his ability to calm himself down. "But all of you believe that there are a group of billionaires secretly running government? Is that what you're suggesting?"

"Are you under the impression it's a secret?" Benjamin turned the questioning back on to his grandson. "Who do you think runs the government?" He emphasized the word "you" and gave his grandson room to process his thoughts.

"Obviously, I work for a senator and I work with a lot of senators who, along with congressmen, enact the legislation."

"And who is writing the laws these days?"

Oliver perused his office desk in his mind and saw the stack of bills sent over by the Corporate Economy

Lobby of America, which represented thirty-five of the largest corporations in the country. Their suggested legislation was deemed the most reliable, and boasted a solid track record of providing well-written, ironclad, and unchallengeable laws. It was a service Oliver appreciated, as did his boss. Without the chore of having to think of and write the actual laws, Rhine and his staff were free to focus all their energies on getting reelected.

Seeing his grandson deep in thought, Benjamin decided to add one more match to the fire.

"You don't have to answer. We all know who's been writing the bills. And we all know your boss doesn't even bother to read them anymore. You read the bills and he votes on them based on your analysis. We get that. But my question is, if the executives of the top thirty-five corporations are essentially contracting CELA to write legislation for them, then who is representing the citizens? You know, the rest of us?"

Oliver's leg started to shake again, but this time Benjamin didn't try to get him to stop.

"Okay, so indulging this collective fantasy for one minute." Once again backed into a corner Oliver turned to condescension for support, a choice that did not go unnoticed but would not be responded to by the group who were quite familiar with the many faces of resistance. Even Craig thought of this allowance as nothing more than giving Oliver enough rope to hang himself.

"The fact that you admitted to being privy to all the supposed evil that has gone on over the last, what, sixty or more years makes all of you and your predecessors complicit at the very least." Oliver believed he had found the Achilles heel of this holier-than-thou group of flaming liberals. Once again he had proven to himself that unintended consequences are an inevitable risk of governing and that any and all steps taken in the name of democracy, be they legal or illegal, were never black or white.

"I'm not going to pretend we all haven't, at one time or another, had to hold back and look the other way for the greater good. And I'll admit I've had many sleepless nights," said the General. Even if Oliver was having a hard time believing everything he was being told, the General knew sleepless nights were an occupational hazard of the Beltway. "But there's a difference, Oliver, between 'complicit' and 'powerless.' We may have known what was going to happen and we may have disagreed vehemently with it, but until very recently we lacked the manpower and the technology to stop them."

"If it was real, you could have called them out. Told the truth. Exposed them."

"Don't misunderstand," the General interjected in defense of both the organization and, more importantly in this case, Benjamin. "We've done what we could here and there over the years. Leaked what we could, stopped what we were able to stop. But just saying it outright, exposing the truth of the *Stratagem*? Which news outlet do you think would have picked that one up and run with it? It's not like you're having an easy time believing it." Everyone, including Oliver, nodded in agreement. "Son, exposing these guys for who they are and divulging their plans, even hints of it, will never work. It'd be like..." The General hesitated. "Like spitting into the wind."

Part 6

When it came to governing corporate behavior, it was the belief in the sanctity of market forces, as opposed to laws, that led to the Congressional decision to leave the NIH, the CDC, NWS, FDA, USDA, and the EPA in the hands of a skeleton crew before ultimately disbanding the lot of them.

With enforcement, inspections, and research no longer being performed, lawmakers set out to inform the public that America, its environment, and its people were healthier and in turn happier than they had ever been before. Without any research to back up their claims, reality had become whatever the government said it was.

Chapter 72

Sunday, March 30, 2025
Oliver Gordon
Benjamin Gordon
Coney Island, New York

While the Strategists had focused narrowly on making money and grabbing power they paid little attention to those doing their bidding, believing wholeheartedly that throwing money at people ensured their loyalty and silence. They never entertained the possibility that those they had wronged in the past, Benjamin's people, were the ones being paid to do the actual work. This not only made Benjamin's group privy to every step the other side was taking, but continually fueled their burning desire to stop them. In fact the biggest problem Benjamin faced over the years, and much more so recently, was convincing his people to wait for the perfect time to act. Time and time again he used the history of the failed Business Plot as an example of an action based on impatience over prudence.

More than once Benjamin had had to laugh at how his advanced age and associated inability to sleep had become a true advantage in his work. So it was that on Saturday night, while Oliver slept, Benjamin and his people worked, meeting and mentoring those charged with monitoring America. This would be their last night together for a very long time, and everyone needed to take advantage of it.

"Ben, look at this." Irvine gave Benjamin his tablet. On the screen the page entitled Hospital Admissions showed clusters of tiny red dots demarcating areas along the Eastern seaboard of the United States. "It's spreading faster than we predicted."

"Predicted, that would be the wrong word." Benjamin flicked his finger to move to the next page.

"They're going public with this tomorrow."

"They're saying twenty-four hours at best. Tell everyone it's time."

"What about the plan?"

"This is the plan."

"Really?"

"Tell everyone 'Plan B.'"

Benjamin worried that soon all the major roads might be closed and worried that Oliver's Congressional employee ID, which had always offered him safe passage through traffic stops, tolls, and checkpoints, might soon become a liability.

Chapter 73

Sunday, March 30, 2025

Oliver Gordon

Benjamin Gordon

Coney Island, New York to Washington, D.C.

If Benjamin had cared to ask his grandson if he was okay with being woken up at four o'clock in the morning to drive back to Washington, Oliver might have admitted he was downright pissed. Too bad for Oliver, though, because Benjamin didn't care. All he cared about right now was getting his whole family to Pennsylvania before it was too late.

"Are you going to tell me now?" Oliver had been driving for three hours and the morning sun was already beating down on the dashboard where Benjamin had placed a sardine can.

"Okay, we're safe."

"Safe?"

"From bugs, drones, any kind of monitoring."

"You found that out from a sardine can?"

"Quite the gadget, isn't it?" Benjamin picked up the

can and inspected it before placing it back on the dashboard. "If anything is detected, we'll know."

"The sardines will tell you?" Oliver displayed one of his rarely-seen smiles and, perhaps due to the stress, Benjamin laughed more than necessary.

"In a manner of speaking. The can will vibrate."

"Seriously?"

"Seriously."

"Where did you get such a thing?"

"Courtesy of my friends in Israel."

"What the hell, Gamps, Israel? They're helping you? Why would they help you? Israel is our ally." Oliver still wasn't sure what his grandfather and his colleagues were planning, but he suspected it would not be supported by an ally.

"Whose ally?"

"America's."

"Whose version of America?"

"Are you going to give me answers or just ask me questions?" Oliver's frustration with his grandfather was obvious.

"Israel is Israel's ally, and never forget that. That sanctimonious politically-motivated rhetoric about being tied to the ancient, oil-free, little strip of holy land in the middle of the desert doesn't fool them. Politicians shout their love for Israel for their own political gain, because it gets them votes they otherwise wouldn't get, period."

Benjamin was constantly amazed at how someone in his grandson's position could continue to be this naive. "Anytime your buddies in Washington want something - bombs, planes, another war - a different foreign country becomes 'the problem.' They can just as easily make up some bullshit about Israel, and then Israel will become the new Iran." Benjamin shook his head in disgust, and Oliver had no immediate response.

"The Iran threat is getting a little weak these days," Benjamin continued. "People are getting tired of funding the threat of war. We need a new enemy. Luckily America managed to drill and frack itself into minimal dependence on foreign oil, so that love affair with our 'ally' in the Middle East is tenuous at best."

Oliver had heard Senator Sherman say the same thing more than once, and considered it the standard response against going to war with Iran, a war that had been on the table for more than a quarter of a century and that had allowed the U.S. to build their troop levels and arsenal beyond immediate necessity. "Was all this in the *Stratagem*?" he asked.

"No, they couldn't have predicted this."

"Just wondering if you got your paranoid delusions from a book, or if you made them up yourself. Maybe it's another stroke?" Though Oliver laughed to cover the feeling that he had crossed a line with his grandfather, Benjamin knew exactly where the biting attack had come from. Oliver had not been the first person brought into the group from the outside, but out of necessity he was being brought in too quickly and without regard for how much he could absorb at one time. Thus Benjamin both expected and dismissed his grandson's comment for what it was, a desperate attempt to maintain homeostasis.

"Israel has been very much aware of American strategy for many years," Benjamin continued. "Though they weren't specifically mentioned in the *Stratagem*, they were given a copy of it and saw the handwriting on the wall. Again, they're not stupid."

"So, what, now you're a spy for Israel?"

Benjamin couldn't help but laugh at being called a spy by his grandson, whose only point of reference for such things would be old movies.

"Not me. Uncle Bernie. My eyes are tired. I'm going to rest for a few minutes."

As much as he wanted to continue their discussion and have his grandfather explain why they had to leave Coney Island in such a rush, Oliver could not help but notice the heaviness pulling on Benjamin's sleepless eyes. At once Oliver went back to seeing his grandfather in a human way, not as the leader he had portrayed for his grandson all weekend.

Self-calming away his urge to disturb his already-sleeping grandfather, Oliver pressed the icons on his tablet until his favorite classical music filled the car and allowed him to process his thoughts and make plans for the rest of the day.

Part 7

Under the banner of 'freedom,' the Federal Government had determined that its citizenry had a right to be informed about just how free they actually were at any given time. The bill, titled the Freedom Level Epidemiological Estimate, or FLEE for short, unanimously passed in both Houses and was signed by the president with as much pomp and circumstance as necessary to get the point across. It purportedly used an algorithm combining economic and social constructs to determine one's ability to be a happy citizen.

Each night on "The News" the number would be presented with the same kind of excitement as the lottery. Low numbers on the screen, which usually hovered around the twenties, meant that everyone was safe and secure and should be happy and optimistic about the future. High numbers, anything above fifty, was supposed to mean duck and cover, or as the bill's name suggested, flee.

Considering that at the end of each FLEE crisis more money had been spent on military appropriations and new surveillance programs were signed into law, it didn't take long for the American public to catch on to the real reason for the system. Its only saving grace was that as soon as the military got what it wanted, the numbers were again moved back to a less-threatening level and the American populace was informed that they could be happy once more.

Chapter 74

Sunday, March 30, 2025
Andrew & Kendall Gordon
Pinewood, Pennsylvania

At first the typecast D-cup, deep-cleavaged bleached blondes trying to read the news phonetically from a teleprompter would leave Andrew in stitches. In fact, he had even made up a game in which whoever could find the most mistakes during a sixty minute time period was the winner. Now, however, Andrew found that listening to these women add their guileless opinions to each news story, as if anyone cared to debate anything other than whether they were 'real' or not, just seemed sad.

As Andrew pulled into the local gas station Kendall noticed the televisions installed over each pump. She also noticed that every screen had the same bleached blond news reporter flashing her large overly whitened smile for the camera.

"Look, 'The News' is on. Again." Kendall had mentioned the obvious, as it was always on in public places.

"As a courtesy to an informed citizenry," Andrew

added, quoting the words that the private company contracted to install TVs at the behest of the Federal Government had engraved in red, white and blue on the bottom edge of each television, just below where the anchor's breasts were.

"They should make those screens bigger. They can barely fit all three boobs on there at the same time." Kendall laughed out loud at her own joke.

"Don't blame her."

"Why? Because she's pretty?" Kendall puckered her lips and made kissing sounds.

"No. I think they are really trying."

"Yes, trying to distract you so you won't notice all the lies being told by the ugly old guys sitting on the couch next to them. It's harder for men to pay attention to the facts when they're being distracted by shiny objects." Kendall flashed a fake smile as she shook the gold heart with the tiny diamond chips that hung around her neck.

"Very funny." Andrew had no intention of admitting his wife was right. "All I'm saying is that I get the impression these women think they're being taken seriously."

"Oh, you think they bleach their hair, Botox their brows, wear tight dresses and push their breasts up to their chins so viewers can take them seriously?" Kendall refused to go along with Andrew's supposition. "Look. When your only qualification for a job is being able to load up a

Ronald Reagan Pez dispenser with male sexual enhancers, you have to know you're not going to be taken seriously."

Andrew couldn't help but laugh at his wife.

"Maybe if they took a few courses in political science or foreign policy they might not feel the need to punctuate each sentence with a giggle." Kendall followed her own words with a mimicked version of the high-pitched laugh.

"I'm sure they are college-educated."

"Oh, I'm sure." Kendall did not hold back her sarcastic tone. "All they have to do is read the cue cards, and they can't even do that right."

"Yeah, they're slaves to these guys."

"Slaves, really? You are going to go there? Look, Gordon." Kendall always called her husband by his last name when she wanted him to know she wasn't going to turn their discussion into an argument. "These women are just glorified hookers who have figured out how to make men come without having to take their clothes off anymore."

Again Kendall followed her words by a giggle, but this time she pushed her breasts together and leaned forward to enhance her growing cleavage and mimic the women on the news. She and Andrew couldn't help but break into laughter together.

"Okay. Well I'm going to go pump some gas now, and stare at some boobs," Andrew said between laughs.

"It doesn't really matter, you know," Kendall called

through the open window of the door her husband had closed behind him. "They may look real in 3D but there's nothing real about them."

Though Andrew didn't let on, he knew his wife was right. They were phony and stupid, which was why Andrew generally ignored the news when he pumped his gas, and why today he found the louder-than-usual volume of the televisions and the beeping sound in the background particularly annoying.

"Doctors are completely baffled as to the cause of the illness and the means by which it is being spread. BEEEEP … BEEEEP … BEEEEP … There is good reason to believe this terrorist-driven pathogen is getting released into the air, as the illness has been spreading in clusters. BEEEEP … BEEEEP … BEEEEP …All citizens are asked to report any unusual activities…"

Andrew couldn't help but wonder if what the woman was saying was true, or if there was another appropriations bill up for a vote.

"We are at an unprecedented FLEE level. BEEEEP … BEEEEP … BEEEEP … It's up to 92, people, let's take precautions. Get your flashlights, water, fill your bathtubs…"

Andrew had never seen a level that high. The fact that the woman on the screen struggled to read the word "unprecedented" as a giant number 9 flashed on the woman's right boob and a giant number 2 on the left, did nothing to convince him of the validity of the warning. Unfortunately, this was not the first time he wished there was another news station to turn to for confirmation, to substantiate the facts or dig deeper into the story.

So in spite of the fact that what he was watching seemed so unreal, Andrew believed it would be best to take the warning seriously.

"We're going home," Andrew called into the car as he topped off the tank.

"What? I thought we were going for ice cream." Kendall shouted back her dismay at Andrew. Her cravings had kicked in, and kicked in hard. "I want ice cream."

"We have to go, the FLEE's at ninety-two," Andrew said as he climbed back into the car.

"Who cares. That stupid number doesn't mean anything. Everyone knows that."

"Usually. But remember, Grandpa said if the FLEE ever goes above eighty we should get home and use the emergency plan. It's ninety-two, for God's sake."

"I thought the emergency plan was for tornadoes and hurricanes."

"Yes, he said tornadoes, hurricanes," Andrew wished he didn't have to finish the sentence, "and pandemics."

Chapter 75

Sunday, March 30, 2025
Oliver Gordon
Benjamin Gordon
Washington, D.C.

With very little traffic on the roads and Oliver's Congressional ID leaning against the windshield of the car, the trip home had been a smooth one.

Mulling over the events of the previous days as Benjamin slept was not what Oliver wanted to do. What he wanted was to have all his questions answered. If nothing else, Oliver was being forced to learn how to be more patient, a lesson his grandfather believed was long overdue.

"What's going on?" Oliver practically tripped over the boxes lining the front hallway of his apartment.

"Missed you too." Abigail ran up to her confused husband and left a kiss on his cheek.

"Hey Abby, guess what?"

"What?"

"I met your father."

Abigail looked at her husband's face for signs of anger. Seeing none, she decided to answer him as if it was not the big deal it was. "That's nice. How is he?"

"Well, the General is fine, actually."

As Abigail braced herself for the inevitable shift in her husband's demeanor for all the omissions and outright lies she'd told about her family, Benjamin came to her rescue.

"Come, sit down everyone. We have things to talk about."

Oliver immediately noticed the sardine can in the middle of the table.

"Okay, Oliver, you wanted to know what the boxes were for. Well, the truth is, we're leaving. Now."

"What? Who's leaving?" Oliver seemed to be the only one in the room who didn't know the plan.

"All of us."

"What do you mean, all of us? Where are we going?" Oliver stood up, "I'm not going anywhere. I have to get back to work on Monday." Oliver doubted he was going back to work, but he needed time to explain to his wife what had been going on.

"Sit down, Oliver. We're going to Pennsylvania, to your parents' farm."

"Like hell I am. I'm not going there. I just drove six hours. I'm tired. I'm going to eat lunch, and do some work. Then tomorrow I'm going to figure out how to be a normal person again. So, no, I'm not getting in the car again, and I'm definitely not going to Pennsylvania."

Benjamin momentarily believed he had finally pushed his grandson too far, and, after looking at his watch, decided to let the television sitting on the kitchen counter explain.

"…the illness has been spreading in clusters with significant concentrations in the D.C., New York and Boston areas. BEEEEP … BEEEEP … BEEEEP … Symptoms include: headache, fever, nausea and vomiting…"

"What the fuck?" Oliver noticed the flashing 92 on the announcer's breasts and the words "Unprecedented FLEE," crawling across the bottom of the screen.

"…There's no word as to the source of the pathogen and the means by which it is being spread. BEEEEP … BEEEEP … BEEEEP … As of this hour, sixteen people have been confirmed dead in New York City, twelve in Boston, twenty four in Washington D.C., and at least seventy-five have been hospitalized. BEEEEP … BEEEEP … BEEEEP … Among the dead are an aide to Senator Borky and two White House staff members. While a terrorist attack has not yet been confirmed, there is some speculation that the unknown pathogen was released into the air…"

"Did you do this?" Oliver's eyes were wide.

"They did it to themselves," was all Benjamin said before asking Abigail to fix lunch so that he might survey all that had been packed.

"Wait. What does that mean?"

"I'll explain it all when we get to Pennsylvania."

Though he wanted answers and presumably the full truth, Oliver couldn't help but believe that perhaps it would be best to accept his grandfather's response for the sake of being able to claim plausible deniability. Besides, right now he really needed to listen to the news.

"Again, we repeat——A terrorist attack has not yet been confirmed and no terrorist group has come forward to claim responsibility for the attacks. However, sources close to the White House are looking toward the Middle East…"

"Do they ever look anywhere else?" Oliver's grandmother had walked into the room.

"They're always from the Middle East, Grandma."

"Statistically? Or is that just what you want to believe?"

"Not you, too? I just spent three days with, well I don't actually know who I spent the last three days with. I thought it was Gamps, but apparently he's some kind of twenty-first century overlord." Oliver rolled his eyes.

"Enough, Oliver. Bring the boxes out to the car. I'll pack your sandwich to go."

"I'm not going."

"You'll go because your grandfather said you're going."

"I'm sorry, Grandma, but I'm not ten anymore."

"Which is exactly why you're going to act like a man and take your wife out of this town before she gets sick and loses the..." Oliver's grandmother stopped herself in mid-sentence and hoped Oliver hadn't noticed what she'd almost said.

So busy with thoughts of trying to right his own life, Oliver had not thought about the possibility of his wife, his grandparents or even himself getting sick from whatever it was that was killing people all around him. Without so much as a nod to his grandmother, Oliver emailed Senator Rhine and told him he would be taking his grandparents out of town to ensure their health, and suggested the senator might also consider leaving the city for a while.

"*Nice touch.*" Oliver congratulated himself. Perhaps his boss would not see him as a threat and would call off the dogs.

He also put in a call to Monty, with the same phony sentiments of concern, though the call went right to voice mail. Then Oliver sent texts to his staff asking for updates on the spread of the disease and waited for the usual immediate responses confirming their intention to "get right on it," but the responses never came.

Oliver told himself the senators were probably photo-op-ing in front of the church at this time on a Sunday morning, and that his staff was probably taking their one day off to sleep in. He told himself that he doubted any of them were aware of what was happening, and pushed away the nagging thought pressing against the back of his mind that he had been thrown out of the loop, a possibility he believed would be a bigger threat to his survival than whatever germs might be spreading through the air. Arguably, he might have been right.

Chapter 76

Sunday, March 30, 2025
Andrew & Kendall Gordon
Tyler & Kris Mayer-Gordon
Gordon Family Farm, Pinewood, Pennsylvania

Though he could not have been more anxious to get home, Andrew made sure to follow all the speed limits so as not to get stopped or arouse any suspicion. For a while he kept the radio on, tuned to the news, but he could see it was unnerving Kendall, who was sitting with her hand on the tiny bump they had yet to acknowledge to anyone in the family. Previous attempts to get his wife to agree to the auspicious announcement had been thwarted by Kendall's fears of losing this baby, too. "Soon," she would say to Andrew. But "soon" never seemed to come.

"We need to tell them about the baby today." Andrew put the car in park.

"Why? Why today?" Kendall grabbed the door handle. "Wait."

"What? We need to get inside."

"We need to tell them because they all have to watch out for you, in case…" Andrew's words trailed off.

Kendall wanted no clarification of what Andrew meant by "in case." The entire ride home her head had been spinning with what was going to happen to them; one scenario after another, and none of them ended well. Subsequently Kendall had no desire to argue with her husband, believing that if the end was near she wanted their lives to be as peaceful as possible until then.

"Fine, you're right. We'll tell them tonight at dinner."

Andrew didn't understand how months of resistance had dissolved so quickly and easily. He had been ready for a long discussion and possibly even an argument, but was truly grateful when neither materialized.

"Just in case, cover your mouth and nose with this." Andrew had taken off his sweatshirt and handed it to his wife.

"What about you?"

"I can hold my breath."

"Let's just pull around to the garage." Kendall released the car handle.

Not wanting to show his annoyance at not having thought of it himself, Andrew kissed his wife. "Thanks," was all he said before putting the car in gear and pulling around the back of the barn just as Tyler was pulling the door open.

"I saw you pull up. Did you get a lot of supplies? Or did you see drones?" Tyler guessed the only two reasons he could think of to pull the car into the garage this early in the day.

Andrew didn't bother to answer as he got out of the car, moving instead into a staccato tirade of instructions. "How much of that plastic sheathing do we have left? Oh, and staples. How are we fixed for staples?"

"Why? What's going on?"

"FLEE is 92."

"Who cares? They're probably just trying to start another war. Idiots. Who is it this time?"

"No one. Some kind of pathogen was released. A bunch of people are dead." Andrew didn't have to look up to know he had put the brakes on his brother's thoughts of being conned. "Kendall, go into the living space and seal all the edges around the windows."

"I'm going." Kendall ran from the garage.

"But don't get up on a ladder. I'll do that," Andrew called after his wife, hoping she'd heard him.

"Where? Who? What people?" Tyler had to run to keep up with his brother, who was heading for the storage room.

"People in New York, Boston, and D.C. I don't know..." Andrew didn't bother to finish his sentence.

"Wait. Andy..."

"No time." Andrew kept walking as he gave his brother instructions. "Get the ladders and all the plastic sheeting we have, and the staple guns and all the staples. We have to cover up every hole in the living space right away. I'm going to start stocking the supplies so we can stay inside till this thing blows over. And tell Kris to check the air cleaners, have him change the filters. Now, go!"

Andrew opened the door to the supply room, which was a good hundred feet from their living area, and started piling boxes into his father's childhood red Radio Flyer wagon, the one with the wood frame around it. It was the same wagon Andrew had used as a kid to cart around dirt, plastic army men, frogs, and, for a while, his seven-year-old brother with a broken leg. Memories embedded in the rusted frame had caused Andrew and his father to advocate for its place on the farm, despite the corroded holes that made parts of the wagon look like Swiss cheese.

"I'll patch it up." Andrew tried to push the memory of his father's words aside as he couldn't help but notice that he had, as everyone predicted, never got around to fixing the wagon.

Chapter 77

Sunday, March 30, 2025
Oliver & Abigail Gordon
Benjamin & Mary Gordon
Washington, D.C. to Pinewood Pennsylvania

It took four hours to finish packing everything into Oliver's compact car and Abigail's minivan. The same minivan that had once taken Abigail and all her belongings to college and then to her first few apartments, was taking her to yet another new home.

Oliver couldn't believe he was driving again. This was the last place he wanted to be right now. Where he wanted to be was in his office trying to figure out why no one had called, texted or emailed him back. He needed to know if he still had any friends or allies in Washington, and if he did he needed to know who they were. By now Rhine was out of church, Mark's touch football game would be over, and his snoozing staff should have at least finished their second cup of coffee. Surely someone had turned on the news and would see the importance of putting their pettiness aside in favor of obtaining Oliver's sage advice.

They're not going to kill me right there in the Capitol; maybe I can smooth things over. The country is in crisis, they're going to need my help. As Oliver drove he silently practiced the words he was planning to say to his grandfather.

"…Three more confirmed dead this hour."

Oliver turned off the radio he had just turned on. Any hope of convincing his grandfather to let him stop in his office before leaving town had just been squashed. Instead he gripped the steering wheel harder, a move not missed by Benjamin.

"Turn here." Oliver had no idea how his grandfather knew the route to the farm, but he sounded confident as he told Oliver which way to turn.

"I gave your grandmother and Abigail directions, but go slow, try not to lose them."

"Do my brothers even know we are coming?"

"No."

"We should call, then." Oliver reached for his phone.

"No."

"Why?"

"Your brother's phone isn't secure."

"And mine is?"

"Of course. And the GPS is blocked."

"How did you do that?" With barely a pause, Oliver answered his own question. "Never mind. The Israelis showed you how. Though I can't imagine why it matters. They can track us if they really want to."

Benjamin smiled. "True, but I prefer not to make it easy for them."

"So does this mean you do have something to do with what's going on?"

"What I'm telling you is that I don't feel it's in our best interest to be followed."

"Our best interest? I have nothing to do with this. Whatever's going on, I'm just the driver. This is all about you and your friends."

"Not about you? This has nothing to do with you?"

"This has nothing to do with me. My issues have to do with my boss and Monty." Oliver was confident in his assertions. "Look, Gamps, no offense, I love you, but I'm taking you to my brothers' house, then I'm turning around and going back to D.C. After that, as far as I'm concerned, you can all plot to take over the world. I just want nothing to do with it."

"So, let me see if I got this right." Benjamin kept his frustrations inside, his voice calm. "You've read the *Stratagem*, and you have seen what they are capable of. They had absolutely no problem killing almost every member of our family, and taking away everything your mother and your father and I worked our whole lives for.

Then they spied on us, arrested your parents, tortured them, and denied them due process." Benjamin watched his grandson's face grimace slightly at the mention of his parents.

"They stole your democracy, Oliver." Benjamin pointed at his grandson. "Your precious democracy. Made your vote, my vote, everyone's, worthless so they could get away with anything they wanted: union busting, privatizing, spying, torture, everything up to and including stealing arms and selling them to our enemies." Benjamin paused then continued.

"So tell me, Oliver, what is it? Just what is it that they have to do to make this about you?"

Chapter 78

Sunday, March 30, 2025
Andrew & Kendall Gordon
Tyler & Kris Mayer-Gordon
Gordon Family Farm, Pinewood, Pennsylvania

As they stacked boxes filled with food and supplies in the corner of the living area, the sound of the staple gun sealing them in plastic punctuated the voice on the radio telling them how many people had died in the past hour.

"It's only in some parts of some cities and in certain towns." Andrew believed it best to track the progression of the disease, and he pulled out two maps, one of the entire U.S. and one of the Northeast.

"Put them up here." Kendall pointed to the only wall that had been covered in sheetrock. The rest of the wallboard was still in their father's truck and more than likely lost to them forever.

"What were those towns again?" Tyler and Kendall responded to Andrew's request by listing all the places they could remember.

"Manhattan: Upper West Side, Upper East Side and Tribeca," Tyler replied, rolling his eyes.

"Bethesda, Easton, and Potomac, Maryland." Kendall had quite a few cousins who lived in Maryland, though not in those particular areas.

"D.C. was on the list, and Green Hills. That's here in Pennsylvania right? Where is that?" Kendall asked absentmindedly as she continued to organize the boxes, not realizing that the proximity of Green Hills to where they were in Pinewood should have caused her worry. "I hope Grandma and Grandpa and Oliver and Abigail are okay."

*I hope **we** are okay,* Andrew thought to himself, but out loud he said, "I'm sure they're fine." He had no specific knowledge that would make his assurances factual, but felt his wife needed to hear it anyway. "Turn on the radio again. Let's get the full list."

"Wellesley, Massachusetts; Sudbury, Massachusetts; West Windsor, New Jersey; Scarsdale, New York; Wilton, Connecticut; Bridgeport, Connecticut; West Windsor and Franklin Lakes, New Jersey; and on Long Island we have multiple deaths reported in the Roslyn Estates area, Sands Point, Old Brookville, North Hills, East Hampton, Amagansett, Sagaponack, Old Westbury and Muttontown…"

As the announcer went down the list Andrew

continued putting X's where each town had lost residents to the pathogen.

"Do you see what I see?" Kris was the first to notice the pattern.

"Oh yeah, I see it. I don't believe it, but I see it." Andrew had stepped back from the map and noticed the pattern too.

"Kendall, come look at this." Andrew called his wife over to look at the map and confirm what he was thinking.

"It's not in the air, is it?" Kendall said, staring at the Xs and trying to make sense of what was really happening.

"No, it's not, the patterns are too sporadic. They would have had to attack every town separately. But look at this, look at the towns." Andrew pointed to the Long Island towns.

"Oh my God, they're all…" Kendall's words trailed off as she felt the need to catch her breath.

Chapter 79

Sunday, March 30, 2025
Oliver & Abigail Gordon
Benjamin & Mary Gordon
Washington, D.C. to Pinewood Pennsylvania

Driving down the road, Oliver couldn't help but remember the tiny people who had inhabited the snow globes his mother used to collect. For hours at a time Oliver would shake the glass bubbles and create violent upheavals in what had once been the static and predictable worlds of the characters inside. Now Oliver knew how they felt.

Though he wasn't quite ready to admit it, Oliver suspected his grandfather was right, this was getting personal. In fact, Oliver couldn't stop wondering how his life might have been different if so many of his relatives hadn't perished in that fire. What would it have been like to grow up with lots of cousins? Maybe, he fantasized, they would have been more like him. Maybe, unlike his brothers, they might have shared his politics, a thought that stopped Oliver cold as soon as he realized he was no longer sure of what his own politics were or should be at this point. The cacophony of disconcerting mental chatter that followed could only be stopped by defending what was familiar. Oliver turned on the radio.

"The President is considering declaring a State of Emergency in an effort to contain the spread of the disease and to stop the anticipated rioting as the death toll increases…"

Why haven't they called me about this? Oliver hit his palm against the steering wheel. *They need me.* Benjamin continued pretending he was asleep. *State of Emergency… State of Emergency.* Oliver repeated in his head, trying to come up with the implications of the declaration. *Frozen assets, property confiscation without having to pay for it. I need to be back there. We can acquire the rest of that land in upstate New York for Holly Gas, maybe even get that Maine project in the bag. Monty will have to blink now, I have dirt on him. Ha. Maybe I can turn this around; blackmail him and Rhine!*

Oliver started to plan how he might turn a liability into an asset. *Align with another senator, someone who wouldn't mind seeing Rhine and Monty take a dive.* Immediately Oliver ran through the list of candidates likely to throw their hat in the ring for President and came up with five names.

Oh no, they're not going to have this crisis without me.

Another hour there, unpack, I can be back by ten, eleven the latest. Oliver consoled himself with the knowledge that he could safely drop off his wife and grandparents, fulfill his obligation to them, look like the good guy, and be back home before midnight. *Gamps said they're looking for me in Philadelphia. By the time they figure out I'm not there, the arms deal will be front page news and everyone working for them will go into hiding for sure.*

"In other news, surveillance reports out of the Middle East show a significant increase in the number of nuclear weapons being produced and stockpiled by Israel. Israel continues to deny the existence of these weapons and continues to deny access to weapons inspectors. The U.S. Generals have issued a joint statement condemning Israel's fraudulent claims and is calling for tougher trade sanctions by the U.S.

At home, the Department of Defense has asked for an increase in their budget for 2026. The currently undisclosed amount is anticipated to be a significant increase over last year's and is expected to gain unanimous approval in both houses in light of the buildup of tensions in the Middle East."

"Anytime your buddies in Washington want something—bombs, planes, another war—a new country becomes the devil. Iraq, Iran. They can just as easily make up some

bullshit about Israel, and Israel knows it." Oliver could not believe his grandfather had predicted this. *What the hell? How did he know that? Our support for Israel was solid; why didn't Monty tell me we were going to start using Israel for military funding justifications? He's on Armed Services for Chrissake.*

"Corporate taxes and taxes for those earning over $250,000 are expected to drop for the sixth year in a row, due to a new set of tax relief laws scheduled to take effect next year."

You're welcome. Oliver smiled and thanked himself for his part in once again reducing taxes.

"The drop is expected to bolster the economy and create significant job growth in the first quarter of next year."

"It's the gift that keeps on giving," Oliver remembered Rhine saying about the trickle down subterfuge that always seemed to garner support from those least likely to benefit from it. *"Stupid bastards,"* Rhine had followed up with as he slapped Oliver on the back and thanked him for the votes that had put the tax cut for the richest Americans over the top.

Even though he knew Rhine was right, Oliver

couldn't help but briefly think about what his grandfather's response to the story would be if he were awake.

"Bullshit. Greedy bastards." Oliver laughed to himself, knowing that his grandfather's thoughts were irrelevant to the real world of Washington. Oliver knew he had done his job and done it well for his boss's constituents, and that was all that mattered.

It's my job. I'm just going with what works. The fact that it's been working for decades and no one is catching on to the fallacy of trickledown theory is not my problem. My concern, and my only concern right now, is getting my boss into the White House. And yes, I'm legislating for the benefit of our biggest donors, but can you name a politician who hasn't?

Oliver played the speech he had previously given to his grandfather in his head, believing he had won the argument and ignoring all he had read in the *Stratagem* about predetermined candidates and stolen elections.

"Foreclosures are up after a brief respite last quarter. The rate has jumped a full 6% over the past three months. In response to the news, Senator Rhine of Pennsylvania has proposed a law that would require homeowners with incomes of under $150,000 to submit a yearly foreclosure prevention audit of their expenses with their tax returns. Those found to have depleted their incomes on purchases of non-essential items would be required to enroll in a money management class. According to the senator, "If people can't be trusted to make sound financial decisions, then the banks should not have to suffer for it." The fee for the online class is expected to be about $75 per person, and all adult members of each household will be required to sign up."

"You're welcome, boss. Now fuck you. I'm moving on to bigger and better things." Oliver said under his breath. The foreclosure prevention audit and class that had, in fact, been suggested by one of his overly-zealous interns was one he continued to take credit for, even in his own mind. Oliver glanced at his phone to be sure he hadn't missed a call from Rhine or one of his other people. *Damn!*

"Stock prices continue to rise, record temperatures heat up March again, these stories and the latest on the terrorist attacks after these messages…".

Chapter 80

Sunday, March 30, 2025
Andrew & Kendall Gordon
Tyler & Kris Mayer-Gordon
Gordon Family Farm, Pinewood, Pennsylvania

The fact that what was happening in the real world was not being reported on the news was nothing new. The Gordons were used to that. What was unusual was that their reality might actually be better than what was being reported.

"Rich? They're rich?" Tyler heard the discussion through the plastic sheeting and stopped work. If it wasn't an airborne pathogen there would be no need for him to continue stapling. "Muttontown, Roslyn Estates, Old Brookville, all of them, really? They're not rich. They're beyond rich. They're like millionaire, billionaire rich."

"So if it's not in the air and only millionaires are dying from it, we should be safe, right?" Andrew smiled as did everyone in the room, elated that their financial situation might actually turn out to be better protection than plastic and duct tape; at least for now, they might be safe from whatever was killing people.

"Well, that's a relief. We should celebrate. Break out the rest of the doughnuts, the ones Kendall hasn't eaten," Kris said, making fun of Kendall.

"We shouldn't be celebrating. People are dying." Kendall hoped her comment would take the focus off her eating habits.

"No one we care about is dying. Let's eat."

"Tyler." Kendall admonished her brother-in-law, and wished she didn't always have to play the role of mother.

"No, Ken, I'm sorry. These are the people who don't give a shit about us. Why should we care about them? If I were lying in the street bleeding, they'd step over me. Fuck'em. Let 'em all die."

Kendall couldn't come up with a good response to her brother-in-law's hatred, nor could she stop it. Instead she issued a warning to Tyler, punctuated with the kind of authority she used when necessary.

"Just be careful, Tyler. You can think whatever you want, but watch what you say out loud."

Everyone knew Kendall's warning was meant to keep her brother-in-law out of jail.

"Here's what I don't get." Kris steered away from Tyler's anger, preferring to focus on the impact the disease might have on his family rather than trying to judge whether those who had succumbed had deserved their fate. "It took ten minutes for the four of us to figure out that whatever the hell is killing these people is not in the air and that it's spreading through the kinds of neighborhoods where the garbage men are the only ones making less than six figures. Not even any of the hospital workers have gotten sick, so it's probably not communicable, or at the very least it's not likely to be highly contagious." Kris noticed he had everyone's attention, and assumed by the look on their faces that they were in agreement with his analysis. "So what's up? Why are they not communicating this information?"

BEEP…BEEP…BEEP

Everyone's attention was brought to the radio.

"The President has issued a State of Emergency Declaration in an effort to contain the spread of the disease and to reduce the possibility of rioting as the death toll increases. White House press secretary Norm Station stated that Martial Law has not been ruled out as a possibility as the terrorist threat increases…"

"Bullshit. Who's going to riot? Everyone's scared shitless. They're duck-and-covering." Tyler's annoyance continued. "They're just going to use this emergency like they use all emergencies, to get what they want."

Too late, they've already got it all, Andrew thought to himself, preferring not to fuel his brother's fire.

"We've already seen it," Kendall added. "Remember, after the last big hurricane the government said they had their hands full with the emergency so they gave a bunch of parks away to Molten Gas?"

"Yeah, except the hurricane was in Florida and the parks were in Montana. Dad went crazy over that one, remember?" Everyone couldn't help but laugh at Tyler's recollection, even though it upset them to think about their father.

"It's the old 'look over there at the emergency, while I steal from you over here' trick." Kendall pointed to one side of the room and then took a doughnut from the middle of the table.

"Smooth." Andrew laughed at his wife's inability to fool anyone. "Too bad the government isn't as bad as you are at stealing."

"Yeah, too bad," Tyler reiterated.

"So, what do you think? Are we safe?" Kris again tried to move the conversation back to the reality they needed to deal with.

"I'm assuming we are for now, but who knows what's next? Let's just finish putting up the plastic and keep the supplies here just in case. Better safe than sorry." Andrew glanced at his wife to let her know he had things under control and that she need not worry. "We'll monitor the news and we'll keep updating the map. That's all we can do for now."

Let's hope that's enough, Andrew said to himself before sending up a silent prayer that his father would soon be home to take charge of things.

Chapter 81

Sunday, March 30, 2025
Oliver & Abigail Gordon
Benjamin & Mary Gordon
Washington, D.C. to Pinewood Pennsylvania

Benjamin conveniently awoke whenever Oliver needed instructions. Turn here, right there. That was the extent of their conversation.

The earth rumbled and the car bucked pushing their bodies full thrust forward against the restraints of their seatbelts.

"What the hell was that? Are you okay?" Oliver had pulled the car to the side of the road, as all the other cars in sight had done.

"Oliver!" Abigail ran from her van parked behind him. "You okay? Is Gamps?"

"Yeah, we're fine. Grandma?"

"She's good."

"What the hell was that?"

"Earthquake."

"Earthquake? You've got to be kidding me."

"No. I told you they have them in Pennsylvania all the time now. Do you listen to anything I say?" While Oliver searched his memory, Abigail laughed at her husband.

"Does the word 'fracking' ring a bell?"

Oliver didn't answer her question. At this point it was clear that nothing he could say would work in his favor. Instead he let his wife offer up some answers.

"So what happens now? Aftershocks?"

"Maybe, but it could be a swarm."

"A swarm?"

"A bunch of earthquakes in the same general area. They don't lessen in magnitude the way aftershocks do, sometimes they get even bigger. It used to be pretty rare, but now, with all this fracking..."

As soon as Abigail said the word 'fracking' she could see her husband's eyes glaze over, a sure sign he was losing interest. Abigail knew Oliver was an avid supporter of the energy industry and she had, on more than one occasion, jokingly accused him of loving its leaders more than her. To which Oliver would always respond that he had been with the energy guys longer. The fact was, though, that Oliver considered energy independence a matter of national security and therefore a priority over everything else.

"Let's take a break, at least till we know whether it's an aftershock or a cluster," Abigail suggested.

Oliver looked at his watch and silently added an

unacceptable hour to his already-obstructed schedule. "Maybe we should go on. What's the worst that could happen?"

"We could crash?" Abigail pointed down the road at the drivers who had parked their cars and were now milling about at the side of the road.

"How do they all know to do this? Not every car has an environmental expert in it." Oliver leaned over and kissed his wife.

"This isn't their first rodeo." Abigail rolled her eyes at her husband.

"I'll get the grandparents' chairs."

Oliver wasn't happy about his decision to join the other stranded drivers, and once again felt himself being pulled further from his responsibilities and his work.

With the beach chairs set up far enough away from the cars, Oliver was happy to see that the land around them was clear of trees and for that matter anything else that might fall. As long as the earth didn't crack open and swallow them up, Oliver was relatively confident they were safe from whatever the shaking earth might bring.

"Come on, let's take a walk while we wait." Abigail never liked sitting still for too long.

Though Oliver had a lot to say to his wife and countless questions about her family, especially her father, he was nevertheless apprehensive about separating from his grandparents.

"Should we leave them?" Oliver spoke quietly and shifted his eyes back and forth from his grandmother to his grandfather. "I'm not sure it's safe to be outside with this terrorist thing."

"I'm old, but I'm not deaf." Benjamin called out. "'This terrorist thing,' as you call it, has nothing to do with the air and has nothing to do with terrorists." Benjamin decided to assuage his grandson's fears.

"Come on." Abigail started running on the relatively flat and barren ground that lined the parkway toward the gently-sloping, grassy hill that blocked the view of everything behind it.

"Hey, I have asthma." Oliver's lie was meant to excuse how out of breath he was trying to keep up with his wife.

"Yeah, asthma. You play touch football every weekend and you go to the Capitol gym every day. Unless you've been lying to me," Abigail jokingly accused her husband.

"No," Oliver pretended to be serious, "I do go to the gym all the time."

"Going to the sauna doesn't count."

"Well, if you're going to be picky."

"Ah–ha, I knew it. Guess I'll have to slow down for you, old man."

Taking his wife's words as a challenge and refusing to be outdone by her, Oliver ran up the mild slope until he reached the top, at which point he was gasping for air.

Abigail, seconds behind him, was herself out of breath now, but mainly from laughing at her husband while she was running.

"Oh, shit." Oliver stood up from the bending position he used to suck air back into his lungs and looked for the first time at the valley below them.

"What?" Abigail followed his gaze to the unnaturally-deep-blue water of the rivers winding around the fracking operation below

Oliver looked at his wife. "Is that SOP?"

"You've never seen it?"

"Only in the brochure." He remembered reading the Solution Over Pollution brochure, the one that showed a babbling brook and an assortment of animals around what looked to be water. "No, come on that's not SOP. What is that?"

"You don't listen to anything I tell you, do you?"

"What? I listen." Oliver feigned innocence but knew his wife was right. When it came to her work with the environment Oliver was never interested.

"No you don't, or you would know this definitely is SOP. Do you want the short version or the long?"

"Short." That was always Oliver's answer.

"Okay," Abigail started her story in the middle, "after the streams and creeks had all been polluted, and all the fish and wildlife were dying. You remember that, don't you?"

Oliver recalled the complaints that had come to his office. The ones he had immediately referred out to other senators like Monty, who preferred to be bothered with such things. "Of course I remember."

Abigail had trouble believing her husband, but kept going anyway.

"We're talking hundreds of thousands of fish and birds, squirrels, cows, horses, bees, even bugs. Basically anything that used the water to drink or bathe in was dying."

"Go on." Oliver wanted to know about the blue stuff below but he didn't really care to listen to what had necessitated its use.

"The gas companies blamed the coal companies, the coal companies blamed the gas companies, then they banded together and blamed the farmers saying it was their pesticides and their GMO'd crops."

"GMO'd?"

"Genetically Modified."

"Oh, you mean WFM."

"Oh, right. Wholesome Food Modifications." Abigail pretended she'd forgotten the replacement name meant to throw off consumers. As much as she wanted to talk to Oliver about the tumors in mice and the virulent strains of mutated bugs from WFMs she forced herself to stay on topic.

"The FDA, God rest its soul, didn't fault gas, oil,

WFMs or pesticides for the animal deaths. Instead they blamed things like algae, water temperatures, fireworks…"

"Fireworks?"

"Yeah, they said they scared the animals to death. The birds just fell out of the sky from fright. They blamed anything and everything but the chemicals they denied were in the water."

"They tested the water, Abby." Oliver defended the facts.

"Yes," Abigail held her fury back, "and that might have meant something if the people testing the water had been trustworthy. However, since the oil, gas and chemical companies were the ones who hired the testers, and since the results from each industry contradicted the others, I think it's safe to assume that their results were questionable at best."

Abigail didn't bother to include the fact that the EPA's closure had been precipitated by a report from Senator Rhine, who had called the agency 'a sham' and blamed its officials for their inability to put their finger on the exact cause of the thousands of fish kills, bee colony collapses and bird deaths that had taken place all over the country.

"That still doesn't answer my question, Abby. Cut to the chase." Oliver was feeling uncharacteristically uncomfortable about having bribed Monty into voting for the closure of the EPA. To calm himself, Oliver remembered all the times he had been sent at the behest of Rhine to stop then-EPA Director Sam Samuels from irresponsibly releasing a report that might negatively impact the economy.

"Okay, well..." Abigail asked herself for patience and took a breath. "No one was going to pay to clean up a mess that no one would admit actually existed. Yet there they were: hundreds of murky, rusty brown streams and lakes, and thousands of dead fish and birds everywhere. The stench was awful. That's where Solution Over Pollution came in. It's a gel that coats the water."

"I know what it's supposed to do. I thought it was going to at least look like water."

"Water, really? You don't read my emails, do you? I sent you pictures." Abigail rolled her eyes and Oliver didn't answer, assuming his wife didn't want to hear the truth. This was how their annoyances with each other stayed petty and never turned into something larger and out of their control.

"It's supposed to be safe for the birds to land on," she continued, " though they can't drink or bathe in it, and the dead fish and their smell get contained underneath. The most important thing, though is, it looks pretty and smells however they want it to smell, perfumy in summer, foresty in the fall. Problem solved." Abigail's sarcasm was obvious, and even Oliver wasn't so sure the unnaturally-bright-blue, stagnating, gelatinous mass below was an acceptable solution to the problem.

"There've been 50,000 wells drilled just like these." Abigail spoke softly and continued to rattle off facts about the environment while Oliver listened and took in the surrounding landscape, amazed at how much of its barren vastness had been hidden from the roads he drove on. For the first time Abigail got the feeling her "environmental chatter" wasn't being ignored.

"In thirty states, including this one, residents pay top dollar to have their water delivered by trucks to huge holding tanks because their tap water has become so toxic from fracking you can set it on fire."

"That's not necessarily from the fracking."

"I've heard that." Abigail knew her husband, like so many others, had bought into the professed innocence of the gas companies. "Though, to be honest, in addition to the pretty brochures from the gas companies' PR departments, I've also read the research. And I have to say the argument connecting fracking with groundwater contamination is pretty compelling, not to mention the fact that it's just plain common sense." Abigail could see from her husband's face that he had taken her last comment as a dig and backpedaled a bit.

"I mean, it's common sense when you look at the big picture. Think of it this way. If you pump poisons into the ground and pretty soon all the water in the surrounding area isn't safe to drink, the wildlife is dying, the cattle are all getting sick, and the human cancer rates in the area are suddenly sky high, and this happens over and over again everywhere they're drilling you start to figure that the gas companies might not be telling the whole truth. They also make the people they lease land from sign special agreements stating they won't tell anyone about what's actually happening to their water and their health, and they stop doctors from reporting on illness in the area. If they would actually let the public know what chemicals they're using we might be able to figure out exactly what's going on, but of course they flat-out refuse to divulge anything. Needless to say when you put it all together the evidence is pretty damning."

"You know, we used to come here every summer." Oliver abruptly shifted gears. He'd heard enough talk about the environment for now.

"You never told me that." Abigail shifted with him, appreciating the time he'd spent hearing things she knew he was uncomfortable hearing.

"I think that's why I wanted to work for Rhine. I wanted an excuse to be back here." Oliver picked up a rock and threw it, wishing it could reach the stream so he could see it skip across the gel.

"My dad rented a cabin every summer. He would work at a nearby camp and my mom would watch us." Oliver laughed at what his mind saw. "She had no idea what we were doing all day. She just figured if we were slathered in sunscreen and bug spray we'd be okay."

Both Abigail and Oliver laughed at his Mom's naiveté in trusting her boys in the woods.

"The three of us got along back then, really got along. We would build a new fort every day, and I remember Andrew collecting bugs and I collected rocks. I think Tyler collected mosquito bites." Oliver laughed as he remembered his little brothers. "One time Tyler tried for hours to convince Dad he had seen King Kong in the woods." Oliver shook his head remembering his brother's excitement at seeing what was more than likely the shadow of a large tree.

"There was no TV in the cabin, so we played a lot of games," Oliver continued. "And of course we were all big into books. *The Three Musketeers* and *Tom Sawyer*, and… oh shit, I just remembered." Oliver stopped to search his memory for the correct version of the story. "We built this raft because we thought we were going to be like Huck Finn and travel down the river. Tyler had broken his leg that summer climbing a tree."

"To look for King Kong?"

"No doubt." Oliver's grin widened.

"Tyler couldn't swim anyway, even before the broken leg, so we put him in my dad's old red wagon and rolled him onto the raft. Then we tried to push him and the raft into the water." Oliver began laughing as he continued. "Mom sees us out the window just as we get the raft halfway into the water, and she comes racing out of the house screaming, her hands in the air, 'Don't do it. Stop. He'll drown. Stop!'" Oliver continued laughing at the image of his much-younger mother screaming at them as she ran, slipping and sliding on the mud and stone stairs that led from the cabin down to the water's edge.

"Well, at least we won't have to worry about our kids taking a raft out on the water and drowning," Abigail added to Oliver's thoughts.

"Yeah, at least." Oliver picked up another stone but didn't bother to throw it this time.

Chapter 82

Sunday, March 30, 2025
Andrew & Kendall Gordon
Tyler & Kris Mayer-Gordon
Gordon Family Farm, Pinewood, Pennsylvania

Even though it was clear the information garnered from the television could not be trusted, there was something about the comfort of seeing other people alive. For now, though, all they had was the radio.

"More than eight hundred people confirmed to have the disease at this point, more than one hundred confirmed dead. And we have unconfirmed reports that a number of high-ranking government officials have been hospitalized. We repeat, more than eight hundred people have been confirmed to have this as-of-yet unnamed disease.

"Eight hundred already? Holy fuck." *How come I can't stop cursing?* Andrew silently berated himself.

Now that Kendall was visibly pregnant, at least with her clothes off, Andrew had decided it was time to start practicing living his life without the boatloads of punctuating expletives he was used to using. He was failing miserably.

"I'm not surprised at the numbers. This is how pandemics start." Kris shared what he remembered from his medical training. "Once people learn about the symptoms, instead of waiting at home thinking they just have the flu, they flood the hospitals. It'll level off soon, watch."

"And if it doesn't?"

"Well if it is a pandemic and we consider the exponential growth of the illness we've witnessed so far, then I suspect we'll soon be up shit creek without a paddle."

"Is that your professional opinion?"

"Hey, what can I say? But realistically, I don't think this is a pandemic, at least in the traditional sense. It's too spread out, and still only a select group is getting sick."

"Pandemic or not, do me a favor, don't share your thoughts with Kendall. I think it would be too much for her now."

"No problem. Where is she anyway?"

"In the loft taking a nap."

"Crashing from the sugar, no doubt."

"No doubt." Andrew confirmed the incorrect assessment made by his brother-in-law instead of sharing the truth that his wife was completely worn out from the worry that her unborn child might be in danger.

"More than eight hundred people confirmed to have the disease at this hour…"

"I can't listen to this shit anymore. I'll update the map later." *Stop cursing!* Andrew yelled to himself in his head. The thought of his current failings as an expectant dad brought with it an unexpected cascade of unsettling questions. What if he couldn't protect his pregnant wife or provide for their baby? What if they never found his parents and he never saw them again? What if? What if? Andrew felt more vulnerable and out of control than he had since his parents first went missing.

"I'm going to start lunch." Andrew needed a distraction.

"Lunch sounds good, I'm starving." Tyler had just walked into the living space. "I finished all the plastic; I'll go back to the list after lunch."

"I'm going to do some work on the stable. Call me when lunch is ready." Kris was getting antsy sitting around listening to bad news all morning, and was happy to get back to work.

"Not me, I'm resting. That stapling was harder than I expected." Tyler flexed his fingers, which were numb from trying to keep his hand steady on the staple gun as it pushed the metal tongs into the two by fours. He also took note of the multiple small cuts in his left hand where the staples had grazed his fingers as he held the plastic sheeting in place. Luckily Tyler had not actually stapled himself, as the daily ribbing regarding his accident-prone nature would have intensified significantly if he had executed such a misstep.

"Well, I'm sure you can muster the strength to peel some carrots." If Andrew was going to be a less-than-perfect dad in the cursing department, he was at least going to provide a healthy meal for his wife.

"Fine. But I'm not..." Before Tyler finished his sentence he stopped to listen. "What's that?"

"I don't know, probably a drone." Andrew didn't want to deal with anything more today.

"No, it's a car."

Andrew and Tyler were out of the living area and at their front door, baseball bats inconspicuously by their sides, just as the car and van doors opened.

"Room for four more?"

The sound of their grandmother's voice was unmistakable, and both Andrew and Tyler dropped their bats on the ground and ran out to greet their unexpected guests with hugs, kisses, and, for Oliver, handshakes.

Chapter 83

Monday, March 31, 2025
Benjamin and Mary Gordon
Oliver & Abigail Gordon
Andrew & Kendall Gordon
Tyler & Kris Mayer-Gordon
Gordon Family Farm, Pinewood, Pennsylvania

While they had been stopped on the road waiting for the second earthquake, the one that thankfully never came, Oliver had told Abigail a little about what was going on with his work; but not everything. Instead he portioned the information out slowly, watching her face for any rise in emotion: a downward curve of her mouth, a widening of her eyes, a finger curling through her hair. With no such visible proof of upset Oliver had assumed she would allow him to return to D.C. later in the day.

Unfortunately, by the time lunch and the tour of the farm were over, Oliver had no choice but to admit to himself he was far too tired to get back on the road, and instead made plans in his head to leave first thing in the morning. In the meantime he had placed another round of calls and texts to Washington, all of which went frustratingly unanswered.

It would be weeks before Benjamin would admit to his grandson that the Pinochle Group had rerouted all his *communications through their virtual offices for suitable responses. After all, Oliver could not be expected to respond appropriately when he had no idea what he was unwittingly involved in.*

Maybe it was the country air, or perhaps it was the all the driving, Oliver wasn't sure. All he knew was that from the time his head hit the pillow that evening until eleven o'clock the next morning he hadn't moved.

"Were you comfortable last night? How was your room?"

Oliver could hear Kendall talking to his grandfather about the makeshift room they had designed out of supply boxes.

"Exceedingly comfortable. The mattress, the temperature, even the privacy. It was all perfect."

As he descended the ladder from the loft to the main floor living area, Oliver thought about his grandfather's inability to ever admit his discomfort.

"Oliver," Kendall greeted her brother-in-law with a smile. "You're up."

"Where is everyone?"

"Kris and Tyler are dealing with the animals that arrived this morning. Most everyone else is doing chores."

Kendall's excitement at the arrival of the chickens,

rooster, goats, three additional cows, and two horses had her rushing around the kitchen finishing the last of her morning routine so she could mingle with her new friends. "I'm trying to get this all done."

Oliver watched as she moved the crumbs swiftly from the dustpan to the large silver metal garbage can before securing its lid back on top. He couldn't help but notice that the can, which would be more appropriate for a curb than a kitchen, shined with newness.

"If I don't keep this place clean and spotless we'll have to deal with all kinds of varmints." Kendall remembered how their initial focus on things other than cleanliness had brought what felt like an endless trail of mice through their supplies, a problem they believed they had finally conquered.

Chores? Varmints? Oliver registered an internal amusement at Kendall's new-found rural vernacular.

"Oh, and your wife went with Grandma to visit her family."

"Her family?" Once again it seemed to Oliver that everyone around him knew more about Abigail than he did. Luckily he was able to temper his frustration by acknowledging the possibility that their lack of communication might be, at least in part, his own doing.

"Yeah, they bought the farm next door."

"What are you talking about?"

"The farm next door. You can see it from the window in the loft. They moved in yesterday."

"What else do you know?"

"I know her father is retired and that some of her relatives are living with them."

"What else?"

"That's it. That's all Abigail said before they left. But I'm done and I'm going to play with the horses, even if I can't ride them."

Oliver missed Kendall's wink, which was intended for Benjamin.

"Why can't she ride a horse?" Oliver asked his grandfather after Kendall left the room.

"I don't know. Maybe she doesn't have a saddle?" Benjamin laughed.

"What's so funny?" Oliver's being left out of things everyone else seemed to know gave rise to his anger, and instinctively he searched his pockets for his keys.

"I'm just imagining your grandmother getting up on one of those horses." Benjamin decided to lie to his grandson, believing it was not his place to tell Kendall's news. "If you were thinking of leaving for D.C.," Benjamin acknowledged the keys in his grandson's hand, "it would be very unwise."

Oliver was getting tired of everyone, especially his grandfather, telling him what to do. Even though he knew he wasn't going anywhere until his wife returned, he nevertheless felt the need to challenge his grandfather.

"And why exactly would it be unwise for me to leave?"

"Come," was Benjamin's only response before getting up and moving toward the door.

Chapter 84

Monday, March 31, 2025
Abigail Gordon
General Baylor
Baylor Family Farm, Pinewood, Pennsylvania

The beautifully renovated yellow and white-trimmed farmhouse, with its freshly painted walls and fine antique furniture, stood in stark contrast to the new home the Gordons had made inside their dilapidated old barn. Each of the fourteen bedrooms in the Baylor home was filled with close friends and relatives, and the basement was filled with a year's worth of food and supplies.

"Oliver's completely confused. He was sleeping when I left. Everyone else is keeping busy at the farm; the chickens, horses and a bunch of other animals arrived today."

"Are you here alone?"

"No, Mom's having tea with Oliver's grandmother."

Abigail was happy to see her father out of uniform.

"Our animals came yesterday. I'll take you to see them when I'm finished." The general had just emptied a box of signed, first edition history books onto the newly-built shelves.

"You can't get these anymore. They're banned. Domestic terrorist propaganda nonsense." The general's words trailed off as he remembered with horror the unanimous vote that had installed the Unified History, Unified English, and Unified Science school curriculums designed by the Congressional Committee on Unified Education.

"The only reason I can have these is because of who I was."

"Because of who you are," Abigail corrected her father as she moved to his side to place a kiss on his cheek.

"So what do you think of Oliver?" Abigail was curious about how the weekend had gone from her father's perspective.

"He's a good man, but stubborn as hell."

Abigail laughed before suggesting that her husband's biggest flaw was also his biggest asset.

"Maybe. If we can turn him around," the general warned his daughter.

"He'll come around. He's almost there. You should have seen him on the way here. Ben's going to show him the bunker today."

"And tell him the plan?"

"Noooo," Abigail elongated the word for effect, "not till it's done. Ben's afraid he'd try and stop it."

"He would."

"It's all about timing, Daddy."

"I couldn't agree more. Come, let's go to the barn. Your sisters have been there since the sun came up. They'll be excited to see you."

Chapter 85

Monday, March 31, 2025
Benjamin & Mary Gordon
Oliver & Abigail Gordon
Andrew & Kendall Gordon
Tyler & Kris Mayer-Gordon
Gordon Family Farm, Pinewood, Pennsylvania

In the hours before Oliver awoke, Benjamin had informed the family of much of what Oliver had been told over the weekend. Though their shock at their grandfather's secret life was no less pronounced than Oliver's, the rest of the family was actually relieved to know someone had their backs. They were also quite willing to accept Benjamin's assurances that the disease, which would soon reach every state in the nation and wipe out entire communities, would leave their family unscathed.

After his talk Benjamin took them all on a tour of the massive bunker, which ran under half the length of the barn and was stockpiled with enough food, water, medicine and amenities to ensure the family's comfort for years to come if it came to that. He knew it wouldn't.

Are you kidding me? Oliver thought to himself as he reached the bottom stair of the bunker.

Benjamin watched as his speechless grandson took in the vision of what had been created decades before, during the time of the Cold War, when everyone believed that digging a hole to live in was a wise, not a paranoid, thing to do. Though all the appliances had been updated and the food was fresh, hints of the past in the form of turquoise paint and wood paneling remained as part of the décor.

"Is this why you won't let me go back to Washington? We're going to hide out in here? Is there going to be some sort of war? A bomb? Don't tell me you're going to drop a bomb." Oliver excused his uncharacteristically frantic thoughts as natural, given the circumstances.

For a moment Benjamin thought about telling his grandson that the initial strategy was to take the government back by force, a plan that had been in the works for decades and might have necessitated the use of a bunker such as this one. Luckily cooler heads, including Benjamin's, had prevailed and convinced the majority of the Pinochle Group that the problem would eventually take care of itself, which it had. And without so much as the firing of one bullet.

"No, this is just storage," Benjamin lied.

"Storage? That doesn't make any sense."

"Did you see the condition of the barn? Before your

brothers got here the roof was like Swiss cheese. I wasn't going to leave this stuff upstairs to get ruined by the leaky roof."

That was still not enough of an explanation for Oliver. "How did this all get here? Who paid for it? Where did you get all this food without anyone getting suspicious?"

"You're going to have to start thinking out of the box, son. You keep thinking we're average citizens with few resources. Our people…"

"Our people? You mean your pinochle friends?"

"Yes. Remember they're not your average citizens. They're just like you," Benjamin poked his wrinkled index finger into the middle of his grandson's chest. "They can drive right through any border with a wink."

Oliver forced himself to listen and not tell his grandfather of the rising indignation he felt toward the questionable actions of his grandfather's pinochle pals. Any anger he directed at them would also have to be placed squarely on his own grandfather, who, much to Oliver's dismay, could be considered nothing less than their ring leader.

Benjamin walked over to the small desk in the corner and pushed it aside.

"Gamps, I could do that."

"While I'm still able, I'll do."

Benjamin effortlessly removed a piece of the wood paneling, behind which stood a large safe cemented into the concrete wall. The door to the safe, which was taller than Oliver and at least six feet across, looked to be brand new.

"What the fuck." Oliver's eyes were wide.

Slowly Benjamin pressed a series of numbers on the keypad and placed his thumb on a small screen before pulling the released door open and flipping on the internal light switch. Oliver's eyes widened to see what he quickly estimated to be at least five hundred gold bars arranged on shelves on the left side of the safe. On the right side were stacks of money piled equally as high, and on the floor was computer equipment. Toward the back of the deep walk-in safe were shelves of old books. And standing in every corner were guns, hundreds of them and all types. A box labeled "handguns" sat near the door. Oliver's heart sank. Before this he could have denied all he had encountered over the past few days as being one man's insane, paranoid, delusional plot to overthrow the government; but the appearance of massive sums of cash, gold, and guns was concrete evidence of wrongdoing that would probably land them both in jail forever.

"What the fuck is all this?" Oliver could feel everything inside him snap. "I listened to all your bullshit about the *Stratagem* and about my stupid great-great-grandfather, and I listened to your crazy take-over-the-world card game friends, and I even listened to you when you said we have nothing to worry about even though people are dying left and right and you apparently have something to do with it."

Benjamin had seen Oliver angry on a regular basis but had not seen this level of rage in many years. He had been expecting it all weekend, so the fact that it had finally surfaced came as no surprise.

"I waited, like you said. I didn't push. I stood back and I waited for you to tell me the whole truth; and this is it? I waited to find out you're a fucking domestic terrorist? You're the reason for the border stops, the wire taps, the cameras, the drones, and the God-damn airport security; and none of it caught you? This is fucking insane. You're fucking insane." Oliver's face had turned bright red. "You're no better than my fucking boss. We're going to fucking prison. They're going to hang us or put us in front of a fucking firing squad." Oliver's hands were flailing, his face was even redder.

Benjamin watched in silence, knowing the rage was pain, pain he wished he could spare his grandson from feeling. Just as he had wished to spare him the pain of seeing his dog Chester put to sleep. The dog that had taken up residence beside Oliver's crib and thereafter never left his side. The dog that had left a hole in Oliver's heart so big that it wasn't until Abigail arrived a full decade later that smiles returned to Oliver's face on a regular basis.

"Calm down, Oliver."

"Calm down? You want me to calm down? You're

stockpiling weapons! There's a whole arsenal in there. Do you even know how to use a gun?"

"As a matter of fact…" Benjamin nodded and smiled.

"What are you smiling at? This is serious. You should not be smiling." Oliver was screaming at his grandfather so loudly his voice was becoming hoarse and his throat painful.

"You can calm down."

"No, I can't calm down."

"Well if you don't, I won't tell you where all this came from."

Oliver was angry, but he had to know more, the truth this time, so he willed himself to gather air into his lungs and breathe out with force, once, then twice, until he was able to listen.

"We stole it." Again Benjamin smiled, but this time he laughed too.

Oliver held his anger, telling himself that the old man had finally lost it.

What's the point in being mad? The jig is up. I can't unsee this. I'm going to have to report all this to the authorities and turn Gamps in. Insanity defense, schizophrenia, dementia, maybe Alzheimer's? In his head Oliver ran through the list of possible pleas that would declare his grandfather innocent by reason of insanity.

"Don't worry, though, it's not like we robbed a bank or anything."

"No? Well it looks like you knocked off Fort Knox!"

"Close."

Oliver didn't want to be close.

"Your buddies in Washington stole it, and we stole it from them. We took a little from here and a little from there." Benjamin didn't think it was a good time to tell his grandson there were other safes on other farms with just as much cash, weapons and gold as was in this one.

"We took it from their under-the-table arms deals, their cash transfers to their offshore accounts, and skimmed it off the top of their illegal kickbacks from the drug traffickers, lobbyists, the corrections and surveillance industries, financial services, water and oil companies, anyone who wanted something. Every time a deal went down, we made sure one of our guys was the go-between."

Who is this man? Oliver no longer recognized the person standing in front of him.

"The weapons deals, they're the big money transactions. Gotta hand it to Rhine, when it comes to making money he's no slouch."

"And no one notices."

"Their focus is and always has been on the airports. Take off your shoes, x-ray your anus. Anyone you know ever try to hide a bomb up their ass?"

Oliver shook his head, still not knowing what to make of what his grandfather was saying.

"It's so much easier to shoot down a plane with a

rocket launcher. Who needs to get on a plane and blow themselves up?"

"What are you saying? You're going to shoot down planes now? You have rocket launchers? What the fuck are you saying?"

"No, no, no. What I'm saying is, you know how every time a plane goes down they say it was mechanical trouble?"

Oliver shook his head.

"Hogwash."

"Shit happens, Grandpa."

"Bullshit. Don't buy their ridiculous stories."

"So what are you saying. Who's shooting planes down?"

"Depends on the plane. There was that one that went down off Long Island... but never mind. I'm not going into that now. My point is that the guys in Washington know for sure that the rocket launchers go through the ports, but they don't want to admit it because then they would have to plug up the holes and start inspecting, inventorying and x-raying the storage containers, like they do everyone's asshole at the airport; and God knows they don't want that."

"Because of the weapons deals."

"And all the other deals sliding through the ports. That's why Rhine and your friend Monty weren't worried about getting caught.

Oliver thought for a minute. "What about the generals? If they could spy on me like Bash did, why couldn't they spy on Rhine?"

"Well, it's a little complicated."

"Try me. I'm a quick study."

Benjamin smiled at his grandson before continuing. "They have been watching Rhine, just like they were watching you. But technically they found nothing."

"Technically?"

"Yes, because Bash gave all the intelligence he collected to his boss, Assistant General Hayes. Now Hayes just happens to be one of our guys. So he took all the intel that was supposed to go to his own boss, General G, and let's just say he redacted it to say what we wanted it to say. Meanwhile Hayes used the real intel to blackmail Rhine and, voila!" Benjamin waved his hand through the air like a magician pointing out the wonders of his safe. "We were open for business."

"Amazing." Oliver shook his head as he thought about what a neat package his grandfather's insane plan fit into.

"Look at these." Benjamin had walked into the safe to retrieve a manila envelope from the shelf, and pulled from it a set of pictures. "Take a good look."

Oliver couldn't help but notice the familiar faces. Senators, congressmen, aids, and the Vice President himself were standing on the waterfront where ships and storage containers were being unloaded in the background.

None had a comfortable look on their faces. They knew they didn't belong there.

"Is everyone on Capitol Hill involved in selling arms?"

"In my experience they will steal anything that's not nailed down. Well, that's not entirely true. They steal land, too."

"But why? Why the fuck? None of these senators are hurting for money. Goddamn Rhine is a fucking millionaire ten times over."

"No, he's a billionaire if you count the Cayman accounts. And to answer your question, this is what happens when opportunity meets greed. Think of it this way. If I told you the bank wasn't going to lock their front door and their vault was wide open would you go in and steal the money?"

"No."

"What if I told you that even if you stole the money and even if your fingerprints were all over the crime scene, you would never get into any trouble for it. Would you do it then?"

"Maybe."

Oliver wished he hadn't been included in his grandfather's bank scenario. He really didn't like to think of himself as having the mentality of a common criminal. However, given this set of circumstances, he knew for a fact he would take the money.

"Why didn't you just tell someone this was going on? Bring them your evidence?"

"Bring it to whom? With all the agencies gone, there's no oversight."

"Big government was wasteful and inefficient."

"And now?"

Oliver knew what his grandfather was getting at, though he wasn't ready to say so.

"Truth is," Benjamin continued, "and you probably don't want to hear this..."

"Grandpa, I haven't wanted to hear anything you've said for the last three days, so go ahead."

"As we mentioned before, Watergate was the last time any president actually got smacked down for something he did wrong. Since then they've broken laws, lied under oath, started illegal wars, spied on, tortured and denied citizens their civil rights, they've made due process optional, imprisoned whistleblowers, impeded investigations, tortured anyone they wanted to, and broken multiple tenets of the Constitution; and not one of them has gotten more than a slap on the wrist. Nope, the vault is open and the guards are all asleep. But Rhine and his mashugenah plans are just the tip of the iceberg. These," Benjamin pointed directly to the books on the shelves in the back of the safe, "now, these are the real deal."

"What are they?"

"Books, documents, journals, history. All the things they thought they'd destroyed so they could make up their own stories and rewrite history. Someday these books and the knowledge they hold will all be returned to society."

Eventually, Benjamin thought to himself, he would share the fact that the books in the safe also documented the truth behind the unprecedented exodus of lawmakers and governors who refused to join the fold. Some left in disgrace of their own making, but most were blackmailed out; their exits generally precipitated by compromising photos. A seamlessly-placed head cropped onto a naked body and a threat of bodily harm generally did the trick.

"But seriously, there must be someone to tell, to stop them."

"Why? So they can call me a traitor or a whistle-blower, and lock me up for a dozen decades like all the others who tried to stop any of the government's bullshit? No thanks, we'll do things our way."

"Our way. See that's the thing that scares me. What is our way?"

"I think you're just going to have to trust me, because right now, Grandson, the fact of the matter is you have no choice."

As much as he hated to admit it, Oliver knew his grandfather was right. He had stepped into the middle of something he barely understood and had no idea how to remove himself from. While Benjamin collected the photos and placed them back in their envelope and onto the safe's shelf, Oliver thought about their conversation.

"If you have access to the Assistant General..." Oliver began speaking as if he were challenging his grandfather. "Why can't you get mom and dad out?"

Benjamin wasn't willing to share with his grandson the enormous upset he faced over his decision to limit the Pinochle Club's involvement with the prison system, a system so large and so corrupt it made the wheelings and dealings of Congress look like child's play. For now the best Benjamin could do was to keep tabs on his son and daughter-in-law and use what influence he did have to see to it that they remained in the country until the impending deaths of the warden and the guards would make their release possible.

"We have to work within parameters," Benjamin explained. "We don't like to run our deceptions past too many people or draw too much attention to ourselves. What I can tell you is they'll be out soon."

Maybe it was an overwhelming accumulation of stress or the fact that he had hardly eaten in days; whatever it was, Oliver's face went suddenly pale and his need for a chair was obvious.

"Dizzy?"

"Maybe a little."

Benjamin grabbed a water bottle and an organic energy bar from the bunker's kitchen and handed them to Oliver.

"I don't drink this stuff, and I certainly don't eat these things. Do you have AcquaO?

Oliver set the bottle down on the table and threw the energy bar, which slid onto the floor. Benjamin picked both up and handed them back to his grandson.

"Drink this and eat the bar. You'll feel better."

As Oliver sipped the water, which tasted significantly less flavorful than the oxygen-infused stream water he was used to drinking, and struggled through the peanuts glued together with honey, he couldn't stop thinking about all the deceptions. Just about everyone he knew, from his boss to his grandfather to his best friend, and even his own wife, had deceived him. In his mind Oliver imagined them all as poorly-drawn caricatures of themselves with big Pinocchio noses: Rhine, Monty, the whole lot of them. Then into his thoughts, but only for a split second, Oliver saw his father's real likeness and wished, for once, that he was there. Despite all his flaws, and as far as Oliver was concerned he had many, Griffin Gordon was an honest man and always had been. He was always himself, which was generally the problem.

"Let's go back upstairs and see about you helping your brothers with the chores."

"Chores? I don't do chores."

"You do now."

Oliver felt the affectionate pat of his grandfather's hand on his back.

Chapter 86

Monday, March 31, 2025
Oliver & Abigail Gordon
Gordon Family Farm, Pinewood, Pennsylvania

After revealing the plethora of secrets including the existence and contents of the bunker below them, Benjamin decided dinner should be a peaceful one. With the radio off and the conversation turned away from politics, the announcement of Kendall's pregnancy had taken center stage, and for a brief period of time everyone forgot about how bad things really were.

"They're all calling it AmeriVirux now," Oliver reported to his wife as they walked on the path that led to the farm road.

The couple had never taken a walk after dinner and had certainly never spent any time in the country together. Oliver wondered if he could get used to this lifestyle. Given that he had no idea who he was or what he believed in anymore, he was hard pressed to answer his own question.

"AmeriVirux? Sounds patriotic," Abigail commented.

"Yeah, I hear they even have a flag."

Abigail punched her husband lightly, pretending to be upset with him for joking about such a serious matter.

"I'm just kidding."

"I know, but people are dying."

For a split second Oliver hoped his boss was one of them, then pushed the thought away and continued. "I wonder why they're calling it a 'virux.' What's a virux?"

"I have no idea. Maybe it's not a virus; last I heard, they didn't know what it was."

Oliver could have no way of knowing the name had come from misread news copy, an inevitable consequence of hiring an anchorman too vain to be seen with his glasses on and a network too stubborn to admit to his mistake. Seeing the 's' in the word "virus" as an 'x' was only the most recent in a cascade of mistakes, which included a three-year-old "doy" who could play the piano and a fire in a "mursing" home.

"I'm just glad our families are going to be safe," Abigail said as she squeezed her husband's hand to emphasize her relief.

"Speaking of families, how is yours? I heard you went over to visit them this morning."

Because Abigail knew right away that her husband's seemingly-innocuous question was just a precursor to a more serious discussion regarding her father, she decided to dive right in. By doing so she hoped to avoid being asked any questions she didn't want to answer.

"I just want you to know I had no idea my father was one of the generals until last year. Even my mother believed he had some low-level Pentagon job and nothing more. I wanted to tell you, but he wouldn't let me."

Oliver knew she was right. There were plenty of things even he, in his position in government, couldn't divulge to his wife, though most were about infidelities, interns, and impotence rather than legitimate state secrets.

"It wasn't until Pinochle started making final plans," Abigail continued.

"Final plans?"

"Don't ask me what they are, I honestly don't know. The only thing my father told me was that they were planning to take over the government. Actually he used the words 'take back.' But he didn't give me any of the details."

The way Oliver looked at her, Abigail knew he didn't believe her.

"No, I swear. He barely told me and my mother anything."

"Well, what did he say exactly?"

"He said Pinochle was being backed up by more than one country."

"Was Israel one of them?"

"I'm not sure. Maybe. Whoever it was, they were getting sick of the hypocrisy."

"What do you mean?"

"You know, the way we go around the world like we're better than everyone else. Telling people how to live, how great our democracy is, and waving our flag in everyone's face."

"Ah. And meanwhile we're selling arms to our enemies. I can't believe Rhine did that, and Monty…"

As his words trailed off Abigail couldn't help but notice the intensity of her husband's sadness. Though she considered Oliver's insight long overdue, she knew it was not easy for him to admit that things had gone horribly wrong in his intensely-ordered world. Her decision to press on was based not on her desire to inflict more pain but on her commitment to helping him understand.

"The arms deals were bad. No doubt countries overseas were angry about it. But honestly, it wasn't the first time Washington betrayed an ally, and no one expected it would be the last. In the end it was the rigged elections that turned out to be the last straw."

"They told? My grandfather told them?"

"Let's face it, things have been fishy around here for a long time. How many times did OSCE have to tell us our elections process was corrupt?"

Oliver couldn't argue with the fact that the independent reports by the international organization had, over the past fifteen years, become increasing damning of the American voting process. What he could argue, and always had in the past, was that involvement with the fifty-member-democracy-promoting organization should have ended long ago. Just like the defunct Voting Rights Act, the OSCE election observers had become a stranglehold on the free will of states to act in the best interests of its citizens. An argument Oliver knew would not fly with his wife as easily as it had with his friends in Washington.

"Your grandfather just confirmed what OSCE had been saying for years."

"So you believe my grandfather? All of it?"

"First I believed my father then your grandfather." Abigail smiled nervously.

"And all their BS about the hollow state You buy that too?"

"You mean do I believe that our democracy is an illusion? Abigail rolled her eyes. "Just because our government is corrupt right down to its core?"

"Sarcasm does not become you." Now Oliver was now the one rolling his eyes.

"Sorry."

"Seriously, Abby. I never thought…"

"They didn't want you to think. They don't want any of us to." Abigail had stopped her husband in mid-sentence, something she never did. "For all intents and purposes our government looks like it's working. But it's not working for us."

"The government works in the best interest of the

majority of its citizens." Oliver's pat answer, the same words he had spoken a thousand times, suddenly sounded wrong to him.

"Sounds hollow to me, what you're saying, compared to the truth. There's nothing to back it up. It is a hollow state, Ol - face it. My father, your grandfather, they were just going to make it right again. Put back what was stolen."

"How, Abby? How the hell were they going to do that? That's what I can't figure out, and no one will tell me."

"I don't know any of the details, and honestly it doesn't matter anymore because it's not going to happen." Abigail tried to sound convincing and looked directly into her husband's eyes as if she were telling the truth. She hated lying to him, but it wasn't her place to tell him. Her only option, as she saw it, was to change the subject abruptly. Push his thoughts from work to home with the news she had been holding back for far too long.

"But I have something more important to tell you." As an anxious smile moved across her face, Abigail informed her husband of her pregnancy.

"What?"

"I'm pregnant." Abigail said again.

"No, really?"

Abigail didn't speak. Instead she nodded her head affirmatively as she braced herself for her husband's reaction. They had not once discussed the possibility of children. She'd assumed it would just happen, he'd assumed it just wouldn't.

"No, really?" Oliver repeated.

"Really," Abigail said as she nodded again to affirm the news, which finally prompted a shocked Oliver to pull his wife into his arms.

"Girl? Boy? Not that it matters as long as it's healthy. Who cares, right?" Oliver really didn't care. He was suddenly just happy, genuinely happy. He was also surprised at his own reaction. For the second time today, and in defiance of his personal belief that children were an annoyance to be avoided, Oliver felt himself being sucked into the excitement of first-time parenthood.

"Won't know if it's a boy or a girl till the sonogram."

"But you took a test, right?"

"Of course. I went to the doctor and I've been taking vitamins, but I wasn't going to have a sonogram without you there."

Oliver was happy his wife had waited.

"We're due in October."

"We're due." Oliver said the words to make it feel more real. "October." Oliver's smile was wide. "Make an appointment for the sonogram next week. We'll be back in town by then."

Oliver may have been sure, but Abigail wasn't.

Nevertheless she agreed to his request, choosing not to argue with her husband.

"Let's go tell everyone." Oliver grabbed his wife's hand and began to pull her toward the house.

"Wait." Abigail pulled back and stopped Oliver in his tracks. "Don't mention the doctor or the sonogram, okay?"

"Why?"

"Kendall."

"What about her? She's pregnant, too, she'll be excited for you. And the cousins can grow up together." Oliver could only see the upside of telling everyone he was going to be a father.

"She's further along than me and hasn't been to a doctor yet. She told me they can't afford it. And there's no way she's going to be able to pay for a sonogram."

"They could afford it if they wanted to."

Abigail became annoyed with the fact that her husband was speaking as if he knew anything about the expenses associated with pregnancy and delivery.

"How much do you think it costs to have a baby?"

"I don't know. What could it cost, a few thousand dollars?"

"Try ten thousand, and they want all of it up front if you don't have insurance like we do. And that doesn't include the hospital and the pediatrician."

Oliver wanted to tell Abigail that his grandfather had plenty of money hidden under the floorboards, but something inside him, that had not been there for a very long time, made him want to step up for his brother.

"We'll pay for it."

In response to his words Abigail's face lit up with a smile as big as her husband's. She didn't know what had changed him, but whatever it was she was happy about it.

Chapter 87

Tuesday, April 1, 2025
Benjamin & Mary Gordon
Oliver & Abigail Gordon
Andrew & Kendall Gordon
Tyler & Kris Mayer-Gordon
Gordon Family Farm Pinewood, Pennsylvania

The news that the Gordons were going to have two new additions to their family was welcomed with tears, hugs, and handshakes all around. The mood was light, and became even lighter after Oliver took Andrew aside and told him he would be paying for Kendall's and the baby's healthcare.

With everyone aware of the supplies stored below, their worries about food, water and even an emergency shelter were gone. Now they could all focus on the farm full time, and the women wasted no time starting on plans to create separate living areas for each couple.

"You're not coming to live here?" Kendall was about to delineate an unused section of the barn where a bedroom and attached nursery could be built for Oliver, Abigail, and their baby.

"That's not part of the plan," Abigail whispered to her sister-in-law after checking to make sure her husband was out of earshot.

Kendall had no idea what Abigail was talking about or why she was whispering. Kendall had been under the distinct impression that even though they were safe from the AmeriVirux it was going to take a long time for the affected cities, including Washington, to recover.

"But I thought…"

"We'll be staying with my parents," Abigail grabbed the lie out of thin air. "They have a guest house on their property."

Kendall's sadness at the news that they would not be living together on the farm showed on her face. She had fully intended to bond with Abigail over their mutual experiences of pregnancy and motherhood, and couldn't help but feel the distance, however small, would sever the connection before it had even begun.

"I will be here every day, though. Early." Abigail tried to put a smile on her sister-in-law's face with a promise she knew would not be kept. They would be back in Washington before her baby was born, and, as far as she knew, Kendall and Andrew and their baby would be there too.

Part 8

This was not the first State of Emergency called, it was just the first time in recent history that the problem was real and not just an excuse to start a war, torture prisoners, spy on citizens, jail reporters, raise oil prices, punish whistleblowers, or ignore the constitution.

Chapter 88

Wednesday, April 2, 2025
Oliver Gordon
Washington, D.C.

Monday's revelations had only served to reinforce Oliver's resolve to return to Washington. He would, he reasoned, need both his income and his health insurance to take care of Abigail and the baby; and if his grandfather's traitorous ways were found out, he would need all the pull his position in Washington had to offer to get his family out of the country before they might be hanged.

So Oliver drove through the black of the night on the steep winding mountain roads of Pennsylvania at speeds far exceeding the limit, flying through abandoned checkpoints and stopping only for bathroom breaks behind what looked to be deserted rest stops. The once bustling hubs of twenty-four hour commuter activity were now homes for the homeless; parents and children grateful for the protection and comfort a roof and four walls afforded them filled the abandoned roadside buildings. Oliver saw their flickering candles through the spaces of the boards covering the windows and assumed that if any of them came out and saw him it would not end well. So his stops were brief and frightening, his steps back and forth to the car quick. Oliver instinctively kept a firm grip on the heavy duty metal flashlight he had pilfered from the farm. Exercises in unnecessary precaution, as those inside the rest stops were much more afraid of him than he was of them.

Aside from his brief encounters with intangible criminals, Oliver's trip went smoothly. Generally, his was the only car on the road, but occasionally a pair of headlights or the flashes of an emergency vehicle would suddenly come into view then fade away just as quickly. If Oliver should have been concerned for his safety, he wasn't. Instead he was focused on the words he would use to smooth things over with Rhine and Monty. Only once his thoughts slipped back to the farm and the worry that might spread over his absence.

Oliver turned his phone off.

The sun, which should have come up an hour ago, was nowhere to be found. Grey clouds hung high above the city and rain fell in steady sheets. Oliver felt lucky to have found an open gas station at the outskirts of D.C. and pumped his almost empty tank full before shooting a hundred dollar bill through the slot and requesting a candy bar and a water from the man behind the glass.

"No water." The man tapped on the handwritten sign taped to the window then pushed the requested candy bar, an unrequested cola, and Oliver's change out through the sliding drawer without further discussion. Though annoyed, Oliver's attention was immediately pulled away by a noticeable increase in street noise. Seemingly out of nowhere, the once empty roadway was flooded with vehicles. From under the shelter of the small gas station overhang Oliver could see all manner of green camouflaged trucks and tanks roll by. He had seen them before, but not so many and not traveling at speeds suggesting a mission rather than a show. After a few minutes Oliver's concentration on the ground was broken by the sound of fighter jets crisscrossing the sky and helicopters filling the airspace below them.

Overkill, Oliver thought. Nevertheless a feeling of uneasiness was growing inside. The unfamiliarity of this familiar setting gnawed at him. Oliver took another bite of candy and a gulp of soda to distract himself, and then tried to focus on how long it would take to get to the office. But his thoughts were interrupted yet again, this time by the sound of a roaring engine reverberating so loudly his body shook and his stomach registered distress. The sight of the huge military plane speeding directly overhead and skimming dangerously close to the top of the gas station caused Oliver to reflexively cover his head and duck.

"What the fuck?" He said out loud to no one. "What the hell is going on?"

Oliver continued to talk to himself as he ran for his car believing the plane to be on the way to crashing into the ground. But the plane lifted up again in time to meet the height of the next tallest building before disappearing into the sky.

Oliver sat behind the wheel of his car and shook for a second before fumbling with the zipper of his jacket. Though D.C. had turned unseasonably cold, Oliver knew the chill he was feeling had nothing to do with the weather.

Chapter 89

Wednesday, April 2, 2025
Benjamin & Mary Gordon
Gordon Family Farm, Pinewood, Pennsylvania

Benjamin wasn't surprised his grandson had left the farm in the middle of the night. He knew the same mechanism that allowed Oliver to deny the human impact of his boss's legislative actions would also allow him to deny the danger he was putting himself in by returning to Washington.

"So he's gone." Oliver's grandmother, Mary, made the statement to Benjamin, not as a question but as a foregone conclusion.

"Yes, as anticipated."

"He'll be safe?"

"Of course."

Oliver's grandmother didn't need to ask twice. Her husband's word was enough.

"When will you be leaving?"

"We're going to give it a few more days, maybe a week. After it's over."

Mary just nodded before moving to make herself a cup of tea.

Chapter 90

Wednesday, April 2, 2025
Oliver Gordon
Washington, D.C.

The roads that led to the city, the ones that usually took Oliver hours to traverse, were clear. Except for an occasional lone car he was free to go in any lane, at any pace. Oliver figured most people had left D.C., if they had a second home or a place to go.

"Deserters," he thought, condemning in his mind their lack of loyalty to God and country.

Minutes after leaving the gas station, Oliver noticed he was being followed. All attempts at trying to believe the drone above was after someone else, some other car, were futile. The aircraft was following his every move. Every left turn and every right, every stop and every start, the drone was there in his rear view mirror. An unnerving feeling that escalated as machine guns conspicuously descended from its underbelly. Oliver's feeling of panic grew, his sense of reality skewed as he fumbled for his phone and searched desperately for an entrance onto the

Beltway. He just wanted to let someone know who he was before some drone-jockey in some office in Utah pressed the wrong button and he became just another statistical casualty on some congressional report.

But his phone wouldn't turn on and every entrance onto the Beltway was closed. Guarded by camo-wearing, automatic rifle toting military personnel and backed up by all manner of tanks and armed Humvees, access to the city seemed impossible. Oliver's fear of itchy trigger-fingered soldiers ran as high as his anxiety over the shadowing drone, so asking for help or directions was not an option. Instead, Oliver drove along the outskirts of D.C., his mind racing, one eye on the road and the other in his rear view mirror as he fumbled with his phone. Still it wouldn't turn on. Cursing, he pulled out the battery and put it back in, causing the phone to light up and slowly resume its functions. Oliver couldn't help but worry that his preoccupation with his phone had allowed him to slip over the speed limit or prompted his driving to become somewhat erratic; two things that would trigger the drone's alarms and alert the operator that something was amiss in the car below. Oliver didn't want to give this flying murder machine any excuse to take him out, but everything seemed too surreal for him to exercise the caution needed to escape suspicion.

By the time the phone displayed a readiness for use, Oliver had found one of the only four remaining openings onto the Belt. The entrance was an army checkpoint and Oliver wasn't sure if he should be relieved or worried. Yes, the drone had not fired at him, and yes, he could clear up any confusion with the soldiers as to who he was, but Oliver had been sweating so profusely he realized he might fall victim to the very same DEAD system that had ensnarled his parents.

Approaching the stop, Oliver thought to roll down his window and allow the driving rain to camouflage his sweat and cool him down. A plan he believed had worked until he heard the words, "Out of the car."

The man in green army fatigues half-covered by a neon-orange rain poncho was serious and seemed angry.

"ID."

Oliver had never been asked for his ID before, usually the sticker on his windshield denoting his Senate parking privileges was enough to allow him to breeze through any check point. Apparently, this was no longer the case.

As Oliver's thoughts and fears moved at breakneck speed and the visceral sensation of fear he had been experiencing continued to grow and distract him, he couldn't help but believe the cool rain was the only thing saving him from being caught by the DEAD sensors and ultimately being jailed.

"ID." The soldier's impatiently stated second request was accompanied by the barrel of a gun inches from Oliver's face. In his absentminded fear, instead of just his identification, Oliver handed the guard his entire wallet.

"Where are you headed?"

As the soldier riffled through the contents of the wallet, Oliver kept telling himself to breathe. He told himself he was doing nothing wrong and tried to convince himself he wasn't about to be taken into custody.

"Work, uh, the capital." Oliver's mouth was drier than he knew and he stumbled to get the words out.

"Who do you work for?"

"Senator Rhine." Normally saying the senator's name was an automatic pass, better than a Senate parking sticker, but today Oliver regretted having to admit the name of his boss. Because, in addition to his other fears, Oliver couldn't help but believe Rhine was somehow behind all of this; the drone, getting stopped, everything.

"He's still alive?"

Oliver didn't know what to answer. Based on the news reports he'd assumed some senators and congressmen had gotten sick but he never thought the all-powerful Rhine would succumb to whatever this disease was. Men like Rhine were carriers of disease, not victims, a belief that made Oliver decide to just assume his boss was alive.

"Yes."

"Well, I hear not many of 'em are. Go ahead." The soldier handed the rain-soaked wallet back to Oliver. "But you'd be better off heading back where you came from."

Without further discussion, and ignoring the soldier's

warning, Oliver got back into his car and headed straight for the capital.

Chapter 91

Wednesday, April 2, 2025
Abigail Gordon and Amanda & General Michael Baylor
Pinewood, Pennsylvania

The usually bright lemon yellow kitchen was bathed in shadows. The storm that had been churning up the coast all night was dumping buckets of much- needed rain on the farm. The general was grabbing the last few moments of solitude before the older Baylors woke from sleep and the youngest of the clan returned from the barn and their morning chores. Over a cooling cup of coffee Michael Baylor poured over the previous night's reports. Arguably there was a case to be made for joy as well as mourning. Such was the conundrum faced by all those in the military, whether they admitted it or not.

You never really win the battle, there's always collateral damage. Innocent people always die, it's just a question of gain. Does the gain justify the loss?" Michael remembered his mentor, General Zeke, saying that every time he was sent to tell a spouse or parents their loved one had died in battle. Based on those experiences, he knew his boss wasn't just talking about actual deaths, collateral damage, babies in the way of a drone strike, or a grandmother standing too close to a car bomb. No, he was talking about the psychic deaths of those the deceased left behind.

Michael wondered if he would ever forget the images of the mothers fainting, the dads admitting their tears were the first they had ever shed. Or the worst, the children, their mothers crying, clinging, gripping them so tight he wanted to turn them loose, rescue them from the tide of soul-drenching tears. The same kind of pain he had heard on the battlefield when a leg or arm had been blown off, severed from the whole of the person. The same pain he had heard from his own mother when a soldier just like himself had come to their door.

A bullshit war. Michael remembered those words repeated over and over again at his father's funeral. Not meant to detract from his dad's service, they told him, but rather to condemn those who sent him to Vietnam in the first place. The innocent sent to die for the guilty. Just like Iraq and Afghanistan, Michael thought. The wars they made him responsible for.

I'm sorry.

How many times had he apologized to loved ones for the crimes of others? He had purposely lost count. But in an ironic twist of fate, staring back at him in black and white were the names—architects, profiteers, those who lobbied for, voted for, and those in charge of all the wars that came after his father's war. Men and women who might have eeked out another ten or twenty years of the excesses and extravagances afforded by their endeavors, had been handed the fate of watching their own loved ones die before succumbing to the ravages of the disease themselves. The same vengeful side that resides in all men and thrives in some made Michael wish to have been there to deliver the crushing blow; your mother is dead, your father is dead, your wife is dead, your child is dead. The same words he had used for them, he now wished to use against them. All their money, powerless against this assault on their bodies, their legacy of supreme wealth slipping through their fingers as each of their heirs passed away one by one.

When Abigail arrived at the back door of the kitchen, soaked from head to toe, Michael barely heard her knock. Without even asking he knew something was wrong.

"Get over by the fire. Take off those wet things." Michael led Abigail to the great room. Even with its expansive space and high ceilings the rustically decorated area adjoining the kitchen warmed up easily thanks to the massive fireplace and wood-burning stove. "Abby, you're shaking." Michael had always been protective of his eldest daughter but since finding out she was carrying his first grandchild, his guard-dog-like instincts were a force to be reckoned with. "Here, take your mom's sweater."

Abigail obliged, removing her now drenched sweatshirt and replacing it with an oversized hand crocheted navy blue sweater, the one with the anchor-adorned gold buttons.

"I'm fine." Abigail knew she wasn't. She'd had a sore throat since last night and had started shivering in the car. Now she couldn't get warm.

"No, you're not. Your lips are literally blue." Abigail's

father grabbed an afghan from the couch and wrapped it around his trembling daughter before going back to the kitchen to make her a cup of tea.

"No Dad, really, I'm just cold, it's cold outside. I'll warm up in a minute."

"You'll have tea."

"Fine." Abigail didn't want tea, but she also didn't want to argue anymore. What she did want was to discuss Oliver. "He left, you know." Abigail could barely get the words out through her chattering teeth.

"I know." Michael didn't care that his son-in-law was in Washington. He expected no less of Oliver and had made the appropriate arrangements for his safety weeks ago, but he could see on his daughter's face she did not share his lack of concern.

"Abby, he will be fine."

"He'll get sick."

"You need to worry about yourself. I bet you have a fever." Michael walked over to his daughter and placed his lips on her forehead the way he had seen his wife do to his daughters hundreds of times. He had no idea what he was supposed to feel, but he was pretty sure it wasn't supposed to be radiating heat. "You're burning up," Michael guessed, though he fully believed he was right.

"Amanda!" Michael bellowed for his wife, who immediately showed up at the landing at the top of the stairs.

"Shhhh. Everyone is still sleeping." Amanda Baylor had her index finger over her lips and tried to get her message across in a loud whisper.

"Don't care. Abby's here, she's sick. Call the doctor." Amanda had rarely heard that level of worry come from her husband, the general. Immediately, the possibility that her daughter might have caught the virus flashed through her thoughts.

"Take her to the guest room," was Amanda Baylor's hurried response before running to get the doctor on the phone.

Chapter 92

Wednesday, April 2, 2025
Oliver Gordon
Washington, D.C.

The remainder of Oliver's trip had been uneventful. Someone, somewhere, had called off the drone and traffic was light. Even the usually filled parking lot at the Capital obliged by being practically empty. Oliver pulled into one of the closest spaces he had ever gotten and pushed away the fleeting thought that perhaps the checkpoint soldier was right about most of Congress succumbing to the disease.

Oliver heard his footsteps against the uncharacteristically less than shiny floors of the Capitol. An unfamiliar antiseptic smell permeated his nostrils. All around handwritten signs saying "Take a mask!" had been taped to the walls. Each sign had an arrow pointing downward to a table beneath. Each table held a box of masks, hand sanitizer by the gallon, and instructions for good hygiene. Ignoring the signs, Oliver moved past the zigzag of ropes and stanchions set up by security, and proceeded directly to the front of the line.

"Sir, you will need to get a mask and go to the end of the line."

The Marine corporal named Bingham, wearing his own mask and gloves, pointed to the space behind the eight people waiting in line. Oliver hadn't even noticed there was a line. He was used to the privileges afforded to those associated with members of Congress. He was used to Jack and Mike, the guys from the private security firm. For years they had been allowing him to walk past their post, sans I.D., with all manner of boxes, bags, and suitcases without once flinching or looking inside, even when the alarms sounded as he breezed through. Oliver quickly realized his security friends were most likely at home hiding under their beds like the rest of America, while the Marines were in place exhibiting the bravery and dedication that apparently had failed to make it from the private security firm's brochures to its staff.

Annoyed with Jack and Mike and assuming the futility of arguing with the Marine, Oliver grabbed a mask from the table and shoved it in his pocket. Then, as instructed, Oliver moved to the opening marked "ENTER" and made his way through the unnecessary twists and turns of the mostly empty line. Eight people ahead of him. Oliver tapped his foot and repeatedly looked at his watch. No one moved. Oliver stretched his neck to see past the line of mask-covered individuals and tried to fathom why so simple a task had caused such a massive delay.

Put your fucking briefcases and pocketbooks on the conveyor belt and walk through the fucking scanner. It's not goddamn rocket science, Oliver said to himself raising his own level of annoyance.

"What the hell," was the only part of his thoughts he actually said out loud but no one on the line bothered to look up from their phones to entertain his frustrations.

Annoyed at his irrelevance, Oliver pulled out his own phone and noticed that there were twenty-seven messages from his wife, the latest of which was open on the screen.

Oliver, I'm sick. Staying with my parents. Call me please!

Oliver didn't bother to check the other messages. He assumed the first ten or fifteen would be doused in Abigail's anger at his having left the farm, and the rest would express her concern for him. And, though for the most part he was right, it was his denial of worry for his wife's wellbeing that led him to ignore the message staring back at him from the screen. Oliver made a mental note to call Abigail right after he spoke with Rhine and Monty, before that he would have nothing new to tell her.

Seven people. "Finally." Oliver's comment was sarcastic in tone. Again the line ignored him.

"Meekens." Out of the corner of his eye, on the other side of the security area, Oliver had spotted Mark Montgomery's Chief of Staff and called out to him. When he received no response, Oliver couldn't help but wonder if Shaun Meekens could be added to the list of people who hated him, even though just last week he would have considered this man his friend. Oliver had known Meekens and his wife Sandra for years and they had spent a considerable amount of time socializing at fundraisers, junkets and simulated charity events staged to create photo ops for Senators. But D.C. turned on its own axis and friendships, like loyalty, were fleeting things in this town that valued money and power over everything else. Nevertheless, Oliver decided to try again.

"Hey, Meekens!" Oliver's second louder demand for attention was also in vain as almost immediately he saw the imposing six-foot-three figure fall to the ground and begin a series of twitching movements. Even though he was too far away to see the pain on Meekens' face, the paleness of his skin or the sweat emanating from his every pore, Oliver immediately knew his friend was sick with the virus, a foregone conclusion that set off a series of racing thoughts of his wife and grandfather warning him of the dangers of leaving the farm. Thoughts that led Oliver to remain perfectly still and silently justify his inaction. *I'm no Boy Scout. Besides, there are plenty of qualified people here to administer aid.*

Oliver looked around, searching to see who would be the first to help his friend. The six people left in line were still preoccupied with their phones, and security was so focused on their own screens and scanners they were totally oblivious to everything going on around them.

Suddenly Oliver's stance for inaction seemed untenable and he found himself obligatorily bending under the stanchion ropes and heading towards his friend on the other side of the security area.

"Sir, stop!"

Oliver didn't answer, but instead pointed as he moved in Meekens' direction.

"Stop!" Two marines were simultaneously yelling at Oliver.

"Over there," Oliver responded, assuming the guards would catch on, as he continued walking quickly and pointing–a critical error in judgment and one that he had no time to correct before being thrown head first to the ground and handcuffed.

Chapter 93

Wednesday, April 2, 2025
Abigail Gordon and Amanda & General Michael Baylor
Pinewood, Pennsylvania

The guest room on the first floor of the Baylor farm was massively large and contained two queen size poster beds, two walk-in closets, and two en suite bathrooms. The walls were covered in beige wallpaper with pink pinstripes and tiny white flowers, and there was a large bay window with a window seat overlooking the man-made lake behind the house. Originally the room had been designed for the twins but they rejected the idea of sleeping on the first floor, wanting instead to be upstairs within shouting distance of their parents. A request they would soon outgrow.

"That Gordon farm is too drafty for a pregnant woman." Michael took the empty cup of tea from his daughter's hands. The porcelain was still warm to the touch. "I should have realized." Michael shook his head. "As soon as I get you settled I'm going to call for Kendall, too. I'm sure she'll appreciate a good night's sleep in a warm, comfortable bed. Now, lie down and get some rest."

"Daddy, I'm fine." Abigail's words were not the least bit convincing to him. "Daddy, I want to talk about Oliver."

"Abby, trust me he will be okay," Michael tried to reassure his teary-eyed daughter for the second time since she had arrived at his doorstep. "Trust me," The General repeated to her again.

Abigail trusted her father but the reality of the situation pushed his assurances aside. There were far were too many reasons to fear for her husband's life.

"They're dying, Dad. People are dying in Washington. And what about Rhine and Monty? Dad, you know they'll do whatever they need to do to stay out of jail and in power." Abigail was crying again. She wanted to be angry at her husband, she was angry, but she kept crying. In fact, Abigail had spent much of the morning crying. A contradiction of emotions she wrote off as being tied to the same pregnancy hormones that now made her sick to her stomach.

"Trust me…" The General tried again to ease his daughter's fears then stopped himself. His bromides were not working. *And why should they,* he thought. When it came down to it he was no longer one hundred percent sure he had actually kept his own daughter safe. Michael allowed himself to wonder if perhaps Abigail had somehow slipped through his protective net. Had she inadvertently been exposed? In his mind, Michael quickly ran through the safeguards he had put in place for his daughter, but the sinking feeling he had missed something made his legs feel weak and his forehead sweat. Thoughts that could have easily spun out of control if they had not been interrupted by his wife's entrance into the bedroom.

"Sweetheart." Amanda Baylor ran into the room and wrapped her soft-pink cashmere covered arms around her daughter. "The doctor will be here soon, baby." Amanda pushed the covers up to her daughters chin and silently prayed that her daughter was not as sick as she looked.

"Mom, Oliver went to Washington."

"He's fine, baby."

"No, no, you don't understand."

"I understand that your dad has taken care of everything and that you need to get some rest. Tell her, Michael."

For his part, Michael could no longer watch his daughter cry and decided to do whatever he needed to do to put his daughter's mind at ease so that she could get some rest.

"Abigail, you can't tell anyone this." Michael made his words sound serious and convincing. "Not anyone. Not even Oliver." Michael took a break to run the impromptu lie through his mind one more time. "When Oliver went to Coney Island he was inoculated against the disease."

"He didn't mention that."

"He didn't know.

"But wait, what about us? Have you been inoculated? Me? The Gordons? Why not all of us?" Until now Abigail had believed Benjamin's assurances that she was safe, that they were all safe from the virus; but the possibility that her sore throat and her fever could be more than just the flu terrified her. "Do I have the virus?"

"No, of course not, Abby; none of us were exposed to the disease, I can promise you that." Michael's lie was convincing to his daughter.

"And Rhine and Monty?

"Rhine's already dead. Most of his buddies are or will be soon. Monty will succumb shortly. I give it a day or two at best." The information Michael had held so tightly, now rolled off his lips as if it was no longer a secret.

In response, Abigail's relief that her husband would be safe was palpable. Her tears dried almost as fast as her shoulders relaxed and a tired smile returned to her face. Yet behind her relief and hidden from her father's view, were still questions, one more disturbing than the next. How was Oliver given an injection without his knowing? Who made the decision not to inoculate the family? Why were thousands of people being allowed to die when there was a vaccine that could save them? Questions Abigail knew her father wouldn't answer without prodding. Luckily for Michael, Abigail was far too sick to deal with anything but sleep.

Chapter 94

Wednesday, April 2, 2025
Benjamin Gordon
General Michael Baylor
Pinewood, Pennsylvania

The stress of the morning and her fever, which registered one hundred and three, had taken its toll. Abigail slipped into a quiet sleep as Michael and Amanda looked on. Both felt it necessary to watch the rise and fall of their daughter's blankets to be sure she was still breathing.

As he waited impatiently for the doctor to arrive, Michael began sending a series of encrypted messages to Benjamin.

> Abigail has a high fever and a sore throat.
> She is resting.
> The doctor has been called.

Then the question Michael didn't want to ask but had to.

> Did we miss something? Could she have the virus?

The answer came back from Benjamin swiftly and definitively.

> Absolutely not.

Michael wished he could feel relieved.

Chapter 95

Wednesday, April 2, 2025
Abigail Gordon and Amanda & General Michael Baylor
Pinewood, Pennsylvania

With her long strawberry blond waves of hair, her short tight skirts, and her three inch heels, Hanna London looked nothing like anyone's image of a country doctor. The only hint of her standing in the medical community was the old black leather medical bag her great-grandfather had given her when she was no more than four years old. At the time, Hanna had used the bag to carry her Barbie dolls and their clothes. A funny sight she was, a little peanut of a girl carrying a masculine looking satchel that weighed almost as much as she did. Yet for Hanna it was the perfect case. Its wide opening clearly displayed its contents, while its ample size allowed her to carry enough dolls and outfits to keep her busy for hours while her parents played in pinochle tournaments. Hanna never thought about why she had been given the doctor's bag, or that its benefactor might have had an ulterior motive, until the day come when she replaced her Barbie dolls with books.

"You're so good in science." "Just try pre-med, if you don't like it you can always switch majors." The messages were not subtle and Hanna realized early on that anything but being

a doctor was never going to be an option. Luckily she loved pre-med and medical school and never regretted her decision; until her residency opened her eyes to the realities of practicing medicine in 2020. In order to obtain privileges at a hospital doctors had to sign on the dotted line and join a hospital-owned practice or be left out in the cold.

So right where her family always intended her to be, Dr. Hanna London was out in the cold.

No matter that she had wiped her feet on the rug multiple times, Hanna's high heels left a dozen tiny wet imprints on the polished dark wood floors of the entranceway. An indiscretion she easily missed due to a distraught Amanda Baylor greeting her at the door.

"He says it's not the virus but, Hanna, I'm not sure."

Yes, Michael had promised Amanda that all her children would be safe from the disease now ravaging their old neighborhood in D.C., killing their friends and neighbors. But now that one of her daughters was lying in bed with a rising fever Amanda couldn't help but worry her husband's assurances might have been nothing more than an empty promise.

"Where is she?"

"In the guest room." Amanda led the way while she ran through her daughter's symptoms.

"Since I spoke to you on the phone her temperature has gone up, it's one O three now. She has chills and she says her back hurts and…" Amanda stopped in front of the guest room leaving Hanna to grab for the doorknob.

"You know she's pregnant, right?" Amanda whispered just as Hanna swung open the door.

"Uncle Michael." Even as an adult, Hanna had not broken the habit of calling close family friends aunt and uncle.

"Hanna." Silently Michael followed her name with the word *banana,* a combination that had stuck in his head twenty-five odd years ago and never left.

After the two hugged, the usual pleasantries were skipped to focus on Abigail.

"Abby." Hanna forced herself to smile at her childhood best friend who looked far more ill than Hanna had imagined she would. "So I hear you're not feeling well." Hanna hoped her bedside manner was disguising her real concern.

"Yeah, not feeling great, Han."

Hanna couldn't help but notice the sweat pouring off Abigail's forehead as she grabbed her friend's wrist to check her pulse.

"Okay, well if you two will leave me be…" Hanna pulled her stethoscope and blood pressure cuff out of her bag. "I will get this patient up and about in no time."

Hanna's lie was obvious. Neither Amanda nor Michael expected their daughter to be out of bed anytime soon.

"Sooo…" Hanna waited to finish her sentence until Abigail's parents were out of the room and out of earshot. "When was my best friend going to tell me she was married?" Hanna placed the blood pressure cuff around her friend's arm. "And pregnant."

Abigail listened to the puffing sound as the cuff tightened around her arm. "Ow." Everything in Abigail's body hurt.

"Your pressure is low, Abby."

"Do I have the virus Han?"

"No. That you don't have." Benjamin had assured Hanna that Abigail wasn't exposed and she trusted his word implicitly.

"Then what is wrong? Will my baby be okay?"

"Patience, Abby, let me finish. My God, you haven't changed a bit."

Abigail smiled weakly, knowing her friend was right, patience was not her virtue.

"How are the kids?" Abigail tried to make small talk to distract herself from the discomfort of the non-stop poking and prodding

"Good. Mia's working on a fourth grade level but she's only six and Ethan is on track to graduate high school in a few weeks."

"How old…ow…is he?"

"Ten. Roll over on your side."

"Ten and he's graduating high school?"

"Yeah, Abby, they've dumbed it down that much, but we supplement his education. Deep breath. When did you get married?" Hanna knew the answer to her question. Being much more on the inside of things, Hanna was privy to all kinds of information.

"Ow! Shit, Hanna."

"Sorry. Here, pee in this." Hanna held up a clear plastic cup with a white plastic lid and waited impatiently, first for Abigail to slowly shuffle back and forth to the bathroom and then for the test strip to yield the results.

"Nitrite. UTI. Shit," Hanna said under her breath as the test strip turned color.

"How long have you had a back ache?"

"A few days?" Abigail didn't want to admit she'd been in pain for the better part of a week and didn't go to the doctor. Like all women, Abigail knew to avoid the medical community in the early stages of pregnancy just in case something went wrong. Better to suffer a miscarriage at home, in silence, than run the risk of being accused of murdering a fetus.

"Are you sure you don't mean a week?"

"Maybe five days?" Abigail could never lie to her friend. "Okay a week."

"That's what I thought." Hanna was not upset with her friend, she was upset for her. The intravenous antibiotics she would have to use to rid Abigail of her urinary tract infection, and save her kidneys and ultimately her life from the onslaught of sepsis, brought with it a high risk to the fetus. No hospital doctor in their right mind would order those meds for a pregnant woman. They would by law have to allow Abigail, and ultimately the fetus, to die in order to preserve the sanctity of human life.

Chapter 96

Wednesday, April 2, 2025
Oliver Gordon
Washington, D.C.

The space Oliver occupied was the newest construction to take place in the Capital. A congressional mandate had ordered the grey double brick walled room to be built inside the security office in the basement of the building. On one side of the room stood a metal table and two chairs that were bolted to the ground, and on the other side was a nine by twelve cell that housed a bed, toilet, sink and now Oliver.

To Oliver, who had both broken his watch and lost his cellphone in the scuffle upstairs, time had become an irrelevant unit of measurement. The only hint that it might be sometime around noon was the arrival of his lunch through the slot in the bars of his cell.

"Hey, wait," Oliver called out to the guard, then immediately regretted his decision to speak loudly as the pain caused by his own words shot through his head.

"What?" The guard named Miller, whose responsibilities were limited to watching one camera trained on one cell and delivering three meals a day to the prisoner in that same cell, was exceedingly annoyed at the prospect of being imposed upon. *Probably wants me to cut his meat.*

"I want to call my lawyer." Oliver responded more quietly so as not to cause his head more pain.

"Yeah, and I want a trip to Bermuda. Looks like neither one of us is going to get what we want."

The guard flashed Oliver a fake smile then slammed the door behind him.

Chapter 97

Wednesday, April 2, 2025
Gordon Farm
Pinewood, Pennsylvania

Oliver's return to Washington, and the news that Abigail was so sick, left the Gordon household in a state of upset. Tempers grew short and much of what was said was not meant. Kendall found it especially difficult to curb her fear-based angry tirades. Out she came with words of resentment and regret, for getting married and pregnant, for being a Gordon and for living on a farm. Everyone was to blame for her worry but no one blamed Kendall for her inability to articulate her real fear for her baby. Instead they blamed her hormones.

The weather had forced the outdoor work off the list for the day. Instead of preparing the soil for transplanting the already late beans, cabbage, cauliflower, and lettuce seedlings into the ground, Kris and Tyler continued framing and dry walling the living areas with the supplies that had been hidden in the bunker. For Kendall and Andrew this was the perfect time to rework the budget based on the additional money and provisions also provided by the storage area below.

"He's such a selfish prick, your brother." Kendall had lost focus on the food list and was at it again.

"He is indeed." Andrew didn't like to hear his own words coming from his wife and he was extremely relieved Abigail was not around to hear them. "We can allocate more food per person, even though we have more people in the house right now." Getting back to the subject at hand was the best way Andrew knew of to calm his wife's negative thoughts.

"It's a total relief. I have to say, I was really getting sick of sandwiches."

"And soup." Andrew ate what the budget allowed for but was always unhappy when soup was on the menu.

"Did you defrost the…"

"I did." Before Kendall could finish her sentence, their grandmother entered the room with a package wrapped in butcher paper.

"Yea." Kendall had craved beef for weeks and finally, thanks to the bunker's freezer, her prayers had been answered.

"I'll put it in the crockpot." Mary crossed the floor to the tiny makeshift kitchen, which consisted of a variety of small appliances and a sink. "It will be ready by dinner. Then I want you downstairs with me for your lessons."

Kendall had actually been looking forward to what

Andrew's grandmother had deemed her lessons but she was not looking forward to spending time in the claustrophobic bunker. Though technically the room was spacious, Benjamin had told her it was more than three-thousand square feet, there was something disquieting about the low ceilings and lack of windows that made Kendall want to be upstairs.

"Can we do the lessons up here?"

"We could. If you can get your husband to bring up the sewing machine, we can pick out the fabric and the yarn after we deal with this roast."

Without being asked directly, Andrew rose from his chair to retrieve the sewing machine.

"You know, eventually we can learn how to make our own wool." The thought of teaching Kendall the crafts she herself had learned as a child was exciting to Mary.

"You know how to do that?" Though Kendall had stopped being surprised at what her husband's grandparents could bring to the table, shearing sheep and making wool seemed far beyond their range of expertise.

"I grew up on a farm."

"You never told me."

"There's a lot I haven't told anybody." Mary's answer was cryptic but not surprising given that there was little doubt in anyone's mind, least of all Kendall's, that their Grandmother knew a lot of things she wasn't telling anyone.

"I think Abby will want to learn too. Have you heard from her?"

"Last I heard they were waiting for the doctor." Mary's usually stoic expression gave way to a level of upset she rarely shared with the younger members of the Gordon family. It was a look that frightened Kendall, and instinctively compelled her to rest her hand on her small bulging stomach.

Chapter 98

Wednesday April 2, 2025
Abigail Gordon and Amanda & General Michael Baylor
Pinewood, Pennsylvania

By the time Hanna had called Michael and Amanda back into the room, Abigail's face was wet with tears. She didn't have to hear the words or be told a specific diagnosis, the look on Hanna's face was all she needed to know that things were bad and were likely to get worse.

"This particular antibiotic is contraindicated for pregnant women. In this case…"

"Then use another one." Michael's interruption did not come as a surprise to Hanna, she was quite used to the behaviors of desperate parents.

"This is a particular type of bacteria, I'll need to use the right meds to fight it."

"So I'll lose the baby?" Abigail closed her eyes and braced herself for Hanna's reponse.

"It's a possibility." Out loud Hanna said half the truth, inside she told herself the rest. *A very strong possibility."*

Abigail looked back and forth between her parents,

her desperation read on her face. But no one moved or spoke, instead they allowed the quiet to absorb the shock.

Five seconds, then ten, until finally Abigail's heart could no longer contain her grief. With fists slamming against the mattress and gut cries of anguish pouring out, Abigail's thoughts tore at her. *Why didn't I go to the doctor? Why didn't I take better care of myself? Why did I...* The list grew larger with each passing second. Abigail's lungs gasped for the air she couldn't find. Michael had to look away.

"Abby, listen to me." Hanna leaned over her patient and grabbed both of her hands. "Abby, breath, slowly, take a breath." Hanna modeled the length and pace of breaths she wanted her friend to take and soon Abigail followed. "Look the important thing is for you not to worry." Hanna squeezed Abigail's hands. "I need you to rest now and leave the worrying to me." Hanna looked right into her friend's eyes but Abigail could barely see her through the blur of tears.

"Now, say goodbye," Still holding Abigail's hands, Hanna turned her head and her comments toward Michael and Amanda. If there was any possibility of her keeping her patient calm, Abigail's visibly distraught parents would have to leave the room. "You two go about your day. I've got this."

Following Hanna's direction, Michael moved to his daughter and kissed the top of her head. "You listen to the doctor and get some rest and you'll be fine in no time." Michael's words were trite and he knew it but he also understood that anything else would have started Abigail crying again.

"Get some sleep, baby." Amanda Baylor kissed her daughter's wet cheek as her own eyes filled with the tears she had willed herself not to shed. "We need to pray and stay positive, Abby." Amanda's words were an order to herself as much as they were for her daughter. "You need your rest. Now sleep."

Chapter 99

Thursday, April 3, 2025
Oliver Gordon
Washington, D.C.

Just before Oliver fell asleep he realized for the first time that no one, at least no one who mattered to him, knew where he was.

"Well, I see you've gotten yourself into a bit of trouble here. Not many people get to spend a night in a terrorist holding cell." The familiar voice forced Oliver to open his eyes and sit up before he was ready to. The striking pain in his head forced him back down.

"Nothing's too good for Senate staffers," Oliver said barely above a whisper.

"Okay, well you want to tell me what happened so I can get you out of here?" Monty was standing inches from the cell's bars taking in the paucity of Oliver's surroundings.

"You're going to help me get out of here?" Oliver sat up again, this time more slowly.

"If I can. It's not easy to spring a terrorist." Monty laughed for the security cameras.

"Ironic, you try to kill me and I'm the terrorist." Oliver only thought twice about the possible consequences of his words after he said them.

"Kill you? Someone tried to kill you?" Though Monty seemed genuinely confused, Oliver no longer trusted anything the senator had to say.

"That was the assumption. He had a gun and he was following me."

"Who? When was this?"

"You want the details so you can try again?"

"I'm telling you, I don't know anything about it. Why would I want you dead?"

Oliver moved off his cot and towards the bars and spoke to Monty in a whisper.

"I guess you don't remember threatening me?"

"Threatening? I was warning you. You were angry, you weren't thinking straight." Monty's words flowed thought his clenched teeth. "I was trying to slow you down, make you think before you started something you couldn't stop." Monty's frustration with his friend was rising and he worked to calm himself down. "What do you think would have happened if you told everyone what you knew?"

"You and Rhine would be in here, and I'd be out there."

"Spare me the fantasy. You think he'd roll over? He

would have thrown your ass under the bus or really had you killed."

"Really killed?"

"I don't know who you think was after you, but it wasn't one of Rhine's guys. They don't miss their targets… ever. Besides, I never told Rhine you knew about the shipments. I figured you'd come to your senses and play along."

Play along. The words stuck in Oliver's thoughts as he tried to figure out if that was true.

"So all that 'remember Jim' stuff was a warning?"

"What else? Did you really think I wanted my best friend to end up like Jim, dead on the side of a mountain somewhere?"

"You didn't exactly sound like anyone's best friend when you were saying it."

"Like we never had an argument before? Please, when I cooled down I texted you. It was you who never responded."

"I didn't get any texts."

"Don't blame me. I sent them."

Oliver worked to process everything he was hearing. Where were the texts? What if he had stayed in Washington instead of going to Coney Island? Who sent the man with the gun? Questions, confusion—and no answers.

"Look, do you want my help or not? I've got a lot to do and not a lot of time to get it done."

"Wait, how did you know I was here?"

"Shaun saw you taken away."

"That was yesterday. Guess you thought it was a good idea to let me rot in here overnight?" Oliver pretended to be joking.

"I was with Shaun all night, at the hospital." Monty's tone turned solemn. "He died this morning."

"Shit."

"Yeah, shit. That's what it's been like around here, a whole bunch of shit. Four of my staffers…" Monty stopped, the way one does when they don't want to hear the truth themselves.

"Dead?"

"Yeah." As Monty rubbed his eyes Oliver noticed for the first time how pale his friend looked. How the normally well rested, health obsessed senator had dark circles under his eyes and seemed thinner than he remembered.

"Are you okay?"

"Yeah. It's just been crazy. We're all dropping like flies and no one knows what the hell this damn AmeriVirux thing is or how to stop it."

"How many?"

"Don't know, fucking can't keep up. Half of Washington left town but we still keep getting calls. They're all dying; at home, here, no matter where they are, they're dying."

"How's my staff?"

"You didn't hear?"

"No."

"Your staff's gone, all of them."

"All?"

Monty shook his head affirmatively instead of speaking.

Immediately, Oliver began thinking about what staffers he might be able to steal from other senators.

"Rhine's dead too." Monty interrupted Oliver's thoughts.

"What?" Oliver stepped back from the bars, his mind raced with possibilities. He had just spent the better part of a week hating his boss's traitorous guts, so feeling anything but relief at word of his death would not have made sense to him. Instead he chose to marvel at the fact that the virus everyone feared so much was going to create huge opportunities for him. Oliver smiled.

"Hey. I see you're all broken up over your boss's demise." Monty laughed at his friend. He knew when Oliver was calculating and it looked nothing like grieving.

Chapter 100

Thursday, April 3, 2025
Abigail Gordon and Amanda & General Michael Baylor
Pinewood, Pennsylvania

In hushed tones around the kitchen table Hanna spoke to Abigail's parents about their daughter's restless night, her virtually unstoppable tears and about how to get Oliver back to the farm.

"I'll be honest with you, the likelihood of Abby maintaining the pregnancy is not good." Hanna issued the dire warning to Amanda and Michael again. "I really think you should see about getting her husband up here."

"I'll go over and talk to Ben. They're going to want an update on Abby's condition anyway, and these things are best done in person. It's his grandchild too." Michael's eyes closed. Tears don't always sting, but this time they did.

"If you don't mind, I'll stay here for a few more days until Abby's through the worst of it." As Hanna spoke, she made arrangements in her head. Her husband would take over her patients and the kids would be fine. Like the Gordons and the Baylors, the London household was filled with extended family.

"Of course you can stay." Amanda's relief took the form of a sigh. "I wish we had a guest room for you…"

"Aunt Amanda, please, your house is as filled to the brim as mine." Hanna's mind flashed to her home. What was once a spacious oasis of quiet and privacy had become a noisy, bustling collection of relatives and all their stuff. "At least this place is quiet."

Chapter 101

Thursday, April 3, 2025
Oliver Gordon
Washington, D.C.

It was much easier than Monty had expected to get Oliver out of jail, mainly because the powers that be, those who would normally hold up the paperwork for days, weeks, maybe months, were gone. "Fled or dead" was the new phrase around town that most easily explained the easing of the constipational grip those in charge generally had on Washington.

"I have some clothes in the office. I'll go down to the gym and get washed up. Meet you for lunch?" Oliver had been in the same clothing for more than twenty-four hours and all he wanted to do was to grab a shower and change.

"Gym's closed, dude. Cafeteria, too. Hell you can't even get a food truck to stop within a hundred miles of this place." Monty couldn't believe how quickly Oliver had become disconnected from the realities of Washington. "Here, we have to wear these whenever we're outside our offices." Monty pulled two masks from a table as they walked by.

"I'm not wearing one of those fucking things."

"Really? You're out of jail five minutes and already you feel compelled to break the rules?" Monty didn't know whether to laugh at his friend or be annoyed with him as he pulled one of the masks to his face.

"I need a phone." Oliver changed the subject as he stretched the elastic band so the mask rested on his head.

"Fine, I'll change in my office and we can go out."

"Out where?"

"L'Enfant, Anacostia's or Jenkin's Grill is fine. Unless you want sushi?" Oliver was suddenly looking forward to a five star lunch. He should, he ventured, be able to put it all on his deceased boss's tab.

"Closed, closed and closed. Do you understand what's going on here? Seriously, a restaurant?"

"What?" Oliver had no way of realizing that his same lack of concern and caring for the untimely demise of his colleagues had also impeded his ability to understand the true gravity of the situation.

"Most of us are dying and those who aren't don't want to stand around and watch us die. I'm leaving tomorrow. If this shit's going to take me I want to see my parents first."

"Who's going to run the government?"

"Does it really matter anymore? What's there to run?

The world out there is standing still. Everyone's at home holding their breaths hoping to have enough food and water to make it through whatever this is." Monty's voice echoed the resignation he felt.

"All the more reason to make sure everything is okay."

"What does that mean? Nothing's okay. Nothing will ever be okay again. Face it, in a week's time there's the very real possibility that we could all be dead, and it's all our fault."

"Whose fault?"

"Us. Congress."

"We don't even know what's causing this thing, but you're going to pin it on Congress?"

"It was us. We lost sight of the big picture."

"What the hell are you talking about?"

"The CDC. If it was up and running, it might have been able to warn us about the virus or stopped it before it got out of hand."

"Yeah, that's what we need, a crew of incompetent government employees guessing at what's making people sick then putting a bunch of rules in place. Like this BS." Oliver pulled the blue preformed mask away from his head and snapped it back. "If they don't know what's causing this thing and they haven't been able to stop it, what jackass decided we needed to wear a mask?"

From behind his own mask, Monty smiled. "You're

right about the masks but I'm still pining for a little science."

"Yeah, well more importantly, what's with the president?" Again Oliver shifted the focus of a conversation to evade an answer.

"Who knows? Bunker, I think? Lotta good it'll do him. Like I said, the boys on Capitol Hill are dying no matter where they rest their head at night, same goes for the White House. Joint chiefs, the cabinet, even the kitchen staff I hear have been pretty much decimated.

Oliver felt like his hearing was playing tricks on him. The neat, easy, orderly world he had come back to Washington to retrieve was, with every word, more and more unrecoverable.

"At least you're okay. That's what's important." Monty forced a smile onto his face. "Maybe your being out of the office for the past few days helped you escape whatever this is. You should leave before it catches up to you. You don't want to get Abby sick either."

"Abby, sick." Oliver repeated the words out loud. *Oliver, I'm sick. Staying with my parents. Call me please!* The words from Abigail's text came flooding back through Oliver's mind, only this time they took on a whole new meaning. Yesterday, "sick" had meant a cold, maybe a stomach ache. And at the time he even considered the possibility that the text might have been a ploy to get him to call. Now the same words rolling around in Oliver's imagination took on only one meaning. Sick now meant virus.

Desperately, Oliver tried to ignore his own thoughts, but his new unwelcomed clarity continued pushing forward. *Fool,* he berated himself for ignoring his wife and ultimately his child. *Asshole,* he called himself for dismissively rejecting the warnings he had been given by his grandfather. *"I could lose them both, Abigail and the baby,"* was the final thought that sent Oliver over the edge, purging his body of strength and plunging his thoughts into a pool of fear so great he could no longer see two steps in front of him. Instead all he could see in his mind's eye was the terrifying image of two white caskets.

"I need to call Abby."

Chapter 102

Thursday, April 3, 2025
Benjamin Gordon & Michael Baylor
Gordon Farm, Pinewood, Pennsylvania

From his sources in Washington, Benjamin knew his grandson had spent the night safely in jail. He also knew Oliver was now flying back to Pennsylvania, courtesy of his deceased boss.

Michael Baylor drove his Mercedes around the back of the barn and pulled through the open door of the makeshift garage.

"Ben." Michael stepped out of his car and offered his friend a lackluster handshake followed by an equally anemic hug.

"General." Benjamin was at a loss to find the steady strength that was the hallmark of his friend. "You look tired."

"I've given up sleep. It's overrated." No one but Hanna knew of Michael's night spent pacing in front of his daughter's doorway.

"How's Abigail?"

"Sleeping a lot. Fever's gone down a bit. Hanna's fairly confident she'll make a full recovery. "

"And the baby?"

"I'm afraid the prognosis isn't as good." Michael wished he didn't have to tell the truth. "She's giving the baby about a five percent chance of survival."

"How's Abigail taking it?"

"Hard, very hard. We all are. Except for Amanda."

"Amanda?"

"Yeah, my wife's convinced everything's going to be okay. Don't know why."

"And you?"

"Honestly, I don't know what to think. I just want them both to be okay."

"God-willing." Benjamin bowed his head the way one does when speaking directly to God.

"So, where's our boy?" Michael's annoyance was clear. Even though he himself had spent many nights away from his family under the banner of patriotism, Michael was on the other side now, uncomfortably watching his daughter desperately need her husband.

"He's in the air now, should be to your place within the hour." Even if he couldn't save his great-grandchild, Benjamin could at least feel like he was keeping a handle on the rest of his family.

"Good."

"Does Abigail know he's on his way?"

"No, I decided not to tell her in case my son-in-law had a change of heart and made them turn the plane around."

"Not going to happen."

"I'd ask how you can be sure…" Before Michael could finish his sentence, Benjamin did.

"The pilot works for us."

For the first time since his arrival, Michael smiled. But it was a short lived feeling as he remembered how much he wanted to be back home watching over his daughter.

"Ben, give my best to Mary and the family." Michael's announcement of departure as he got into his car felt too abrupt.

"Sure I can't tempt you with some of Mary's homemade coffee cake?" Benjamin took a stab at slowing his friend down.

"I'll take a rain check." Michael called from the window as he backed up the car significantly faster than he should have.

PART 9

During the flight to Pennsylvania Oliver bargained with God. In exchange for the health and safety of his wife and child, he would, he promised, get his spiritual house in order by attending temple with his grandfather every Friday night and church with his wife every Sunday. He also intended to make amends to his family, his brothers for starters and his father, if he was still alive. He would be perfect, he vowed. He would do anything, if only God would stop trying to destroy his life.

Chapter 103

Sunday, April 6, 2025
Oliver Gordon
Baylor Farm, Pinewood, Pennsylvania

Oliver sat at his wife's bedside for three days as she moved in and out of a restless, fever-driven, sleep. Whenever Abigail would awaken, she would do so with tears in her eyes and Oliver would start apologizing again. Any further conversation between the two centered around Oliver's insistence that his wife eat the latest hot meal sitting on the tray on her bedside table. Eventually Abigail would think to ask how the food was always waiting, and always hot. Then Oliver would tell her that he had watched her so carefully that he could sense when she was about to wake up. An admission that offered Abigail the sense of wellbeing she knew her husband had always been capable of providing.

In low toned whispers, Oliver spoke with Hanna about his wife and his baby, and about all manner of things the two couldn't agree on. An unnerving mix of oil and water they were. Unlike Abigail's palatably subtle and easily ignored approach to all things political, Hanna's overly confident, straight forward, shoot-from-the-hip, in your face style made Oliver's blood boil.

"Are you f'ing kidding me?" Oliver's restraint from using actual expletives was in deference to Hanna's gender and had nothing to do with the outrage he felt.

"Are you kidding me? You think smashing our healthcare system to smithereens was a good idea?"

"Medicaid and Medicare were bullshit. Too expensive. It was thirty percent of the federal budget when we finally pulled the plug on that socialist nightmare. And the ACA, what was it called, Obamashitcare? Don't even get me started about that commie train wreck. Good riddance to all of it."

Oliver's wall of deflection was familiar to Hanna. "Yes, use words like socialist and commie instead of cogent arguments for having taken everyone's health insurance away. Brilliant."

"Not everyone. I have insurance. I'm sure you'll be billing them for all this."

Selfish, egotistical prick. Hanna worked to keep her worst thoughts to herself.

"You are so clueless. You think I'm here for the money?"

"That and the fact that for some reason the General seems to trust you." Oliver didn't bother to mention how much praise the general had heaped on Hanna.

"I came so your wife didn't have to go into a hospital.

Because if she did, they wouldn't have given her the antibiotics she needed because of the risk to the baby. And no, I won't be billing the insurance company because if they figured out what I did, she and I would both go to jail. And if, God forbid, your wife were to miscarry, all of us would be on trial for murder. Me and Abby for sure, and the rest of you as accessories."

"Murder, oh please, you know as well as I do the General could get his daughter anything she needed without consequence. Laws don't apply to everyone, you know." Oliver smiled as if he had already won the argument, but continued nonetheless. "And as for payment, look around." Oliver scanned the room with all its designer fabrics, expensive knickknacks and original oil paintings. "The General has deep pockets, so you know you'll get paid with or without insurance." Oliver had quickly and skillfully moved the conversation away from his wife and back onto the subject of money. "Face it, doc, you liked the old system because you could charge an insurance company an arm and a leg for an office visit. Now you're lucky if you can get, what, twenty-five when someone walks through your door?" Inside, Oliver praised himself for manipulating the argument back to a more comfortable and winnable position. "Guess you won't be getting that country club membership anytime soon."

Asshole. "We're not talking about me, or even Abby,

we're talking about the hundreds of millions of people who have no access to healthcare."

Oliver didn't answer but instead offered a condescending laugh. A win in his book.

"Good comeback." Hanna rolled her eyes. *What a massive jerk.* "You didn't save the government any money. All you guys did was take the money from healthcare and move it to defense."

"To keep us safe."

"From who?"

"I have to tell you?"

"Yes, considering that half of Washington is dying, I'm thinking whatever invisible enemy you thought you were fighting was apparently the wrong one. I'll bet even the president is dead by now."

Oliver had no way of knowing Hanna had already won that bet, instead he believed her comment was a low blow aimed right at him. "I don't want to talk about this anymore."

"Why would that be?" Hanna knew it wasn't like Oliver to give up that easily.

"My friend is dying, okay? My best friend. At least I think he was. I'm still not sure, but it doesn't matter. And, yes, he had healthcare so I guess that shit doesn't matter." Oliver stopped. His rage at Hanna was equal to his own anger at himself for using a personal matter to win an argument; a golden rule he never broke because he had watched it backfire in Washington over and over again.

"I'm sorry." Hanna softened. For the past three days she herself had feared for the health and safety of her best friend and still had frightening thoughts about her friend's baby, so her empathy, even for the likes of Oliver, was right there.

"I don't need your pity. You're a doctor, just tell me how I can save him."

Chapter 104

Sunday, April 6, 2025
Oliver Gordon, Benjamin Gordon
Gordon Farm, Pinewood, Pennsylvania

By afternoon, Abigail seemed to have turned a corner. Her fever finally broke, her appetite came back and for the first time in three days she stopped crying every time she looked at Oliver. It seemed as good a time as any for Oliver to make a visit to his grandfather.

"What does Hanna say?"

Oliver wanted to tell his grandfather he didn't give a shit what she had to say. But the fact of the matter was that his wife was getting better and his baby was still alive, so for that he was willing to show her a modicum of respect.

"Abby is pretty much out of the woods, and we'll know about the baby in a few days but so far, so good."

"Excellent."

"Yes." Oliver's subconscious made him take a deep breath.

"Gamps, I have to ask you something."

"Of course."

As Benjamin moved away from the laptop that had been holding his attention since early that morning Oliver couldn't help but notice the speed at which information was popping up on the screen. There would be a name, last then first, followed by demographic information and then what looked to be a family tree with some names in green, some black, most flashing red.

"What's that?"

"Once you know something, you can't un-know it."

"I'm standing in your bunker next to millions of dollars in stolen money and an arsenal that could take down the Pentagon. I think that ship has sailed."

Benjamin couldn't help but smile at his grandson before returning his eyes to the screen.

"It's the names of all the victims."

Oliver was surprised at how easily he accepted the fact that his grandfather had that information, and he couldn't help but wonder if Benjamin's deviance had normalized in the wake of the ongoing crisis or was just an anomaly dismissed as too hard to process.

"And are those family trees?" Oliver pointed to the screen.

"Organizational charts. The flashing names are those who have died. Black means they're sick. Blue is so far so good."

"What organizations?"

"Businesses." Benjamin's answer was purposefully incomplete. "You never told me the reason for your visit." Benjamin turned off the screen to ward off any further questions.

"The virux, or virus, or whatever the hell it is…"

"What about it?"

"Is there a cure?"

"A cure?"

"Yeah, like once someone is sick."

"I don't know; but I'm assuming if there was a cure, some medicine, some sort of drug or treatment, then they'd be using it."

"No, I'm not asking if they have a cure; I'm asking if you do." Oliver worked to keep his frustration in check, but he was overtired. "You and your Pinochle buddies. Maybe your Israeli friends are hiding something?"

"I don't know what you're insinuating, but be sure to keep these thoughts of yours to yourself." Benjamin's words were strong, his look frightening .

"I asked because of Monty." Oliver wanted to give his grandfather an excuse for stepping across what he suddenly recognized as an invisible line.

"He's sick? How long?"

"I found out today." Oliver had to look away. The last thing he wanted anyone to see were the tears that kept forming in his eyes every time he thought of his friend.

Benjamin shook his head. "Sorry, if I could help him, I would."

Oliver wasn't convinced his grandfather was telling the truth.

Chapter 105

Monday, April 7, 2025
Oliver & Abigail Gordon
Baylor Farm, Pinewood, Pennsylvania

When he wasn't worrying about his wife or arguing with Hanna, Oliver spent his time trying to figure out what he would do when he returned to Washington. Now that Rhine had died, the possibilities seemed delightfully endless. He could look for a senator with presidential aspirations, or work for a first tier congressman with a lot of clout and money to burn. If that didn't work out, Oliver knew he could call on his many contacts to secure a job on K street. Though being a lobbyist didn't carry with it the same cachet as working on Capitol Hill, the hand over fist money he would be making would surely make up for any loss of prestige. No, getting a job would not be a problem for Oliver; the big obstacle would be convincing Abigail the job he chose was the right one.

"His phone keeps going to voicemail." Oliver didn't want to talk about Monty anymore.

"Do you have his parent's number?" Abigail only wanted to talk about him.

"I'll find out more when I go back to Washington,"

was Oliver's subtle way of changing the subject and informing his wife that he would not be staying on the farm for very long.

"I'm not going to bother to try and stop you from going." Abigail feigned frustration by rolling her eyes.

"Good." Although he wished that was the end of the conversation, Oliver knew better.

"Just wait okay? Don't rush back there. There's no reason to."

"Except that technically I no longer have a job."

"We'll be fine."

"Not unless we win the lottery." The thought of money hidden in the bunker crossed Oliver's mind.

"We can live here. You can help my father manage the farm." Abigail couldn't help but laugh at her own suggestion. "I'll buy you a pair of overalls."

"Throw in a tractor and I'll consider it."

"The way you drive? You'll kill yourself and every living thing in a hundred mile radius."

"I drive fine."

"You drive like a maniac."

Now it was Oliver who was laughing and rolling his eyes.

"Okay, but seriously," Abigail added, "all I'm asking for is a couple of weeks. Besides, you said everyone was clearing out of Washington anyway."

"I can promise a week. This thing should be over

by then." Oliver wanted to be in D.C. just in case any impromptu job opportunities came his way.

"Just promise me that no matter what, you won't leave in the middle of the night." Abigail was not sure why she was asking her husband to promise her anything. She was well aware of the fact that Oliver had been trained by Washington to make promises, not keep them.

Part 10

In just three weeks, America had been brought to its knees...

The upper echelons of corporate America were all dead and fear that the virus might trickle down on the masses, just as they had promised their wealth would, kept most people inside. The only rational reason to emerge from one's residence was to find food. Some hunted or fished, some stole from local farms, and still others found ways to barter. The mega-sized big box and grocery chain stores had all been closed when top management succumbed to the disease and workers chose their lives over minimum wage. These once bustling centers of commerce were nothing more than mirages of unattainable food and water, as well as the fuel behind a starving neighborhood's anger. Even law-abiding citizens thought about looting the stores. Only the knowledge of the heavily armed drones deterred them. Eventually, though, entrepreneurial store managers took it upon themselves to sell all that was left of the inventory through a burgeoning black market. A perfect crime since no one would be coming from corporate to see that the store was virtually empty or to look for the money they pocketed.

In the world of the media there were no more live

broadcasts of surgically-enhanced, make-up-basted television and movie stars chatting up the airwaves, recounting all the funny things that happened as they gallivanted through the award show circuit or romped down the Canadian ski slopes. Gone were the stick-their-tongue-out specials featuring mega-sized mansions, exotic cars and multi-million dollar clothing closets. Even if anyone cared to hear their stories anymore, there was only one story left to tell and they couldn't tell it because they were all dead. Televisions ran a continuous loop of reruns. Whatever happened to be on TV the day everyone went home to hide was what continued to play.

Stocks traded for a while in the US. Money hungry traders seeing a window of opportunity took their chances on the virus and went to work. But as the rich died off and the smaller investors made survival a priority, there was little reason to remain open. On the other hand, foreign markets seemed to be celebrating America's misfortune. Public acknowledgements by world leaders regarding their new-found freedom from the self-appointed leader of the free world abounded. Calls for a new world order and currency came from a number of fronts in South America and the Arab world, but most loudly, and least surprisingly, from China. The only thing standing in the way of their attacking the U.S. and starting a full on war were the messages sent from the oval office reminding them that the president still had his finger on the button and he wouldn't hesitate to blow them all up if need be.

At home a Rooseveltian pep talk or comforting words from the president, or any other government official for that matter, asserting America's ability to withstand the menace that had besieged the country would have been helpful. Instead, what the populace got were rumors that swirled through towns like twisters, destroying faith and promoting the notion that the president and his staff were no more, and that the government in any recognizable form had also ceased to exist. Rumors that became cemented into the public's consciousness despite the prerecorded protestations of TV and radio announcers whose smooth voices begged the country to ignore all reports of discord and take up the official meme of "All is well."

Chapter 106

Tuesday, April 22, 2025
Benjamin & Mary Gordon
Oliver & Abigail Gordon
Andrew & Kendall Gordon
Tyler & Kris Mayer-Gordon
Gordon Family Farm, Pinewood, Pennsylvania

On April eighth, Washington officially shut down its offices and Congress announced it was taking an impromptu recess for Members to check on their respective constituencies. It was also reported that the top three rungs of the country's chain of command were all safe and sound in their secret, individual, secure locations. Oliver had no good reason to rush back to Washington. Instead, he helped his brothers install the solar panels that had been hidden in the bunker. Though they didn't generate much power, it was more than enough to keep the lights and the refrigerator going when the local power went out.

After that Oliver put himself in charge of the farm's security, installing the surveillance equipment and alarms he found in the bunker, and setting a schedule and protocol for the 9:00 p.m. to 5:00 a.m. shift. Generally, it was Oliver and one of the other Gordon men in the overnight eight hour slot, staring at the security screens, loaded shotguns by their sides.

Though Oliver knew how to operate a shotgun in theory, he had no real-world experience doing so. In fact, it was Oliver's justifiable firearm insecurity that prompted him to insist everyone sleep in the bunker instead of the loft. But only his grandparents agreed to do so, the others citing the claustrophobic nature of the bunker for their refusal. Instead, they compromised with Oliver by agreeing to keep a pistol under their respective pillows up in the loft.

That left Benjamin and Mary alone in the bunker each night, and also for a good portion of the day, as it had been decided long ago that they would keep watch over the country through shortwave radios and encrypted messages via their network of secure servers. As a result, the Gordons were privy to a comprehensive picture of the truth, one that was far more accurate than the one being disseminated over the public airwaves. Their grandparents' attentiveness in monitoring the national situation allowed the rest of the family to distance themselves from all that was going on in the world.

In fact, life on the farm was so cautiously peaceful that if it were not for Benjamin's nightly updates they might never have known how bad things had actually gotten.

"The total count is over 150,000 dead." Benjamin was standing at the head of the long wooden table reading from his notes. "That number will probably triple by the weekend."

Everyone sat in silence, absorbing the gravity of what they were being told and wishing they didn't remember the number had been in the low thousands just a week ago. Despite their distress and their belief that Benjamin had some magic bullet to stop what was happening, no one dared question his decision to keep it to himself. They all knew he had his reasons.

"The highest concentrations of the disease are in the New York metropolitan, Los Angeles and D.C. areas, although all major and even secondary cities have relatively large pockets of impact." As he spoke, Benjamin pointed to each area on the map with a crooked stick he had detached from a tree limb. "When you get down to the town level of things, you have entire communities and areas left unscathed while others are completely wiped out."

Benjamin would not describe how the hospitals were overwhelmed with patients they could do nothing for. Everyone affected eventually succumbed to the illness, no matter what the medical profession did for them. Benjamin also spared his grandchildren the knowledge that previously abandoned school buildings had been turned into makeshift morgues, where bodies wrapped in white sheets were laid in neat rows on the dulled wooden floors alongside deflated basketballs and errant sneakers.

Instead, he read off the numbers, city by city,

believing that circumventing the details of the dead might spare his family the sadness he himself wished to avoid. He was wrong.

One by one the Gordons found themselves taken down by their emotions. Leaving Oliver to squirm and look away. The truth was that Oliver had been more at ease at Senate hearings in which stoic faces routinely and expeditiously excused the deaths of hundreds of thousands of victims of indifference, wars, and corporate encroachments by dismissively describing them as collateral damage.

After wiping his face with his handkerchief and clearing his throat multiple times, Benjamin was once again able to continue speaking, and Oliver was once again able to look at his grandfather.

"Obviously all attempts to call back expat researchers from the CDC, the FDA and the EPA have failed."

"Why's that?" Kendall, who had momentarily stopped crying, queried her grandfather.

"All of them, at least any of them worth their salt, tried to let people know what was going on for years: the corporate takeover of their agencies, the co-opted research. For their due diligence their lives were destroyed."

Their grandmother, who generally kept silent on political issues and allowed Benjamin to lead the way, found this particular issue so disturbing she felt compelled to add to her husband's comments.

"Their work was discredited and destroyed, and they were told to keep quiet about it or they would be charged with treason. What's the point of having a Constitution if the government can ignore it whenever they want by saying the words 'national security'?"

Benjamin continued. "In the end they all accepted an offer of deportation, or 'relocation' as the officials termed it, in exchange for their passports. Not one ever looked back, nor should they have."

Benjamin did not share his ironic thought that the same people who had made the lives of these researchers a living hell were now in their own hell as a direct result of their actions. He had never seen karma work with such a swift and decisive hand.

"As far as the possibility of any foreign intervention is concerned," Benjamin continued, going down his list of items to be discussed, "our protectionist policies, which included throwing the members of the UN out on their keisters, put the kibosh on the possibility of the international community coming to our aid. Small countries, the ones we used to bully in exchange for our support and protection, are getting a kick out of watching us squirm; and the larger countries see this sickness as either an opportunity to become the world's next superpower or, just as important, the next superpower's best friend. No one's coming to help us. Oh, and American citizens, our ambassadors, ex-pats, people who were out of the country on business or pleasure, have all been sent back to the U.S. out of fear that they're carrying the disease. No one is able to leave the U.S. either. Overseas airports are not accepting our planes, and the secured borders we were using to keep illegal immigrants out are now being used by Canada and Mexico to keep us in. Essentially, we've been quarantined."

Not sure if his grandfather was happy or upset about this turn of events, Oliver decided to share his own disgust with the situation.

"We gave away billions of dollars' worth of aid. We spread democracy all around the world."

"Even to people who didn't want it," Kris said under his breath.

"Now they owe us."

"Just remember, it was that kind of arrogance that got us into this situation in the first place," Benjamin warned Oliver before silently wishing his grandson had not spent so many years in Washington.

"The New York Stock Exchange is closed," Benjamin said as he watched Oliver, hoping for any sign of contrition. "The banks were closed because they could no longer handle the run on cash. The supermarkets are out of everything, so they're all closed, and the streets are empty except for emergency vehicles. People are hoarding food, cash, gas, soap, bleach, toilet paper, weapons and water. Looting's been minimal, though, because people are too afraid to go out, believing they'll either get sick or get shot."

"Well, we've all seen the un-camouflaged drones with their cameras and machine guns pointing at the ground." Kris added, confirming that the fears of the citizenry were not unfounded.

"Power and water deliveries have been sporadic at best, not because of any specific shortages, but because there's no one to run the facilities." Benjamin continued his report. "We haven't been affected by any of these things for obvious reasons." Benjamin was referring to their rainwater recovery system, composting toilets, and solar panels, which were all operating better than expected.

"Now, this is the important part."

No one could imagine what was coming next, and each person at the table looked around to see if they were the only ones afraid of what Benjamin was about to say.

"Almost all of the largest corporations, about a thousand of them, are currently without a CEO or board of directors and the upper echelons of their management teams are either currently sick or have already died."

Benjamin looked around at his family and took a deep breath before continuing. "The Cabinet, Secret Service, about three quarters of the Senate and Congress, as well as their staffs and much of our national security force, Special Ops, spy agencies like the FBI and CIA, higher levels of law enforcement, and prison officials are all gone at this point."

The response in the room was a collective gasp followed by a pin-drop silence. Later, much later, everyone would agree that the best description of the experience was the feeling of jumping off a swing, of letting go of the chains and flying off into the air without knowing exactly how or when you would land.

Chapter 107

Wednesday, April 23, 2025
Benjamin Gordon
Oliver & Abigail Gordon
General Michael Baylor
Washington D.C.

On Benjamin's say so they drove through the night, flying through abandoned checkpoints and stopping only for bathroom breaks behind deserted rest stop buildings. By the time Oliver pulled the car into the empty Capitol parking lot, they were all ready to get to work.

Passing one closed door after another reminded Oliver of Christmas Eves spent in the Capitol before he met Abigail. He and just a handful of his staff, too afraid to leave before their boss, would always be the last ones out of the building and the parking lot. Then, like now, the small space under every office door was dark, and the sound of Oliver's leather-soled shoes was conspicuously loud in the empty halls.

"Oliver, wait," Abigail yelled down the hall after her

husband. Her annoyance at his not waiting for her was obvious.

He's in work mode, Abigail said to herself.

As Oliver walked past each senator's office he sped up his pace in the hopes that the images of the dead flowing past him in his mind would disappear if he could just move fast enough. But the harsh and painful expressions he imagined to be a part of their final days on earth were resilient. As a last resort, Oliver tried to override his thoughts by counting his footsteps—1,2, 3, 4, 5, –19, 20, 21, – 48, 49—until he reached Monty's office door, at which point he had no choice but to stop and endure his grief. Although quick to deny his feelings if anyone were to ask, the tears that dampened his face spoke a different truth.

Abigail, too, as she caught up to her husband, couldn't help but break down and cry. Despite the fact that she'd known for some time that Monty had become Rhine's partner in the arms deals and had worried incessantly that he would bring her husband into the mix, she had enjoyed his good-humored personality and appreciated what his friendship had meant to her husband.

"I'm so sorry." Abigail kissed her husband's cheek, and Oliver could not help but be momentarily distracted by the smell of his wife's perfume.

"Yeah, well." Oliver didn't know what to say. There were too many words, too many thoughts, and he had yet to have enough time to sort them all out.

"They finally got a taste of their own medicine." A familiar voice echoed through the hall and made Oliver turn around quickly.

"Senator Sherman?"

Though Oliver had never been a fan of the old man, seeing a familiar face gave him hope that perhaps there were more people alive than his grandfather had told him.

"Oliver, how are you?"

Oliver moved toward the senator and shook his hand.

"I'm the only one left. They're all gone. Sorry."

Sherman didn't sound sorry to Oliver and he couldn't really blame him. After all, there wasn't a man or woman on the floor of the Senate who hadn't at one time or another verbalized their impatience with Sherman's ability to work even into his eighty-fifth year. The fact that this much-reviled old politician was still alive, while all his enemies who had wished him dead were now themselves deceased, was an irony not lost on Oliver.

"Ben, General." The senator walked toward Benjamin and Michael, and unlike his greeting for Oliver, offered the two approaching men large bear hugs.

"You all know each other?" Oliver asked himself why he was surprised.

"Abigail." Sherman hugged Oliver's wife, too. "I hear you are going to help us with our environmental issues. You'll be heading up the Green team with Marissa and Nigel."

"See you later." Abigail leaned against Oliver, whispered in his ear that she would miss him and wished him good luck, before heading down the hallway like a woman on a mission.

"Where are you going?" Oliver had no choice but to call after her because she moved so quickly.

"I'll see you later," was his wife's only response as Oliver saw her turn into an office as if she were well aware of her direction.

"We have a lot to do, son; we'll see you later," Benjamin told his grandson as he and the general left for yet another room down the hallway.

"Come, we have a space for you to work in my office until we head over to the White House this afternoon."

As they walked down the hall at a speed far exceeding what he would have anticipated a man in his eighties would be capable of, Oliver tried to keep up with what Senator Sherman was saying to him.

"Your office will be in the West Wing. Not all VP's choose to be there, but I want you close by."

"West Wing, sir?"

Oliver wasn't sure what Sherman was talking about, though he couldn't help but believe his grandfather did.

"You'll be my Vice President. Ben told you, right?"

Oliver could barely swallow, let alone speak, but managed to eke out a "No" before stopping dead in his tracks.

"Son, we have no time. Keep up." The Senator kept walking and seemed annoyed at his charge.

"Of course, the Constitution says you have to be thirty-five to be VP, but what the hell. I don't remember the Order of Succession going all the way to a senator from Vermont, either, but you have to make allowances when everyone else is dead." Sherman let out one of his signature chuckles. "I'm putting you in charge of elections. I have a team that's been working on getting this democracy back on its feet, and I believe they have a pretty good plan in place. It will just need your oversight."

"Yes, sir," Oliver responded as he struggled to keep up with the senator.

"I will be making the announcements this afternoon."

"Announcements?"

"I'll start with death tolls, and how the outbreak has already peaked and virtually stopped its progression at this point."

"Is that true?"

"Essentially. Then I'll go into our plans to restart the government by next Monday, and I will introduce you as my choice for VP. Then we'll have the swearing in. Of course, there's no Supreme Court Justice to officiate because they're all dead." Again the senator laughed and made Oliver uncomfortable. "We'll use a lower court judge from my home district. Any port in a storm as they say, right? Son, you look white as a ghost." Sherman had finally looked at Oliver as they rounded the corner to enter his open office door.

The large office was filled with young people hurrying about their business: typing on laptops, making copies, texting, and talking, while a plethora of Sherman's own secret service professionals as well as a spattering of Marines lined the walls.

"Michelle, get Oliver some water," Sherman instructed the intern who quickly fetched a glass of water and tried to hand it to Oliver.

"No, get me an AcquaO." Oliver punctuated his annoyance at the intern by waving the back of his hand in the air.

Immediately Oliver's words brought the buzzing of the office to a silent stop.

"Gordon, get in here!" The senator bellowed through the sudden silence of the outer office.

Oliver moved quickly, ignoring the shocked intern and the glass of water she still held in her hands.

"Holy shit. Close the door and sit down. I'd ask you what else you don't know, but I guess we will just have to figure that out as we go along."

The senator had no idea Oliver hadn't known about the water, or what other important information Benjamin had left out. The only thing Sherman did know for sure was that Benjamin never left anything up to chance, and if he hadn't told Oliver these things he must have purposely left it up to him to do so.

"It was in the water, son, in the bottled water. You know that expensive shit rich people drink? I don't drink that crap, never have, never will. Rainwater, filtered rainwater, that's what my intern offered you. I ship it down from my farm in Vermont. It's delicious." The senator took a swig from the clear glass of water sitting on a bamboo coaster next to his right hand. Oliver couldn't help but wonder if one day Sherman would be pitching rainwater purifiers on television the way other former politicians pitched sexual enhancers.

"Anyway, the thing that killed everyone was an amoeba in the expensive water." The senator exaggerated the word 'expensive.' "Those amoebae, they're crazy. Accomplished what I could never do. Got right through to their thick-headed brains. Here's the press release that's being sent out now."

Oliver grabbed the paper the senator slid across his desk and read, appreciating the distraction from Senator Sherman's brazen disregard for the deaths of his colleagues.

"FOR IMMEDIATE EMERGENCY RELEASE FROM THE OFFICE OF THE PRESIDENT"

"The cause of the disease that has taken the lives of so

many American citizens has been isolated and steps have been taken to prevent any further spread."

Well that's good news, Oliver thought to himself before he continued.

"It should be noted that this deadly disease was not a result of any terrorist action, but rather a naturally-occurring amoeba. Similar to Naegleria fowleri, this brain-eating protozoan known as Retae niarbi developed in waters that would normally be too cold to host its predecessor. This new breed of amoeba infested the same spring waters the UnesteCope Corporation had been filling from for years. However, higher water temperatures brought on by global climate changes created conditions favorable for hosting and transmuting the amoebae into a virulently-lethal form. Unfortunately, this situation went unnoticed by company inspectors. Unlike other similar organisms, this heartier, more deadly strain of amoeba is able to enter through the mouth and move at a rapid pace through the various systems of the body, ultimately arriving in the brain where it causes incapacitation and death within a matter of days.

All citizens should be aware that evidence of the amoeba has only been found in luxury bottled water varieties sold by the UnesteCope Corporation under the following brand names: A+Amenity, VigorousPlus, ChicD and AcquaO. Anyone still in possession of any of these brands of water should contact the government hotline immediately for information about proper disposal. All remaining bottles of water at the UnesteCope's processing plant have been seized and will be treated before they are discarded.

As he read the press release, Oliver envisioned the stark white UnesteCope water trucks. Oliver, like all of the company's customers, had believed the ads that said its product had the best flavor of all bottled waters, and had trusted its claims of purity and consistency. 'The best water money can buy,' the company had boasted. What they had failed to mention was that it was also the most expensive, prohibitively expensive for those having to live on less than a million dollars a year or those not getting supplies gratis from the U.S. Treasury.

Oliver had seen UnesteCope trucks delivering to the Capitol, as well as to offices around town. Places like K Street, where nothing was too good or too expensive for the Washington lobbyists. He had also seen the conspicuous trucks delivering to areas like Georgetown, Spring Valley and Rock Creek, where the residents of multimillion dollar homes had their kitchen staffs accept deliveries of the massive glass jugs and cases of to-go bottles through their back door service entrances.

Oliver also recalled the bottles of AcquaO that had

taken up most of his office refrigerator alongside his secretary's yogurts and bag lunches, and the cases of it that had made their way home from the corner of his office to the shelf on the door of his and Abigail's refrigerator.

"Shit," Oliver said in response to what he had just read. "When did you find this out?"

Sherman's briefly-closed eyes were a tell Oliver couldn't read.

"Let's just say we've known for a while this was going to happen."

"And you said nothing?"

"Oh, son, we said a lot."

"To whom?"

"Everyone."

"No one told me. And if you told Rhine, I'm sure I would have heard about it."

Again the senator laughed, but this time at Oliver.

"So you don't remember hearing about Global Warming? Does 'Climate Change' ring a bell?"

"Of course." Oliver was not happy with the senator's sarcastic tone.

"Remember hearing that the balance of life in the oceans and lakes would change? That whole species were dying off and water levels were rising?"

Instinctively Oliver wanted to deny it all, knowing that any major impact had not been predicted for at least another century. In fact he and his staff used to joke about how their inland homes would be worth so much more when they became waterfront property. Oliver also knew from all the data he had been handed that the warmer temperatures they'd been experiencing in the Northeast for the last decade and a half were an anomaly.

"I remember that, but..."

"But nothing, son; stop right there. You and all your buddies were warned. And, quite frankly, if it hadn't been for your grandfather convincing me you were the right man for the job, we wouldn't even be having this conversation now." Senator Sherman wiped his brow, annoyed with himself for getting so irritated, and took a breath.

"For decades I tried to tell all of you: look at the earth, look at what you're doing to it. The bees were dying off, birds fell from the sky, millions of fish were floating on top of the water. I showed you all the pictures, but that wasn't enough. Then the tap water was on fire, the ground was shaking. I begged you. You know I did."

Oliver nodded his head, affirming the fervor with which the senator had pleaded with his colleagues to vote for his bills. The same fervor they had all laughed at and called him crazy for.

"And whenever I thought I'd have enough votes, that I had Minsk or Tether or Wellheart convinced, one of those assholes from K Street would roll in with a monosyllabic brochure full of bullshit and pictures, denying all the science while happening to mention their list of supportive campaign donors. Before I knew what was happening another damn law written by those K-holes was being used to clear a hundred acres of protected land, frack on top of another aquifer, or clear the way for another scum-sucking oil company to screw up the ocean. Did you ever eat a shrimp with two heads, son?"

"I–"

"You don't have to answer. Of course you haven't. Do you think they'd have them in your local neighborhood food market? Hell no, because the oil companies bought up the sea food distributors so they could save that two-headed shit for chopped shrimp salad."

The senator's face was red, the same shade of red Oliver had seen so many times before.

"Not to change the subject, but I'm still not clear on when you found out about this amoeba water. I'm sure someone's going to ask me."

Sherman was well aware Oliver was trying to change the subject. He was also well aware of the fact that Oliver was correct: people would want to know exactly when and how they came upon the Retae niarbi protozoan. And because they couldn't really tell the truth it was imperative they were all on the same page.

Chapter 108

Wednesday, April 23, 2025
Oliver Gordon
Washington D.C.

I'm not sure he's the right one for the job. Can we really trust him to keep this to himself?

We have no choice. We need someone from the other side of the aisle to minimize suspicion. Besides, we don't have to tell him the truth, we just have to tell him what we've told everyone else and we're golden.

I don't know. He might start to question things. I heard he already has.

No, he believed all the shit the energy lobby idiots fed him for years. He's not going to question this.

What if someone else does? We're releasing all the real journalists from jail soon. They're going to want to know.

You really think so? Because I think all they are going to want to know is where all the money is that the legal system stole from their bank accounts. My guess is if we set each of them up in a nice cozy apartment and give them all their money back with interest they're going to see this little amoeba thing as their hero and leave it alone.

We could threaten them to make sure they don't dig.

We could. I'm sure they'd be terrified of going back to

jail, but I'm telling you we won't have to. We're good. We know how to deal with their questions. For Chrissake, we figured out how to kill off the entire government and save democracy without firing so much as one bullet. I think we can figure out how to keep one naive Vice President and a handful of reporters in the dark.

As soon as Oliver was sure their conversation had ended he hesitantly peeked around the bend in the hallway, only to find the two individuals had disappeared entirely. Though Oliver might have recognized their voices if they hadn't been whispering, all he was able to do at this point was distinguish that one was male and the other female.

Chapter 109

Wednesday, April 23, 2025
Senator Sherman
Benjamin Gordon
Oliver & Abigail Gordon
General Baylor
Washington D.C.

Instead of crowds, there were TV cameras. Instead of pomp and circumstance, there was a quiet resignation that what was happening was necessary, if not inevitable. Senator Sherman raised his right hand, placed his left on the bible, and became President Sherman. Oliver Gordon raised his right hand, placed his left on the bible, and became Vice President Gordon. It was not the first time a President of the United States was not voted in by a democratic majority election, but everyone in the room hoped it would be the last.

"While we mourn the loss of those we love, we must rejoice in the knowledge that the ills that have befallen this country will soon be no more." President Sherman began his speech of promises for a better America, the one Oliver had listened to over and over again, and helped him revise until the perfect words were spoken. Though exceedingly proud of himself and relieved that he hadn't lost his God-given skill of turning a phrase, Oliver struggled to listen as his thoughts kept shifting back to the conversation he had had with his grandfather only minutes before the ceremony, an intrusion that had chopped his attention into sound bites:

"We have seen what greed can do. How it can destroy our common sense and strangle our democracy."

"Oliver, nothing more happened. I told you everything. I don't care what you heard. It could have been two stupid interns talking. There's no way to know."

"We have seen what the lust for power can do. How it can make men do what their oath of office made them swear they would never do."

"Okay, even if something happened here, why would you want to know? What purpose would it serve at this point? It's time to move forward."

"My promise to you as President of these United States is that I will uphold the principles upon which this democracy was founded."

"Whatever's happened has already happened. Think plausible deniability."

"For the first time in a very long time you can be assured that your representatives in Congress and in the Senate will be voted for, not paid for. You can be assured that practicality, good sense, reason and compromise will rule the day."

"Come on, Oliver, it's me you're talking to. Don't try to pass off your upset at being left out of the loop as some kind of sanctimonious moral outrage."

"The only way to move forward is to take a good look at ourselves. Acknowledge the dysfunction that has engulfed our system and allowed the few to profit mightily from the blood, sweat and tears of the many."

"Lobbyists loved you. You made their wet dreams de jour come true. You gave them a blank check: steal, sure; pollute, no problem; kill, you made up extenuating non-culpable circumstances; break the law, no worries, our judges are on it. Whatever it was they needed, you gave them.

"We can no longer surrender the core of who we are as Americans and allow corporations to dictate our every move."

"Remember that speech you wrote for Rhine, the one about the lazy food-stamp moms who needed to go out to work to show their kids the path to independence? You did it, Oliver. You put the kibosh on food stamps, while corporations and the rich became the real welfare queens."

"Responsibility will rule the new dawn of this American Republic. No longer will we allow corporations to claim to be what they are not. Until they eat, drink, breathe, feel, and pay taxes we will no longer buy into the misnomer that corporations are people."

"A lot of kids went hungry without food stamps. They got sick and even died, Oliver, because that was the same year McKarrey saw to it that the school lunch program was squashed."

"We must take care of our citizens, prioritize their welfare, and keep the focus on people over money. Health care, education, Social Security. We have lived without them all, and found they were not the unaffordable luxuries we were told they were but rather that they are necessities. To desire a world without them is to desire to a world without humanity."

"For God's sake, Oliver, they handed you prepackaged bills that compromised the health and wellbeing of every man, woman, and child in America. Clearly the world's a better place without them – without the whole lot of them. Stop trying to turn this on Sherman, like it's some sort of conspiracy. If there's blood on anyone's hands, it's on yours."

"Nor can we arrogantly go around the globe insisting other countries behave as we would like them to. Waving the flag of democracy while we underhandedly dictate who their leaders shall be, steal and destroy their resources, and pay their people an unlivable pittance to make our goods. We will either be a good neighbor or we will continue to find ourselves alone, as we have been these past weeks."

"In ten minutes you're going to be Vice President of the United States of America. You do realize the impossibility of that, don't you? You were never going to make it to the White House with Rhine; he was looking to dump you. Even before you found out about the arms deals, your good buddy, Mark, told your boss about your parents being arrested. Rhine was just waiting for the right time to replace you. You can't blame him, though, he couldn't exactly get into the White House with the son of domestic terrorists working for him, now could he? By all rights you shouldn't even be allowed to set foot on the White House grounds, let alone be the Vice President. You've got to buck up and see this as your opportunity to fix the insanity that labeled your parents DTs in the first place, and to fix everything that has been broken for too long. You can actually do what your great-great-grandfather tried to do and couldn't. This is your opportunity to make America live up to the values it's always espoused."

"Our government must stop spying on and terrorizing its own citizens. We must close the loopholes that send innocent people to jail, and we must take away cash incentives to imprison our citizens. We must rid ourselves of the prejudices that have permeated our system of justice for far too long."

Plausible deniability… Vice President of the United States…you don't want to know…more than a hundred thousand Americans dead…sanctimonious moral outrage…blood's on your own hands. The words swirled inside Oliver's head and he imagined himself yelling and telling everyone he had no idea how this had all happened. How he, how we, had gotten to this place.

"Ensure equal protection for every citizen under the law."

It wasn't until Oliver stopped contemplating his own

thoughts and looked out at the faces in the small group of chairs, that he noticed his brothers. The unmistakable look of pride on their faces held an admiration for their big brother that Oliver had not had the pleasure of seeing in many years. The answer to the question of where it had all gone so wrong, though, still escaped him.

"With your help, their deaths will not have been in vain. We will rise together as one nation, one America, a family united at last."

Then he saw them. They were barely recognizable. Old and fragile. Thinner. The skeleton-like shadows of their former selves barely filling the clothes they wore. They looked as if a breeze as light as one that would blow out a candle could knock them out of their chairs and onto to the floor. With weak smiles and eyes straining against the light, their emotions remained trapped inside them. Oliver would have to rely on his brain to tell him what his eyes could not: that his parents were indeed proud of him.

Without warning, his lack of sleep combined with the unrelenting upheaval of all he knew to be true broke his wavering will not to cry. Small tears, water for his dry eyes at first, then a small stream down his cheek that he brushed with his sleeve. Whether he was up to the task or not, here he was, looking out at his family, the worse for wear, but also better, with a new generation waiting in the wings.

Later, at the reception, Oliver would hug his mother gently and shake his father's hand as tightly as he thought he could without causing damage. He would whisper in his wife's ear, prompting her to tell his parents the good news about their being grandparents, and the subsequent raised glasses and impromptu celebration would be magnified when Kendall and Andrew shared their news.

Before the end of the evening Oliver would thank his grandfather, and assure him that he would willingly put the past aside, no matter what it was, and move forward. Oliver would seal this promise with a handshake, followed by a hug.

Chapter 110

Thursday, April 24, 2025
Oliver & Abigail Gordon
Blair House, Home of the Vice President, Washington D.C.

The morning online papers showered Senator Sherman with praise for his inauguration speech, and characterized Oliver's appointment as an olive branch to the opposition. After the former senator's long history of fighting with everyone on the right and those who should have been on the left, the question of whether Sherman and Gordon could actually work together was the topic of every editorial written that day. Though the consensus touted Sherman's pick as a bold and impressive move, showing his willingness to hear all sides of an issue, it was also clear the editors regarded the pairing as one deserving of nothing more than guarded optimism. Ultimately, no matter what they had written, it came as no surprise to anyone that the opinions expressed were nothing more than wishful thinking and posturing for the good of the country rather than the propagating of any innate truths or beliefs they possessed.

After too many consecutive hours awake and far too much excitement, Oliver and Abigail continued their sleep between the intermittent annoyances imposed by the snooze alarm. Soundly past their usual wake-up time, their bodies would have it no other way.

Later Abigail would tell inquiring reporters that being in the Vice President's home that first morning was like waking up in a hotel room where the unfamiliarity of the bed beneath and the ceiling above colludes to spark fear before the recognition of reality set in.

Taking more time to shower and dress than usual and blaming their unfamiliar surroundings for both, Oliver and Abigail intended to make up their lost minutes at breakfast.

As they descended the grand stairway of the Vice President's home for the first time, neither of them could help but notice the secret service agents lining the walls below, a slightly-unnerving sight in what was now their home.

Before he could reach the bottom of the stairs, Oliver's newly-assigned aides swarmed, calling out to him his schedule for the day and updating him on issues that needed to be dealt with immediately.

Realizing his wife was no longer at his side, Oliver glanced back to see Abigail had been stopped in her tracks by the onslaught, and he immediately responded.

"This is how it's going to be, people," Oliver called to his new staff. "My wife and I are going to have breakfast alone every day. You'll wait here or in the car. I don't care which."

Oliver then ascended three steps back, took his wife's hand, and walked her down the rest of the stairs and into the formal dining room, closing the sliding double doors behind him.

With more chairs than anyone would bother to count and three large vases overflowing with flowers gracing both ends and the middle of the massive dining room table, Oliver commented, "Not exactly the table at the farm."

Instead of addressing the resurgence of her husband's arrogance, Abigail acquiesced to her burgeoning cravings.

"This all looks so good." Abigail's eyes were wide as she lifted the silver lid and perused the eggs, sausage, bacon and French toast, perfectly arranged on her plate and garnished with a sprig of parsley and slices of strawberries. "If I eat this way every morning, I'm going to have one big fat baby." Abigail looked down on her still-flat stomach.

"And our baby is going to have one big fat mommy." Oliver laughed while leaning over to pat his wife's belly.

Abigail never minded Oliver's teasing, and was in fact relieved to see his sense of humor had not been compromised by his meteoric rise to the Vice Presidency.

"Just a little. Then, I know, we have to go."

Abigail was talking to herself because Oliver was

already reading, unconsciously replacing his wife's morning banter with the overnight reports and morning briefs on the tablet that had been placed next to his plate.

After brief conversations with various members of the household staff who hovered about filling and refilling their coffee cups, and after eating more of their breakfast than they had planned to, Abigail and Oliver headed outside, flanked on all sides by the Secret Service. Their limousine was the third vehicle in the vice presidential motorcade that stretched the entire length of the block.

"This is so weird," Abigail said just before ducking her head under the top of the limo door. "Are we ever going to get used to this?"

Without explanation Oliver knew exactly what his wife meant. While he had ridden in plenty of limousines before, the fact that this was going to be his life every day and not a vacation or some sort of special occasion made his entrance into the roomy and plush vehicle seem surreal.

"Ready for your first day, Mr. Vice President?" Abigail's smile was broad and Oliver could feel her excitement without looking up at her.

"Yes, of course," he replied rapidly, trying not to dull his wife's excitement as he scanned the last of the morning's emails.

"Me, too." Abigail hoped she was up to the task of

overseeing the cleanup and preservation of what was left of the environment she had been reporting on for years.

As the car slowly pulled away from the curb, Oliver's patiently-waiting staff began a frenzied dialog of needs, wants, and have to's; all of which demanded his attention and prompted him to dictate a list of orders back to each of them.

Abigail's comments about looking for a more energy-efficient limousine were summarily ignored by Oliver and his staff, who deemed the Second Lady's concerns secondary to their own. A somewhat disappointed Abigail consoled herself with assurances that there was a more environmentally-friendly ear waiting for her in the Oval Office.

Amidst the muffled sounds of the sirens surrounding them, Abigail instead chose to observe her husband as he took command of his office, listening closely for any chinks in the armor of the new and improved man everyone was counting on. *So far so good*, Abigail thought to herself, relieved that their plan was actually working.

Suddenly, and without warning, the limo rounded a turn more quickly than all the previous turns. Abigail grabbed for the armrest to stop herself from sliding across the shiny leather seat and into her husband. As the other riders in the car took similar actions to keep themselves steady, the surrounding sirens grew alarmingly louder. It was then that all the phones in the car began ringing, vibrating, and displaying texts, causing the neophyte aides to look with widened eyes back and forth between themselves, afraid to look down at their phones to find out what had gone wrong already.

Before Oliver could touch the ALERT icon flashing on the center of his tablet to learn what disaster lay beneath it, the automatic transmission of the limo seemed to skip a gear and lurch forward to an excessive speed, the momentum of which pushed Oliver against the back of his seat. Yelling from the front of the limo to request fastened seat belts, the Secret Service Agent got all to comply immediately.

"Hello," Oliver heard Abigail say into her phone as the air in the car became thick with panic. His first worry that he had exposed his wife and unborn child to unnecessary danger quickly transformed into a myriad of other concerns as he read aloud the message on his screen from Prescott Mason, Sherman's newly-appointed Chief of Staff.

President Sherman pronounced dead. WH doc confirmed heart attack. Order of Succession protocol directive attached. Swearing-in 9 a.m. Awaiting your arrival at the WH for briefing. GBA